TOTTENHAM BOYS

John Kinski loves history, blues, rock, and football. He studied history at the London School of Economics. At present, he is writing a novel on the English Civil War.

To Hen. J.

Thanks for all your

help.

Love

John

John Kinski

TOTTENHAM BOYS

Published by Ivinghoe Press.

ISBN 9781974077014

For my wife, Mary.
Her love and encouragement were indispensable.

1

I won't tell you where I am now or what's about to happen to me. Later maybe, but that depends. I will, however, describe the events that led me here. My story begins with the Tottenham riots of 2011.

I wasn't in Tottenham that night to cover the riots. I was there to take pictures for my physio friend, Mike. I owed him for three treatments and he wanted a record of his son's housewarming-cum-engagement party. His son, Danny, would've preferred Archway but couldn't afford it. Don't laugh, N17 was supposed to be the next up-and-coming place. After I'd snapped the happy couple and an assortment of their juvenile friends in idiotic poses – standing on one leg, poking out a tongue – I bypassed the mums with partners and called upon the unattached ones to step forth. I wanted to pull, so I trowelled on the charm and flattery: are you sure you've never done any modelling, Gloria? You're a natural, Dee. That smile, Jasmine. Wow, sensational. I'd put on a clean shirt and trousers for the occasion and combed what was left of my hair (the last time I went to a drycleaners Glen Hoddle was kicking a ball for Spurs). I'd even sucked hard on extra strong mints. And what was my reward? Not so much as a peck on the cheek. I might as well have gone in soiled long johns.

You can't blame a man for trying. I would say stupid old git but velvet-hips Sir Mick Jagger has pushed back the boundaries and Basset Hound skin isn't an insuperable obstacle to getting laid by someone half your age any more. Of course, it helps if you've got fame, money, a great bluesy voice, and can prance around the stage like a meerkat on a hot tin roof. When Mike had the youngsters doing *Knees up Mother Brown* to Snoop Dogg, I spat my extra strong mint into an ashtray and skulked off into the night. I would have stayed longer if the music had been more to my taste. I could listen to Hendrix or Pink Floyd at full volume but Girls Aloud? No wonder none of the revellers were aware of what was unfolding a few streets away. The billowing smoke and the red glow on the skyline had me in work mode and sober before I reached the front gate. I was all too familiar with the cacophony of cries and the sounds of explosions and shattering glass. My first assignment was back in 1985 when I was asked to cover the Brixton riots; where my naivety left me with a bruised cheek (courtesy of a rioter) and a smashed camera (courtesy of the cops). I'd heard that a demo was planned outside the police station but this was way bigger than that. It had scoop written all over it.

By the time I'd started taking pictures hundreds had already swarmed onto the High Road. They bopped between the flames and broken glass; a dance floor for unchoreographed mayhem. Give them a lick of paint, plant axes and swords in their mitts instead of rocks and petrol bombs, and *voila*: your archetypal pagan warriors await. But this mob wasn't invoking the spirits of the ancestors before going into battle, or preparing themselves for a journey into the afterlife. They lived for the here and now. And for me the now is highly profitable. I positioned myself at a safe distance from a burning police car: a firewall between the crazies and me. Ducking and skipping from side to side, I got some great shots of looted premises and trashed vehicles. But devastated people sell more copies than devastated buildings and my luck was in. An elderly man had returned to protect his grocery store. When his pleas went unheard and as his business disintegrated before his watering eyes, he dropped to his knees and raised his arms. He reminded me of that luckless sergeant in *Platoon*. I snapped him at various angles and meandered further along the High Road before he had the chance to vent his fury at me.

A young woman in a taupe business suit and high heels cut across my path and stopped abruptly. She was battling a shopping trolley loaded with dresses that had become jammed in a crack in the pavement. She pushed, pulled, and shook the trolley but it wouldn't budge. A man in a maroon woollen hat grabbed the top dress, a thin, gypsy-style summer garment. One of the girls at the party had thrown up over something similar, reminding me of my hippy days. The man held it up, dropped it back on the pile and roared 'never fit my bitch', and gave the trolley a shove. The woman thanked him in Polish. To my left a youth with a scarf wrapped around his face was vandalising a travel agents. Perhaps he'd been jilted by a travel rep, or had something against Greeks (a poster of a sun-drenched beach in Rhodes had caught fire in the window). Whatever his motive, Greece was never this hot.

The young and the not-so-young were emerging from shops whooping and laden with armfuls of swag. A thin line of police officers strove to halt the carnage but they were retreating under a hail of missiles. Before I reached the next corner the man in the maroon hat sprinted past me stacked high with cigarettes, his pockets leaking giant Rizlas. A packet of Benson and Hedges became dislodged and landed at my feet. The light cast by a burning police car was so bright that I could read the warning on the packet. I had no qualms about joining the ranks of the looters, but as I stooped to pick it up, something struck me on the top of the head. Bent double, I staggered a few paces, determined to stay on my feet because I'd seen too many people get a good kicking when they hit the deck. I glanced behind and glimpsed a clutch of hooded men. In my confusion, I'd strayed too close to the burning police car. I covered my face with my arms, as much to protect my eyes from the light as from the searing heat – and ran like fuck.

Many gasping yards later I stopped and looked back. The four hooded men were silhouetted against the flames sheeting from the police car. One of them pointed at me. He was a good foot taller than the others and for that reason alone I took him to be their leader. I had no idea what I'd done to offend them, taken one picture too many maybe? I patted my head and checked my hand. My skin was tinged red in the firelight but I couldn't see any blood. I didn't know what they'd hit me with, but thought myself lucky that my entire skull hadn't caved in. Another car was torched.

'This is our street!' was the cry from those around me.

I was in no position to argue. By now I was choking on the smoke. My heart was thumping as hard as the camera, which continued to pound against my chest with every stride. If my mind wasn't groggy and my hands hadn't got the yips I would have taken a picture of a burning bus. I might have made a tidy few bob there if it hit the wires first. I hoped the four hoodies would succumb to temptation and help themselves to the goodies on offer. No such luck. When I glanced back again they had set off after me at a casual pace. I tried to speed up, but loping they still steadily gained ground. I needed to get my bearings. The Tottenham that I'd grown up in had long since gone, but some things hadn't changed. I was nearing Bruce Grove Station. Should I attempt to take a train? Were the trains even running? They might corner me on the platform. They might hurl me onto the track for all I knew.

I pumped my arms and prompted my legs, but I was reduced to a laboured jog. The way ahead was illuminated by a fire which had engulfed a large building. The innards were unrecognisable but the outline was familiar. The apex was on a corner and the flames fanned out many yards along two roads. I recalled a decoration similar to a large snooker triangle placed beneath a kind of bell tower, but they had gone up in smoke too. Shaped like the bow of a mighty liner, the Art Deco building barely stood erect. When I was a boy, the very same building was owned by the Co-op. I'd charge inside and sail across the ocean to the land of cowboys and Indians. I'd hide behind the clothes racks and furniture, form my fingers into a gun, and order my mother to put her hands up or else. On that wretched day in 2011 it looked as if the store had been bombed to oblivion. Come morning it would be a burned-out shell, a ransacked hulk; tangles of charred concrete and gaping holes for windows. God, it felt as if I'd passed through a time portal to the Blitz. I imagined men in tin hats and baggy uniforms scouring the piles of rubble for survivors.

People were crowded onto the pavement opposite the blaze taking pictures with mobile phones. A woman in a burka bemoaned the fact she'd put a deposit down on a carpet just the other day. Another voice prayed that the people in the flats above the store got out alive. Some just wept. In the middle of the road a photographer braved the heat. He snapped away, twisting his torso and crouching on his toes to get the best shots; camera clicking away at the rate of a semi-automatic. I recalled once sharing a flask of tea with him on some bleak winter's evening as we shuffled our feet outside The Ivy. I wanted to scream out to him for help but my throat was parched and not enough air was reaching my lungs. I knew that if I kept going in my present direction I'd reach the Spurs ground, the tiny enclave that frustrated and delighted in equal measure. But if I headed in a straight line they'd catch me for sure. I needed to zigzag. Lansdowne Road and the warren of streets that surrounded it were a better option. I knew these streets inside out. At least, I hoped I did.

Nearly every house I passed showed a light. I could see the flicker of television screens in the few with open curtains, the news programmes most likely. I thought about banging on doors but doubted that the inhabitants would dare open up, especially to the press. I would have thrown my camera away before knocking if I'd had enough money to buy another one. I was tempted to hide in a front garden but not even a ten-foot-high wall could dull the sound of my wheezy breath. I cursed the stitch which gripped my side. The gang emerged in Lansdowne. Like puppets silhouetted before a backdrop of red, they ran straight through the flames shooting from the old Co-op. I was in full view and it would have only taken them a minute or two to catch me up. But instead of waving his three mates forward, the giant held out an arm and formed them into a huddle. I could tell by their frantic arm movements that his mates weren't best pleased.

My head throbbed and I was too disorientated to think straight, from exhaustion or concussion or a mixture of both. I'd made a good hundred yards before they'd set off again. I took a sharp left and stumbled on.

A harsh voice from not too far away hollered, 'Spread out! The cunt ain't gone far!'

The row of houses ended, replaced by a large brick building protected by railings. I shook the railings like an innocent man cast cruelly behind prison bars. I didn't recognise the name on the sign above my head, which read "Primary Academy", but that gloomy pile of dust was my old junior school. If only Mr Gasson could have seen me then. He used to say that I'd meet an untimely end if I kept on picking my nose.

I wasn't aware of the man's approach until a gun dug into my ribs and a hand seized me by the collar. He was a good three inches taller than me and considerably broader. He wore skin-tight leather gloves and shades, which covered a good third of each cheek. The peak of a baseball cap poked out from under a raised hood, casting his face in deep shadow. I couldn't see his lips move as he held out a hand and spoke to me in North London tinged with West Indian; third generation Afro-Caribbean, possibly in his mid-twenties was my guess.

He growled, 'The camera, chief. Pass it over.'

I had the yips bad and fumbled with the strap. Losing patience, he snatched the camera and threw the strap over his shoulder. He waved the gun in front of my nose and ordered me to sit on the pavement. I slumped to the ground; my mind was neck and neck with Usain Bolt but my legs and lungs were grateful for the rest.

I peered up at the bloke who held my life in his hands. If I managed to make eye contact, I might be able to get through to him, to stop it before it started. A thin light brushed his cheeks as he scrutinised my picture gallery. He stopped rolling the images, jabbed me in the shoulder, and asked what I'd seen. When I didn't respond he repeated the question. I'd photographed a Muslim woman once while on assignment in East Ham. She told me she poked her tongue out at white people beneath her burka when they gave her nasty looks. If I did capture him throwing petrol bombs or firing a gun no one could have recognised him under all that clobber. He might as well have worn deep-sea diving gear over a space suit. I wondered if his eyes were bursting with hatred behind those shades. I was convinced they didn't hold a mischievous twinkle. When I insisted that I hadn't seen anything he pointed at the screen. I reached up to take the camera but he moved it out of range and wafted a hand in front of his face.

'Your breath stinks of whisky, chief. I'm surprised you can still walk let alone run.' A voice giving directions on a Sat Nav exhibited more emotion than him as he raised the gun and continued, 'Shouldn't feel much as the slug shatters your skull then, chief.'

I'd often wondered how I'd react if I was assigned to a killing field. Would my hands remain steady enough to capture the slaughter? Would I have the guts to even board the plane? Sweat trickled from my clammy armpits as piss seeped into my pants. I closed my eyes and pressed my trembling frame against the railings. I heard a pathetic grovelling voice: mine.

'Please don't. I'll make it worth your while…'

I waited a few seconds and squinted up at him. He was using his mobile as a torch to read the name printed on the side of my camera case.

'This you?' he barked.

I nodded.

'Yes.'

'Funny name, Kuchy. Can't be many of them around.'

'I have a long Polish name. It's hard to pronounce. You can call me Ricky if you like.'

'Prefer Kuchy. Who lumbered you with it then?'

'Someone at my paper. Funnily enough the nickname was first given to me by a kid at this school … I can get a debit card. I haven't got it on me.'

'No thanks. Just mugged an old lady … you went here, to this school? When? Who was the kid?'

'In the fifties. A Pakistani boy called Mushtaq.'

'Year?'

'1957.'

'Mushtaq, is it? Can't be many of his kind around in those days. I want to hear all about the first brother off the boat.'

'Notting Hill already had a large black community but he was the first non-white in our school.'

'Not interested in them brothers. I want to hear about this Mushtaq and how he was treated by you white boys.' His mobile chimed some jarring rap song. He looked at the caller's name and his finger hovered over the green button. He put the phone on silent before he slipped it back inside his pocket. 'Pass me your mobile and get your white arse over these railings.'

I promptly handed it to him.

'Please … you can have anything you want.'

None too impressed by my Casio, he stamped on it and threw the remains cricket-style into the overgrown garden hedge opposite. He looked up at a surveillance camera.

'CCTV ain't working and no one would give a shit if it was tonight.' He caught the fear in my eyes and beamed. 'Don't worry, chief, I'd have done you here if I had a mind.'

I patted my head. It was no less tender to the touch.

'Was it you that struck me?'

'My bitch. Said she weren't dolled up enough to have her picture taken. She's gone shopping. Heard there's rich pickings down at JD Sports.'

He wasn't ranting and raving, but my sixth sense told me he was on the edge. You need a sixth sense in my job, especially if you catch one of those macho film stars or a crazed rock drummer unawares.

From close by someone shouted, 'Raz!'

'Your choice, chief. My friends'll be here soon.' He ran his fingers across his throat. 'They don't take prisoners.'

He tucked the gun into his belt, covering it with his coat. He obviously didn't consider me much of a threat. It wasn't so long ago that I could bench a hundred kilos and knock seven shades out of a punch bag. He bent and formed his hands into a stirrup.

'Last chance, chief.'

How deep the reserves of human energy when your life is about to be snuffed out. I placed my foot in his interlocked hands and he gave me a leg up. I wanted to tell him that I'd make it to the top without his help. I'd have liked to have sprung upon him like a caged tiger. As it was, I tottered on the edge and agonized over the ankle that Noel Gallagher's mate had kicked as he left The Ivy. Mike said I might get arthritis if I hurt it again.

'Raz! Where the fuck are you, bro?'

There was that voice again, but it was a hell of a lot closer this time. My assailant prodded me in the calf.

'It's now or never, chief. You're not leaping from the fucking Twin Towers.'

I wondered if Raz was an extreme Islamist. Had I inadvertently photographed him beating up a Jew? Stamford Hill was only down the road from Tottenham police station. Whoever he was, I decided to take my chances with him rather than the pack of snarling wolves he called friends. I bent my knees and jumped. Images of the souls who leapt from the Twin Towers flashed across my mind. Unlike those poor bastards my feet felt concrete. Raz landed beside me and pointed to an area of darkness.

'This way, chief.'

I dragged my weary legs across the playground and we squatted in the gloom. He put a hand over my mouth to stifle the sound of my breathing. Almost immediately his three mates appeared.

One of them said, 'Best let him know, blud. That cunt don't look much, but he might've got Raz.'

He made a phone call and the gang set off down the street. Raz forced me to sit with my back against the wall and cuffed me across the side of the head.

'How much do you remember?'

'I told you, I didn't see anything.'

'I meant about this school. When you were here in the fifties.'

'Why?'

'Start from the beginning, from your first day and work through. No need to squeak but give the young Ricky his boyhood voice, add a touch of the vernacular now and then. And tell me more about this Mushtaq kid. I bet you white boys made his life hell.'

'You're joking. Right?'

'Do it.'

He didn't seem mad, more maddened. It occurred to me that he might be on drugs. If so, I hoped he toked on mellow weed and didn't get blitzed on skunk. Who was I kidding? He was probably on crack. These hoodies don't exactly exude peace and love. I reckoned there was plenty of room inside this guy's head for mind expansion. At least his jeans weren't at half-mast and he wasn't showing off lurid underpants; flaunting the attitude that went with it. And he'd kept his shades on and hood up. If he were going to bump me off, surely he wouldn't care if I saw his face. What did he want to hear? What didn't he? Where to start? Never mind where to start, I thought I'd better take a long time finishing. If I ran out of memory I'd make it up as I went along. Best make it simple and entertaining. The guy probably had the IQ of Baldrick's turnip and the attention span of a noughties teenager. Hopefully the police would start patrolling the streets at dawn. Dear God, there were sirens going off all over the place by now and up popped yet another red glow on the skyline. Judging by the way the riot was spreading, they'd need water cannon, or failing that, armoured personnel carriers. Whatever happened to the spirit of the Blitz?

2

The bricks were cold and painful against my spine. My headache was slightly better; at least things weren't spinning now. But my neck was stiff and there was a shooting pain beneath both shoulder blades. I wanted to find a more comfortable position but my body, as with my mind, was going nowhere. Raz shook me by my shoulders.

'Why you hunching up, Kuchy? Relax, man. Little Red Riding Hood wore a hood.'

'But she didn't have a fucking gun in her hand.'

He tutted and wagged a finger at me.

'Language, Kuchy. I bet you wouldn't have said that to a teacher in the 50s. Tell you what, chief. Let's go inside and you can have a proper sit down.'

I tried to stand but my knees buckled. I could smell coffee on his breath as he seized me under the armpit and hauled me to my feet. I expected weed or alcohol. I expected him to scout for a way into the main building, break a window or a glass panel, but he led me across the playground to a low-level structure with a flat roof. As we got closer, I recognised the boys' toilets. In my day, the entrance had no door. It was now fitted with a metal one which looked capable of withstanding a bomb blast. He took a bunch of keys from his pocket, carefully selected one, and opened the door. I managed a clumsy backward step and a clumsier half-turn before he dragged me inside. He closed the door behind us and locked it.

The toilets reeked of disinfectant and stale piss. He switched on a torch and aimed it at the ground like a cinema usher showing a patron to their seat. As we walked alongside the row of green cubicles our long shadows slid across the wall and ceiling. Small pools of water glimmered on the concrete floor as if someone had been sloppy with a mop. He stopped and opened a cubicle door, shone the torch inside, and pushed me in. I gripped my belt and begged him not to. In the next breath, I told him I wasn't big on Boy George. I may have been quaking with fear but fool was in my DNA. It was a well-known fact amongst my dwindling circle of friends that the greater my stress or distress, the greater my capacity for playing the clown. I was the sort of guy who was grateful they had a minute's applause at football matches instead of a minute's silence for the deceased. Danny Blanch-flower was one of my all-time heroes, yet I nearly bit my tongue off trying not to laugh when he passed.

Raz pointed the gun at my face. He ordered me to sit on the toilet and make myself comfortable. I didn't dare object but my quads and hamstrings complained as my bottom felt for the seat, any lower and I'd have been sitting on the floor. I was on the verge of convulsing, and petrified that he'd take down his joggers and make me suck his cock. I was shrivelled, rooted and doomed, like the slug I'd smothered with salt in my bedsit the previous morning. He remained motionless, neither of us speaking. What wouldn't I have given to instead be standing slap bang in the middle of the riot with an orchestra of police sirens blaring in my ears?

Raz shone the torch in my face.

'You'd better start remembering, Kuchy.'

I covered my eyes to ward off the glare. I swear if my trousers and pants weren't up I would have shat in that toilet bowl. I have no idea how and why he came into possession of the toilet key. But I doubted that he was the caretaker, because we had to scale the railings. If he was a pervert seeking sexual gratification he was going about it in a strange way. Was he a cop or working for the cops? If he hadn't got his mates into that huddle they would have caught me for sure. Had he been cut off from the police station and was I under investigation? If so, his methods and line of enquiry didn't make any sense. Advances in forensic science had helped to solve ancient crimes, but childhood memories from the 1950s?

'Remember what? I don't know what you want. Who are you?'

'This Mushtaq was the first, weren't he? He's what you call a trail-blazer. If he weren't a Pakistani we'd build him a statue. If the people in your recollections ain't met Mushtaq I don't want to know. Don't try telling porkies or padding it out, chief. You don't want me to come in there with you.'

How would he know if I was telling the truth? How could I be certain that my memory wasn't playing tricks on me? As you get older reality becomes blurred at the edges. When I taught history in the 70s I'd make up yarns to keep the little darlings interested. I told one class that Henry the Eighth got hit on the head by a piece of falling monastic masonry, and that's why he dissolved the monasteries. Half the class wrote it down as fact before they realised they'd been had. If Raz was in the dimwit league I thought I might have half a chance of surviving the night. If I could've seen his face and it was half presentable, I'd have offered him a free photo shoot and assured him that he'd make a fortune as a male model. There are no greater flatterers than people photographers. It was all too mad for words. Would he kill me? After what I'd witnessed on the street I wasn't taking any chances. Forget cop, it occurred to me he might be a Yardie and a new batch of paranoia was thrown onto the pyre. Right then I would've worn an Arsenal shirt in exchange for a bottle of scotch. If he wanted a story he'd get a bleedin' story. Ah, the idyllic past: long summer holidays when the sun always shone and kids played in the street without fear of being run over or abducted by paedophiles.

3

'The weather was as dreary on my first day at junior school as my mood. It had rained overnight and there were puddles in the road. Mum held my hand as we crossed in case I jumped up and down in one. Money was tight and she'd used the last of her Co-op "divi" points on new socks for me. She straightened my grey pullover and gave me a cuddle close to a bear hug at the gates. If that wasn't humiliation enough, she pecked me on the cheek and combed my hair with her hands. Everyone saw it. For the umpteenth time that morning she made me promise to behave or she'd tell Dad, and for the umpteenth time I replied with a sulky, "Yes, Mum". She then stood in line with the other mums and waved as I went into the playground. I'd begged her not to, but she waited by the railings long after all the other mums had left. She was quite right not to trust me. Most of my mates from the infants were from my street (which was a stone's throw from the Spurs ground), but we'd been split up and packed off to different schools. Disruptive is the word they used to justify my exile here. I have a notion that what was disruptive then would be considered tolerable behaviour these days. One weedy boy asked me if I knew the woman wiping her eyes with a handkerchief. I told him she wasn't with me and to fuck off.'

Raz placed the gun over his heart.

'I'm touched, Kuchy, but Mushtaq better pop up soon.'

I kind of understood how an actor felt when he forgot his lines and had to ad lib. The difference was that the actor might get ridiculed if he dried up, whereas I'd get a bullet in the head. My mind went blank for a few seconds. If it had stayed that way any longer, I could very well have had a panic attack. I blinked. I don't know why but blinking helped clear my mind.

'I'm leading up to him.'

'Carry on then, Kuchy. You don't have to make it complicated. Pretend you're telling a child a bedtime story.'

Get an audio biography of Ice Cube, motherfucker. Go curl up in bed with a nice warm cup of arsenic-fortified cocoa. My thoughts.

***

'Before Mr Gasson had a chance to bring the class to order and separate the chatterboxes from the petrified, I checked that Mum had left and did a bunk. The caretaker was at the gates talking to another man in overalls, so I decided to hide in these toilets until the coast was clear. I hoped that if I acted naughty enough they'd pack me off to the school where my mates had gone. A boy was blocking the doorway as I tried to sneak out of the main building. He was my age but at the time I thought he must be a 2nd or 3rd year because he was much bigger than me. He had smudge marks on his cheeks and forehead, stained teeth, and his big toes poked out of plimsolls that looked a size too small. I would have been as grubby as him if Mum hadn't made me have a bath in front of the fire. My teeth were only whiter than his because we'd started using Colgate instead of salt. When I think of him now, I'm reminded of the street kids I photographed in Naples. We sized each other up. He might have been bigger than me but I wasn't going to back down. In Tottenham of the 1950s, kids proved themselves by fighting or playing football. I gave him a Tottenham Look. It was like the evil eye but with serious menace (your cheeks came towards your nose and your eyes slowly narrowed as you held a glare). He gave me a Tottenham Look back. You could only hold a Tottenham Look for so long and we both burst into laughter.

He stepped aside and said, "I've been for a crap. Blimey, bogs with seats are well plush compared to doing it in a bucket like me old man." He followed up with an astute analogy. "Ain't much difference between this dump and Pentonville Prison except the screws and a bleedin' high wall. Me old man's banged up in Pentonville. Shot a security guard in the leg, he did. Weren't his fault. Had an itchy finger."

There were no high fives in those days, just a friendly slap on the shoulder. After we exchanged names and slaps I made my way across the playground to the toilets, grateful that I was on the right side of Harry Hooper.

At Parkhurst Infants' School one of two teachers had policed the boys' toilets. Mr Hart was teeny and his gut wobbled like jelly. He was so short that he could only see over the top of the cubicle doors by standing on tiptoe. He preferred to bellow at the entrance if a boy sneaked off to the toilet without permission. He'd warn them that they'd better come out in a minute flat or there'd be no football at break. Although Mr Dicks was as tall as a prefab he preferred to look under the doors. Make of it what you will, but if he'd done that post-Jimmy Saville fifteen detectives would have raided his house and confiscated his computer. I had no idea who policed these toilets but that morning Dad told me they gave you the cane if you really played up. I'd been too hyper to take it in at the time, but his words suddenly came back to freak me out. Goose bumps spread across my milky thighs and there was a growing fear raging inside my brain. I needed to go, but try as hard as I could my bum just wasn't having it. It started itching. I was forever scratching my bottom. Nanna blamed it on the *Daily Mirror* and said Mum should cut down on the fags and buy proper lavatory paper instead. At home Mum came with me to our toilet. It was in the back garden and was freezing cold in winter. In the torchlight the spiders looked as big as mop heads, but she would tell me not to be scared because we're all God's creatures. I tried telling her that when she caught a mouse nibbling on her Yorkshire pudding, but she wasn't so brave then. It was the first time I'd sat on a strange toilet without Dad being there. When I couldn't go, he would stand outside the cubicle and tell me scary stories about an Italian monastery on the top of a big hill, and how many evil monsters he'd pulverised before his tank blew up. He meant Nazis. I'm talking about guns on swivelling turrets and not angelfish or thick-lipped gourami.'

Raz took a giant stride towards me.

'Don't push your luck, funny boy. You better not dis me. Did your parents and Nanna meet Mushtaq?'

'Did they just. I'll never forget it.'

'I hope so for your sake.'

'If I don't tell you this bit, none of what happened to Mushtaq will make sense.'

'Proceed under caution, Kuchy.'

So much for spellbinding soliloquy. Bloody Hamlet never had it this tough.

***

"I pulled up my short trousers and galloped out of those loos like Crepello, the horse which won the Derby that year. Dad backed the horse which came third from last."

Mum said, "At least you didn't come last, dear".

Mum told me to never repeat what Dad said in reply. It sounded like the name of the winning horse, but wasn't. I got as far as the chalk goal on the playground wall when my guts started playing up. A few feet past the goal there was a shelter where the teachers left their bikes. Squeezing my bum cheeks together, I dashed inside and downed my trousers. After executing the first ever rendition of the twist, a turd shot out of me and lay steaming at my feet. The bloody thing was as slippery as the gudgeon we fished in the River Lea. Dad only seemed to catch a whopping great carp when I wasn't there. Looking back, it's likely he told whoppers rather than caught them. But this was no gudgeon. It was a ruddy great pike. Poo bags weren't invented when I was growing up. When you played in the street you had to scrape your shoe on the curb to get rid of the dog shit. Luckily for me, mine was a hard one. As every schoolboy knew, before soft toilet paper was a standard commodity you didn't have to wipe your bum if it was a hard one. What to do with it? More importantly, had anyone seen me? If I kicked it away it might disintegrate and deposit bits on my shoe, or even worse, on a teacher's spokes. Mum worked part-time in the Whitbread Brewery and had saved long and hard for the shoes on my feet. Nah, I'd stitch some bugger up instead. The caretaker was still yakking at the gates, but I figured I could make the main building without him seeing me. I sprinted across the playground and dashed into my classroom. I informed Mr Gasson that I'd got lost and stood by the door awhile to find me a dupe. I ignored the girls and studied the boys' faces as closely as Dad studied the racing form. Mum said you could pop a balloon in front of her Ziggy's face when he had his nose in the racing pages.'

Raz clapped his hands with such force that my ears rang.

'Stop right there, Kuchy. Why did you ignore the girls? Their toilets inside, were they?'

'No. In the playground like ours. I figured the teachers would know it's not one of them because they didn't fart like us. You rarely heard a girl popping off. That meant their poo would behave itself better. Once I heard a loud fart coming from the other side of our garden fence. There was brief silence and then Betty Harris said indignantly, "Ladies don't blow off. It must be you, Fred." I thought girls must wee more than us though because I heard Mrs Harris telling Mum that she saw the comedian, Tommy Trinder, and pissed herself laughing.'

'What you on about, Kuchy? If I struck a match my bitch would turn into a flamethrower.'

'Boy, if ever there was an age of innocence. These days I expect most seven-year-olds have seen porn movies and can operate the computer on the International Space Station. But without a bombardment of information via social media, you could argue that there was a greater sense of mystery in my day. I didn't know what female genitalia looked like until I was seventeen and it came as quite a shock, I can tell you. Sharon Bullock was her name. I'll never forget it. She had her legs wide open and I knelt on the bed holding her ankles in case she closed them again. I kept gawking at it, gormless, as if it was some strange animal …'

He grabbed me by the collar. I weigh a good sixteen stone, but he lifted me clean off the toilet and hoisted me so high I could see into the next cubicle. I swear he had the strength of a small crane.

'Stop throwing this useless shit at me, Kuchy! Mushtaq had better put in an appearance soon.'

My shirt was choking me and all I could manage in response was a nod and a stunted gargle.

He lowered me back on the toilet and hissed, 'And don't make things up about him. I'll know if you're lying.'

My university days may have passed me by in a haze, but my junior school days were clearer, and appeared to be getting clearer by the minute. It didn't bode well.

**

'The fat boy at the front reminded me of Billy Bunter. His piggy eyes were set deep into his blubbery face and his chubby knees were pressed against each other. He looked as if he might shit himself at any moment. The fidgety kid with the pudding basin haircut at the back looked like he'd already done the business. Either that or he was sitting on a drawing pin. None of the others really caught my eye, and I'd just decided to plump for Billy Bunter, when a puny brown kid stood up. He had gelled black hair combed flat and he wore a smart jacket and long trousers with sharp creases in them. Harry Hooper was on one side of him and a girl with ginger hair and freckles on the other. Harry winked at me and made his fingers into a gun. He pretended to vomit and pointed the imaginary gun at the brown kid who was shivering as if he'd just stepped out of an ice bath. Under normal circumstances a Carrot Top would have borne the brunt. I winked at Harry, widened my eyes, and nodded back. None of us had ever seen a face that colour around our way before. It wasn't quite as black as the golliwog on a Robertson's jam jar. I thought a lightly fried Walls' pork sausage came closest. Mr Gasson made him spell his name out and wrote it on the blackboard: M-u-s-h-t-a-q. I naturally called him Mush and conjured up some choice wind-ups in my mind: All right, Mush? You've got an ugly mush, Mush.

I managed to keep a straight face as I cried, "Nice to meet you mush."

It had everyone in stitches. I might have felt like taking a bow but Mush didn't get it. Mr Gasson got it all too well. He stopped writing, turned around, and slapped away a chalk mark from his brown corduroy trousers.

"From what I understand your father was an immigrant, Ricky. Please show some consideration."

I had my reply off pat.

"We might never have won the Battle of Britain without the Poles, sir."

I glared at Mush.

"What did his lot do in the war?"

Hitler's mob had their Jews as scapegoats and I had this brown kid. No need to look any further than Mush, then.'

4

Raz slipped his hand into his inside pocket and removed an object.

I thought it a large pen at first until he said, 'So the white suprema-cists were at it from day one then, were they?' and casually fitted a silencer to the end of the gun.

I recoiled so violently that my buttock slewed off the edge of the toilet seat and my shoulder rammed into the side of the cubicle. I pushed a hand against the partition to regain my balance, and then jammed my hands between my thighs to stop my knees from knock-ing together. He strolled into the next cubicle, returned with a roll of loo paper, and positioned it vertically at the entrance to my cell.

Smirking, he said, 'I would have taken your one, chief, but I think you may need it.'

He propped the torch on the roll and adjusted the angle till it shone at my chest.

'What did you say was on the jam jar, white boy?'

My breathing became shallow and erratic, and my voice quaked and stuttered like it does when Mike uses his heavy massage machine on my upper back.

'A little black boy. Very cute. I believe Queen Victoria had a collection.'

'Why'd they put a golliwog on the jar? Nigger haters were they?'

'To sell more jam. Attitudes have changed. We know better these days.'

'Reckon?' He cupped his balls. 'Do you think my cock's bigger than yours?'

'How would I know? Can't we call it a dead heat?'

His silhouette filled the entrance to the cubicle.

'Let's find out, shall we? Stand up and pull down your pants and trousers down. Better still, strip naked. Let's take a good look at you.'

My scrotum contracted so tightly around my balls that I thought they were going to pop. Some feat for a man of my age. I hugged my raised knees and rocked back and forth like the homeless smack addict I'd snapped behind Selfridges when the snow was a foot deep. My bum cheeks may have been well padded but they weren't designed to withstand this kind of punishment. My hamstrings cramped and the dull ache in my arse became a burning pain. I caught the glint of his gun as it cut the beam, and begged him not to shoot or abuse me. Each plea was met with silence. I struggled to my feet, took off my jacket, and draped it over the top of the partition. As I fought to undo my shirt a button flew off. Raz caught the button before it hit the ground. He swallowed it whole in one movement and licked his lips. Think of a lizard catching a fly. I rushed to hang my shirt over the jacket, begged again, promised him all kinds of rewards, swearing I'd never tell a soul if he let me go. I hesitated at the vest, horrified at the thought of being found dead and stark naked in the boys' lavatories.

He broke the silence with a curt, 'And the rest, Grandad, or I'll put a slug in your bingo wings.'

I fumbled to unfasten my belt and unzip my flies. Once they were undone, I clung onto the top of my trousers to stop them from falling. He lunged forward and jabbed the barrel of his gun into my upper arm. I lost my grip on the trousers and they tumbled down my legs, depositing themselves around my ankles. He grinned at the sight of my XL Y-fronts. I tried to humour him by telling him I pressed the wrong button during my Amazon order. Whether that singular noise he made was a laugh, a grunt, or a growl, I'm not sure. He told me he'd put a bullet in my head if I didn't do exactly as he said. I lowered my pants and once past my hips they didn't need much persuading to join the trousers. The torch was aimed precisely at my genitals, which compounded my discomfort, as did the warning not to cover them with my hands. I stood there exposed and shivering as he removed my camera from his shoulder and took pictures of my privates from several angles.

'When you were a very big boy, did you show your cock to very small boys, Kuchy?'

'No…no way. Only when I was a small boy and with boys of a similar age. Most boys compare penises. It's natural.'

I dreaded to think that he was trawling the area for sickos and wanted me to join some twisted club. You'd hardly call it protection, more like self-preservation, but I decided to tone down the explicit and keep the imagery to a minimum – and the procrastination to the maximum.

'Douglas Noble got his cock out in his garden shed and asked to see mine and Bill's. I didn't mind. After all, I thought, they're only made of skin just like our ears and nose. Bill was convinced that he'd grow balls any day soon. He knew it for a fact because it prickled down there, similar to how our skin felt when we played football on a field by the gasholder. Sometimes the air would be tinged orange on that field but no one thought twice about it. Douglas asked him how big testicles were.

"The size of marbles? Conkers? Ping pong balls?"

I recalled Grandad Ink telling me a German sniper could shoot your nuts off from six hundred yards.

Thinking a sniper would have more difficulty hitting a target the size of a marble or a conker, I replied, "Has to be ping pong balls, mate."

We also tried to get the girls to show us a nipple. I offered Jenny a tanner to see her chest and she told me to get stuffed. Bill told me to go back with an improved offer. I think he must have remembered the conversation they were having at the estate agents when we pretended to be collecting for the cubs. If we'd had one of their uniforms on we might have collected more than a clip around the ear and a threepenny bit for cheek. Douglas had a longer feel of mine than Bill's, but I sort of prodded at his because it didn't look very nice. I said his reminded me of an earthworm popping its head up after it'd rained. He got all sulky and replied that mine was like a worm cut in half.'

Raz stooped and picked up the torch.

'Things ain't changed that much then, Kuchy. I should have done you a favour and used the zoom.'

I tried reminding myself that he had a girlfriend, but my paranoia only abated when he unscrewed the silencer, put the gun in his pocket, and ordered me to pull my trousers up.

When I was fully dressed, he growled, 'Now get your pasty arse back on that toilet seat and tell me how you stitched poor Mushtaq up.'

Since Maggie kicked me out, life on Earth can be summed up in two words: random futility (or who gives a fuck?). Far from inducing desperation, the concept of an arbitrary, godless universe provides humongous scope for debauchery and a modicum of wellbeing. Of course, "who gives a fuck!" can be interpreted in many ways. For example, who gives a fuck if this hoodie is deprived? Or, who gives a fuck if this hoodie comes from a broken home? And last, but not least, who gives a fuck if a police marksman riddles this pervert with bullets? (I might even get some choice snaps of the body if my camera remains intact). That said, if one puts one's mind to it, there are circumstances in which random futility isn't the be all and end all of existence. For example: when an old man's mind is fixed on killing the bastard who's standing before him.

5

Being scared out of your wits while enduring prolonged physical pain is not conducive to planning a well-thought-out and cleverly executed murder. I did, however, retain enough acumen to realise that if I was dealing with a madman whose actions were triggered by random, illogical impulses – possibly the product of substance abuse – there was little point in trying to reason with him. If that were the case, he'd have to be eliminated sooner rather than later. Easier said than done. The exit door was solid metal and locked, and even if I caught him by surprise, there was little chance of me overpowering him without employing a weapon of some kind. A good old-fashioned lavatory chain that I could have wrapped around his throat might have come in handy, but they'd gone the way of Betamax long before the turn of the new millennium. I thought about stealing his keys but that would have required him to fall asleep and there seemed to be sufficient adrenaline surging through his body to withstand a quiver full of tranquiliser darts. My life in the 50s was but a tiny piece of social history, hardly a saga. My hope was that he had a goal in mind dependent upon me finishing the story. If so, I could bide my time before I pounced. Close to the end, but not at the climax of my story being the prudent option, for I was convinced he would kill at its the conclusion. A tricky thing the truth, especially when it may get you killed. But it rolls off the tongue much easier than thinking up lies for hours on end. The truth would have to be censored, bits snipped off and falsehoods glued on here and there. Though not to the extent that I was seen to be hesitating and stuttering over passages of make believe. I figured I'd introduce more characters into the mix – the longer I could spin it out, the greater my chances of survival. "I think therefore I am" is an undeniable truth. In my case: I talk therefore I am.

During my stints as a journalist and press photographer, I'd witnessed first-hand the aggro between Afro-Caribbean and Asian youths in North West London. Mush was a Pakistani who had a good thirty years on Raz – which made Raz's black power trip and his apparent affinity with him even more puzzling. Raz was punishing me for being white both in the present and the past, and judging me when I was a seven-year-old kid. I thought if I could make him understand that I was simply a boy of my time he might ease up and drop his guard. I was determined to show him how multiculturalism was a term that didn't get airtime in my formative years. If it had it would've been as popular as gay marriage with the Good Old Boys in the Bible Belt.

***

'The first book Dad gave me was published in the 30s when we still had India. It had pictures of elephants and tigers and there was a long procession to honour our king. We were the rulers and black people were the domain of the *Pathé News*. The Notting Hill riots broke out in the late 50s and various rebellions erupted in the far-flung reaches of the Empire. Suddenly the fruits of imperialism didn't taste so sweet. Dad may have been Polish but he was also an ardent Anglophile. He consoled himself by showing me an atlas in which huge chunks of the Earth were still displayed in pink. Later on, I borrowed Dad's atlas and shoved it under Mush's nose. He mightn't have been too impressed but I felt proud to be British. It was true, there were countries in the world that we hadn't colonised, but, except for America, they didn't count for much. Mush looked just like the Indians in Dad's book, and boys back then loved playing cowboys and Indians. I always chose the cowboy because they were smarter than the Indians and invariably won. I was too busy slaying redskins with my spud gun to take into account greedy gold prospectors, weight of numbers, repeating rifles, or the cavalry's Gatling guns. Indian, Red Indian, what was the difference? They were inferior and Mush was no different to a whooping savage on horseback. The Lone Ranger was the boss man, not flamin' Tonto.'

'Grandad Ink used to say that God was an Englishman; a feeble hypothesis maybe, but one that bore fruit when Mush raised his hand and asked to be excused. It was just the opportunity I'd been waiting for.'

Raz's forearm smashed against the partition and the whole cubicle shook.

'Did your Grandad meet Mushtaq? Did he live with you?'

I thrust the flats of my hands in his direction, like a man trying to stop a reversing juggernaut from demolishing a wall.

'Easy, man... he was Nanna's husband. The old couple lived upstairs. They both met Mushtaq.'

'In your house?'

'Yes.'

'Did anyone else live there?'

'Only my dog, Sandy. He came with Mum and Nanna to meet me from school and spent a lot of his time sitting on the top of walls, or cars if one happened to be parked up. That way he could keep a lookout for cats. He had a body the colour of sand and a red mane. I wanted to dye it blue but Mum wouldn't let me. He was like the brother I never had. Sometimes I loved Mum, Sandy, and Dad in that order, and when I was mad with Mum, I loved Sandy most of all. I told Dad that once and got upset.

He said, "I k'now you didn't mean that. You k'now your mother and me love you, don't you Ricky?"'

'What's with all this k'now business, chief? Got some Special K stuck in your throat?'

'Dad spoke excellent English although he did pronounce silent kays: "k'neel in church"... "the K'nights of the Round Table"... "I was k'nocked spark out when that shell hit my Cromwell tank." And my favourite one of all: "Betty next door has been k'nocked up by her Uncle Fred!!"'

'Did you have a back garden?'

'More like a tiny patch of scrub.'

'Did you never consider putting a kennel in it?'

'No way. Sandy was part of the family.'

'I meant for your old man. Describe the layout of this hovel.'

Hovel isn't a long word but it wasn't one that I expected him to use. I was too badly shaken up to think beyond that.

'As you went in through the front door there was a room on the right which housed the best furniture. Mum spent a good hour each Sunday polishing in there. It was used for entertaining the more prestigious folk in the community, the doctor and vicar being top of the list. Don't forget, in those days the C of E had a flock worth talking about and doctors made home calls for measles and chicken pox. I recall Doctor Miller dropping in when I had a painful foot. I overheard him telling Mum that I had a verruca and couldn't go swimming. When Dad got home I asked him what a verruca was. Thinking it was a homework question he said he'd never heard of it, but it was probably like a small bazooka. The next room on the right was the bedroom, which I shared with my parents (one double and one kiddie's single). After that came a titchy kitchen with a rusty, slim-line cooker and sink (cold tap only). A transit van had more room in it than our kitchen. And finally, the heartbeat of the house: the back room.'

'We lived in there, as did a pre-war radio with huge dials set in a wooden cabinet (it had most of the capitals of Europe on its display, none of which we could pick up), a settee and matching armchair with faded grey cloth upholstery, and a working fireplace. We toasted white bread and crumpets on the fire, and on Sundays I'd bathe in the tin bath in front of the blazing heat. Mum scuttled to and thro between the kitchen and the back room with saucepans full of hot water to fill the bath. Once her relay race was run, she'd towel me dry while Dad emptied the dirty water down the drain in the yard. The bath was then stored upright by the door between the bedroom and kitchen, which led to the yard. The layout upstairs mirrored downstairs, although their furniture was older and of higher quality. There wasn't a door at the bottom or top of the stairs, so I could go up and visit Nanna and Ink whenever I wanted.'

Raz played an imaginary violin.

'Okay, Kuchy. I get the picture. You were as poor as shit. Tell me more about Nanna and Ink. Make it brief.'

'They weren't actually related to us but they were like grandparents to me. Nanna's real name was Dot. She gave me milky tea and malt biscuits with cows on them. According to Ink she was from snobby Hertfordshire and hadn't fully adapted to slum life. She had white hair, a plump face, and tufts of fine hair on the base of her chin and above her upper lip. Ink used to say her stockings laddered because she rode horses in Hertfordshire as a girl and got bandy-legged. She was well into horses and was forever dusting the china ones on the mantelpiece. She named them after kings and queens. They were called Henry, William, George and Elizabeth. The only horse around our way pulled the coal wagon. They didn't have children of their own. To this day, I don't know Ink's real name. Apparently, I called him that when I was a toddler. I sometimes wonder why a two-year-old would call someone by the name of a writing fluid. Most of his nose and cheeks were covered in thread veins while the rest of the skin was pasty white and dotted with liver spots. He was tall with bushy eyebrows. He drank lots of hot water and could burp for England. If they had company, Nanna would say it's better than blowing off. One of his many mottos was "don't look a gift horse in the mouth", which, in effect, meant don't steal from a lorry unless something happens to fall off the back. Know what I mean, squire'

'When he twitched and mumbled in his sleep, Nanna would say that he was dreaming of the trenches in the Great War. Sometimes he'd sit in his armchair with his eyes closed talking to the friends he'd lost. He had a leather-bound photo album held together by string. The pictures were black and white; the faded ones not much bigger than the snazzy stamps Mum bought at Christmas. From time to time he'd get the album out to show me a single photo, usually of a man in uniform.

At other times, he'd turn the pages over and mutter in a broken voice, "He was a good lad," and repeat it on nearly every page.

On occasion he'd chirp, "I wonder what happened to him after the war."

He didn't say that very often. He hadn't been to a Spurs match since the great push-and-run team because of his pins. He used to lean out of his bedroom window to ask passers-by the score when the game was over. He'd grumble for ages if we'd lost. Nanna said our new manager had better win the cup or she'd push Ink out of the friggin' window.'

'I was at Bill Nicholson's first home match; the start of the glory glory days. We beat Everton 10–4 and Ink wanted me to run through each goal in turn. He fell asleep before I'd reached seven. Mind you, it took me ages because I had to re-enact the goals in their backroom. Nanna stopped me diving around like their goalie in case I broke her china horses.

Ink would sit me on his lap and say wistfully, "I hope I live long enough to see you grow up, son."

While Dad told me stories about the last war, Ink told me tales of the one before that. Ink said he had it much worse in those trenches with all that mustard gas. And bloody no-man's-land, he would lament, that was Hell on Earth. You'd either cop one straight off, drown in a shell crater, or get tangled up in all that barbed wire. Dad retorted that he should try being k'nocked senseless in an exploding tank. When a Tiger had you in its sights you needed a steady nerve and the ability not to shit in a confined space. How many of them were tall stories I couldn't tell you, but I'm pretty sure Ink never shot down the Red Baron and Dad never single-handedly captured Mussolini...'

Raz hauled me to my feet by my left earlobe and forced me back down again. His fingers were like pliers.

'I said make it brief! I didn't want their fucking life histories – although it served a purpose. Now get back to your school days with Mushtaq. He'd asked to go to the toilet, right? What happened next?'

***

'Mush asked to be excused and Mr Gasson asked him if he knew where the lavatories were. The teachers were forever trying to get us to say "excused" and "lavatory" instead of bog. Some people around our way said lav but none of them used the longer version.

I shot my hand up and said, "I know where they are, sir. I'll show him. Mum says I'm to keep trying 'cause I'm all bunged up."

Mr Gasson replied, "Have you tried Milpar, Ricky? Very well, but don't be long."

As I was closing the classroom door behind us, I heard Mr Gasson say, "What a nice polite boy. I hope you will all follow his example."

I knew he couldn't be talking about me. If anyone deserves to be fitted up, I thought, it has to be this foreign kid. Never mind the odd colour, he talks posh and says lavatory. He had about as much chance of being accepted in Tottenham as a kid wearing an Arsenal rosette.'

Raz stopped me.

'Tell me a bit about Mr Gasson. Did you like him? Did he ever hit his pupils? Describe his appearance.'

'He'd just qualified but he was the best teacher we had. He never caned us or snitched on us to the headmistress unless we'd done

31

something really bad. And when I left the juniors I remembered more of what he'd taught me than any of the other teachers. He even returned my spud gun after he caught me using a snail for target practice. I promised I wouldn't bring it to school anymore. And I kept that promise for a whole month. With any of the other teachers, I would have snuck it in the next day. He had a shock of black hair and a beard. I overheard Jenny's mum calling him a beatnik behind his back. Why did you want to know?'

I waited for a response but none came.

After a delay Raz snapped, 'I ask the fucking questions. Carry on, what happened between you and Mushtaq?'

If he thought Mr Gasson had any direct bearing on what happened to Mush, then he was wrong. In the extended words of Lord Tennyson, "Mine is not to reason why. Mine is but to do and hopefully not die."

***

'We didn't say much until we were in the playground. I think Mush was either shy or scared, probably both. Not only did he look and talk funny, he walked funny too. For starters, he never put his hands in his pockets and was as erect as a girl with a book on her head in a posh deportment class. I held back from taking the piss because there was less chance of him seeing the turd with his chin up. I wasn't taking any chances though, and as we approached the bike shelter I started talking nineteen to the dozen.

"Come far?" I said, positioning myself between him and the offending object.

"Bruce Grove," he replied.

I called him an Indian twit, which didn't go down too well. I pointed at the boy's bogs and informed him that the girls went separate. I figured he needed some educating.

He queried the word bog and I retorted, "Are you thick or something?

What's not to understand and who taught you to speak our lingo anyhow?"

He had me on the back foot by responding, "If you are referring to my diction a retired British Colonel my father employed."

He had me scratching my scalp.

"Your what?"

He poked his head inside the toilets and gasped.

"Oh dear, I'm used to relieving myself in private. They don't appear to have any locks. Someone might disturb me."

I wondered if he'd ever been to a proper school before. As it turned out he hadn't because he was educated at home.

"The bogs have doors, don't they?" I said, thinking this colonel of his weren't all that.

He replied, "That's not what I meant, Ricky. There are so many of them and they are in such close proximity and so adjacent."

He might have used long words on me but I thought I'd try a bit of Tottenham cunning on him.

"Don't think I can go now. Tell you what, Mush. I'll hang around here and tip you the wink if anyone comes. That way you can have the bogs all to yourself." After I explained what "tip the wink" had meant, he thanked me and begged me not to call him Mush again. Some chance, I thought, as I watched him tiptoe into the toilets.'

'The moment I heard the cubicle door close, I was off. It was important I got to the classroom before him and played it cool. I was a fair distance across the playground when it occurred to me that he'd find the turd on his return journey. What if he took offence and sounded the alarm? Unless you were as cunning as Fu Manchu you'd hardly sound the alarm if it came from your own arse. On the other hand, there was every chance he'd walk straight past it without batting an eyelid. Ink had served in India and said their shit was everywhere. There was an episode of *Dixon of Dock Green* where a bent cop planted something on a bloke to get a conviction. It wouldn't have made sense to stuff Mush's pockets with shit, so I came up with another way of landing him in it. Thinking Fu Manchu has nothing on me, I decided upon an ambush and hid in the shelter.'

'I was brought up on punch-ups and rough and tumbles, but he was as soft as feathers. When I got him in a headlock he just crumbled.

I dragged him up to the turd and cried, "Filthy brown git! Did you do this?" I forced him to kneel and gripped him round the back of the neck. He begged me not to, but I pushed his nose in it. I let him lift his face a few inches before pushing his beak in it again.

I hissed, "This was you, weren't it, Mush? Admit it. No Englishman would do it."

They say you can't smell your own but I could smell that one all right. He was choking like someone who'd just been pulled from the water and even that Good Samaritan in the *Bible* wouldn't have given mouth to mouth. By the time I'd finished his face looked just like mine after I'd stuffed it full of Nanna's chocolate pudding. As I went into the main building I caught a glimpse of him clutching his guts and fleeing into the toilets. I remember thinking I'd missed a trick because I didn't make him sit in it and dirty his nice trousers.'

'When I entered the classroom, Mr Gasson was writing the times table on the blackboard. He swung round and asked Harry what 2 x 6 made. Harry had been goading Carrot Top by showing her something nasty he kept in a box of Swan Vestas.

He mumbled "Err" and looked blank.

Dad taught me numbers so I decided to help him out. Dad was ace at mental arithmetic and could work out the racing odds in a second flat.

"12!" I cried, hoping Harry didn't think I'd showed him up.

Mr Gasson looked pleased and said, "Well done, Ricky. Life is full of surprises."

He reflected for a moment and enquired where Mush was. I told him I couldn't go but that he was having trouble. I said his gut sounded like the noise our plunger made when Dad unblocked the sink. Just then classroom doors started slamming along the corridor and I heard the headmistress, Mrs Law, bellowing. She had a deep voice for a woman and had acquired the nickname Bing (after Bing Crosby).

I looked sheepishly at Mr Gasson and said, "I shouldn't tell tales, sir, but Mush has had an accident. I think Mrs Law ain't that happy about it."

'I'd hardly finished the sentence when Mrs Law frogmarched Mush into the classroom. His face was more red than brown, probably because he'd scrubbed it clean, and the sobbing didn't help his complexion much either. He was holding a shoebox with both hands at arms' length and hunching his shoulders as if he was walking through a blizzard. She ordered him to raise the lid and show Mr Gasson the contents.

"The caretaker scooped it up. I wouldn't come too close," she railed.

"Is that what I think it is?" replied Mr Gasson.

His nostrils went into spasm for a good few seconds, like Dad's had when Ink offered him a slice of stinking bishop cheese.

Lifting his face in search of fresh air, Mr Gasson said, "From what I understand, poor Mushtaq was having difficulties."

I had to hold my knees to stop my hands rubbing together in glee.

"Mushtaq!" barked Mrs Law. "I think there are things you need to know about our Christian customs. Cleanliness being top of the list."

A dozen excited voices shrilled the same question: what's in the box, miss? Some reckoned it was a dead rodent he'd been playing with. Harry Hooper had made a dash to the front after it was opened and saved me the trouble.

He bawled, "He's shit himself and missed the bog. Thought he smelt funny. Reckoned it was coming from his mouth but must have been his arse."

35

Tears were streaming down Mush's cheeks and he was shaking in his shiny shoes, which had miraculously remained contamination free.

He spluttered, "It wasn't me."

Mrs Law shook him by the shoulder. "Who was it then? Speak up, boy!"

I was preparing a Tottenham Look in case Mush pointed the finger at me.

But he mumbled, "I don't know, miss."

I was well chuffed when Mrs Law threatened him with the cane if he ever lied to her again. I sat at my desk, which was directly in front of Harry's.

He leant over his desk and whispered in my ear, "We're going to have all kinds of fun with this brown cunt."

I cowered as Raz sprang forward.

He snarled, 'Welcome to England, nigger,' and repeatedly head-butted the knuckles on his clenched fists.

He ranted some more, spitting out unintelligible words for the most part, and then stormed up and down the building kicking cubicle doors. The clatter reminded me of those old steam locomotives in the rush hour when a line of carriage doors opened and slammed as they spewed hordes of commuters. It also sparked a memory of Northumberland Park Station once, when some mates and me stuck two fingers up at the stationmaster as we tore along the platform and jumped onto a moving train. Over fifty years had passed and I could still smell the clouding steam, hear the clank of the wheels on the track, and the chuffs of the engine as it toiled to pick up speed. The more aggressive Raz's behaviour became, the more memories were triggered in my mind. I could have taken the opportunity to stand up and ease the burden on my glutes and lower back, but I just sat there in that narrow space trying to piece together the images; desperate to sketch out the next chapter before that maniac gathered whatever wits he possessed and resumed tormenting me.

Raz was so light on his feet that he could have been wearing moccasins instead of black Nikes. A rap on the partition wall made me jump and a shadow the size of a grizzly bear formed on the ceiling. He took the torch from behind his back and shone it at my face. After the glare had subsided I blinked and tentatively opened my eyes.

He hissed, 'Imagine you've been sentenced by Judge Jeffries and I'm papist King James.' He raised a clenched fist above his head, lifted his chin, and extended his neck as if a noose was stretching it. 'If I think you're telling lies there'll be no royal pardon. I want every recollection of Mushtaq you possess, no matter how bad you look. Get my drift, chief?'

His knowledge of history was admirable, so much so that I considered telling him I once taught the subject. But the word boring follows history teachers around like that old incontinent dog you can't bear to put down. First rule of teaching it: convince them that a salient date is more appetising than a dried fruit. Second rule: teach them what salient means. To clear the apathy from my pupils' eyes I indulged them with tales of bloodletting, backstabbing, and graphic sexual excess. I'd never get away with it today, of course. A shudder, which stood comparison to the Severn Bore ripped through my body. Was Raz older than I thought? He wasn't that Year 7 pupil who'd eavesdropped on my sixth form class, was he? I never did catch that little bugger (the lesson included a discussion of nymphomania versus the playboy, and an account of Catherine the Great's relationship with her horse). If it had been Raz, my teaching combined with a liberal intake of crack, could easily have been pushed him over the edge. Just in case, I decided to give history a miss and Raz got far more of the truth than I'd intended. It was as if my vocal cords had become routed into my autonomic nervous system.

'Within a week of starting school, six boys in our class had formed a gang. Harry Hooper was the leader and I was second in command. Every boy who joined had to have scabby knees and be capable of punching someone in the face. Mush kept well clear of us whenever he could. He never used the toilets at break and asked to be excused during lessons if he couldn't hold it in. He'd check where we were huddled playing knuckles, or paper, scissor, stone, or where we were kicking a ball around before venturing into the playground. He'd make sure not to stray far from the teacher on duty. Although we were only seven we ruled half the playground, the dividing line being the edge of the netball court. The bigger boys and girls were made to share the rest. Not even an eleven-year-old was going to face up to Harry because it was common knowledge that he was a nutter and his dad wielded a sawn-off shotgun.'

'As time progressed, a whole series of misfortunes befell Mush: shoulder barges; stamping on his feet; headlocks; and placing all kinds of creepy crawlies in his desk. Once Harry and me dragged him into the bogs to administer Chinese burns. We bet gobstoppers on who could make him scream the loudest. Jenny volunteered to be judge. She wasn't quite brave enough to come inside but stood in the playground guarding the entrance. She called it a dead heat and proposed we give him another dose on both arms. Harry wanted to piss in his desk but I talked him out of it because the smell would have alerted Mr Gasson. Instead, I suggested everyone had to take the piss out of Mush each time we passed him in the corridor.

Things like, "You're the colour of shit" and "You smell like shit."

It was agreed that "shit" should always be in there somewhere. Mush tried to make friends with Billy Bunter and Carrot Top but they were having none of it. I couldn't blame them because with Mush taking the brunt it took the heat off them. Jenny embarrassed Mush by asking to see his winkle and Jane brought a pumice stone to school so that he could scrub the shit off.'

'There was no chance of us getting him before or after school because his father dropped him off and picked him up in a spanking new Austin Princess. The car was huge and gleaming white – top of the range – fit for royalty in our eyes. The whole gang stood gaping at the railings the first time he turned up in it. We all thought it: how could one of them afford that 'cause our dads can't. His dad was a small, wiry man who wore a dapper suit and tie. His hair was jet black with white streaks around the edges. Looking back, I suppose you would say he was distinguished, but all we could see was an old brown cunt that should've been pedalling a rickshaw. Mush even brought his own food and sat by himself at dinnertime. I overheard Mr Gasson say that he didn't like segregation and Mrs Law reply that his food might be blessed but it didn't do much for her blessed nostrils. It was unusual for Bing to make a joke and it wasn't much of one. Mush became so withdrawn that Mr Gasson asked him if anything was wrong. Harry had been earwigging and reckoned he'd brought some horrible disease over with him. Mr Gasson scolded Harry and told him not to be so cruel, but still got the nurse to check Mush over. I don't think a day went by when Mush didn't sob gently to himself. He did gain a grudging respect from Harry because he didn't grass on us. Even so, we weren't going to let up until he went back to where he came from.'

I'd often wondered why people dig their own graves as the killer or killers look on. Now I knew. It's being overwhelmed by a force so great that it crushes your will to resist. I'd been in hair-raising situations in the past and had managed to cope without turning tail: aggro at West Ham-Millwall, the poll tax, and G20 demos for starters. Abject cowards don't make good press photographers. Yet I'd been incarcerated for less than an hour and my shovel had already broken the earth. He sensed my capitulation and said I could stand up if I bowed to him, like prisoners of war were made to do by their Japanese captors. I used the cistern for leverage and remained head bowed and cowering before him as I recounted my story ...

'Something unexpected happened a few days after my eighth birthday... in case you're wondering, but nothing else of consequence happened when I was seven. If it had, I'd tell you about it...'

'Go on, Kuchy. I've got all I wanted out of your seventh year on this earth. Let's hope you reach your ninth year in one piece, shall we? As you were saying?'

'I'd been kept behind after school to do a hundred lines: "boys must be kind and behave gently towards girls". I'd put a dead frog originally intended for Mush in Carrot Top's desk because she'd made me miss a penalty in the playground. Her screeching could wake the dead. She screeched even louder when she found the frog, so loud that the cook dropped a plate in the kitchen. Anyhow, Mush was waiting for me in the playground after my detention. There was no one else around and no sign of his dad. Saying it was time for a powwow, he took two liquorice pipes from his pocket and offered me one. I loved liquorice but refused because I didn't know where it had been. I pulled a face and then pulled out my spud gun. I would have brought my cap gun to school but that made too much noise (if you shot someone with a cap gun they had to stay dead for a count of a twenty). I thought I might bring a peashooter and a water pistol with me the next day. I'd ping him in the neck and aim the water pistol at the front of his trousers so that it looked like he'd wet himself.

Mush held his hands out to show that he was unarmed and said, "There's no point in us indulging in violence, Ricky."

I didn't know what indulging meant and thought he was taking the proverbial.

I retorted with a "Fuck off!"

To which he responded, "Let us put our differences aside and make peace." I told him to fuck off again and he said that God would punish me for profanity. That latest long word really got my dander up. I was about to pull the trigger when he informed me that his father had fought for the British.

I soon regained the initiative by countering, "Bet my dad killed more Germans than your weedy dad. He can hardly see over the top of the bleedin' steering wheel. And where did he get the dosh to buy a car like that anyway?"

If anyone had badmouthed my dad I'd have landed him one, but Mush fought with his mouth rather than his fists and trumped me with a sarcastic, "My dad fought the Japanese, *Kuchy*. They were crueller and tougher than the Germans, *Kuchy*."

It goes without saying that I wasn't going to stand idle while this brown tosser called me names.

Kuchy sounded like the beginning of kuchi kuchi ku so I aimed the spud gun at his chest and barked, "One false move and I'll let you have it, mush."

I only had one round in the magazine so I had to make it count (Bing had confiscated my potato as I dribbled it through the school gates). Mush caught me on the hop when he knocked the gun out of my hand and tried to shove me over. He gave it a good go but he was easy meat.

I threw him to the ground, cried "Bundle!", and landed on of top of him.'

'He struggled a bit first, but then I sat on his chest and pinned him down. I was going to punch him in the face but thought that might really land me in it. Thinking they wouldn't notice the bruises on his skin, I pinched his arms instead and he squealed and pleaded with me to stop. He started panting like an old dog in a heat wave and I got a blast of curry breath. It made me want to puke. Don't forget, these were the days before curry had become our national dish. Both liquorice pipes were lying next to us on the concrete. I was on the verge of stuffing them up his nostrils when Bing came storming out of the main building. I copped her first and jumped to my feet.

Clutching my face and groaning, I sobbed, "He attacked me for no good reason, miss."

She wasn't interested in excuses and hauled us off to her study.'

'We had it easy compared to those public schoolboys because the cane hurt more across the arse than across the hand. I knew this because I'd met up with Harry after school one day and we'd bet each other who could take the most whacks with his dad's snooker cue. I retired hurt after the first two.

I remember rubbing my behind and exclaiming in a very high-pitched voice, even for a prepubescent, "Why's it called six of the best, Harry? It hurts like buggery."

The cane was an accepted method of punishment then. Just the threat of it was often enough to get an unruly child to behave.'

Raz lifted my chin with his middle finger.

'Is that right, Kuchy?'

And pushed my head down so that I was staring at his feet again.

In my hippy days I had a girlfriend who believed in spirit guides. It made no difference whether she was straight or stoned. Raz had got me so befuddled I considered the possibility that he was my guide to Hell. Of course, from a Marxist perspective it was more likely that I'd suffered brain damage. It entered my mind that I wasn't in the toilets at all, but lying on a pavement in Tottenham High Road with blood oozing from the back of my head. Rioters were running over and around me and ambulances were whizzing by without stopping. Raz rapped the partition so hard that the whole building appeared to shake. The golden rule for the over-60s is if you think of it write it down quick. I didn't have a pen but I knew where I was, all right: in the shit.

***

'Mrs Law asked us who'd started it. I blamed Mush and he apologised and took responsibility for his own actions. You'd have thought Mush's contrition might have got him off the hook but Bing was a Presbyterian and he'd never seen the inside of a church. She used to work in Leeds and thought she was bettering herself by coming to Tottenham. Nanna reckoned Mrs Law might have letters after her name but she was as daft as a brush for thinking that. Before flexing her elbow, Bing used to toy with her victims by hurling tautologies at them from the moral high ground, iterating words like guttersnipe and hobbledehoy. I hadn't the foggiest what they meant and reckoned even that British colonel who taught Mush wouldn't know either. Our lecture was interrupted by a rap on the door.

"For heaven's sake. What now?" she moaned, as she opened the door and gave Mrs Rose, the secretary, one of her stiff smiles.

As the two women discussed the comparative cost of pilchards and sheep's hearts, I told Mush to listen up, putting on the same voice I used to convince Mum that I was too sick to go to school.

"You get more respect in these parts if you don't take your eyes off the cane."

"Like the cricketer who watches the ball all the way onto the bat, Ricky?"

"That's right, Mush. If you manage that without yelping then no boy will ever pick on you again, including Harry."

The stupid idiot believed me.

"Do you promise, Ricky? I think I would rather keep them closed,"

I replied, "Scout's honour. Men in the trenches stick together, mate."

I'd conveniently forgot to tell him that Bing had a rule: any boy who moves his hand out of the way of her cane gets one for luck.'

'Mrs Law took a roster from the secretary and gave another of her forced smiles, which vanished the moment she closed the door on her. She put the roster on her desk and selected a cane from the cabinet.

"Right", she said, looking at each of us in turn and taking a practice swing, "Who's first?"

Mush flinched but I raised my hand.

"I will, miss, so that Mush can see how it's done."

Mr Gasson insisted I call Mush by his proper name, but Mrs Law never bothered. My arm went limp when it suddenly dawned on me that I'd have to keep my eyes open or Mush would know I was pulling a fast one.'

'Bing had a swing borrowed from the tennis smash. How I never withdrew my hand or yelped I'll never know. Mush's face went whiter than mine as he held out his hand and she lined up the cane. Just as I'd anticipated, Mush saw her arm twitch and shot his hand back. Bing called him a cowardly guttersnipe and told him to show some backbone, to take it like a man as Ricky had done. One compliment was more than enough for Bing and she ordered me to go home, saying she'd be having a word with my father. As I closed the study door behind me, I shook my hand like fuck and thought it's no wonder we conquered half the bleedin' world if wimps like Mush stood in our path.'

'I put my ear to the door and giggled as she let fly, punching the air each time Mush yelped. Harry Hooper was passing by at the time. He'd been kept behind and was running some errand or other as a punishment for swearing. I gave him the thumbs up and displayed a red palm, my medal for valour.

Swaggering towards him, I said nonchalantly, "Didn't make a murmur, mate. Which is more than can be said for Mush. He squealed like Sandy does when someone treads on his tail."

Harry slapped me across the back and replied, "I'd expect nothing less of you Ricky, me old son. Why do you think only boys get the bleedin' cane? Ain't fair. The girls are supposed to get the slipper but I ain't never seen it happen."

I reflected for a moment and said, "Come to think about it, neither have I, Harry. Wouldn't mind Carrot Top getting a few choice ones."

Harry tapped his nose.

"Can be arranged. I'll borrow one of me mum's slippers and we'll slap her across the bare arse a few times. Once we get the hang of it we'll give Mush a dose because he's a big girl. We'll wear balaclavas so they won't recognise us." Talk about a chip off the old block. Harry waited with me till Mush slunk out of the headmistresses' study. Mush was blowing on his hand and trembling. His tears became a salty torrent as I embellished my triumph with a large measure of indignation.

"Fucking coward. If your dad's anything like you, he hid up a tree when the Japs approached."

Harry hit him with "Fucking cry baby", and scarpered before Bing caught him.'

'Mush wiped his eyes and stared at the red welts on his hands.

He sniffed up snot and muttered, "May God forgive you, Ricky. I shall pray for you."

I was having none of that crap.

"Just you fucking try, mate."

I tracked him as far as the main exit, continuing from where Harry had left off.

"Cry baby"…"Cry baby" …"Cry baby."

I would have pursued him across the playground if his dad's car weren't parked up outside the gates.'

'The next day, Harry got busy organising a surprise for Mush and me. After school he lined up ten boys outside the main doors. They formed a guard of honour for me, and a guard of dishonour for Mush. I walked between the two lines soaking up the accolades and holding my hands above my head as if I was displaying the FA Cup to the Spurs crowd. The cheering and clapping turned to jeers and catcalls when Mush appeared. I expected him to retreat inside the building, but the fool chose to run the gauntlet. Billy Bunter was one of the boys Harry had put on parade. His lips hardly moved at first and I could tell his heart wasn't in it, but after Harry gave him the Tottenham Look fatso joined in the chorus with gusto.

"Cry baby!"…"Cry baby!"…"Cry baby!"'

Raz switched off the torch and all I could hear was the sound of my breathing interspersed with a dripping tap. I half expected him to come careering towards me through the black curtain which had unfurled – knife or gun in hand, or extending those giant hands to grab me around the throat. I covered the top of my head, like a boxer bent double on the ropes, trying to dodge the flurry of blows raining down on him. I endured his silence until it became unbearable and lifted my chin to speak. The moment I did he switched the torch on and thrust a broom handle in front of my eyes. He snapped it in two over his knee, tossed one half into the next cubicle, and slid the smooth end across my cheek.

'Greased. It'll go up a treat. Can't say the same for the splintered end. Or would you prefer six of the best? Take care, chief. If you yelp, I'll give you an extra one for luck. Now turn around like a good little boy and drop your trousers and pants. Make sure you untangle your feet when you bend over or you won't be able to spread your legs.'

In a blink the temperature dropped several degrees and I criss-crossed my arms as if constrained by a straightjacket.

He barked, 'Do it!'

I responded instantly, like a new recruit to a sadistic sergeant major. Goose bumps crawled across my legs as I lowered my pants and trousers and kicked them free of my ankles. Naked from the waist down, I placed the flat of my hands against the tiles and assumed the position of a man about to be frisked by a cop.

I'd been fucked up the bum once before. She wore a strap on and got through half a jar of K-Y Jelly in the process. She didn't put it in straight away, but donned surgical gloves and inserted her fingers to expand the back passage. That bit was quite pleasant but the reality of a huge leather penis strapped to a naked gyrating woman wasn't half as enjoyable as the fantasy. It hurt a little at first and a lot more as she built up speed. My anus throbbed for ages afterwards and the thought of that splintered broom handle being shoved up there… it was bound to rupture blood vessels, never mind a vital organ.

I heard a swish and he said, 'Well, what's it to be Ricky? Buggered or six of the best?'

Dribbling piss into the toilet bowl, I closed my eyes and blurted, 'Six of the best. Make it six of the best.'

My body tensed as he ran the jagged edge across the lower half of my buttocks, not hard enough to leave a scratch mark but it had me begging.

'Brace yourself, Ricky.'

'Please! I said I prefer the cane.'

He coasted the splintered handle across my flesh three more times and on each occasion stopped within an inch of my anus. It may not have been as cruel as a terrorist holding a gun to a captive's head and pretending that he was going to pull the trigger, but the sentiment was similar. By now my palms had become so sweaty that they were slowly sliding down the tiles. My nails dug into the grouting but failed to get any purchase. Any further and my chin would have smacked against the cistern. He burst into laughter and patted my right buttock. I couldn't have jumped more if he'd penetrated me.

I glanced over my shoulder. He had his back to me and had taken off his shades to wipe his eyes. I could have sworn I glimpsed pink fish scales on his cheek as he cleaned the shades with one of those silky optician's cloths. I wondered if that acid trip I took while watching *Stingray* in the 60s had done some serious damage. He replaced the shades and swung around, curling his upper lip and flaring his nostrils.

His next gargoyle impersonation involved a demented grin, which remained riveted to his face until he said, 'If you saw my eyes you'd witness two black holes that lead straight to hell. Would you care to look into the Devil's eyes, Kuchy?'

Like a tenderfoot gunslinger, I managed an air shot before biting the dust.

'Dunno. What colour are they?'

'To quote Oscar Wilde: Sarcasm is the lowest form of wit. To quote me, chief: Any more of your insolence and I'll rip your fucking head off. Shift it. We're relocating to the main building where you can have a proper sit down. Get your shit on. I'm going to check out the playground for intruders.'

He wiped his hands with toilet tissue and turned off the torch to leave me staring at that black curtain again. As I groped for my clothes and scrambled to dress, I heard the metal door being unlocked. When I'd finished dressing, I poked my head out of the cubicle and could just make out a pool of light at the far end of the building. I staggered towards it and a breeze chilled the sweat on my face, while the wail of a solitary siren could be heard in the distance.

7

I wanted to hurl myself into the cool night air, but my shredded nerves screamed caution and I stood limply in the doorway. After a while I started counting slowly in my mind. If I reached ten and Raz hadn't returned it was my intention to work my way around the back of the toilets. Edmund Hillary probably looked up at Everest with trepidation. For Everest read school railings and it was unlikely that Sherpa Tenzing would appear to give me a bunk up. I paced the count at snail and was stuck between a cowardly eight and nine when Raz materialised in front of me. He clapped to hurry me along, then closed and locked the metal door. Rid of the smell of sickly disinfectant I took several deep breaths, catching a whiff of smoke as it drifted invisible over the playground. There may have been stars, a full moon for all I knew, but all I saw was the blackness overhead and a red glow on the skyline. My lungs were sucking in oxygen when he clamped my lips closed with his hand. He dragged me backwards on my heels to the main building and deposited me in a recess cut into the brickwork.

Forcing me onto my haunches, he pressed down on my shoulders and whispered, 'Button it, Kuchy. We've got company.'

One in three of the streetlights was switched off and a large proportion of the pavement was enveloped in darkness. A group of five hoodies appeared through the gloom to congregate beneath a lit streetlight. One of them ran his knife along the railings and scowled.

'Still no sign of Raz. Where the fuck is he?'

A languid voice replied, 'Dunno, bro. Can't be far.'

Two of the gang members crumpled their empty lager cans and tossed them into the playground. The more frugal among them were still drinking theirs as they ambled off. When the expletives tarnishing the night air had faded, Raz removed his hand from my lips. I swallowed what little saliva I could muster and went to scream. He slapped the hand back over my mouth and squeezed the top of my shoulder. A burning pain shot up the side of my neck and for a moment I was paralysed.

'I'll snap your turkey neck next time,' he hissed, slowly removing the hand. 'Sit on that fat arse of yours and get on with the fucking story. Get my drift, chief? Don't stray too far from Mushtaq, but include something about your old man. I think he needs a bit of attention.'

***

'Dad had a shock of blond hair which got shorter year on year. When teenagers were flicking their quiffs and rocking around the clock he was well on his way to becoming an American marine. He was a stocky man who wore braces, but his loose-fitting trousers somehow stayed up when he had a strip wash at the kitchen sink. Some mornings he would only be wearing his long underpants and then he would put his hands over his crotch and say something in Polish, which sounded like "no dollars". Strange, I can't remember ever seeing Mum strip wash although she always smelt soapy fresh. Mum used to say that the bookies were his second home. His bookie didn't operate from a betting shop but a house in Lorenco Road. That road had some of the worse slums in the country and all sorts of nefarious activities went on there. Ink and Nanna went on a charabanc ride to Southend before the war. The driver lived in Lorenco Road and got arrested on the pier for selling fake jewellery from a suitcase. Ink boasted that he drove the charabanc back to Tottenham himself. Nanna said that he couldn't even get it out of first gear and that he only did a tiny stretch of the A13.

She'd chuckled. "Never mind getting it out of first gear – these days he can't even get it in to start with."'

'Mrs Law put Mush and me in separate classes after the caning and warned us about our future behaviour. Dad said if I got into any more trouble he wouldn't take me to see Spurs play for the rest of the season. Talk about holding an H-bomb to your head. I'd already missed the Wolverhampton Wanderers match because I nicked little Susan's doll and strung it up by its feet to a lamppost. They were much shorter and chunkier than present day lampposts, painted yellow and green as I remember. Susan was Bill's little sister. Bill Reeves was the leader of the gang in our street and, as was the case at school, I was second in command. Dad looked out of the window at the doll and said it reminded him of Mussolini's mistress ...'

Raz pinched the top of my shoulder with just enough pressure to serve as a warning – don't stray too far from Mushtaq! I raised my hands.

'Stay cool, I've got the message ... the strange thing is I never told my parents, or anyone else in our street, that Mush was a Pakistani. For one thing, I didn't know if Dad would like me mixing with one of them. You'd probably call him a racist but I prefer to see him as a man of his times. We'd recently seen a film about blacks on the *Pathé News*. They were chanting and dancing around a fire. The men had bones through their noses and the women's bare breasts were bouncing everywhere.

I asked Dad why these black women were allowed to show off their chests and the man next to him said, "I'll start a petition and send it to Harold Macmillan."

Dad called them monkeys and the same man made monkey nois-es. I thought they were funny, and so did most of the other people sitting nearby because they joined in the laughter. Dad may sound as if he was a follower of Enoch Powell, but if he'd witnessed a Negro being beaten up by white people, I'm positive he'd have come to his aid. In truth, if Mush had blacker skin and plumper lips, I'd have called him a monkey. Luckily for him he wasn't that much different in colour to Douglas Noble after he returned from his foreign holidays. The Nobles flew on the Comet and Douglas and his parents would come back with deep suntans. Their house was so big that you could fit two of ours into it (it included a bathroom and off-street parking for one car). When they felt like showing off they'd take their flash Jag for a spin around the neighbourhood and Douglas would sit in the back like royalty. The kids would run after it, touching the shiny green paintwork...'

Raz shook my sleeve and whispered, 'Quiet, Kuchy. We've got company again. Just the one this time, but a Girl Guide's more than enough to put paid to you.'

He sprang to his feet. Keeping to the islands of shadows dotted across the playground, he moved swiftly. He reached the railings at the same time as a slightly built hoodie appeared beneath the street-light. As Raz beckoned him closer, I could see that the newcomer was a sallow white youth, probably in his late teens. I couldn't hear what Raz said to him but the young man, who I christened Oik, gave a wave of acknowledgement and put his face up to the bars. In a blur, Raz shot his arms through the bars, grabbed Oik around the back of the neck, and slammed his forehead against the metal. At least I had time to be shocked. Poor Oik was flat out on the pavement before he knew what hit him. Raz scaled the railings, flung Oik over his shoulder, and climbed back up with ease. He balanced on the top of the railings for a moment to look up and down the street. I assumed it was all clear, because he jumped back into the playground without a sideways glance.

During my career as a press photographer I've seen the occasional dead body, but I'd never witnessed a murder before. My back was pressed so firmly against the wall that, if made of wattle and daub, it would have collapsed on top of me. A cowering wreck I may have been, but a few dregs of professionalism had survived and I cursed the maniac for pilfering my camera. Assuming my drink-deprived hands had stopped shaking long enough, I might have captured some wonderful images for the murder trial. In terms of artistic merit, I preferred the shot where he posed on top of the railings carrying his victim like a hunter does a slaughtered deer, muscular frame silhouetted against the orange glow of the streetlight: savage beauty, primeval, gladiatorial. Scary as fuck!

Raz weaved his way towards me and stopped about two yards from my recess to inspect a section of the wall. He hoisted Oik over his head and I got the impression that it took an enormous measure of self-control for him not to slam his prize onto the concrete. As it was, he bent his elbows, flexed his back, and placed him none too gently on the ground. Crouching, he shook Oik by his hoodie and slapped him across the face, two, three, four times. The last blow was so fierce that I feared it had fractured a cheekbone. When that didn't elicit a response, Raz drilled his knuckles into the side of Oik's head. He should have signed up for the CIA at Guantanamo Bay and saved on Uncle Sam's water bill. If Oik had been playing possum he wasn't any more. A loud grunt and his eyes started open. He blinked and rubbed his forehead, but before he could speak Raz seized him by the hood and shook him even more violently.

He hissed, 'Were you there? Were you one of them?'

Oik turned his head and looked pleadingly at me. His face dropped when he realised we shared a matching set of large, terror-stricken eyeballs. Raz clenched a fist and drew his arm back as if he was about to administer a knock-out blow.

'Last chance. Were you there? Were you one of them?'

Oik batted back a feeble, 'Fuck you.'

It's a well-known fact that you can't rely on the testimony of a man under torture. Unfortunately for Oik and me, Raz didn't share that adage.

Raz was in no mood to swap pleasantries. He knelt on Oik's chest, delved inside his hoodie, and removed a length of rope that was tied around his waist. In the same movement, he used his other hand to retrieve a leather gag from his pocket. Oik threw a lame punch but Raz seized his arm and looped the end of the rope around the wrist. He spun Oik onto his stomach and planted a knee between his shoulder blades. Oik tried to scream but Raz inserted the gag into his mouth, tightening it until it looked as if Oik had just completed a course of Botox. I felt like vomiting and dreaded to think what would happen if Oik puked up. Raz secured the spare end of the rope around Oik's other wrist and hauled him to his feet. He hooked the rope around an overflow pipe situated a good six feet up the wall, leaving Oik standing on tiptoe with his arms drawn half way up his back. Heaven only knew what Oik had done to piss Raz off. At the very least he must have raped and mutilated his little sister. To be punished that cruelly it was a fair bet that he hadn't merely dented Raz's bumper in Tesco's car park. Raz prodded him in the chest.

'When I remove that gag, you'd better start talking. If you don't I'll hang you up by your fucking neck.'

He turned to me.

'Carry on, Kuchy.'

'Don't think I can. You're freaking me out.'

'It's either that or I'll finish that little cunt off and you can take his place on the butcher's hook.'

My blood pressure was way too high the last time Mike had taken it. He told me to cut back on the booze and saturated fats. My diastolic must have been way over a ton as I forced myself to look at poor Oik, who was performing a ballet pointe to take some of the load from his shoulders. His head started flipping from side to side and a muffled groan signalled yet another assault on sorely stretched tendons and ligaments. I expected to hear a crack as a ball was expelled from a socket. Oik's physical anguish only served to heighten my mental torment and a terrifying image of Oik and me stuffed into a car boot came to mind, followed by an equally disturbing image of two shallow graves in the woods. I took solace in the knowledge that it was a good seven miles to Epping Forest, but there then followed an image of two corpses being discovered by a screaming teacher in a stationery cupboard on Monday morning.

Raz squatted by my side.

'Strung up like a pig in a butcher's shop. For his sake I hope he squeals like one. You sure you ain't a junky, Kuchy? You've done a hell of a lot of shaking. Cold turkey, is it?'

'Have you ever been scared out of your wits? Probably not. You're the big brave action man who never cracks under torture and escapes in a blur of karate chops.'

When he spoke again there was a foreboding chill to his voice.

'Do you call this torture, Kuchy?'

'What do you fucking call it? I'm sure poor Oik would agree with me.'

'Oik? Is that what you've named him? Can't think of a better name for this creep. Would you like me to show you some real torture, Kuchy? Mike's your physio and best friend, ain't he?' He didn't wait for me to query how he knew about Mike and continued, 'I'll kill him if you don't agree to have your little finger cut off. It's only a pinkie and you can still work.'

Praying it was an idle threat, I didn't reply. I didn't know how to reply. He pulled out a knife.

'If you don't hold out your hand before I've finished counting to ten, I'll spare your pinkie and move on to the fourth digit. Another ten seconds the third, and so on till we reach the thumb. If you chicken out altogether you'll keep all your digits, but Mike will endure a very painful death.'

If I refused to make that sacrifice for my best friend, I'd drown in guilt. And as the counting progressed, that guilt might become too much to bear. I'd then be faced with the prospect of losing an index finger or a thumb. He'd reached nine when I turned my head away and held out my left hand. I tried my best to keep the hand still for fear that he'd slice through another finger, but my arm tremored as if I had Parkinson's disease.

'I wouldn't want to be a nurse giving you an injection,' he scoffed, seizing the other four digits and separating them from my little finger. 'I'd keep turning your head away if I were you, Kuchy.'

My breathing was as shallow as Boris Johnson and my forearm went into spasm as the flat of the blade glided across my fingertip. He withdrew the knife and there was a heart-stopping pause before he pricked the little finger with the tip of the blade. The spasms had traversed my elbow before the knife made contact for a third time.

I felt a scratch and was close to passing out when he said, 'All over. No more quaffing champagne for you, chief.' He let go of my hand and placed my arms at my side. 'Don't want to drip blood on your trousers, do we Ricky? What would your mummy say?' He roared with laughter. 'Only kidding. Have a wiggle. It's still there.' As I held my hand up to check, he added, 'There are many ways to torture a man into submission.' He took a syringe and a phial from inside his hoodie and quickly replaced them. 'No need to cut off a finger if you can fuck with their mind, Kuchy.'

Had he injected me with something? My sleeves weren't rolled up and I hadn't felt a needle puncture my exposed skin. Had he injected himself? I'd read accounts where people taking angel dust had acquired the strength of ten men and gone completely loco. Imagine you're sitting next to an unexploded bomb and it starts ticking. Talking to it won't stop it from going boom, but talking was the only hope I had with that monster.

8

'In early December Dad was taken into hospital. It came as quite a blow because I was counting the days to my Christmas presents. Not that I didn't love Dad, but I was hoping to get a pedal car like Douglas Noble. His was red and he only drove it around his enormous back garden. The garden obviously wouldn't look that big to me now, but back then the path around it was a veritable racetrack. If I owned one it would have been blue, because one in Arsenal colours wouldn't have lasted ten seconds on the street. I was good at spelling, but Dad had something with a very long name wrong with him. I'm not certain but, on reflection, it could have been gastroesophageal reflux disease caused by esophagitis.'

The point of Raz's finger played ip-dip-sky-blue on my ribcage.

I winced as he snapped, 'Do you think using long words makes you superior to me, Kuchy? For all you know I could be writing a novel or doing a degree at Oxford.'

No matter how hard I tried to prepare myself, the speed of his movements always caught me unawares. Picture a moonless night, and a deer runs out in front of your headlights on a country road, not once but several times in quick succession. Each time, you gear yourself up for a collision that never comes, until you can't think straight let alone react. But I had to think straight. My life depended on it. And my thoughts led to the realisation that he didn't use much gang speak in my presence, innit being a prime example. He certainly didn't strike me as a novelist, but with the onset of E-publishing the country was sprouting wannabe writers faster than people were losing interest in county cricket. Crazy I know, but I considered the possibility that he was studying at Oxford, researching for some quirky PhD in psychology and had gone native. Oik let out a groan which sounded like a Harley Davidson revving up in the distance. Oxford postgrad or street thug, I prayed that Raz would spare Oik's life. The poor bastard had suffered enough and even Jeffrey Archer drew the line at murder.

***

'The next day, Mum was laid off at the brewery. I helped out the best I could but it wasn't easy. Dad was the one who shovelled the coal into the scuttle and carried it into the house. I told Mum that I'd take over from him for a tanner a day and, after a cuddle, she agreed. The bunker was almost full to start with but it was a bitter winter and the coal heap soon dwindled. I got covered in black powder trying to capture the dregs with a dustpan and brush, and was attempting to wash it off in the kitchen sink when Mum returned (she'd been out looking for work). Her expression was the same as when that mouse ran over her foot.'

'Had it hard, did you Kuchy?' I lowered my eyes as the loathing in Raz's voice intensified. 'Not as hard as poor Mushtaq, I'll wager.'

'Compared to a starving Rwandan, perhaps not. Compared to this day and age, you tell me. Besides toast and jam I normally had two boiled eggs and buttered soldiers for breakfast. We didn't have yogurt and granola parfait in those days and two weeks before Christmas it was down to bread and dripping. All sorts of people popped in offering us things but Mum insisted we were fine. Nanna reckoned she was too proud to accept charity.

It wasn't until Nanna commented, "Are his legs getting bowed? He hasn't got rickets, has he?", that Mum started taking the food and cigarettes on offer. And just in time, too. Our Sunday roast had been replaced with pig's trotters and the fruitcake she baked on Sunday morning had disappeared altogether. When she stopped singing along to Billy Cotton and laughing at *The Goon Show* and Tony Hancock I knew things were bad. The Goons creased me up but Hancock bored me half to death. The Goons were a zany comedy act. Spike Milligan was the zaniest of the lot and my favourite…'

'I'm not frightened of pussycats. They only eat up mice and rats. But a hippopotamus could eat the lotofus. Mine too, Kuchy.'

I doubted that there was another gang member in the whole of North London who knew that poem. Were the shades and raised hood a mask that did more than simply hide his face? What if he really was studying at Oxford and had OD'd on Rousseau? It's an easy thing to do.

***

'The turkey and all the trimmings that Mrs Beaker and Mrs Harris brought round on Christmas Eve put the smile back on Mum's face. I told her that I didn't expect a lot that Christmas, not meaning a word of it, though I was determined to hide my disappointment. As it turned out I got an Indian chief's feather headdress from her and a rubber tomahawk from Dad when we visited him in hospital. I told them that they were what I'd always wanted and wondered what Tonto got for Christmas. Whatever it was, I figured it must have cost way more than mine. So when the new term started, I offered my services as Mush's bodyguard and asked if he'd do a swap. He said they didn't celebrate Christmas and he hadn't received any presents.

"What!" I exclaimed. "No bleedin' presents? Me Indian headdress would have fitted your bonce a treat."

He knew straight away what I was getting at.

"Is it because I resemble a Red Indian more than you, Ricky?"

I replied, "Sort of," and did a sulk.

I was doubly pissed off because I was looking forward to seeing Tonto peppered with potato bullets by a posse of cowboys.'

'The front of my shoe came apart in January and started flapping. If it'd happened before Christmas, perhaps Mum might have got me a pair of shoes from the jumble instead of that naff Red Indian stuff. It was only a little flap at first – until I kicked a leather ball the men were playing with over Bruce Castle Park. Kicking those old leather balls really hurt your feet. Bill heard that there was a ward at St Anne's Hospital full of boys with broken toes. Rumour had it that one of them had his whole leg sawed off when it turned green. But the goal was gaping and the centre forward had collided with the goalkeeper. For a boy who used jumpers for goalposts the opportunity to whack a ball into a real net far outweighed fear of amputation (we did use the Spurs gates in Worcester Avenue as a goal but nothing beat a bulging net). You should have seen me. I ran around the penalty area waving my arms in the air pretending I was Tommy Harmer after scoring the winning goal at the Cup Final. I ran even faster when the flamin' goalkeeper chased after me.'

'There I was at school with mud-caked knees and half my shoe hanging off. Dad was out of hospital by now and I was dreading having to tell him. The girls gave me the most grief.

"Can't your Mum afford new shoes?" sneered Jenny, looking at me as if I'd trodden in dog shit.

"You look like the stinking tramp what begs outside the Florida," said Doris, with a look to match Jenny's.

I called her a bitch and told Mr Gasson that Mum allowed me to use that word.

"Only when referring to dogs," he replied.

Doris was a bitch all right, but I loved dogs and decided not to call her one again. Mr Gasson asked Mrs Law whether someone should pay my family a visit. He said I was thinner than I was a month ago. At least Mum won't have to get me new clothes, I thought.'

'By the end of the first lesson it was already the worst day of my life. A note had landed on my desk in the shape of a paper aeroplane. It said they could smell my rotten feet from the back of the class. When I turned around they were all sniggering at me, including Harry who'd just got a new pair of pumps.

When I told Ink about Harry's new plimsolls, he said, "I bet his old man's stashed some of the dough he got from that security van heist."

I wanted to tell them to get knotted but Mrs Law was present. By lunchtime I was seriously thinking of joining the Foreign Legion. I asked Mr Gasson if I could be ink monitor and excused myself from lunch because I had a funny tummy. He agreed providing I promised to not get it everywhere. I might have escaped the welcoming committee in the playground but it didn't get me off lessons.'

***

It had been as if I was on the outside looking through a window into my past. Suddenly I was on the inside and my responses and emotions were as intense as they were on that day in the 1950s. When I got really upset or angry back then, I would drop more aitches and imagine horrible ways of extracting revenge on whoever or whatever.

***

'Teacher made me read aloud the story of a dog what saved a baby from wolves. The bleedin' farmer came back 'ome and saw blood everywhere. He looked around for his son and when he couldn't find the baby he assumed the dog had killed 'im. He shot the faithful dog, but soon after found the baby safe and the wolves dead, slain by the dog in another room. I kept thinking that dog was Sandy. I didn't blame the wolves because they were only big dogs but I 'ated that fuckin' farmer. I drew him in my notebook and jabbed me pencil in his head. The tip splintered and it could have done some serious damage if I'd stabbed it into Jenny's eyeball. I didn't know if I was the only one crying and I wasn't going to turn around to find out. I wiped me snotty nose on me sleeve and raised me arm. When Mr Gasson asked if I was okay I clutched me stomach and begged to use the bog.'

61

'Before I knew it, I was in the street and praying to Jesus that Sandy never dies over and over again, in case the Son of God hadn't heard me the first time. I couldn't go 'ome because Dad might get his belt out. He didn't look that strong when I left for school but he did 'ave a bottle of Lucozade by his bed. It would fuckin' snow, wouldn't it? Pretty soon I couldn't feel me big toe. On cold nights, Mum would fill up the stone hot water bottle. I couldn't go to sleep unless me feet were warm. I thought about taking shelter in a tunnel that went under the railway, but that led to the Marshes and I might 'ave been ambushed by the Edmonton mob. We only called a truce when Spurs played at 'ome. Then I had a brainwave. What if I went to Mrs Harris's and claimed political asylum? I'd 'eard that a Russian geezer had claimed that on the radio and he couldn't be touched. Everyone knew that the Russians ate their own babies and drank rats' blood. Even Sandy didn't do that. Just a quick shake and that rat were as limp as little Susan's rag doll. But Mrs Harris was Mum's best friend and she was bound to grass me up. On the other hand, if Betty was home alone she might do me a good turn. Betty had given me two Crunchies on condition I didn't mention to a living soul that her Uncle Fred came around to fix her something or other (I'd caught Fred sneaking in through her back door while I was crunching snails with Dad's hammer). Fred wasn't her real uncle but a close family friend. He'd fought alongside Reginald Harris at Arnhem and both men had received medals for gallantry. Dad often met up with them in the Railway to discuss football and the war. Trouble was, Mrs Harris had lost her job at the same time as Mum so she was bound to be in. I burst into tears for a second time and set off to cuddle Sandy. I'd only gone a few paces when a hand tapped me on the shoulder...'

Raz gave a Communist clenched fist salute.

'Who was it, Ricky? Joseph Stalin?'

'It was bleedin' Mush. He was holding a black umbrella that was rapidly turning white.'

9

The first slap smarted. The second jerked my head to one side and stung like hell.

'Stop the blubbering, Kuchy, or I'll hit you for real next time. People pay hundreds of pounds to be regressed and you're getting it for free. Are you aware that you were dropping your aitches and hurling expletives at a faster rate than Frankie Boyle? If you're not careful you'll be making cooing and gurgling sounds and saying ah-ah and ooh-ooh before too long. Whatever happened to the Dunkirk spirit? Did you ever see that picture of the two Tommies taking thousands of Italians prisoners? With all these cuts I doubt if we could even beat the Argies these days. What do you put it down to? Immigrants diluting the bloodline?'

Raz shone the torch into my face and moved it from side to side. I glimpsed my own reflection in his shades; for an instant, it looked like me when I was a small boy. He handed me a few sheets of toilet paper.

'Blow your nose and get on with the fucking story.'

An abundance of fear and hatred are supposed to imbue us with incredible strength. Given Superman powers, I'd have ripped his head clean off his shoulders and hurled it over the railings. Not so easy when all the joy and inner strength has been sucked out of your very being. I used to consider myself tough and self-assured. My split with Maggie had put a huge dent in my self-esteem and my experience with Raz had obliterated what was left of my self-respect. It should therefore come as no surprise that I meekly dabbed my eyes and apologised for having a croaky voice. The Ricky in my story was now approaching nine years old, but even he had more balls than me.

***

'I said to Mush, "What are you and that stupid umbrella doing here?"

He replied, "I saw you from my classroom window. I have a dental appointment and they let me leave early."

That pissed me off. They'd never let me leave unaccompanied. I scowled at him.

"What, all by yourself?"

I was kind of hoping he was pulling a fast one. That way if he snitched on me I could snitch back. But he pointed at the Austin Princess parked further along the kerb.

"My father is taking me."

He looked at my flapping shoe and offered me his umbrella while he had a word with his dad. I was well on my way to turning into a snowman by the time he returned.

He said, "The dentist's receptionist has telephoned to say that due to the inclement weather the appointment has been put back by a few hours."

For ages after that I thought inclement was a posh word for snow. I told him to stuff it but he either didn't hear me or chose not to.

He then put his foot next to mine and said, "I have large feet for my build. They should fit."

Baffled, I replied, "What should?"

He informed me he had several pairs of shoes and that I was welcome to a pair. I told him to sod off and that I wasn't accepting charity from the likes of him. I thought, who does he think he is? He has a telephone. Except for the Nobles no one has a telephone for miles. He's been in the country for five minutes and he has a bloody telephone. He rubbed it in by stating that the Lone Ranger and Tonto were meant to be friends and that I should come back to his house to dry off.

Playing hard to get, I retorted, "No bleedin' chance."

And did he let up? Not him. Saintliness oozed from every pore. He said his mother made lovely desserts and that I should try some.

Seeing me hesitate he tempted me with a new football game called Subbuteo. He said the players swerved and shot just like the ones he saw at Tottenham Hotspur. I was sickened. If word got out amongst the Arsenal that we let brown people in at Spurs we'd be a laughing stock. I screwed my face up as if I'd just tasted Doctor Miller's flu medicine.

"They let you in at Spurs!"

His response really had me going.

"We had seats, Ricky. I noticed that most of the people had to stand. I think it comparable to the Hindu caste system."

I was gobsmacked.

"A bleedin' seat! You had a bleedin' seat?"

He nodded towards the Princess and a brown hand with a silver ring waved back.

"My father thought that I should join in with the locals. When I grow up I'll invent Subbuteo for cricket. It's a far more civilised game."

I half wanted to get my tomahawk and plant it in his bonce, but instead offered it and ten cigarette cards for his Subbuteo. He turned me down flat and said I could play with it if I wished. He had two teams, one with white shirts and blue knickers like Tottenham Hotspur, the other red shirts and white knickers like Arsenal. He said I could be Tottenham.'

Raz tapped me on the top of the head. Thankfully, he missed the bump.

'Knickers? Were there a lot of cross-dressers in your day, Kuchy?'

'That's how shorts were described in the programme.'

'How did you respond?'

'I tried to make it sound as if I was doing him a favour. I shrugged my shoulders and said, "Oh, all right then," and followed him to the car.

He even opened the back door for me. I saw a chauffeur doing that for some nob once, so I was right chuffed, thinking that's the way things should be between us: me and the likes of him.

When I got into the car, Mush's dad smiled and said, "Nice to meet you, Ricky. I'm Mr Mohammed and I've heard a lot about you."

He gave me the kind of look Constable Warner did when a window had been broken and no one was pointing the finger.

"I hope you aren't playing truant," he continued, keeping the look.

I shook my head. I wasn't sure he believed me and hoped he didn't mind the wet patch on his leather seat or the wet fart sound my foot made. I bit my lip to stop myself from giggling. Once I started I couldn't stop. As the car picked up speed I began to panic. What if they'd called the school? What if Mush had told his dad that I got him an extra stroke of the cane? What if Mush told him I pushed his face in shit and that I'd set him up for a fall? As far as I could tell, Mush had never mentioned the incident to anyone, including me. Perhaps he was too embarrassed. Perhaps he was biding his time to get his revenge. I would have smashed a cricket bat over his head if he'd treated me like that. My paranoia continued unabated. What if they were taking me on a one-way trip to the Epping Forest! Ink served a year in India and said they did one of his mates in on patrol. He said the only thing worse than the smell of the nosh was the smell of the people. He said they had it in for him the moment he got off the boat: "All the railways we built them and they were as grateful as shit."

He didn't actually say shit but mouthed it because Nanna was in the room. Mush turned his head and looked at me over his shoulder.

"Here we are," he said.

I couldn't believe my eyes. He lived near the cinema in Bruce Grove. They didn't have houses at that end of Bruce Grove. They had bleedin' palaces, even bigger than the Nobles.'

'The smell of their cooking hit me as soon as he opened the front door. I hadn't smelt anything as strong since Mum smashed a bottle of TCP on the mantelpiece, or as horrible since Nanna forgot she had cabbage on the boil. And it was bloody hot in there. Despite having something called central heating, Mush's mum still had her head permanently covered. The Nobles had plug-in radiators but Mrs Noble didn't wear a funny thing on her bonce that hid her shoulders. Nor did anyone else in our street for that matter. Headscarves for church or to cover curlers were common (Mrs Noble didn't do either because it would ruin her hair, beautifully styled by Brian of Hampstead Garden Suburb). I thought that maybe Mrs Mohammed had gone barmy like Mrs Harris's mum. As they carted her off, the old girl screamed that the Devil had taken Glen Miller from her and she wasn't going to heaven without him. I was about to complain about the smell when Mrs Mohammed helped me out of my coat and started drying my hair with a fluffy towel. The towel was warm and smelt of flowers. She then took off my shoes and washed my feet in a bowl of warm water. Then she dried and sprinkled them with a powder similar to talc but even nicer. And then she gave me a pair of soft slippers to wear. I was half expecting her to shake some of the powder over my head in case I had fleas. Her little cakes were delicious. She served them up on a silver tray. They were green, yellow, pink, and all sorts of other colours. The pink things might have been an awful colour but they tasted the best. The cakes were called cham cham. I didn't know what was in them and I didn't want to. I had one of each before we went up to Mush's room, and I had to give it to Mrs Mohammed, because she never moaned about the crumbs like Mum did.'

'Mush's bedroom was enormous with a fitted wardrobe and bright drapes. The wardrobe at home would have toppled over without a folded up *Daily Mirror* propping up one side. The Subbuteo was all laid out on the carpet: goals, teams, and a pitch that was as green as the Spurs pitch on the first day of football season.

It was love at first sight, and I exclaimed, "Cor! Show me how it works, Mush. 'Ow do they move without magnets? Is there a motor in the base?"

He knelt and flicked one of the red players with his finger. It swerved just like he said it would, but how he missed from that range was beyond me. If a real football were as big as a Subbuteo ball in comparison, it'd knock the players' heads off. I picked up a goal and stroked the net.

"Do you pin it down, Mush?"

He replied, "Oh no. That would ruin the carpet. You hold it in place with one hand and operate the goalkeeper with the other."

Sensible. I'd never seen a plusher carpet than his. The only colour in our frayed back room carpet was where I trod tomato ketchup into it. Compared to their gaff we lived in a poxy cupboard.

'I soon picked up the hang of things and after a few practice goes, we were almost ready to kick off. I ran through the two line-ups. I began with our goalkeeper, Bill Brown, and ended up with Johnny Brooks. I gave Tommy Harmer a pat on the back. He'd patted me on the head once. It was bath night, but I didn't let Mum wash my hair without a struggle.

"And what of my Arsenal players?" asked Mush.

I listed them off.

"Let me see. There's Bashful, Doc, Dopey, Grumpy, Happy, Sleepy, Sneezy…"

Before I could add Snow White, King Kong, and Tom and Jerry, he cottoned on.

"Disrespecting your opponent isn't the gentlemanly thing to do, Ricky. The English invented cricket. I thought they had better manners."

He'd never fit in with an attitude like that, so I replied, "What you on about? Not around here we ain't, squire."

He went on to tell me all about the hatred between the Hindus and Muslims. I felt he was talking down to me.

Drowning in my own ignorance, I said, "Who are they when they're at home? Some pathetic Indian teams, I suppose?"

He said his father had walked a thousand miles to escape the fighting. People were burning houses and attacking one another with machetes. Even the women and children weren't spared the hate mobs.

What else could I say but, "So what? That's nothing compared to Spurs and Arsenal, mate."

Determined to win my friendship, he enquired, "You are an only child, Ricky?"

He was heading for a place I didn't want to go. I had a sister but she died before I was born. I once saw Dad comforting Mum as she looked at a picture of her. Her name was Mary and she died of pneumonia. Nanna said she was a pretty butterfly and every time I saw a butterfly I was to think of her. Which I still do.'

***

Raz put his thumbs together and flapped his hands like wings. He fluttered the "wings" high above his head and then made them plummet. As they spiralled closer to the ground he made a noise that was meant to sound like an aircraft crashing.

'What happens in the winter, Kuchy? Do clothes moths count?'

I half clenched one fist, loathing myself for being so weak.

Having failed to provoke a response, he continued, 'How did you reply to Mushtaq's overtures of friendship?'

'I said, "Yeah, so what?"

Mush had this knack of absorbing aggression and diffusing it.

And replied, "I'm an only child, Ricky. I didn't lose a sister but I lost two close friends to cholera. The disease strikes in many poor countries. I was lucky. We had a big house with live-in servants and didn't mix with the villagers when disease struck. My father worked for our government and now he's on a project over here."

My imagination was working overtime.

"Blimey! Is he a spy?"

69

He sighed and asked me if I would like to kick off, adding none too optimistically, "I hope you will play the game like an English gentleman."'

'He was useless. I won the game 8–1 and he only scored because I gave away an own goal. I told him he should have sought divine help like Mrs Harris's mum did before she was carted off. Dad was a Catholic and Mum C of E. Dad took me by bus to Westminster Cathedral every Christmas. I remember him pointing out Big Ben and the River Thames and thinking how massive the church was.

I told my mate, Bill, "Didn't think much of the wafers. You'd starve to death if you had to live on them. I swear there were as many candles in there as there are ants in our backyard."

The teams shook hands at the end of each Spurs match so I thought I'd better do the same thing. I wished I hadn't bothered because Mush's skin felt soft and his grip was limp (Dad always taught me to shake like an Englishman or a Pole, and not like an Italian).

Hoping to steer Mush in the right direction, I said, "Better pray to Jesus next time, mate. You could do with a bit of help."

He replied, "We don't pray to Jesus, Ricky. We pray to Allah, our God, and his Prophet."

Dad had a painting of Jesus and his mother above the bed, so I said, "Show me a picture of this Prophet geezer."

He mumbled something which could have been a prayer and replied, "We are not allowed to show his likeness."

I responded, "I hope you have better luck with this Prophet geezer than I had with Jesus. Terry kicked the ball into the river. Jesus can walk on water so I prayed that he'd appear and get our ball back. He never turned up. So what's this geezer's name, then?"

He said, "Mohammed. And please be more respectful, Ricky. I would never demean your God."

As far as I knew the name Mohammed was as uncommon as my last name. Thinking they might be related, I replied, "Wouldn't have minded being related to Jesus because he can turn cod liver oil into Tizer. Bet your Prophet geezer can't do that."'

'Before Mush could have another go at me the door opened and in came Mush's dad. He was holding a pair of white socks and black shoes. I couldn't tell whether the shoes had been worn or were brand new.

He smiled and asked, "Who won?"

I must have had a brainstorm because I replied, "It was a draw."

Mush patted me on the back and said, "Ricky is an English gentleman, father."

If he thought he'd turned me into one of them he had another think coming.

"It's snowing harder," said Mr Mohammed. "I'll drive you home, Ricky. You live in a road just off Park Lane, don't you? The dentist has his surgery in Park Lane."

Hold up, I thought. Tonto and his dad meeting my dad ain't so clever. If Dad catches me with one of this lot I'll be in for it.'

***

I was sitting on cold concrete in a drab playground, and yet I could feel the soft pile of Mush's carpet beneath me, smell the curry, the incense and flower petals. I couldn't grasp how I'd recalled my distant past in such detail, the minutiae of boyhood experiences, down to the most routine and obscure conversation. Then it hit me. What was the name of that truth drug? What if Sodium Pentothal was in that phial he put in his coat? He could have used a very thin needle. I had bloods taken by Nurse Rosie once and didn't feel so much as a scratch. Another thought gripped me: can you wear shades and still hypnotise someone?

10

'To avoid Dad catching me with the Pakistanis, I got Mr Mohammed to drop me off outside Bill's. Thank God for small mercies or, in this instance, the big snowflakes which tumbled from the sky. Believe me, no one saw me getting out of their car, otherwise it would've done the rounds by teatime and we'd have been besieged. I waited till the Austin had turned into Park Lane before venturing out of Bill's front garden and skating home on my new soles. When I opened the front door, Mum homed in on my shoes and there was more than a touch of anxiety in her voice. Some might call it blind panic.

"Where did you get those? You haven't stolen them, have you?"

I replied, "Mush's dad gave them to me, Mum."

She went from yellow alert to red.

"Who's Mush? Not one of Harry Hooper's acquaintances, I hope?"

I heard Ink belching upstairs. He'd just come out of the lav and was doing up his braces. He cupped a hand over his ear.

"Did you say mash, Margaret? Are there bangers and fried onions to go with it?"

When Nanna's rheumatism got too bad Mum cooked for them.

"It's the name of a boy, Ink," she called back.

"Oh," replied Ink, sounding disappointed. He said, "Oh" again and traipsed along the landing towards their back room.

"Well, young man, who is this Mush?" said Mum, arms folded.

She'd really caught me on the hop.

I swallowed my words for a bit and then replied, "He's a boy at our school and his surname is… Hammer."

She opened the front room door, peered out of the window, and patted my shoulders and hair.

"Mm, you should be soaked through walking in that snow."

I nipped in.

"His dad gave me a lift home in his Austin Princess. It's like a Rolls Royce and can drive through anything. Fit for a queen and tough as Cromwell tanks, then some."

She was still well on my case.

"Where are your shoes?"

I wasn't going to tell her that darkies had disposed of them.

Mum was a proud woman so I said, "Chucked them over the wall of that boarded up house. It was already full of rubbish and a dead cat. Don't think Sandy did it."

It came as no surprise when she went into one.

"Why did you throw them away? I had them repaired just last month and they still fit you."

'One had come apart.'

She looked really hurt.

'I would've bought you new ones, Ricky. We're not beggars.'

I curled my upper lip and sniffled to make her think I was about to cry.

"I did it for you, Mum. I heard you telling Nanna that you're skint and you don't like charity."

She put an arm around me and kissed my cheek.

"How thoughtful of you, dear."

'That was the first battle won.

Outright victory seemed improbable when she enquired, "Did you go to their house?"

In my excitement, I couldn't get the words out fast enough.

"You should've seen it, Mum. It's one of them big ones in Bruce Grove. I had cakes and played Subbuteo. They're even posher than the Nobles. They have central heating and fly on the Comet when they go on holidays." Realising I was sinking deeper into the proverbial, I tried to cover my arse by adding, "They have better suntans than the Nobles after a foreign holiday and accents that sound Welsh... but ain't."

73

Her eyes widened.

"Did you say like a Rolls Royce? One of those big houses in Bruce Grove? We must repay their generosity. I know, I'll ask them around for tea."

I tried to convince her that it wasn't such a good idea, but she was already playing hostess in fantasyland.

"Nonsense," she said. "We've got nothing to be ashamed of. I keep the place spick and span." She looked towards the back room and crinkled her face. "We'll entertain them in the front room. No need for them to see the rest of the house." I was running out of ammunition fast and fired one last round.

"Supposing they want the lavatory?" I said lavatory instead of bog to please her and then ruined it with, "They'll freeze their bleedin' knobs off."

I knew what was coming. And it did.

"Language, Ricky. How many times have I got to tell you? They won't stay long, just enough time to swap pleasantries. To be on the safe side, I'll put a new battery in the torch." She rubbed her hands together. "That's settled then.'"

'Her next move was as predictable as Halley's Comet. She went half way up the stairs and called out to Nanna.

"We're going to have well-to-do company soon, Dot. They live in one of those big houses in Bruce Grove."

Nanna came out of their kitchen drying her hands on a tea towel. She was well impressed.

"A big house in Bruce Grove? They'll want salmon sandwiches and fruitcake then, Margaret."

Mum tapped her chin and looked as though she was working out a sum in her head.

"I'll have to go to Sainsbury's. If this snow gets any worse the buses will stop running again."

Nanna replied, "If the weather doesn't improve get a large pork pie from Alf's. I heard it's snowing in Rome. We've had so much of it recently that Ink thinks the Russians are behind it."

Mum was playing the big day out in her head: entertaining well-heeled, well-educated Aryans with white-collar jobs.

She said, "We'll wear our Sunday best. I must press Ziggy's trousers. I know. I'll open that bottle of sherry that you got me for Christmas."

Nanna replied, "If it doesn't stop snowing soon they might not be able to get here anyway."

Mum was on a high and wasn't going to be deflected or deflated. "They've got a Rolls Royce, or as near as damn it."

Nanna nearly toppled head first down the stairs.

"Did you say a Rolls Royce, Margaret?"

Mum was a simple farmer's daughter and not usually prone to pretentiousness.

"Ricky told me. He knows all about cars. I'll send him to the greengrocers on the corner to get some cucumbers and tomatoes. Ziggy can bring a fresh loaf from work. I'll write a note for Ricky to give to his friend asking the Hammers around on Saturday. I don't suppose Spurs will play in all this lot. Mush is a funny name, Dot. Isn't that what Eskimos say to their huskies?"

Nanna thought for a moment.

"I dare say it's really Malcolm or Marmaduke. You know what boys are like with their nicknames. Marmaduke, now that's a real toff's name."

Ink joined in the conversation.

"Did you say Hammers? I hope they ain't bleedin' West Ham supporters. People round here have worked hard all their lives and they can't afford a big house in Bruce Grove, let alone a bleedin' Roller." He burped. It wasn't one of his long ones and he could grumble away without gasping for breath. "I wonder how they came by their dosh?"

Nanna snapped, "How many times have I asked you to say excuse me?" Ink pulled a browbeaten look. When his teeth were in a glass of water a constipated pug best described his boat race.

"'Scuse me, I'm sure.'"

'The more I thought about it, the more shit I realised I was in. The Mohammed's smelt nothing like us and they came from a place so hot that it toasts your face. Mush's mum might be nice but she was barmy. And what about the fact I'd played truant? If it weren't for the snow, I'd have had Bing knocking on our door by now. Please let it snow for a month, I prayed. I can build a snowman and Mum might forget all about asking the Mohammeds over for tea. But it relented overnight and Mum walked me to school through the slush. She'd taken ages composing her invite and almost as much time finding a place in her handbag where it would remain flat. Luckily for me she'd forgotten to write Mr and Mrs Hammer on the envelope. When we reached the school gates she carefully retrieved the note and smoothed it out, although it didn't need smoothing, and peered into the playground.

She said, "Is your friend Malcolm here? Perhaps I should give it to him personally. I bet he's smartly dressed and polishes his shoes. That reminds me, I must get you a new cardigan at the jumble sale, Ricky."

She'd got it into her head that Mush was called Malcolm and I wasn't going to contradict her. I couldn't see Mush anywhere and was scared that his dad's Austin Princess would roll up at moment.

"He's not here yet, Mum. I'll give it to him."

Mum knew that if anything didn't need crumpling or creasing, I'd crumple and crease it.

She said, "I think I'll wait here a while, dear."'

***

Raz sprang to his feet and twisted Oik's earlobe.

Lifting the youth's chin, he snarled, 'Just checking you're still alive. Hang on in there, blud.'

Oik groaned. It was the first sound he'd made in a while. Scared that Raz might finish him off, I was almost relieved when he turned his attention back to me.

'So how did you get out of that one, Kuchy? You were obviously going to dispose of the note the moment your mummy left.'

'Dead right I was. I'd planned to tell Mum that the Mohammeds had thanked her for the invite but were too busy to attend. All that went out the window when Bing spotted us from her study window and charged across the playground.

Handing Mum a note of her own, she folded her arms over her heaving bosoms and boomed, "Ricky played truant yesterday. The facts are all here. He will be kept back after school and made to write a hundred lines." The old windbag scowled at me. "My study during lunch break, young man."

I was going to get a double dose of pain, from Dad and the bleedin' headmistress. I say pain, but when Dad got his belt out it made a lot of noise and that was about it. Mum would never have let him really hurt me. Mrs Law's cane, as I knew to my cost, was the genuine article.'

'Mum was more miffed than the time I broke George (Nanna's favourite china horse).

She handed Bing her note and said, "I obviously can't trust Ricky. Would you kindly give this to Ricky's friend, Mrs Law?"

I cut in before she could say Malcolm.

"She means Mush, miss."

As luck would have it, Mrs Law had other matters to attend to. Using Carrot Top for cover, Harry Hooper was letting loose with a water pistol, shooting at everyone who came through the gates. By the time the Austin Princess appeared, Mrs Law had Harry by the ear and Mum had left. I watched Mush getting out of the car and wondered how he'd get on with the spiders in our bog.'

11

'Did the big day arrive, Kuchy? Or did you talk your mother out of it?'

'The lady wasn't for turning. She even made Dad give the bottom of our front door a coat of primer. We couldn't afford gloss. He moaned a bit at first but did as he was told.'

'What was wrong with the rest of the door?'

'Nothing but a few chips. The bottom looked as if someone had attacked it with a chisel. If he were out by himself, Sandy would scratch the bottom panel to be let back in. Sandy was in and out quite a lot.'

'Did you try and get the note from Mushtaq before he gave it to his parents?'

'No. I'm not sure why.'

'Course you do. You thought things through and decided to get your old man back for all those beatings he gave you. A troop of monkeys turning up on his doorstep? What better way of getting even?'

Raz's use of language left a lot to be desired, but his insight was uncanny. Drugged, or otherwise. It felt as if I was on a psychiatrist's couch being deconstructed under hypnosis. For once Raz was keeping his cool, whereas I was close to losing mine.

'I loved my father. Hated him sometimes. But how could I ever love him again after he'd committed the most heinous crime known to man?'

'Rape and pillage? Incest? Genocide?'

'Worse.'

'This is turning out better than *Silence of the Lambs*, Kuchy. I wish I'd looted a tub of popcorn now.'

***

'It was the day before I played truant. I'd been upstairs with Ink and as usual the conversation flitted between football, food, and the Great War. He was about to tell me what he did after he was demobbed when he nodded off. Fed up with Mush springing new words on me I thought I might turn the tables on him. So I went downstairs and asked Dad what demobbed was. When he told me it meant leaving the army, I asked him what he did after he left. He said they gave him a choice of staying in England or going back to Poland. He said if he'd gone back I would never have been made.

I asked him how I was made and he said, "You k'now."

When I said I didn't, he said ask your mother. The reality was that he went to Northampton and found work in a bakery. That's where he met Mum. He skipped the next few years and started talking about their life together in North London. He said he took me to my first football match when I was just three years old.

"Who were we playing?" I asked. 'And do you know what he said?'

'Why are you shaking, Kuchy? Are you coming down with something?'

'He said, "Arsenal were playing Manchester United and I sat you on a bar. Don't you remember? We caught a trolleybus to Finsbury Park."

Some bastard started rolling snowballs up and down my spine. Dad often talked about the Russian terror and how they massacred thousands of Polish officers. He should have tried that terror out for size.'

'I couldn't have hollered any louder.

"My first match was at Arsenal! Don't tell me I wore a bleedin' red rosette. Have you told anyone in our street?"

I must have freaked Dad out big time because he put an arm around me.

"You cried all the way through the match. The next week I took you to Spurs and you were as happy as happy can be."

Fuck me, was I seeing red.

"You took me to bleedin' Arsenal!"

He did his best to explain away his betrayal but it was a hopeless cause, even before he said, "You were only k'nee high."

I stamped my foot on the floor and it hurt like buggery. Ten angels stroking my hair couldn't have calmed me down.

"You don't love me! Can't do!"

He didn't know where to turn and pleaded, "Please stop crying like that. You k'now it upsets your mother. What about we go to Alf's and I'll buy you two chocolate bars?"

He could've bought me every chocolate bar on Alf's counter and it still wouldn't have done him any good. Lord Haw-Haw's treachery paled into insignificance. There was only one thing left for me to do.'

'Club him to death with your rubber tomahawk, Kuchy?'

'I headed for the dresser drawer and scrambled around for socks and pants. I heard him pitter-patter into the bedroom after me. He was a stocky man but he wore thick tartan slippers around the house.

I threw an elbow back to stop him coming too close and spluttered, "I'm off and this time I really am going to join the Foreign Legion."

'How ungrateful can you get? Your poor daddy was only doing his best for you, Kuchy. You really were a right little so-and-so.'

'I was only a nipper. You can't hang me for what I did when I was eight years old.'

'I could shoot you though. Go on, you delivered the note. And?'

'The Mohammeds accepted our invitation and Mush gave me a letter to take to Mum confirming the following Saturday. At the top of the page they'd put their surname so I chucked it in a dustbin on my way home without bothering to read it all. I assumed it only contained a thank you and how much they were looking forward to meeting my parents. Mum was thrilled when I told her that we had guests and was up early that Saturday morning. I helped pull out the table leaves, but Mum arranged the food and drink herself. My hands had a mind of their own when there were goodies on show. She'd given up trying to stop me from dipping my finger into the cake mix before she put it into the oven on a Sunday. She made me stand well back as she got things just right. I couldn't understand how moving a plate an inch to the right or left made the slightest difference.'

'A feast fit for a king, was it Kuchy?'

'A large pork pie cut into equal slices, cucumber and fish paste sandwiches, and bowls of crisps and salted peanuts. Alf's pork pies were something else. Mouth-watering didn't come close. Mind you, the thought of eating one of them these days, that awful jelly...'

'Turned veggie, have you?'

'When I'm on a shoot beggars can't be choosers, the corner shop, bakers, even McDonalds at a pinch.'

'Bet you fancy taking a chunk out of me, Kuchy.'

Yep, I thought, I'll start with a meat cleaver, progress to a chainsaw, and finish you off with a fucking rotavator ... black boy.

***

'The sherry and the posh glasses which Mum had borrowed from Nanna were next to the peanuts. I reckoned Mum probably did that because we'd recently seen a film at the Florida where someone went mad in the desert after running out of water and eating peanuts. Nanna said the last time she saw such a fine spread was at the street party to celebrate the Coronation. Besides cleaning the window, Mum had also polished the table till it squeaked. It was so shiny that I could poke my tongue out at my own reflection. I kept peeking out of the front room window to see who was going to turn up first, Dad or the Mohammeds. Mum was worried that I might steam up the glass because she'd just given it another good going over with Windolene. But I needed to keep a look out because the Mohammeds thought I lived at Bill's. If they'd knocked on his door the reception would have been none too friendly. Bill's dad was the coal merchant and his face was often so black that Dad reckoned he should audition to be in the *Black and White Minstrel Show.'*

'What were they, Kuchy? A mix of black and white singers?'

'Something like that, yeah. He may have looked like a Negro at work, but after work, Mr Reeves scrubbed up patchy pink and headed for the boozer.

After downing a few pints his many mantras included, "Those coons in Notting Hill belong in the jungle".

Bill told me that his dad had had a bad experience in a Kenyan witchdoctor's hut while serving in the army. Ink and Dad spent a cold winter's night drinking hot milk and whisky conjecturing what it might have been. They must have overstepped the mark because Nanna ordered them both to bed.'

'Did no one in your street think to put this coalman right, Kuchy?'

'Don't think so. But he wasn't very popular.'

'Didn't you think to warn your mother that brown aliens were about to pay her a visit?'

'She was angry with Dad because he hadn't returned from his walk and wouldn't have time to change into his best suit. He never stayed out for long on a Saturday unless he'd won a bundle. Mum made sure he gave her the housekeeping money on payday so his losses were never more than a few quid. By bundle I mean anything approaching a score. I thought news that the Hammers were really the Mohammeds might push her over the edge.'

'Do you often set people up, Kuchy? Especially your nearest and dearest.'

'I did my best to protect Mum.'

'How did you do that? Blindfold her?'

'She grew up on a farm and hadn't served in India like Ink, or been blown out of a Cromwell tank like Dad. I figured she'd be more accepting. Don't ask me why.'

Raz held his nose.

'All those animals, was that it?'

'That never crossed my mind. I thought she could cope with the visual shock but it was the Mohammed's odours that really concerned me. I'd got used to their pong but if Mum got a whiff … I'd thought long and hard about tactics. If Custer had done that he mightn't have got a No.1 from the Sioux. Clever me had a secret weapon, which I'd requisitioned from Ink to help Mum out. And it was far more effective than any scalping knife. But for it to be deployed effectively I had to make sure she wasn't near the front room window when the Mohammeds arrived.'

'How did you do manage that, Kuchy?'

'Milk. The Nobles had a fridge and so did we. Theirs was called a Hotpoint and ours was called a backyard. In our fridge you had to cover the milk up or the birds would peck through the bottle tops. Mum used to joke that ours was ten times bigger than the Noble's in the winter. In the summer it was a fraction of the size because she left the perishables in a bucket, which she refilled with cold water several times a day. When I spotted the Mohammeds' car turning in from Park Lane, I told her that the sparrows were at it again. I waited for her to make a beeline for the back door and headed for the front.'

'What was this secret weapon, Kuchy? A gas mask?'

'I'm coming to that. Before their Austin had even pulled up outside Bill's house, half the people in the street were looking through their curtains admiring the car. When the Mohammeds got out of the car, the same people were on their doorsteps, more interested in what had just hatched. I ran down the pavement, shouting and waving my arms. Mush saw me and waved back. He was wearing a suit and tie. The closest I got to a suit was when Mum bought me a grey coat from a jumble sale to match the grey trousers she'd bought from a previous jumble sale.

I called out to Mr Mohammed, "Oi! I live further down."

Mr Mohammed already had one hand on Bill's garden gate. If he pushed too hard it'd come right off its hinges.

"Didn't I drop you off at this house, Ricky?" he replied.

I told him I was just visiting.

"Then lead on, young man," he said.

We passed many of our neighbours on the way. Shall I describe them or push on?'

'Such close encounters might prove useful. You have my permission, Kuchy.'

***

'I was dreading the walk back to my house. Mrs Mohammed still had that "silly" thing around her head. It was perishing cold so I reckoned she might get away with it. The previous week a Tory came down our way drumming up support. If the Mohammeds were alien to our street then the Tories weren't far behind. Ink said they fed on the poor and hung out in Highgate and Hampstead. I wasn't sure what a Tory did and even though the geezer wore a blue rosette, I knew I didn't want to be one. Mr Wilson had to stop Mrs Wilson from hitting him with a rolling pin.

Mrs Beaker chimed, "Not today, thank you," and Mr Beaker offered him a jar of coronation jam that had turned.

Mr Mohammed gave a little wave to Mrs Beaker who was standing on her doorstep. She waved back. For one awful moment I thought she was going to offer him some of her jam. She'd made that latest batch using bitter green things in a big black pot. She stirred it with a long wooden spoon, licked the spoon from time to time, muttered, "too sour by 'alf", went "mm", and added more sugar.'

'Mr Bentley was lurching on the doorstep directly opposite the Beakers. He'd lost his glasses yet again and was squinting. Tall and thin he was stooped from arthritis, which was why the glasses kept falling off his shiny nose and why he had such difficulty retrieving them. Shot by a fanatic while on active service in Rangoon he had the scar to prove it. Mum told him never to show it to me again. Mr Bentley reckoned people looked just like ghosts if he hadn't got his glasses on. Mum reckoned he'd be a ghost soon if he didn't stop knocking back the hard stuff. He insisted the booze eased the pain. Mum said it's not his war wound that set him on the slippery path but his wife running off with a Yank. Mum, in her pinny, would go into his house once or twice a week to clean and cook. He'd inherited a few bob from a relative in Australia but she never asked for any money. He kept his inheritance in a battered brown suitcase under the bed. Everyone knew about it, but it was safer there than if he'd deposited it in a bank. I nipped in after Mum once. The place smelt of cat piss. Mr Bentley didn't own a cat, but he often left his back door wide open and a big tom would make itself at home. It was especially fond of the scraps lying around in the kitchen, notably cheese with the texture of concrete. After Mum had chased the cat out with a mop she shooed me out of the front door, but not before I caught a glimpse of the old drunk sprawled out on the settee. His shirt had vomit and what looked like blood or tomato stains on it. His glasses sat askew on his nose and a bottle of Bell's was dribbling whisky on his lap. I sneaked a look through his front room window after I'd finished my game of flickers with Roy. The empty bottles had gone and he was sitting up eating tomato soup. He had fresh trousers on and a clean shirt. Mum propped a broom against the wall, wiped her brow, and had a drag on the cigarette burning in the ashtray. He smiled and squeezed her hand as she put her coat on to leave.'

'A few doors along on our side of the road, Mrs Ripley was with Mrs Harris. Mrs Ripley had her hair in curlers. She wouldn't be seen dead in them if the tallyman were in the neighbourhood. It was common knowledge that she paid him back in instalments but no money changed hands. It wasn't until we were at my front garden that

I deployed the secret weapon. I took Ink's tin of Fisherman's Friend from my pocket, undid the lid, and offered them to the Mohammeds.

"Here, have one of these," I said. "They'll put hairs on your chest."

Mr Mohammed put his nose close to the open tin. He didn't need a second invitation. Neither did Mrs Mohammed or Mush. They licked the end first and soon decided that a Fisherman's Friend was indeed a friend.

"What a delightful aroma," said Mr Mohammed, sucking away. "I must remember to get a supply of these sweeties."

Well, that was one obstacle out of the way. But I wasn't out of the woods yet. The front door wasn't locked. I opened it slowly and poked my head inside the hall.'

'Not locked? Trusting lot in those days, weren't you Kuchy? Why didn't you just go straight in?'

'The only time it was locked was when Dad slept into the afternoon after a night shift. Otherwise Mrs Beaker or Mrs Harris would pop their heads inside our hall and wake him up by calling, "Cooeee! Fancy a fag and a cuppa Margaret?" I'd promised Mush that Sandy wouldn't be inside the house. As far as I knew, Bill and the others had taken him with them to Bruce Castle Park. But I wasn't taking any chances.'

'Vicious, was he?'

'Sandy liked to be introduced to strangers before they stepped across the threshold. And there were no stranger strangers than the Mohammeds. A set of canine gnashers hurtling down the hall at the speed of the Caped Crusader would have ruined everything. There was no sign of him so I ushered them inside. Mush looked nervous and remained at the back. He'd seen Sandy often enough when he came with Mum to meet me from school. Sandy loved children. Above all he loved being made a fuss of by them. But while the other kids patted and stroked him, poor Mush stayed well clear. I suppose Muslims have a thing about dogs.'

I regretted saying it the moment the words left my lips. For all I knew he may have been a Muslim. His line of questioning did nothing to dispel the possibility.

'Does that put you off them, Kuchy? Do you hate their guts?'

'No way. I look upon it as a cultural thing. Though, like Gandhi, I believe a civilisation should be judged on how it treats its animals.'

'When Gandhi came to this country wearing only a dhoti, Winston Churchill called him a half-naked fakir. I wonder how old Winnie treated his animals. From what I hear he wasn't too fond of black dogs.'

'How do you know all that?'

'Heard all about Churchill on *Kiss*.'

'You'll be telling me you've read Bertrand Russell next.'

'I drew the line at Jeremy Bentham. I'm the inquisitor and if you get too inquisitive your story might have a nasty ending.'

'Gandhi was a pacifist, you know.'

'And Hitler was a vegetarian. Your point being? I won't tell you again, chief. The aliens have invaded your hovel. What happened next?'

***

It struck me that if Raz overcame his psychopathic tendencies, he'd make a bloody good teacher in a deprived inner city school. None of the kids would dare answer back, that's for sure. Clearly, I had to acknowledge the fact that all hoodies weren't dumb or ill-educated, although I suspected Raz was the exception that proved the rule. It wouldn't have surprised me if he watched the *National Geographic* channel while snorting up. By hoodie I mean the jeans at half-mast brigade and their slouching swagger, the ones who travel in packs, the ones to avoid eye contact with in case you "dis" them. But were my preconceptions and prejudices hindering any hope I had of reaching out to him, mad or otherwise? His mates may have been yobs but why would an educated person like him come down to their level? He obviously had street cred, which in their world meant he'd gained their respect, which meant that he'd earned his spurs doing things best left unsaid.

**

'I tried to put the Mohammeds at ease by copying how Mum greeted Doctor Miller and the vicar. A smile and a polite, "Won't you come in? Please make yourself at home." Doctor Miller was an Irish Catholic, the vicar an Ulster Protestant, so Mum never asked them round at the same time. Ink said the Micks should shoot each other and get it over with. Mum, meanwhile, had brought the milk in and was busy making herself presentable. Once the Mohammeds were inside the hall I hurried them along in case Ink copped an eyeful.

"Can I get you anything?" I asked them, opening the front room door with one ear on Ink's landing.

Sure enough a sound emanated from the top of stairs, which could easily have been mistaken for a creaking door in a haunted house.

"Blimey O'Reilly, it's one of them," said Ink, glowering down at them.

Mr Mohammed smiled up at him.

"I'm very pleased to make your acquaintance."

Ink hadn't put his teeth back in and his scowl resembled a gurn.

"Thought I'd seen the last of you lot when I left India. Me guts ain't been the same since."

Nanna peered around Ink's shoulder. Her eyesight wasn't what it used to be.

"Stupid old fool. They fly on the Comet and have suntans."

Mr Mohammed looked at Mrs Mohammed and they both looked at Mush. Mr Mohammed opened his mouth but all he could manage was an, "Ah."'

'Mr Mohammed's jaw had just slackened when Mum came out of the bedroom adjusting her hair. One look at her guests and she completed a full circle. She glanced at the back room, then at the front room. Locked in suspended animation, she did her best to smile but rigor mortis was setting in. Her hand twitched as if it wanted to shake hands but her brain thought otherwise.

"It's nice to make your acquaintance. Refreshments?"

Mum had a slight Northamptonshire accent and dropped fewer aitches than the rest of the street. The last time I heard her talk that posh was when she met the bishop.

Rocking into action, she opened the front room door and said apologetically, "I would've laid on salmon sandwiches and fruitcake but I couldn't get to Sainsbury's."

Fiddling with her hair, she kept glancing towards the street hoping Dad would come back from the bookies. If I were a Mohammed, I'd have already made a break for it. I think they might have done, if it hadn't been for Dad stumbling through the front door. He was as pissed as a newt and there was a fat unlit cigar sticking out of his mouth. He hadn't seen the Mohammeds. He couldn't see much of anything. Mum propped him up against the wall and hastily ushered the Mohammeds into the front room.

"You can serve our guests, Ricky," she said, pushing me in after them and closing the door behind me.'

'If the Mohammeds hadn't been ensconced in our front room, Mum would have screamed at Dad.

As it was, she half hissed and half growled, "Go to bed and sleep it off, Ziggy."

I could imagine Dad puckering his lips as he replied, "Give us a kiss, Margaret."

She might have suppressed a faint smile at this stage. After all, he did have a fat cigar and it boded well. Cigar or no cigar, she was having none of that kind of behaviour when we had guests.

"Do as I say, Ziggy."

Dad played his trump card.

"We're rich, Margaret. I did an acc-cum-urater and the last horse won by a short nose."

He had her undivided attention now. Mum wasn't greedy but we needed every penny we could get.

"How much did you win?"

"Fifty squid," he replied.

It's highly probable she held her hand out at this stage.

"I'll look after it. Where is it?"

Dad patted and then slapped his pockets.

"Bugger. It was here."

Mum hadn't given up hope but it was draining away fast.

"Try the pockets again. Is there a hole in the lining?"

Dad was only slurring every other word by now. The loss was sobering him up fast.

"That's odd. I don't k'now what happened to it."

Mum's growls were getting louder and a mega hiss wasn't far behind.

"Think, Ziggy. You obviously didn't come straight home. Where were you?"

Dad had climbed the gallows steps and placed the noose around his own neck. Now he was about to plummet through the trapdoor.

"I stopped at the Railway Tavern for a quick one."

The hiss arrived right on cue.

"How many did you have?"

I imagined Mum bracing herself for the reply.

"Just three pints."

Dad couldn't drink more than two before his mind went blank.

"And he calls himself a Pole," mocked Ink, who'd returned to the top of the stairs.

Ink rarely came downstairs because it took him most of a day to go back up again. Mum had given up on talking proper by now.

"You went into the bloody Railway Tavern and flashed fifty quid!"

There was scuffling in the hall and a sound resembling the mice that scuttled about at night, only ten times louder. The mousetraps going off woke me up sometimes. Dad cleared the dead bodies away when he got back home from work. Mum wouldn't touch them. Ink joked that she wasn't a real farmer's daughter. There was that scuffling again and this time it was followed by the sound of people charging down the hall. I turned to face the Mohammeds. One thing's for sure, I'd never call Mrs Mohammed mad again. Not while she was in our house.'

'The week before, Mum had taken me to see a film called *Thank you, Jeeves!* The way the butler and the servants performed their duties gave me a good idea of how to dish up the food. Mum had scrubbed my hands and cut my nails but I was still careful to use the spatula. I put a portion of pork pie on a small plate and offered it to Mrs Mohammed. She held the plate at various angles, observing it as if it derived from Mars. I was well up on me *Quatermass*.

"What is it?" she asked.

"A pie," I replied, thinking no one can be that thick.

She kept the offering at arm's length.

"Yes, but what's in it, Ricky?"

I thought if ever proof was needed that she was mad then this is it. Still, I owed it to Mum to be polite and assumed she was put off by the jelly.

"It slides down a treat," I said.

Her nostrils pinched and her brow furrowed as she moved her face closer to the plate.

"I meant the meat," she replied.

What else could I say but, "Pork."

She took an instant turn for the worse. Nanna had those. I offered it to Mr Mohammed and he started batting away flies. Mum had removed the flypaper before they arrived but I couldn't see any flies.

"Our religion forbids us to eat the flesh of a pig. Didn't you read our letter?" said Mush.

"Not all of it," I replied.

"It's not your fault, Ricky," said Mr Mohammed. "We should have been more precise."

Mrs Mohammed would probably have liked to use her plate as a discuss, but with admirable restraint, she placed it gently back on the table.

"Yes," she said, "it's all our fault."

I rushed to the table and snatched up the bottle of sherry in the hope that it would soothe the nerves.

Not quite grasping the terminology in the Jeeves' film, I enquired, "Would you care for an imperative?"

Mr and Mrs Mohammed were on the settee and Mush was in the armchair. They shook their heads in unison.

"We don't partake of alcohol," said Mr Mohammed.

Bloody hell, what do they bloody partake of? I thought. A fish paste sandwich was closer to a pork pie than a crisp. In desperation, I picked up the bowl of crisps. I wasn't that optimistic but I offered it to them anyway.

"A party game, anyone?" I said chirpily. "First one to find the blue paper with the salt in gets first go at the peanuts."

Mr Mohammed smiled thinly, took the bowl, and offered it to his wife.

"Thank you, Ricky," he said. "We all like crisps."

You can't go wrong with a nice cuppa was another of Ink's mottos. He reckoned that's what made us civilised. There was only one thing for it: the infusion that built the British Empire.

"Tea?" I asked. They had mouthfuls of Smith's finest so all they could do was nod. "I'll be back in a mo," I said, rushing into the hall and closing the door behind me.'

'Ink was still on his landing peering down. I went a little way up the stairs to make sure he could hear and the Mohammeds couldn't.

"Blimey, they're a fussy lot," I said to him.

"We had to eat their muck in India. Make them eat ours," he growled.

I was feeling sorry for Mum because she had gone to so much trouble and it meant a lot to her.

"Mum would never forgive me if I'm rude, Ink."

He heard Nanna pulling the chain and limped back along the landing. As Nanna came out of the lavatory, a generous whiff of disinfectant followed her.

"Pay no heed to Ink, Ricky," she said. "The mark of a man is politeness. Be a good boy and go and help your mother."

When Nanna told me to do something I did it without question.

I found Mum in the kitchen. She shooed me away and I poked my head into the back room. It was empty.

"Where's Dad?"

She throttled a hiss.

"Sleeping it off in the bedroom. The tea's just brewing. Did they enjoy the pork pie? Alf said it was fresh yesterday."

I took a step back. Mum never hit me but I wasn't taking any chances.

"They don't eat pork because of their religion. Same with the sherry. And Mum, they're called Mohammed not Hammer."

She slapped her head with one hand and covered her face with the other.

"You might have told me they were *that* different. What are they doing now?"

At least I've kept them entertained, I thought. That was no small

93

feat considering we didn't have a telly and the Xbox hadn't been invented.

"Munching crisps and looking for the blue paper."

She fitted the caddy and placed the teapot on the tray beside the cups, milk, and sugar. Adjusting her hair, she picked up the tray.

"I've put an extra spoonful in for luck. It should be strong enough," she said, setting off down the hall.

I'd never seen her move so fast. I reckoned she must be a strong contender for the egg and spoon race come sports' day.'

'She stopped outside the front room door.

"Get it for me, will you dear?"

I opened the door and peered inside. Mush was sitting cross-legged on the carpet at his mother's feet, the bowl of crisps between them. He punched his fist in the air and held up the blue paper.

"I win," he cried.

I don't think Mrs Mohammed could have tried very hard because she hadn't got bits of crisps stuck to her hands. I stepped into the room and nearly swore in polite company. Dad wasn't kipping in the bedroom. He was sat on the arm of the settee next to Mr Mohammed. I'd seen him but Mum hadn't. She headed straight for the table and the uneaten pie.

"I must pay you for the shoes you gave Ricky," she said, fixing her eyes on the mutilated centrepiece of her gourmet meal (I'd fitted Mrs Mohammed's portion back into place but hadn't done a very good job of it). That, and the embarrassment of being given charity from a Pakistani family, had her well flustered.

"I'm really sorry. Ricky should've told me. I would've got real salmon but for the snow. Would you care for a fish paste sandwich?"

She put the tray on the table and turned around. The semblance of a smile on her lips vanished as quickly as a last Rolo when I was around.'

'No words can describe the look on her face when she copped Dad with his arm around Mr Mohammed. She whistled (I can't begin to tell you how many times I'd tried to teach her to whistle).

Mr Mohammed said to Dad, "Really, and you were catapulted out of the tank? Thank God you survived. I was deafened by a Japanese artillery round."

Dad gave him a shoulder squeeze and replied, "K'nock me down with a feather. It could only have been God that saved me. I was deaf as a post for three days after my tank went boom. Did you have that ringing in your ears, Mr Hammer?"

Mr Mohammed removed his face from the vicinity of Dad's breath. I could smell the beer from across the room. Though it didn't dampen his enthusiasm for reminiscing none and Dad seemed to be enjoying breathing in Fisherman's Friend. They might have been all lovey-dovey, but I wasn't chuffed because I'd hoped Dad would insult the Mohammeds, perhaps inadvertently mention men with bones through their noses. If he'd done that Mum would have gone ballistic and he wouldn't have got a sniff of a toad in the hole for weeks (his favourite). Mum's mood mellowed when she earwigged the nature of their conversation. Her hands had steadied by now and she poured the tea nicely and without spilling a drop.

Before serving up she muttered to herself, "Thank God for the bloody war.'"

12

Raz knelt and moved his hands towards my throat. I'd already felt like puking before he straightened my collar and contoured my neck with his fingertips.

'We have company again. Close your eyes and count slowly to one hundred in your head, Kuchy. If you open them before that, or try to escape, I'll rip your eyeballs out of their sockets.'

I sensed rather than heard him leaving and had just completed a twenty count when voices sounded. Any hope I had of being rescued was extinguished when I sussed the nature of the banter. Mum used to say that I came down the stairs like a herd of elephants. God knows what she would have made of that din. Judging by their raucous laughter and the magnitude of swearing, I gathered that his so-called friends had returned. A hand patted me on the top of the head and another covered my lips.

'Good boy, Kuchy. Stay nice and calm until they pass.'

I opened my eyes to see the curtains in the house opposite, part and close in the same motion. Further down the road the lights in two houses were switched off simultaneously. Tottenham was still under siege and the blue coats had been confined to barracks. I looked to my left. I could just make out the outline of the overflow pipe but there was no sign of Oik or the rope that bound him.

The first of them came into view; a ghoulish figure slowly transforming into something vaguely human. It was followed by five more of its kind, bunched as tight as a rugby scrum. I was anticipating a tempest of hate and bravado, the main topic of conversation looting and the joy of burning police cars. But for them, as for me, the world revolved around Raz.

One of them moaned, 'Ain't making no sense, blud. Can't see Raz slipping.'

Another gobbed on the pavement and spread the phlegm with the sole of his shoe.

'Maybe the feds got him. Done for carrying a mash or something. Sooner we get out of this hood the better, bro.'

The first hoodie replied, 'The consignment arrives in the morning. Without him the fucking deal's off. This looting shit's small time compared to what we'll make on this, blud.'

It became apparent that Raz wasn't a looter at all and I doubted if he was a religious freak or political activist. He was most likely a simple criminal, possibly engaged in a drug or arms deal. Reflection gave way to panic as the bloody alarm on my wristwatch sounded. I thought I'd set it for two in the afternoon, but I must've gotten my pm and am mixed up. I chose that model because its yowling wakeup call was piercing enough to rouse even the likes of me from a drunken stupor. Someone should have recommended it to the medical profession, because it could have come in handy for stirring patients out of comas. My jabbing index finger located the off button, but not before the bloke at the back of the pack had shot to attention.

His hand reached inside his pocket and he hollered, 'What the fuck's that?' His outburst was followed by a discordant gabble of voices and a stampede. A torch blazed into life, its rays sweeping the playground like a searchlight in a prisoner of war camp. Raz seized me under the armpit and hauled me to my feet.

He pressed his gun into my hand and whispered, 'Safety's on. Stick the barrel in my back and stay directly behind me. Let me do the talking.'

Even if I'd wanted to I don't think I could have spoken. Any words that happened to escape my lips were unlikely to belong to someone capable of pulling a trigger. Raz put his hands in the air moments before the torchlight struck him full in the face.

He called out, 'Easy Jess, he's got the drop on me.'

One of the gang members broke from the scrum. His face was

obscured by a fashionable hood, which covered his baseball cap. He wasn't wearing shades and as he passed beneath the streetlight, I could tell that he was fair-skinned. He sounded incredulous.

'That old cunt got the drop on you, blud? Ain't possible.'

'Don't get fooled, Jess,' replied Raz. 'He's ex-SAS and knows how to handle himself. Lower the fucking torch or I'll go blind.'

The owner of the torch guided the beam to either side of us. Jess darted his eyes, tracking the beam as it criss-crossed the playground.

'Is he alone? Did he get a picture of me doing that fed?'

'I told you not to join in the street party, blud,' retorted Raz. 'We're on a mission, remember?'

Jess scratched his cheek. I think it was intended as a signal for Raz, telling him to drop to his knees so that he could put a slug in my chest.

'Better that we blended in,' said Jess defensively. 'Only banged that fed. Fell awkward like. Could have shanked him.'

He gave a quick nod of the head and stepped out of the light. Another signal?

'Don't sweat, blud,' replied Raz, attempting to soothe Jess's nerves. 'This guy ain't a real photographer and he didn't capture nothing on camera. That's just a cover. He's holding me as a kind of insurance policy so we don't double-cross them. I'm to phone you with the location at the last minute.'

'He's muscle for the suppliers? Why were we chasing him, then?'

'He was simply leading the way, bro. Didn't want us caught up in the riot and needed a quiet word with me. I'm the one what set up the deal. He don't want to do business with anyone else.'

The expression on Jess's face could have belonged to a contestant on *Countdown*. An unlucky bugger who'd been given two letter u's and a heap of consonants. His body was silhouetted, but the gun in his hand glinted as it caught the rays from the streetlight.

'Don't get it. Why does the boss want the deal done in this swag hood? Where do we hang out while we're waiting? We'll be dead if we get caught around here.'

'Swing a right under the bridge at White Hart Lane Station and then first left after the Irish Centre,' responded Raz. 'There's a bit of wasteland they use as a car park when the football's on. Cool it. Last I heard the locals were trying to storm the nick. Their bitches are helping themselves at that shopping estate near Tottenham Hale.'

Raz's crew wanted to avoid the local gangs, which suggested they weren't from Tottenham. Raz, on the other hand, seemed very familiar with the area. From what I'd gathered, the most notorious local gangs were a Turkish gang and one loosely connected to the Yardies. The former were having some sort of feud with a gang from Hackney. I hadn't seen much evidence of Turkish involvement. If Raz was part of the Afro-Caribbean mob, he sure had a hell of a lot of white acquaintances. If the young men on the other side of the railings owed allegiance to a gang from outside "the hood" they probably couldn't call for reinforcements. And who was this boss they mentioned? An old-time gang boss in the best East End tradition or a young usurper collapsing under the weight of headphones and drowning in bling? Raz may have been top dog amongst that little lot but he obviously wasn't pulling the strings.

Jess began moving from side to side. Fearing that he was trying to get a clear shot at me, I ducked my head.

'Can't he speak for himself?' asked Jess suspiciously.

Raz's reply was couched as an order rather than a request.

'Do what I say or the deal's blown. If you take him out we'll never have those gangster wheels the man promised us, blud.'

Jess shrugged and tipped the peak of his cap.

'If you say so, bro.'

He returned to the pack and they reeled away to form another huddle on the far side of the road. Raz whispered to me.

'If they start climbing the railings pass me the gun and hit the deck.'

Jess left the scrum and tapped his gun on the rails.

'Listen you old cunt,' he snarled. 'If we're scammed...'

'Nothing'll go wrong, Jess,' interjected Raz.

'Don't like it, bro.'

Raz slapped him down.

'Don't want to repeat myself. And keep the fucking noise to a minimum.'

Jess straightened his baseball cap.

'Whatever you say, Raz. You're the man.'

Jess ambled back across the road. He said something to his friends, which involved a lot of arm waving. I guessed that he'd conveyed Raz's instructions because the gang set off with scarcely a word spoken between them.

It's a funny thing, you can hold something in your hand and after a while you hardly know it's there. Raz hadn't forgotten.

'You can return the gun now, Kuchy. And give me that fucking watch while you're about it.'

I stepped back and fumbled for the safety. It took me a while to locate it in that light and at any moment I expected him to rush me. Once the safety was off I pointed the gun at him and steadied my aim by clamping a hand over my wrist.

'Don't come any closer. Story time is over. Now, why the fuck do you want to hear about my school days? And what's happened to the poor bastard you strung up? Is he dead? What was he meant to have done, anyway?'

He took a couple of casual steps towards me. I swear I put all my strength into pulling that trigger but the bloody thing might as well have been set in concrete because it didn't move a jot. Believe me, I couldn't have strained any harder if I was anchor in a tug-of-war team. The yips had spread up to my shoulder by the time he grabbed my wrist and plucked the gun from my grasp. He sighed.

'Really Ricky, you'll get double detention if you carry on being a naughty boy. Mrs Law wants me to administer the corporal punishment from now on.'

He pointed the gun at my temple and pulled the trigger. There was a click and I remained cringing well after he'd grinned and added, 'This is your final warning.' Tucking the gun into his belt, he slapped me across the back like a buddy. 'Move! We've got to relocate to that patch of shade over there. Walk behind me and use your fingers as a gun.'

I strained my eyes to see into the shadows either side of the streetlight.

'We're safe here, aren't we? They've gone, haven't they?' I looked down. And so had my watch. 'How the fuck...'

It was in his palm. He clenched his fist and there was a grinding sound followed by a crack as the insides burst the casing. He stuffed the parts into my pocket.

'Ugly thing, ain't it? Aesthetics obviously ain't your cup of tea, Kuchy.'

He kept a tight grip on my arm as we traversed the playground, moving stealthily when in shade and picking up speed when exposed to the rays shed by the functioning streetlight. He frogmarched me the last few yards, made me sit, and squatted beside me.

'Pay attention, Ricky. I'm going to tell you a parable. A group of settlers were drinking whisky when they found themselves surrounded by Apaches. One drunken clever arse told the others that the Indians were too scared to attack at night and he sang *Dixie* at the top of his voice. The Apache are clever, insightful people with acute hearing and a taste for liquor. They overwhelmed the settlers, kept the whisky, and let everyone go. All except for the clever arse, that is. They stripped him naked and bound him to a tall cactus with lengths of hide. The whole war party took turns pissing on him. Do you know what happens to hide if it's soaked in piss and the sun gets to it?' He made a circle by linking the tip of his middle finger with his thumb and gradually made it smaller till it shrank to nothing. 'I returned to the toilets and paid Oik a visit after I left you just now. There wasn't a cactus or strips of animal hide to hand, but I still managed to initiate him in the ways of the Apache. If you're sitting comfortably, Ricky, then you may return to the days when only fishermen wore hoods and a man could stroll down the road in winter wearing a balaclava without triggering an armed response unit.'

13

'The love between Dad and Mr Mohammed didn't survive the excesses of peacetime. Dad wasn't scared of anything, except Mum, so it wasn't the gossipy neighbours that bothered him. Both men had the war in common but after that they were struggling. The bookies were definitely out and so was the dog racing at Haringey and the horseracing at Ally Pally. Mum said he should take him along and only look at the nice dogs and horses. You can imagine how well that went down. It was the same with the Railway Tavern and, as for cricket, Dad didn't know one end of a middle stump from the other. When I tried to show him he gave me a clip around the ear for my trouble. He did get a good look at a cricket ball, though. It was when Mrs Thompson took a short run up to our front door and plonked one in his hand. He examined it this way and that and asked if it was edible. After she'd finished her rant, Mrs Thompson told him it was a cricket ball and not a Cox's Orange Pippin.

Dad had another feel and enquired, "What's this k'nitted thing around it?" Mrs Thompson informed him it was a seam but she didn't know what it did. Dad was impressed by the hardness and the weight of the ball.

He said, "If you run out of grenades you could k'nock a German senseless with one of these babies."

He wasn't that surprised when she replied, "The blooming thing broke my window and hit my Cyril's ashes. It was only by the grace of God that the urn didn't smash. Your Ricky's the culprit."

From that day on Dad considered cricket a force for evil.'

'Dad got his belt out and stopped my pocket money for a whole month. But what really pissed me off was the fact that I didn't do it. We'd nicked the ball from James Carpenter. James wasn't really one of us. He spoke posh and rumour had it that he drank mock turtle soup and ate munchmallows for tea. He would run home crying if he so much as grazed his knee. His family had moved from a big house in Highgate and James had gone to private school before his mum fell down on her luck. Mr Harris told Dad that James's dad had run off with a tasty harlot to Bournemouth. I asked Mum what harlots were and could I have one for supper. Funnily enough I was toasting a crumpet over the fire at the time. She muttered something under her breath that I couldn't quite catch.'

'My woes began with our street gang sitting in a circle on the pavement admiring the shiny new ball (we played cricket with a length of wood and a bald tennis ball). Frank reckoned it wouldn't be out of place in a trophy room.'

Raz raised a hand like an Indian chief greeting John Wayne.

'Who were "we", Kuchy?'

'Besides me there was Bill, Roy, Frank and Terry. As already stated Bill was the leader. He was the tallest with messy dark hair and freckles on his face that no one dared rib him about. Roy was quietest. He had blond, pudding basin hair and was dependable in a scrap. Frank and Terry were brothers and joint smallest in the gang. Both had brown hair but Terry's eyes were blue while Frank's were black. Terry was the oldest of the two, loved scrapping, and half the time he'd be the one to kick things off. Frank, on the other hand, had an evil tongue, preferring to bait other boys rather than fight them (he positioned himself at the back during a scrap). Terry wasn't the sharpest tool in the box and was held back at school for poor reading. They called Frank a gifted child and his parents were considering sending him to a special school. When he went to the library he'd nick books from the adult section when no one was looking. He could play chess while his older brother struggled at snakes and ladders. Mrs Beaker thought they must have different fathers. In case you were wondering Mush wasn't part of our gang yet.'

Raz leant towards me.

'But he is soon, I hope?'

'He was kind of conscripted.'

'I dare say. Mushtaq doesn't sound like the type of boy who'd mix with the likes of your friends.' He paused, waiting for my response. When none came he snapped, 'Don't even think of dissing my friends, Kuchy. Now shift it!'

'Sandy had been sitting by my side ogling the ball when the temptation to have a chew became too much for him. They say foxes are sly but they had nothing on Sandy. He got up and stretched, took a casual look around, and grabbed it before any of us could move. He sprinted down the road with us haring after him. I was screaming for him to give it back, worried he'd bury it over the allotments. But instead, he dropped it in Mrs White's garden and started howling outside her front door.

Terry said, "Reckon her Spaniel bitch has overheated again. Must have stood too close to the fire."

None of us thought to correct him. I'd seen Sandy humping Mrs White's dog and thought they were playing piggyback. It may be hard for you to believe, but children in those days thought procreation had something to do with the birds and bees. Once, when Mum was working at the brewery, I came home early from school and disturbed Dad in the bedroom. He had his braces down and the top of his white underpants was visible. He was looking at a picture of Jane Russell in a magazine. She was flashing her teeth but nothing else of great interest to modern man, because she was wearing a one-piece bathing costume that denied the ogler even a hint of cleavage. I tried to take a closer look but Dad said it wasn't for my eyes. He locked the door and tried the knob for good measure after I'd left.

'Kuchy! How many times have I got to tell you? Stop playing for time.'

'Right. So, there we were huddled around Mrs White's front gate. Bill crept inside the garden and had just retrieved the ball when she emerged carrying a bucket of water. The weight of it had made her go lopsided. We all had a good laugh, safe in the knowledge that she'd never lift the bucket high enough to throw the water over us.

She scowled at Sandy, whose tongue was hanging out, and cried, "Filthy beast. Come any closer and I'll chop them off!"

Later, when I told Ink, he tapped his nose and said she was a spinster. Yet in that moment of angst, she'd somehow gained superhuman strength and the bucket was at shoulder height before we knew it. Sandy took the brunt, but Bill got a good soaking. Sandy stopped howling and panting and shook himself over Mrs White. Her stockings had rolled down her legs but that didn't stop her. Nothing could. She rushed back inside the house with the bucket. Sandy didn't hang around for a second soaking and turned his attention to the ball in Bill's hand. Sandy could knock you flying when he was on a charge. Bill tried to chuck it to me but he was on one leg and it sailed over my head and smashed Mrs Thompson's front window. I was the nearest and so she thought I'd done it.'

Raz held his thumb and index finger millimetres apart.

'You're that close, Kuchy. If Mushtaq doesn't make an appearance…'

'Soon, I promise. One minute, max.'

'We'd always intended to give the ball back to James. The next day, Bill pleaded with her but she'd already donated it to the Salvation Army. Don't ask me why. We were scared stiff that James would call the police, and during a hastily arranged meeting in Terry's front garden, Bill made a suggestion.

"What about that sissy brown kid what was round your place, Ricky? I heard he can't kick a ball for toffee but he's good at cricket."

"Yeah, he tried to get Bing to play cricket at school. He wanted us to all wear long white trousers and clap each other. Bing turned him down flat. No way was she going to let Harry Hooper get hold of a cricket bat."

"Perfect. We'll get him to join our gang. He's bound to have a real cricket ball to spare."

Frank said the brownie would have to be initiated and thought up a test of unimaginable cruelness.'

Raz turned his hands into claws and slashed at the air.

'Did Mushtaq have to fight a lion? A rabid gorilla, perhaps?'

'Worse. He had to go scrumping in the vicar's garden and nick one of his big green apples. I'd rather have faced a rabid lion with tooth-ache than our vicar.'

14

'Frank figured Mush needed protection and reckoned he'd jump at the chance of joining our gang. He had a point. It was a bloody miracle that Mush hadn't already been beaten up and it was bound to happen sooner or later. The first Negro family of African descent had just moved in down Northumberland Park. Their son, Denzel, never went to my school and didn't ask to join our gang. He was done over by the Edmonton mob when he strayed too far into the Marshes. They called him jungle bunny and made him hop like a rabbit. Frank thought it hilarious. He rubbed some coal dust over his face and did "the jungle bunny hop" while singing along to his very own version of *Jailhouse Rock* – "Let's hop, everyone, let's hop". It never made the rounds on the Royal dance floor.'

Raz pulled a knife from his hoodie and snarled, 'I'll leave nigger-hating Frank to later. That Edmonton gang needed sorting out, chief.' He put the tip of the blade against my throat. I couldn't move my head any further back because it was already wedged against the brickwork. 'You let them roam uninvited into your hood? You sure you come from Tottenham? Didn't your generation take the North Bank Highbury some years later?'

'I was more of a hippy than a football hooligan. I don't know what I am now… but we sorted that Edmonton mob out, all right. We bought bows and arrows from the hardware shop in Park Lane.'

He put the knife back inside his hoodie and grinned. He grinned more and more as my story unfolded – the kind of crazed grin which sometimes cracked Charles Manson's stony face.

'What else could you buy in that hardware shop, Kuchy? AK47s?'

'The bowstrings were literally made of string and the bow only had a range of about ten feet at most. The arrows were blunt and resembled kindling on sale at present day garages. Kids improvised in those days. We took off the flights and tied darts to the end. We shot two of the Edmonton mob in the arse at close range and they all scarpered.'

'Was Mushtaq there?'

'No way. He would have had kittens. And we didn't want him praying for us either. Frank thought Jesus's dad might get angry. The vicar had told us all about plague and pestilence. Most of us couldn't wait to get away from the vicar's sermons but Frank lapped it up. His favourite bit was when Cain killed Abel.'

'Terry, right? I get the picture and fratricide's not a pretty one. And don't look so bemused, Kuchy. We use the word fratricide on the street all the time. This Denzel, tell me more about the brother and his family.'

'Ink reckoned Denzel should change his name to something more Christian and suggested Matthew or Mark. There was a waiting list to get a job on the "dust" but Denzel's dad wangled it somehow. Rumour had it that his wife was a nurse and had tended to a leading council member. The story involved a bed bath and rubber lips the size of donuts. I remember Ink winking and Nanna scolding him for repeating idle gossip. All the dustmen knew Sandy and he knew them. Well, he did until this dark stranger with the brilliant white teeth turned up crooning in his native tongue. Ink looked out of the window and chuckled as Sandy chased Denzel's dad towards the dustcart.

"Blimey, look at that blackie go. I thought Jesse Owens was a fluke but I ain't so sure now."'

Raz jabbed a finger in my chest and repeated the dose.

'Find that funny, do you Kuchy?'

It wasn't the pain that caused me the most distress, rather the life force he was sucking out of me. I was weakening both in body and mind. I know it sounds implausible but it was as if he fed on my energy. I shook my head.

'Maybe I found it amusing at the time but not anymore.'

'Frank seems to be the brains behind the operation. What was his next move?'

'He said we should make Mush an honorary member, and as such, he mustn't have any voting rights. When I told Ink, he said we had to draw the line somewhere. He insisted the Second World War had nothing to do with us losing India. It was because we allowed the buggers the vote. Frank gave two reasons for why Mush shouldn't be granted full membership: he was the colour of a lightly fried Walls' pork sausage (my analogy had sprouted wings), and he lived streets away. Frank also said we should have an oath to make us look the part. It would be nothing like the naff oath they had in the cubs. He said it was called a promise. I promised Mum that I'd join the cubs and stay out of trouble. I had no intention of keeping that promise. Frank had nicked *The Three Musketeers* from the library. The Musketeers had an oath that went "All for one, one for all". We were all well in favour. Although it was Frank's idea, even Terry went along with it. Musketeers had sword fights and ran people through. Ink was always going on about the "good old days". I thought that must be when these Musketeers lived.'

Raz yawned and stretched lazily out. I'd taken pictures of lions doing that in Tanzania after they'd gorged on their kill.

'Ah, this night air's so bracing, ain't it Kuchy? How old was Frank at this point?'

'I was a year older than him, so he must have been eight going on nine. Believe me, he was a cocky little bleeder.'

'Takes one to know one.' He didn't need to raise his voice to have me flinching. Just a slight change in intonation could do it. 'Eight going on nine, you said? That means you must have been nine going on ten. This story appears to be advancing at a rapid rate.'

'You wanted to hear about Mushtaq. There were long periods when I hardly saw him. I can tell you more about Dad and Ink's wartime reminiscences, if you like.'

'Not unless you want me to wring your neck. Explain Mushtaq's absence.'

'When things became too unpleasant, Mr Mohammed arranged for Mush to be educated at home. He was out of school for a good year or so prior to this. Billy Bunter and Carrot top weren't best pleased because they got it in the neck instead. I thought you wouldn't want to hear about my schooldays if Mush wasn't there. I'm not sure why he returned, or would want to return. I dare say the Local Education Authority had a say in it. Anyway, I was surprised to see the Austin Princess pull up outside the school gates. Mush looked glum as he got out of the car. He hadn't changed much and, unfortunately for him, neither had Harry. Harry tripped him up in the playground and would have gobbed on him if Mr Gasson hadn't intervened.'

I could've lied, told him Mush got out of the car, waved merrily as he skipped across the playground and into his classroom, up to his desk, which had a smoking joss stick in the inkwell and was filled with lotus flowers courtesy of Harry Hooper, recently converted to Buddhism by the Dalai Lama. But whoever Raz was, he wasn't a fool.

'Carry on till the end of the road, Kuchy.'

'What's at the end of this road? A bullet in the head? I'll take the M25 if you don't mind.'

'Like going round in circles, do you Kuchy?'

'Perhaps I'm taking a leaf out of your book.'

His spittle sprayed my cheek.

'Don't need no bullet, white boy. If I clap any louder you'd die of fright.'

I threw my hands up to stop that juggernaut from reversing into the wall again.

'Take it easy, man. Everything's cool.'

'That dude with the tassels in *Easy Rider* weren't no hippy. And neither are you if you've got any sense. You were saying, man? Tell me more about the Bash Street Kids.'

'After Frank had explained what honorary member meant, we had a vote and all agreed that Mush was in on condition he was fully initiated. Terry reckoned that, as Frank was the youngest member, he should be made an honorary member and therefore lose his voting rights. Terry lost the vote and Frank was promoted to corporal. Terry's rank was corporal so he said he should be made whatever comes next. He got outvoted.'

'And what rank were you, Kuchy?'

'I was a captain and Bill was a general. It was left to me to deal with Mush. I couldn't act overfriendly with him or Harry might have turned against me, but whenever I could I asked Mush how he was doing, that kind of thing. After a week of pleasantries Mush invited me round for a game of Subbuteo.

"Fell right into our lap," said Frank when he heard the news. "Butter him up a bit first, Ricky."

He then convinced Bill and the others that we needed a plan B in case I failed.'

'Did that entail giving Mushtaq a few slaps? Did you draw blood, Kuchy?'

'No way. Not wishing to humiliate Mush, I only beat him 4–2 at Subbuteo. Ink said, "Humiliated, that's what we were after Hungary thrashed us 6-3 at Wembley."'

'Ink this, Ink fucking that. I get the picture, Kuchy. What happened next?'

'Frank suggested I should box clever in case Mush suspected I had an ulterior motive. I was to act as if I was his best friend and tempt him into joining our gang with promises of KitKats and Mars bars. Frank had read up on the ingredients and stated categorically that there was no pork in either of them.'

'What was your subtle opening gambit?'

'I asked Mush whether he wanted to join our street gang and if he had a real cricket ball we could borrow.'

'Einstein had nothing on you.'

'I didn't know what ulterior motive meant and I wasn't going to let on to Frank. If he knew something you didn't he could be a right know-it-all.'

'How did Mushtaq respond?'

'He said his father had opened the batting for Pakistan and possessed loads of new cricket balls. He asked me what my gang was called. That posed a problem.'

'Why?'

'We didn't have a name and I had to think one up pretty fast.'

'What did you come up with? The Park Lane Tearaways? The Park Lane Savage Bunch?'

'I said the first thing that came into my head: Tottenham Boys. Before you scoff, it wasn't such a bad shout. Park Lane this or Park Lane that wouldn't have cut it. But Tottenham Boys rule the whole borough. Get it?'

'How did Mushtaq respond when you told him your gang ruled as far as the eye could see?'

'He said, "Peacefully, I hope. I don't want to get into any trouble."

That was typical of him. It was time for me to play the fear factor. I asked him if he ever got hassled. He replied that the Jewish boys who attended school at Stamford Hill picked on him occasionally and the Devonshire Hill mob had made threats.

"Not to worry," I said, forcing myself to put an arm around his shoulder. "Bill's the leader of the gang and he's going to be a weight-lifting wrestler when he grows up. Not even Harry would dare take him on."

I qualified that statement by assuring him that we mostly played games like football and "it" and when it was pissing down we played flickers and marbles in someone's hall.'

'Flickers?'

'You stood a cigarette card against a wall and the one that knocked it down kept all the cards that missed. We developed a wrist action and they really flew through the air.'

'And what was on these cigarette cards?'

'Mostly footballers with the odd picture of a racing car or cricketer. You could collect whole sets if you were lucky enough.'

'And was Mushtaq hooked?'

'He said he didn't play football and neither of his parents smoked. He said many people in Pakistan had the habit but his father considered it a vice. Perhaps the makers of e-cigarettes should think about re-introducing the cards.'

'And get the kiddies hooked on nicotine? What kind of human being are you? All that shaking. You absolutely certain you ain't a junkie, Kuchy?'

I was sweating so much that I could smell the Vindaloo I had for lunch.

'Mush liked marbles best because they had such pretty colours. I wasn't impressed because that's what Bill's little sister, Susan, would have said. I was beginning to wonder about Mush. Dad had recently nudged Mum when we came across this bloke wearing a bright yellow collarless shirt with green palm trees on it. I knew they were palm trees because I asked him.

The bloke walked funny and Mum said, "Come away immediately, dear."

Dad winked and replied, "I bet he's one of *them*."

To make sure Mush wasn't one of *them* I sneaked a look inside his wardrobe after he'd popped out of his bedroom. There was no sign of a yellow shirt with green palm trees on it. Blimey, I couldn't bring one of *them* back with me to meet the gang.'

'Are you homophobic, Kuchy? You're not one of *them* are you?'

'You should've seen the babe I went out with last Saturday.'

'Had a dummy in her mouth, did she Kuchy? Okay, so Mush agreed to join the Tottenham Boys. That right?'

'Not straight off. He wasn't sure whether his parents would approve. He asked me if it cost anything to join. I told him he had to be initiated and that it was on the house. After I explained nothing was on a real house he enquired if the initiation was painful. I told him it was easy as piss and all he had to do was pick one apple.'

'I see you've omitted to mention the vicar, Kuchy. I hope you ain't leaving important things out of your story. Did you produce the Mars bars at this stage?'

'He wasn't convinced and anyway, he preferred KitKats. The best I could do was to persuade him to meet the others. I wasn't hopeful that he'd say yes and quickly surmised that the situation required Frank's plan B.'

'Roy had been stationed across the road from Mush's house because he was the fastest runner. He held a *Daily Mirror* up to his face with two eyeholes cut into it. While Mush was putting the Subbuteo men back in the box, I snuck over to the window and gave Roy the signal. He'd been reading the sports pages and the wind had really picked up. The sports coverage was only a few pages in total at the end of the paper and they moulded onto his face. The more he tried to fight it off the more it came back at him. In a moment of inspiration he did a pirouette that Nureyev would have been proud of and the newspaper sailed past the cinema, which was showing *The Magnificent Seven*. All the kids in our street wore their cowboy gear while that was on. The sound of cap guns going off got so bad that some mums and dads imposed a curfew. Roy gave me the thumbs up and set off like Roger Bannister.'

15

'To get home from Bruce Grove, I'd normally walk along the High Road, cross Lansdowne Road, and swing a right into Hampden Lane. But Frank's plan B entailed leading Mush along Lansdowne and into an overgrown passage, which ran behind the houses. Mush was a bit hesitant at first, but I allayed his fears by telling him it was a short cut that we used all the time. I didn't let on that the passage was known locally as Hell Alley and could be dangerous, especially if your face didn't fit. A group of kids hung out there led by a lunatic called Jason who had long grubby nails and was forever scratching his head. Ink reckoned he'd been watching too much *Laurel and Hardy*. Mum thought he must have a rare skin condition because nothing visible jumped off him. When Sandy had fleas, Dad would smother him in powder and Mum would dab camomile lotion on my lumps with cotton wool. She'd tell me not to scratch them because I might get blood poisoning. I hated it when that lotion dried because it hardened and left pink patches.'

'While our gang played cowboys and Indians, Jason and his mates played a game called "kill the Jap". Basically, any kid that strayed down the passage who they didn't know or like was a Jap. One unlucky kid from outside the borough was punched in the face till both nostrils bled. He was then tied up and had ants put down his pants.'

Raz held his hands to his face and pretended to sob.

'Poor Mushtaq. Like a lamb to the slaughter. Let me guess. He got a good hiding, wriggled a bit, and concluded that Tottenham was as lawless as the Old West. After his wounds healed he begged to join your crew.' He hissed, 'That right, Kuchy?'

'Frank had a sly, callous nature and was cleverer than that.'

'At some point soon we're going to pick the flesh off young Frank's bones, but for the time being tell me more about this Jason character.

He had a skin condition but it appears he also had a brain condition to go with it. I reckon Doctor Miller should have referred him for a lobotomy. Speed it up, Kuchy, or I might carry one out on you. Nah, why bother when the alcohol's doing such a fine job of finishing off your remaining brain cells.'

He'd smelt whisky on my breath and I had the shakes bad. But who wouldn't when imprisoned by that nutter? It irked me to think he assumed I was an alcoholic on such flimsy evidence. If only that Doors song would stop playing in my head … well, show me the way to the next whisky bar.

'Jason's dad, Ernie, was taken prisoner by the Japs and went a bit mental. Nanna said that when he returned from the war, Ernie was as thin as a rake and no one could recognise him. He was fatter by now, a porker in fact, but just as mental. Mum said he must have poisoned Jason's mind with horrible stories drawn from the Japanese prisoner of war camps. I asked Ink what a poisoned head looked like after someone had scratched it for too long. He said he saw plenty of poisoned limbs in the trenches. Rodents, insect bites, and leeches were the main cause. You had to burn the bloodsuckers with fags to get rid of them otherwise your arms and legs resembled rotten pears. I had a nightmare about Jason's brain that night. Old man Glover hit Jason over the head with his stick and cracked open his skull like an egg. Old man Glover was evil. He'd attack kids with his walking stick if they went into his garden to get their ball back. In my nightmare Jason's poisoned brain plopped out and ate Mr Glover. It was the biggest, smelliest pear imaginable and I woke up screaming. Mum reached across from her bed and held my hand.'

'I've changed my mind. I think you were the one with the brain condition, Kuchy. I killed a man once and left him to rot. He couldn't have smelt too nice by the time he was found.'

Had he just confessed to murder? If so, then my chances of survival had gone from slim to non-existent. I had no idea what time it was.

Gone two and nowhere near sunrise was my best estimate. Another red glow appeared above the rooftops and I heard the wail of a siren reach its zenith and fade away. He tilted his head like a dog when its owner mentions treats.

'Don't expect help any time soon, Kuchy. I could slow roast you on a spit in the middle of the playground and none of the people in the houses opposite would risk calling the cops on a night like this. They say it's healthier if you cook bacon in its own fat.'

You might conclude he was only out to scare me. I didn't.

'Did you? Did you really kill someone?'

He laughed.

'Ate him alive. He finally croaked when I took a chunk out of his liver. Okay, Kuchy, so you've led Mushtaq into the alley. What next? How many bottles of camomile lotion did it take to bribe Jason into thumping him one?' When I didn't reply, he gnashed his teeth. 'You better start moving those lips, Kuchy …'

***

'Jason and his gang of four weren't expecting us. Unless it was pouring it down, they were normally there playing marbles and flickers on a concrete slab surrounded by weeds. Jason took one look at Mush and jumped to his feet.

He waved his crew forward and cried, "That's a fucking Jap if ever I saw one."

Mush took one look at Jason and said, "He doesn't look very friendly, Ricky. Perhaps we should turn back."

I'm still confident at this stage. They might be circling us like Red Indians around a wagon train but the cavalry was due to arrive at any minute.'

'For Roy read Paul Revere. Bill and the others, right?'

'Especially Bill. "We don't want any trouble with you, Ricky," snarled Jason. "Why don't you bugger off and let us take care of this filthy Jap."

Mush replied, quite politely considering the slagging off he'd received.

"If you think I am Japanese then you are very much mistaken. I come from Pakistan. My father fought the Japanese in the war."

Jason wasn't impressed. He knew a bloody Jap when he saw one.'

'What did you do, Kuchy? Leave Mushtaq to his fate?'

'Frank's idea was to show Mush that we ruled the streets. The way things were going the poor sod would be too scared to show his face in this part of Tottenham again. I played for time by facing up to Jason like that cavalry officer I saw challenging the Indian chief one-to-one at the Florida. It might not seem possible to you, but I'd earned quite a reputation back then. For starters, I developed a sinister growl, which I'd learned from Sandy.

I growled at Jason and said, "He's going to join our gang, Jase. You lay one finger on him and it'll mean war."

I nearly said Tottenham Boys but we weren't known as that yet and Jason might have felt left out. He may not have been right in the head but he did come from these parts.

"You and whose army?" he yelled, clenching his fists.

I quickly weighed up my options.'

'To run or not to run… that right, Kuchy?'

'In a nutshell, yes. Why shouldn't I do a runner? I thought. Mush ain't from around here and he's a funny colour. Douglas Noble's suntan will fade but Mush will be stuck with his for the rest of his life.

I was still dithering when Mush stepped in front of me and said, "Thank you, but I can fight my own battles, Ricky."

He couldn't because Jason shoved him in the chest, which sent him flying. Mush landed awkwardly on the concrete, but after rubbing his knee he got straight up.'

'Do I detect a twang of conscience or a bonfire of the moralities,

119

Kuchy? In case you're wondering, the DJs at the XOYO are always going on about bonfires.'

'Tell me you're from the Planet Zog and I'd believe you. What was uppermost in my mind was replacing Jack Carpenter's ball before the police came knocking. Kids were genuinely scared of the police in those days. Never mind a clip around the ear, they'd nearly pull your whole ear off if they caught you misbehaving on the street. I gave Jason the Tottenham Look and it seemed to be working because he didn't take a swing. He'd lost none of his bravado though and spat close to Mush's shoe.

He scrubbed his head with his nails (the only time you couldn't see dandruff on the tops of his shoulders was when it was snowing), and snarled, "So what's the name of this filthy Jap, then?"

I replied, "Mushtaq."

Mush smiled, pleased that I'd used his proper name I guess. Jason wasn't smiling.

"Knew it!" he exclaimed. "That's a fucking Jap name if ever I heard it."

'Did you and Jason slug it out, Kuchy? Or did Mushtaq surprise everyone by picking up a long stick and demonstrating his mastery of the quarterstaff?'

'The cavalry came to the rescue in the nick of time. I heard Terry first because he screeched when he charged. I think it was meant to be a bugle. And Frank was singing something I'd never heard before:

"Bash up Jason's mob 'cause they're all queer. Bash up the Arsenal 'cause they're all queerer still."

'A catchy little number, Kuchy. I can envisage it being accompanied by a gay flautist. Did Jason stand and fight?'

'Jason copped Bill appearing at the head of the alley and made a break for it. Just as he turned the corner he did his Stan Laurel routine and shouted, "You'd better watch your step, Jap."

Mush shrugged and turned to face the bushes. As he rolled up his trousers to check the damage to his knee, I got a glimpse. Talk about ugly. His knees reminded me of little Susan's tortoise that got squished by a dustcart.

I said, "Blimey, I didn't think Jason pushed you that hard."

He replied, "It's only a graze and Allah made my knees this way."

I thought this Allah geezer wouldn't get a skilled job down at Gestetner's factory. The others were only a few feet away by now, so Mush quickly pulled his trouser leg down.

He pleaded, "You won't mention my knees, will you Ricky?"

I was tempted but shook my head and replied, "Nah. I know how to keep a secret, mate."

Now that Jason and his mob had scarpered, Frank dashed in front of Bill and gave a second rendition of his new bash them up song.

Mush held a hand over his mouth and whispered, "I think that boy needs help, Ricky. And what does queer mean? Do these Arsenal boys look peculiar?" I hadn't got a clue. Frank was always coming up with new expressions. I took Bill aside and told him my idea for our new handle. He patted me on the back.

"Love Tottenham Boys, Rick. And that little git can't claim this one.'"

Raz clapped his hands inches from my face.

My ears were still ringing as he snarled, 'Frank, right?'

'Who else? Bill winked at me, turned, and offered his hand to Mush. "You won't get any more grief with us around, mate. Tottenham Boys are the pukka mob in this borough."

Terry was even more confused than usual.

"Who?"

Bill and I replied at the same time.

"Shut it, Tel!"

Mush may have shaken Bill's hand but he was just as confused as Terry.

He drummed his bottom lip and mused, "But how did you know we were in trouble?"

Bill wasn't as bright as Frank but he wasn't dumb either.

He stuck out his chest and replied, "We patrol these streets regular and have scouts everywhere. So, you want to become a Tottenham Boy? Safe."

Mush thought for a moment and said, "I accept the apple challenge."

Over Mush's shoulder I caught Frank winking at Roy.

Roy wasn't prone to getting overly excited but he nudged me and whispered in my ear, "If that fool thinks Jason's scary then wait till he sees our bleedin' vicar.'"

16

'Kuchy, have you ever been to Hampton Court? Wonderful history, don't you think?'

I hesitated. He was bright enough and possibly knowledgeable enough to discuss the relationship between Cardinal Wolsey and Henry VIII, but I sensed he had a motive which had very little to do with the Tudors.

'Yes... a long time ago.'

'Imagine you're in its maze and there's no escape. At each turn all you see is a burning hedge that reaches way into the sky.'

The sweat on my brow had pooled and was streaming down my face.

'I've got no way out of this and you're going to kill me? Is that what you're saying?'

'Whether you roast or not depends on the ending, Kuchy.'

'What ending?'

His eyes may have been hidden behind those shades but I just knew that they'd narrowed.

'The ending to your story, of course. And don't try making one up to please me. For all you know I might hate happy endings.'

'But when does it end?'

'Are you leaning more towards the physical or metaphysical?' He punched his own palm. If the blow had landed on my chin it would have knocked me senseless. 'I'll fucking tell you when it ends, chief.'

'Who the hell are you? If you're trying to scare me then you've succeeded. If you want physical proof have a whiff of my underpants.'

'No need. I can smell them from here. Just like I can smell your fear. Tell me more about this vicar. Did he wear a six-gun on each hip? Was he burning with passion for the Lord?'

'The Ulsterman was all fire and brimstone; an opinionated man consumed by the Word of God and caged in the Old Testament. I remember him dropping in on us for tea and running his sweaty hands through my hair.

"Ricky's a good lad really," he said. "But I think he should come to Sunday school for moral guidance."

I wanted to guide my rubber tomahawk across the top of his bonce. Not that I could've done because Dad had confiscated it after I hit Bill's sister on the leg. It was a tragic accident. I was aiming at James Carpenter who was on his way to the cubs.'

'Stick to the vicar, Kuchy, providing his path converges with Mushtaq's.'

At least, I thought, the vicar had the comfort of believing in a utopian afterlife. After my split with Maggie, I didn't believe in anything anymore. I'd even lost faith in Harry Redknapp.

'The vicar had a chubby face, fleshy hands, and a bulbous nose. He wasn't a small man by any means, but he walked taking tiny, rapid steps. We christened him Mr Wimpy after the character in *Popeye*. He may not have had a hamburger in his fat paw all the time but he normally had something; a sausage roll or pork pie would do it. Mum felt sorry for him and said the poor chap should have a proper sit down meal. The vicar believed God's work could never wait.

"No wonder there's mice in the vicarage with all those crumbs," Mum told Mrs Harris.

"I heard he chases after them with a poker. Rodents obviously ain't God's creatures, Margaret," replied Mrs Harris, causing both women to fall into hysterics.

If the vicar caught you scrumping in his garden, he'd reach for an old tennis racket. He had them dotted around the place. If it were your first offence he'd just use the strings. They made a twanging sound as they bounced off your cranium. For a second offence it would be the wooden frame on the back of your leg.'

'Frank said the hardest wall to climb over in the whole world was the Great Wall of China. I think Mush might have contested that assertion as he stood staring up at the vicarage wall.

He said timidly, "Oh dear. How am I supposed to get over it?"

Aware that Frank was waiting for him to bottle it, I stepped in.

"I'll give you a bunk up, Mush. Once you're up the top, swing your legs over and jump."

Mush's language skills may have served him well with school lessons, but they didn't do him many favours on the street.

I think he thought a bunk up was a kind of hoist because he looked up and down the pavement and asked, "Where do I get a bunk up?"

Frank replied, "Why don't you ask Betty Harris?"

The gang all giggled but I doubt if any of them, including Frank, got the joke. Bill bent down and formed his hands into a stirrup.

"Here Mush, slip your foot in."

Mush stood rooted to the spot.

"If I'm caught the police won't arrest me, will they? My father has taught me honesty and to respect the law."

Roy chipped in.

"Nah, you'll just get a ticking off. Honest Injun." He looked around to make sure we'd got the joke. Just in case we hadn't he repeated honest Injun and pointed at Mush, "Get it?"

Roy was proud of that one because he didn't tell many jokes. We may have all laughed but Mush wasn't amused, or reassured.

"But how do I get out?"

Terry pointed at a tree which grew on the other side of the wall.

"Climb that, mate."

Frank nudged Mush with his elbow.

"Go on then. We've all done it."

Mush mumbled something with the word "forgive" in it and put his foot in Bill's clasped hands.'

'Bill raised him up easily enough and Mush sat on top of the wall looking down into the garden.

I asked him if he could see anyone and he replied sheepishly, "It appears to be clear, Ricky. I don't know if I should be doing this."

He began rocking back and forth, trying to summon the courage to jump.

Frank cried, "Bollocks to this!" and sprinted across the pavement. I swear he ran up that wall.'

'I think you've been watching too much Dynamo, Kuchy.'

'I'm telling you his little legs didn't stop at the pavement and he gained enough height to tip Mush into the garden. Mush didn't yelp so I guessed he hadn't landed in the nettles.

Frank called out after him, "And make sure you get the biggest green apple you can find. You won't be initiated if you bring back a tiddler."

Mush's feet had barely touched the divine sod when Jason poked his head around the corner and shouted, "I've stitched that Jap up good and proper. I'd scarper if I was you."

Terry scratched his head in sync with Jason and mumbled, "How's he done that?"

Frank had already retreated several strides.

"Clot! He's rung the vicar's front door bell and grassed us up."

Bill was in two minds as to what to do. He'd have clobbered Jason if the little rat hadn't beaten it.

"Not even Jesus can save Mush now," he said.

I had some news for him.

"He don't believe in Jesus, Bill. He believes in some prophet or other."

Bill cried, "Bleedin' heck! The vicar'll skin him alive.'"

'The next voice was the vicar's.

"Boy!" Followed by, "Come here you little thief!" The tree nearest the wall shook and Mush's head popped up. The vicar must have grabbed hold of his foot because he disappeared as quickly as he appeared. After Frank, Terry was the next boy to scarper, closely followed by Roy. Bill urged me to do likewise.

"Come on, Rick. There ain't nothing we can do for him now. We're okay, the vicar ain't seen our faces."

I looked down at my new shoes and gripped Bill's jumper.

"I owe him. Give us a leg up first. One for all, and all for one."

Bill wasn't a deserter. He made a stirrup and helped me up on the wall.

As soon as the vicar glimpsed my face emerging over the top, he said, "I thought you'd be involved, Ricky. I heard you were entertaining Muslims. I was meaning to have a word with your father about that. Come down this instant and we'll see what he has to say about this latest transgression."

Bill called out to me, "Hold out your hand and help me up, Rick. We might as well all swing together."

The vicar overheard him and bellowed, "Is there another boy involved? Show yourself!"

The vicar must have loosened his grip because Mush's head and shoulders popped up again.

He tossed Bill down the biggest green apple I'd ever seen and cried, "Better make your escape, Jason."

It would have sounded more authentic if he used "scarper" or "leg it" but it had the vicar fooled.

"Jason, is it? Aren't you the boy who's just rung my doorbell?"

Bill would never become a Rory Bremner but his impression of Jason had the vicar fooled when he replied, 'Yeah, that's me. And you ain't no Mick, you're a flamin' Jap if ever I saw one.'

'What was that? I think I'll pay your father a visit, young man,' cried the vicar.

Bill saluted Mush and Mush smiled, or I think he did. It's hard to tell when an Ulsterman's got hold of your ankle.'

'And that was how Mushtaq gained your respect and was welcomed into the fold? That right, Kuchy?'

'Not quite.'

127

17

'Dad was already upset with me. Despite his best endeavours I'd failed to grasp the rudiments of Polish. He'd even bought me a shiny book with big letters and short words. I still couldn't get the hang of it. Mum was kinder. She said Dad gave up too quickly and she'd teach me herself if she could.'

'Nudge me if I snore, Kuchy.'

'Sorry, I never know what you want or don't want to hear.'

'Just stick to Mushtaq unless I tell you otherwise. Do you understand? Or shall I have a nibble on one of your vital organs?'

'Understood … there we were, Mush and me, standing outside my front room door while Dad and the vicar decided our fate. Anyone would think we'd robbed a bank or done someone in. Mush couldn't stand still and I was praying that Mum would come home soon. Nine times out of ten when I was naughty she'd get Dad to keep his belt around his trousers and give me a ticking off instead. Mush kept telling me to come away from the door, said I was being rude. I told him to get stuffed and my ear remained stuck to that wooden panel like Bostik.'

Raz covered his ears.

'OMG. What did you hear, Kuchy?'

'It may only be an apple but theft is theft. Thou shalt not steal, and all that crap. As the vicar ranted on I imagined Dad calculating the odds at Kempton Park, because there was a delay before he replied, "I k'new that nothing good would come out of Ricky mixing with them. I bet that Hammer kid put him up to it."

The vicar crunched on a rich tea. I knew it was a rich tea because the only other treats on offer were sponge fingers. There was a further delay, probably caused by the vicar wiping crumbs from his cassock and reaching for another biscuit.

"Do you mean the Muslim boy?" he said.

For Muslim read guttersnipe. The rest of his words were incomprehensible because he'd crammed the second biscuit into his mouth before he'd finished the first.'

'Do you believe in God, Kuchy? There must be something more to life, don't you agree? I so would like to be a good man.'

'Are you being serious?'

'Never dis religion, chief, no matter what it is. One of them has to be right. Which one would you plump for?'

Once I'd overcome my shock, I realised religion was the perfect tool with which to idle away hostage time. Buddhism, Judaism, Christianity, Islam - bring them all on. I opened my mouth to theologise and just as quickly closed it again. Teller beware, religion is a subject that can get you killed. What was I on about? Hoodies aren't religious. If they were, *Sky News* would have done a special feature on them by now. He shook my sleeve.

'Well?'

'Did I hear you right?'

'That's not an answer, Kuchy. I need an answer.'

When in doubt throw it straight back at them was one of Dad's mantras, although I think he was referring to German stick grenades.

'Are you seeking God's forgiveness for your sins?'

'Oh, is that what I'm doing, Kuchy?'

'What do you want with me? I don't think you're just some common-or-garden street thug. A criminal mastermind, maybe?'

For devotee of divinity now read Gestapo interrogator.

'Flattery alone won't keep you on this mortal coil, white boy. The Buddhists seek nothingness, ain't that right? If you don't get on with the fucking story you'll experience it without having to meditate once.'

'Please, just give me the answer to one question. Are you really capable of shooting me?'

'Do you believe the Archangel Gabriel visited Muhammad in a cave?'

'Do you?'

'Stranger things have happened. Carry on, Kuchy.'

Did that mean he was more, or less likely, to be a Muslim? Little did he know that I was one once.

***

'Mush was worried that he'd get the blame as he was a different colour. I tried to reassure him that it'd be me for the high jump because this was my third offence. He abandoned his scruples and asked me what I could hear and if his religion was being discussed. I told him it wasn't. Of course, it was. Dad kicked off the Muslim bashing with a bit of Polish bragging.

"Jan Sobieski k'nocked the hell out of the Turks at the Battle of Vienna. We'd all be praying towards Mecca now if he hadn't, vicar. The pope hailed him as the saviour of Europe, you k'now."

I may not have been able to string two words together in Polish, but Jan Sobieski had been rammed down my throat often enough. Now the vicar was getting a dose. After referring to the Garden of Eden and quoting Calvin, the Belfast man returned to the subject of his stolen apple. Dad was more than willing to do Jehovah's work.

"I k'now. I'll take my belt to the little bugger."

The vicar informed him that he had something else in mind. Dad tried to second-guess him.

"I k'now, I'll ask Mrs Harris if I can borrow one of the sticks that hold up her runner beans."

Dad was way off the mark, for the vicar intended that I should regularly attend Sunday school. I'd rather have had Mrs Harris's runner bean stick across my backside. Dad was having none of that and told the vicar that he wanted me brought up as a Catholic. I thought, thank God for Jesus' mother, the bookies, and night shifts. Dad'll never find time to take me to Catholic Sunday school. It's all he can do to take me to that big church in London once a year. Just when I thought I'd got away with it, Mum returned home. She smiled at Mush, scowled at me, and went straight into the front room. The vicar couldn't wait to fill her in.'

Brought up in the Church of England she responded by uttering the dreaded words, "Hush, Ziggy. I'll make sure he attends Sunday school, vicar. I think I'd better walk Mushtaq home. I'll phone his parents from the box in Park Lane on the way."

Traumatised, I turned to Mush and asked, "Do Muslims have Sunday school?"

His reply gave me cause for hope.

"As far as I know religious schools for Muslims do not exist in this country, Ricky. I suppose there aren't enough of us. My father instructs me in the Koran at home. It's like your Bible."

There was only one thing for it.

"I want to become a Muslim. Can you arrange it on the quiet, Mush?"'

'You couldn't expect me to keep a secret for long at that age. In fact, I must have kept it for all of three minutes. While Mum got changed and Dad terrified Mush with stories of Polish lancers and exploding tanks, I pretended I was going to the bog and nipped upstairs.

I sat on the arm of Ink's chair, looked around because walls have ears, and said; "I don't think the vicar's going to speak to me anymore, Ink."

He replied, "Lucky you. Why's that, son?"

I had another furtive look around.

"Don't tell anyone, but I'm a secret Muslim."

Ink had a swig of hot water. He aimed a burp at the china horses on the mantelpiece.

"Excuse me. I'm sure." He winked. "It'll be our little secret."

Nanna was sitting in the armchair directly opposite.

She stopped knitting and said, "Stand up, Ricky. I think I have a pullover that'll fit you. I got it at the church jumble sale." She reached down and patted around the side of her chair, which was besieged by battalions of woolly pants, greying long johns, vests, and stitched socks. "Now, where is it?"

I stood up as instructed, but Nanna was taking ages so I carried on talking to Ink.

"They want me to go to Sunday school. I'll miss playing football and things. Did you ever go, Ink?"

He had another sip of hot water and replied, "Not if I could bleedin' well help it. They asked me to run one after the Great War. The vicar was taken and people were dropping like flies from the Spanish flu.'"

'I'd failed to notice Nanna conducting a frontal assault on my position. Before I could scarper, she held a red pullover against me and I became as stiff as a frozen asparagus. To get out of wearing this red shit, it'll have to appear either too big or too small, I thought. I breathed in, then out, and tried hunching my shoulders. None of it did any good.

"Lovely," she said, "it'll fit like a glove."

I looked at Ink and winked. "Muslims don't wear red, do they Ink?"

He raised his chin. He always did that when he talked about his army days.

"When I was in India they wore nothing much at all, son. Or was that the Hindus? I get them all mixed up."

Nanna had already set off in the direction of the kitchen sink.

"I'll wash it and give it to your mother, Ricky."

My only hope was that it'd shrink in the soak. I used to pray to Jesus, but now I prayed to the Prophet. I knew what Jesus looked like but I hadn't an inkling with this Prophet. Still, I gave it a go and said a silent prayer: please Mr Prophet geezer, don't let me wear this red crap. Ink's body jolted.

"He can't wear that, Dot! It's bleedin' Arsenal colours."

I yelled, "It works! The Prophet has spoken through Ink."

I wanted a telly more than anything in the whole world and thought I'd give that a whirl next. Mum came to the foot of the stairs.

"Ricky, are you up there? I'm walking Mushtaq home now. You can either stay here with your father or come with us."

Dad was well pissed off at the prospect of me attending a C of E Sunday school, so I decided to steer well clear of him. Ink watched me as I made a dash for the door.

"Where you off to, son?"

I looked over my shoulder.

"Mush has to face the music and I'm going with him. He's lucky. They don't have Sunday school."

Ink was none the wiser.

"Who's Mush?"

Nanna started patting around her armchair again.

"He means Marmaduke, dear."

Ink wasn't impressed.

"What kind of name is that for a darkie? He hasn't bought a bleedin' peerage, has he?"

I shouted down the stairs, "Coming, Mum."

Ink tapped his nose.

"Your secret's safe with me, son."

Nanna held up a ball of red wool.

"I might knit Ricky a pair of red socks to go with his nice, red pullover."

As I galloped down the stairs, Ink called out, "Don't worry son. Me old army mate, Bernie, is paying me a visit tomorrow. He blew up a bridge over the Meuse and made an entire German infantry unit disappear, know what I mean?'"

'Mum made that phone call to the Mohammeds, which turned out to be a right palaver. We have mobile phones these days but it wasn't so easy back then. Mum was nervous because she'd never made a call from a red phone box before. Her farmer dad had a phone in North-amptonshire, but all you had to do was pick up the receiver and ask the operator to connect you. She got Mush to write his number on a scrap of paper and told us to wait outside. Mush said he could make the call if she liked but she refused. I guess she wanted to retain control. We had to help her open the door though. It was as heavy as the one at the Florida. I had to shoulder charge them to get those buggers open. The inside of the box even smelt of piss like that cinema. Mum wasn't short-sighted but she put her face right up to the directions, read them twice, checked that the penny in her hand was a penny, and dialled the number. Later, when I told Ink about the trouble Mum had had with the phone box, he said he couldn't get the hang of the Electrolux vacuum cleaner when it first came out. He said it went berserk in the showroom. Nanna said he deliberately set it on the salesman when he refused to accept that Arsenal was a South London club.'

'Mum might've appeared to be frozen in time – phone glued to her ear and penny glued to her hand – but she wasn't going to be beaten. Mr Mohammed must have said, "Hello, is there anyone there?" at least three times before she sprang into action and rammed the penny into the slot. It was a wonder it didn't come out the other side. The actual conversation couldn't have lasted more than twenty seconds. When it had finished, she put the receiver down, jiggled it, and pushed the door open with her back.

"Your father is expecting us in fifteen minutes, young man," she said to Mush. "He wants a strong word with you."

Mushtaq hung his head and Mum didn't utter another word as we traipsed over there. She loved a good chinwag so the omens weren't good.'

'When we arrived she ordered me to wait by the gate and led Mush up the path. Mr Mohammed answered the door on the first ring. She had a brief word with him and pointed back at me. I couldn't hear what she said to him but "Ricky", "led", and "astray" were probably in there somewhere. He thanked Mum and told Mush to go to the study and read aloud from the Koran for two hours. I thought Muslims must be the nicest people in the world because Mr Mohammed didn't even give him a clip around the lughole. Mrs Mohammed came to the door and invited us over for dinner at the weekend. I decided it'd be a good time to tell Mum and Dad that I was a Muslim. We'd outnumber the Christians 4 to 2 and Dad could hardly land me one with all those people present.'

18

'In the eyes of the vicar, stealing an apple was a grave sin, especially if it came from his forbidden tree. Compounding it with a lie was a one-way ticket to eternal damnation. He'd been to see Jason's father and one look into Ernie's eyes had convinced him that Jason preferred pears and thus was as innocent as the Virgin. In response, the man of God had then paid the Mohammeds a visit to ascertain which boy had remained in the street during the robbery. Whilst there he re-counted to them (over copious quantities of chai and pink cakes) how Mush had told him a bald-faced lie and was a sinner in need of urgent redemption. To achieve salvation he deemed it essential that Mush inform on the boy who'd scarpered with his apple. Mush, to his credit, insisted Jason was the culprit. Whether his actions were based on a fear of reprisal or a strict observance of local customs is open to debate. Mouth stuffed with pink cake and recoiling at the prospect of meeting Jason's dad again, the vicar decided to leave the judicial enquiry to God. Luckily for me he'd left a couple of hours before we arrived for our dinner date.'

**

'Mum picked one of Sandy's hairs off Dad's jacket sleeve before she let him ring the Mohammed's bell. As we waited for the door to open, she told him in no uncertain terms not to mention Jan Sobieski. Dad may not have retreated in the face of German machine-gun fire at Monte Cassino, but he took a step backwards when Mr Mohammed opened the door flashing his pearly whites and a large carving knife.

Mr Mohammed placed the knife behind his back and said apolo-getically, "Oh dear, I meant to put the knife down but my thoughts were elsewhere."

Mush was standing rigidly behind his father, arms hugging his side. He had the same kind of expression on his face like I did when Spurs lost, and his complexion resembled a Walls' pork sausage in the packet rather than one sizzling in a frying pan.

Without a backward glance, Mr Mohammed said sternly, "Go and await your punishment, Mushtaq." He smiled at Dad and Mum in turn and frowned. "My son has disgraced Islam with his behaviour. As you English say, he is in for the chop."

Wait a minute, I thought. Islam rings a bell. Didn't I read about them lot in the *Daily Mirror* before I wiped me bum with it? Hold on! Ain't they the ones what stone you to death and chop your hands off for stealing? As I watched Mush climbing the stairs it dawned on me.

From a safe distance I asked Mr Mohammed, "Is an Islam the same as a Muslim, sir?"

Mum had told me I had to say "sir".

I nearly shat my pants when he replied, "All followers of Islam are Muslims, Ricky."

I was pretty nifty on me feet, but Mum had hold of my hand and wasn't letting go. After running on the spot for a few seconds I became resigned to my fate and trooped into the house with Mum and Dad.'

'I was familiar with the smell in their gaff but Dad was caught unawares. Up until that moment he'd thought curry smelt like Fishermen's Friends. He stepped into the hall and pulled up like a horse gone lame. It took one of Mum's looks to make his feet move again. She had a talent. The rest of her face stayed the same, but she did something with her eyes that made him come around to her way of thinking. Mr Mohammed showed us into the dining room where Mrs Mohammed greeted us. She sat us down and told us to make ourselves comfortable. Mr Mohammed left the room to check on the food, or so he said. You could see into the kitchen through a serving hatch. A good minute must have passed but there was no sign of

Mush, or his father. I tried telling Dad that we should do something because Mush was being chopped up but he told me to button it.'

'Their dining table was three times the size of the one in our front room and there wasn't a single scratch on it. The cutlery was all neatly laid out, along with wicker mats, napkins, glasses, and a big jug of water. I sat clutching the base of my chair, bracing myself for Mush's screams. I was used to the sight of blood. I'd grazed my knees countless times playing football in the street and I'd sliced my finger open with Dad's razorblade once. Mum wanted to put a plaster on it but Nanna said it was best left to the air. I glanced at Mrs Mohammed who was sitting opposite Mum. She seemed to be taking it better than Mum did when I slit that finger open. Blimey, I thought, how much blood is there when a hand's chopped off? I reckoned it was gallons and gallons, enough to fill the tank of an Austin Princess. Mum's face wasn't showing much of anything and I figured she was too polite to complain. My mind was going at it full tilt trying to solve the puzzle of how Mush was going to eat using two stumps. If Mr Mohammed chopped both his hands off he'd need to hold a spoon in his mouth and have food that didn't need cutting up, like mashed potato with a knob of melted butter or oxtail soup. A knife and fork would be useless. And so would a spoon come to think about it. How was he going to get the mash or soup from the spoon when he had the spoon sticking out of his gob?'

'I was still trying to work it out when Mr Mohammed's head and shoulders popped through the serving hatch. He was still holding the knife, but this time there was blood on it. Admittedly, it wasn't quite as much as I expected and it appeared to contain little pips. I reckoned as their skin was different to ours so must their blood. Perhaps he'd just settled for a finger.

Mr Mohammed said as casually as you like, "I've finished dicing. It shan't be long now."

I nudged Mum and whispered, "What does dicing mean, Mum?"

She replied, "It means chopping things fine into little cubes."

Crikey, I thought, he's not only chopped Mush's hands off but he's dicing them up fine.

She added, "They blend in better with the food that way, dear."

Mrs Mohammed joined in the conversation.

"We're having aloo keema for dinner."

She might, but I weren't.'

'Ink once said, "Never take food from these Indian types because you never know what's in it. And it's so bloody hot that it all tastes the same."

He didn't actually say bloody but mouthed it because Nanna was in the room.

Mrs Mohammed rose from her chair and said, "Will you excuse me. I must give my husband a hand."

Fuck me! I nearly said it out loud. She's going to get Mush's other hand and add it to the pot. It was a miracle I didn't go into shock. I spoke to Mum out of the corner of my mouth.

"Do we have to stay for grub? I seem to have lost me appetite, Mum."

She replied, "Just have a couple of mouthfuls, dear."

I looked to Dad for support. He didn't want to come in the first place so there was hope yet.

"It's more than poor Mushtaq can manage, Dad." I pulled my sleeves down over my hands and waved my arms like semaphore. "Get my drift?"

Since she'd discovered that Mush's name wasn't Malcolm, Mum had made me promise to use his proper name. If it wasn't for her I think Dad would have made some excuse and left.

Like it or not, he was part of the fathers' union and said, "Mushtaq had to be punished. They do it differently here, Ricky."

My bottom edged closer to the front of my chair and my restless feet brushed the carpet.

"No kidding they do, Dad."

At that moment Mr and Mrs Mohammed arrived with trays of food.

Mr Mohammed said, "There are two curry dishes. One is hot and spicy, the other mild. I suggest you start with the mild one."

'Mrs Mohammed put some of the mild curry on my plate. It was like a lumpy brown soup with spuds in it. Well, I assumed they were spuds, and there were green and red things, and rice, definitely rice. I knew that because we had Ambrosia creamed rice for afters sometimes, although the Mohammeds' rice was as dry as a bone in comparison. I poked at it with my fork looking for fingernails. When I couldn't see any, I thought Mr Mohammed must have either taken them out or had done a good job at dicing. Perhaps Mush's hands weren't in there at all. They might be in the hot stuff the Mohammeds were eating. I wanted to warn Mum that she was about to become a cannibal but she'd already swallowed a spoonful. A second spoonful would have to wait because she was busy waving a hand in front of her face and wheezing as if she was having an asthma attack. Usually reserved in the company of strangers, she lunged for the water jug without so much as an "excuse me".

She filled her glass to overflowing, took a large swig, and croaked, "Very nice."

Just then there was a knock at the door and Mush poked his head inside the room. I reckoned he must have used his elbow.

He said, "I've finished copying those pages from the Koran, father."

His father ushered him into the room.

"Then you may eat. After you have eaten you will copy the same passage ten more times."

When I saw that both of Mush's hands were securely attached to his arms I gave him the thumbs up. It was my tenth birthday in two days' time and somehow Mush had found out. He handed me a card, which he'd drawn himself.

140

Raz clapped once. It sounded like a retort from a rifle.

'Your tenth birthday already! I hope there ain't yawning gaps in this story, Kuchy. I hope you ain't hiding things from me.'

By now I'd lost all concept of time and looked at the horizon for the emergence of dawn. If there was a moon overhead, the cloud cover and smoke had prevented its light from reaching Earth. Besides the streetlight the only brightness to be had was from a red glow mushrooming above the rooftops.

'You can't expect me to remember everything. I'm doing my best to get the events in the right order.'

'You'd better have. What was on this birthday card?'

'A drawing of a football player with a cockerel on his chest. I think he was meant to be Cliff Jones. Underneath it read, "To my best friend. Thank you for looking out for me."'

Raz patted his heart the same way that modern footballers pat the badge when they want to convince fans that they'll lay down their life for the club.

'Didn't that tug on your heartstrings, Kuchy?'

'Sort of. But I hid it from the other Tottenham Boys. Too girly by half.'

'And did you eat all your nice curry up like a good little boy?'

'Are you kidding? A kid brought up on spam, corned beef, chips, and baked beans? Mrs Mohammed kindly made me beans on toast and said there were cham chams to follow. While she was in the kitchen, Mum waited for Dad to finish his account of the Normandy Landings and asked Mr Mohammed what he did for a living. Mr Mohammed replied that he was in the middle of a project but it was a bit hush-hush. That did it for me. He was a spy and the evidence was overwhelming. Ink said Pakistan ain't got a pot to piss in so how could he afford a big house in Bruce Grove? When the moment was right I intended to expose him like that Englishman did with those German spies in *The 39 Steps*. If Mr Mohammed was an evil foreign agent, the Queen might even pin a medal to my chest.'

Raz grabbed a handful of my stomach roll, stretched it, and let it flop back to join its mates.

'And how many cham chams did you scoff? Judging by the proportions of this gut you're still going strong, Kuchy.'

'Half a dozen at least and that was a few too many. They made me feel sick and I vowed never to eat another pink thing so long as I lived. As soon as we got home I ran upstairs and cried, "Forget this Muslim lark, Ink! I'd rather be a flamin' Leyton Orient supporter. Guess what? Mr Mohammed's a spy and he's got a secret poison weapon called hello something or other. It nearly put paid to Mum."'

'The effects of this devastating weapon were felt the next day when Mum and me took the bus to Sainsbury's. We sat upstairs at the front. We'd had chops for lunch and they'd gone down a treat.

I stopped pretending that I was driving the bus and said, "How stupid are the Mohammeds for missing out on a nice bit of pork?"

She replied, "They're just different, dear. Live and let live."

Someone farted, silent and deadly. The passengers took sly looks at each other. Mum's expression didn't change a jot but she couldn't fool me. That fart had "hello something or other" written all over it.'

'The day after that I pretended to be Dick Barton, special agent, determined to track Mr Mohammed to his HQ. Mush's father was the evil foreign spy and I was the brave Englishman who'd bring him to justice.'

'How patriotic of you, Kuchy.'

'People used to stand for the national anthem back then.'

'Did that include Mr Bentley? Go on, Kuchy. Continue serving your country.'

'To help catch the spy, I decided to borrow Ink's hat and scarf as part of my disguise. Nanna was out with Mum and Ink was snoozing in his armchair in their living room. Ink's flat cap would've been useless but he kept a homburg and a silk scarf on the top shelf of their wardrobe. Nanna had a tear in her eye when she showed them to Mum once. She said he'd worn them when he came courting and how dashing he looked. The problem was, I wasn't tall enough to reach them and the bed was too far away to use as a trampoline. Dick Barton had a similar problem with a castle wall and he used a rope and a grappling iron. The best I could come up with was the three-legged stool by the dressing table. It wasn't the healthiest of stools but Nanna said it had sentimental value. Ink said she wouldn't think it so sentimental if she landed slap bang on her arse. I put the stool by the wardrobe and tested it out with one foot. It was a bit wobbly and it creaked when I put both feet on it, but it did the trick. There was all manner of things on that top shelf; shirts, gloves, towels, folded sheets, and an enormous brassiere with cups as big as two large hairdryers in a woman's salon. There was also a garment like Mum's corset but softer and flimsier. It was an orangey colour with frills around the edges. *The Tiller Girls* wore something similar when they kicked their legs high in the air. One Sunday afternoon, I was invited to Douglas Noble's to watch *Maverick* and those stupid dancers were on before him. I got so impatient that I hoped they'd kick their own noses and be carted off to casualty.'

'Once a misogamist always a misogamist, eh Kuchy?'

'That's not true. I respect women. I've had my disagreements but ...'

'Touched a nerve, have I Kuchy? Carry on. Did the Queen pin a medal to your chest?'

'The hat didn't put up much of a struggle. Well, not until I tried it on and discovered that it was ten sizes too big. Blinded and tottering on the edge of the castle parapet, I prised it off my head. For it to fit snug, I calculated that I'd need to stuff a whole *Daily Mirror* inside it (I'd remove Dad's racing pages first). If that still wasn't enough paper then I'd raid the bog for more pages. I lobbed the hat into the moat (the bed) and reached for the scarf. The bloody thing had got tangled up with the corset thing so I threw them into the moat as well and jumped down from the stool. I'd fished them out of the water, and was about to begin untangling them, when I heard voices in the street. Scampering to the window, I copped Mum and Nanna talking to Mrs Harris. There wasn't time to put the corset thing back in the wardrobe, so I left it on the bed with the hat and scarf and rushed to put the stool back. I'd just flown down the stairs and into our front room when the front door opened. Mum went into the kitchen and I heard Nanna climbing the stairs (she stopped halfway to catch her breath), and there followed slow footsteps on the landing heading in the direction of their bedroom. They were then followed by a shriek that would have wakened Rip Van Winkle.

Nanna screamed, "He must be joking!" The footsteps quickened in pace as she made a beeline for their back room. I imagined she thrust the corset thing under Ink's nose as she bellowed, "Ink! You'll do yourself a mischief." Her voice became all soppy. "Let's just settle for a cuddle, shall we?"'

'Before I got to sleep that night, I heard Mum say to Dad, "I wonder what drugs Doctor Miller gave Ink for his gout, Ziggy?"

Dad responded with, "Do you think Doctor Miller can write me out a prescription, Margaret?"

Mum giggled.

"You don't need drugs, Ziggy."

There were times when they probably wished I didn't sleep in the same room.'

19

'Do we need drugs, Kuchy? What did you make of Timothy Leary?'

'Turn on, tune in, drop out.'

'That's the dude. I see it this way. There's a carer looking after a frail old press photographer. He takes a trip now and then and acquires the ability to cut through the baggage in his life, which makes him a better carer, more tuned in with the needs and fears of his charge. But without warning this carer decides to follow Professor Leary's advice and the crazy LSD world becomes his entire existence. What do you think will happen to the poor old bed-ridden press photographer then? Abandoned? Crying alone in the dark as his lifeforce slowly ebbs away? A tie-dyed pillow pressed over his face? Ripped off to pay for more drugs? All his precious memories carted off down the pawnbroker's in a cardboard box?'

'Did you take a drug, just after you pretended to cut off my little finger? Are you flipping out? Maybe I can help.'

'Maybe all I need is religion.'

He held his hands out before his face as if reading from a book. It struck me that I'd seen Nayim doing that after he'd scored against Arsenal from the halfway line.

'Wasn't that a Muslim symbol you made just then?'

He made the sign of the cross.

'That better?'

He delighted in giving me mixed messages, laying smoke screens to conceal some deeper purpose. He waited to see if he'd succeeded in teasing me up another blind alley. When I didn't respond he gave me a hurry up gesture.

'Yeah, yeah. The Prophet came through and you got that telly.'

'How do you know?'

'Just a hunch. You haven't said if the Mohammeds had a telly.'

'They didn't. It surprised me because they could definitely afford one. Mum reckoned Mr Mohammed didn't want Mush distracted from his studies.'

'Did Mushtaq's father let him watch yours?'

'Only on the first day we got it.'

'I bet you couldn't wait to show it off.'

'What do you think? I had something expensive that Mush didn't and it beat his Subbuteo hands down. The Nobles apart, no one else owned a telly.'

'Tell me all about that day, when the outside world invaded your modest abode. Did things go to plan?'

'They could have gone better.'

***

'I flew up the stairs with the good news.

"Ink! Nanna! Auntie Sheila's new husband has copped it and she's come into money. She's sent us enough dosh to put a deposit on a telly and Dad can afford the rest."

Death isn't that important when your balls haven't dropped and *Tom and Jerry* is on offer. I sprinted along the landing to the front window, looked up and down the street, and rushed back again.

"No sign, but it'll arrive any second now. Just know it will."

Nanna glanced up from her knitting.

"Heart attack, was it?"

I tried to recover my breath, but a mayfly has more chance of celebrating Christmas.

"Don't know, Nanna... happened while they were in bed."

She raised her wispy eyebrows and said, "Figures. Ziggy won big on the gee-gees, has he dear?"

I had one foot inside and one foot outside the room straining to hear a van engine. She repeated the question and I came up with a vague "What?"

146

She sighed and tried again.

"Ziggy won big on the gee-gees, has he dear?"

I knew better than to disrespect Nanna. That was one crime Mum wouldn't forgive me for. I startled into life.

"Sorry, Nanna. He's going to be a commie chef at The Savoy. One of his old wartime friends works there."

Ink looked horrified.

"The commies have infiltrated the Savoy?"

Nanna put him straight.

"I think Ricky means commis chef, dear. The Savoy, is it? They'll have fresh sardines at The Savoy. Those tinned ones give Ink terrible heartburn."

I dashed between the two of them imparting more good news.

"Dad says he'll even have enough dosh to take me and Mum to Lyons Corner House up London. It's right flash. There's music and the waitresses wear smart uniforms with fancy hats. I'll have a cream bun with me tea."

'I was licking the cream off an imaginary bun when Mum came into their back room without giving her customary "co-eee". She'd heard a good chunk of our conversation and couldn't get the words out fast enough.

"Ziggy will be working days at the Savoy and we'll be able to afford more things. He says he'll buy me a new frock. And listen to this, Dot. He's promised not to gamble as much. And to think, Princess Grace stayed there. Ziggy said he might even get me one of the teacups she drank from. I'll keep it out of harm's way on the top shelf."

Nanna cocked an ear.

"Hark. Is that a van I can hear, Ricky?"

I don't remember haring down the stairs or hurtling through the front door. I do recall standing on the pavement with my head going from side to side like I was watching the men's final at Wimbledon. When no van materialised I pouted and trudged back up the stairs.

Nearing the top, I heard Nanna's funny little laugh. It was the same one she made when she spied Fred turning up to fix Betty's something or other, and when that tallyman called on Mrs Ripley. She always spoke in a hush when she made it or shooed me out of the room if it drew my interest. I crept up a few more steps and stopped to listen.'

'Nanna chirped, "I wondered why you were so perky yesterday, Margaret. Ricky said he couldn't get into your bedroom because the door was locked. The last time Ink locked our bedroom door was during the war."

"It must have been sticking, Dot."

Nanna gave that funny little laugh again.

"Between you and me there was something about a doodlebug that got Ink up and excited. It didn't last long because that doodlebug's engine stopped popping and we headed for the Anderson shelter pretty damned quick." There was a silence and when she spoke again her voice trembled. "The poor sods in St Paul's Road copped that one." She was a tough old lady and perked up in the next breath. "Have you considered turning your front room into a second bedroom, Margaret? Ricky's getting to be a big boy now. It would give you and him more privacy... Ink! Stop doing that with your hand."

Mum coughed and cleared her throat.

"I'll get Ziggy to fix that door, Dot. Must fly."

As Mum made her getaway Nanna called after her, "Thought that must be it, Margaret."

I was going to wait at the bottom of the stairs for Mum and act all sulky and annoying, but decided to round up the others for a game of football and a bit of boasting.'

'We put the jumpers down outside our house so I wouldn't miss the van. Every boy in the street took part in the kickabout and that included Roy who was running a temperature (he stayed in goal). I'd just hit a thirty-yard screamer into the top of the Arsenal net when the delivery van pulled up. It had a long ladder attached to the top. Bill wanted to swing on it but couldn't reach. Boy, we had the van surrounded before the driver had time to switch his engine off. Mrs Lambert (Terry and Frank's mum) and Mrs White left their houses to have a gander. Terry and Frank were on the far side of the van which meant Mrs Lambert could have a moan:

"Typical, just when we've started to make ends meet. Frank has his books but I bet Terry will want a flippin' telly now."

Mrs White replied, "All these modern gadgets. In our day we made do with jigsaw puzzles and a good old singsong."'

'The van had *Father and Son* written on the side and you wouldn't believe the size of that television. Twice as deep as it was wide and it took both men to get it off the back.

I led the way as they carried it towards the house, furiously waving them on, shrieking, "This way, this way," and becoming irritated when I had to stop for them to catch me up.

The son was fit enough, but the father was puffing and panting as if he'd just climbed to the top of Muswell Hill.

"More like last legs and son if you ask me," said Ink, peering down the stairs as they negotiated the telly through our front door.

Nanna joined in.

"I hope they aren't going to send that poor man up on the roof with the aerial. He looks like he could do with some of my Scotch broth."

Ink replied, "He should try some of Mrs Beaker's jam. That'll get him going."

Dad tapped the top of the beast as they carried it into the front room.

"It's a Bell. They don't come any better than that, you k'now."

The whole gang would have filed into the house if Dad hadn't shut them out. Mum organised a turning on party for later.'

Raz toked on an imaginary joint.

'Smoked weed did she, Kuchy?'

'The only joints she knew were the ones she served up on a Sunday.'

'Be a good boy and run through the guest list for me, Ricky.'

When he called me Kuchy he was brutal and sadistic, but when he called me Ricky it was if he was talking to a small boy. I couldn't make up my mind as to which was the more threatening.

***

'Top of Mum's guest list were Nanna and Ink, followed by Mr and Mrs Harris and their daughter, Betty. Thinking the Harris's were going to Clacton for the day, she'd originally invited the Beakers (there wasn't room for all of them). It worked out okay in the end, because Mr Beaker developed a bad case of the trots (Mrs Beaker blamed it on Alf's pork pie). Braving the red telephone box on her tod, Mum had also invited the Mohammeds. I'm sure Mr Mohammed only accepted out of politeness and because he took pity on her – Mush had told him Mum making that trip to that phone box in Park Lane was the equivalent of Columbus setting sail for the New World. Doctor Miller couldn't make it because he was busy at the hospital and the vicar wasn't invited because he considered television to be an abomination, as morally corrupt as a two-piece swimsuit. After the party she had Dad set it up in the back room. There it would out of sight, if not out of mind, and in a future sermon the vicar cited a TV in the *Book of Kings*.'

'To complete the set, Mum borrowed four chairs from Nanna and Ink and requisitioned the rest from the Harris's. She had Dad put them in two rows in front of the telly and told him to space them out so that no one was elbowed if the excitement got too much. He did his best, but there was less legroom in the back row than on an Easyjet flight. The chair nearest the screen was slightly ahead of the others and there was a large piece of paper with the words "Reserved for Margaret" written on it. Queen for the day, she wanted to have easy access to the controls (the delivery men had showed her how the knobs worked). The telly had been tested and the aerial fitted to the chimney, but she insisted the screen remain blank until the allotted hour: *I Love Lucy*.

Dad moaned, "You're not turning on the Christmas lights, you k'now Margaret."

She'd fussed for ages about the seating arrangements. If she went by size alone then logically herself, me, Mush, Nanna, and Mr and Mrs Mohammed would occupy the front row with Dad, Mr and Mrs Harris, Betty, and Ink at the back. The Harris's were a tall family (Mr Harris had served in the Coldstream Guards) and they could see over the top of most heads. But Mum considered the front row to be more prestigious and in consequence she'd placed Nanna's Chippendale oak chairs there. Humming and harring, she wrestled with her conscience, swaying this way and that, filling half a notebook with sketches of various seating arrangements. Dad suggested a game of musical chairs and got "the eyes" for his trouble. Mum was still faffing around minutes before the guests were due to arrive. I'd begged her to let me watch *Tom and Jerry* first but she had her mind set on Lucy. I was cheesed off because I'd told Mush we'd be watching cartoons and I would lose face. To be fair to her it couldn't have been easy. The Harris's were part of our community while the Mohammeds were from another planet, and we survived hardships by looking after our own. Yet the Mohammeds had been exceedingly kind and hospitable and she didn't want to relegate them to a restricted view. As it happened it was Ink who determined who sat where.'

'It took him ages to conquer the stairs and he'd clung onto the banister for dear life at every step. Dad offered to help him down but Ink growled and deployed an expletive favoured by Cockney soldiers in the trenches. Nanna scolded him and for the zillionth time he promised never to use it again.

Dad watched Ink shuffling towards the chairs and said to Nanna, "I don't k'now how he's going to get back up again, Dot."

151

Nanna replied, "After a few sherries he could scale Mount Everest, Ziggy." Complaining that his peepers and lugholes weren't what they once were, Ink stooped to squint at the blank screen. The screens were minute in those days. Ruse or otherwise, he plonked himself down next to Mum's chair and jiggled his bottom till he got comfortable. That he didn't sit in Mum's seat suggests ruse. Once set, he called me over and patted the chair next to him.

"Come and keep an old man company, son."

I'd just taken my seat alongside him when Dad answered the door and ushered the Mohammeds in.'

'Mush's parents entered the room smiling but Mush kept glancing nervously around. When Mum assured him that Sandy was locked in the back room he relaxed a little. I waved at Mush and called him over. He took one step towards me, turned, and looked to his dad for permission. Mr Mohammed agreed, providing he didn't chat during the programme and ruin it for everyone else. Mr Mohammed saw Ink and said, "Ah", and when nothing else issued from her husband's mouth Mrs Mohammed took over.

"Mr Ink, it's nice to make your acquaintance again."

Without waiting for a reply, or to be seated, the pair then made a beeline for the back row. Nanna sat beside Mrs Mohammed because she wanted to apologise for Ink in advance and quoted a medical condition. Mum didn't intervene. She had more chance of swimming The Channel than getting Ink to budge. She couldn't swim. While she was distracted the Harris's had occupied the seats next to me in the front row. When she saw them she sighed and threw her arms in the air. But her annoyance was only fleeting because the decision had been taken out of her hands by an act of God.

She whispered to Dad, "We can always ask Nanna for a few of her thick cushions for the back row. Sandy's moulting and a flea jumped off him yesterday so we can't use any of ours."

'While I forced back my sulks, the grownups waited expectantly for *I Love Lucy* and the dawn of the modern era. With military precision, Mum dished up the salmon and cucumber sandwiches exactly fifteen minutes before the start of the programme. Not wanting to be caught out a second time, she offered them to Mr and Mrs Mohammed first and held her breath.

Mrs Mohammed took a dainty bite and said, "Lovely."

Mr Mohammed flipped up an end, had a bite, and said, "Just what the doctor ordered."

Just as well because the remains of a beef roast were on standby and I think Mum would have had a seizure if Mr Mohammed had referred to halal. Dad followed Mum around with a tray of blackcurrant cordial. Mush had told me that his family loved Ribena and Mum had seized upon the opportunity to appease the Prophet. Ink snarled when Dad offered him a glass. I acted drunk and swayed in my chair, pretending it was red wine. Mush looked perplexed when I told him I was drowning my sorrows. He asked if I wanted to talk about what was troubling me. No mate had ever done that before and it made me feel uncomfortable.

I wanted to swear at him but said, "Give over," and shook my head instead.'

'Dad went back to the table and loaded the tray with sherry.

Ink heard the clink of glasses and grumbled, "About time. An Englishman could die of thirst around here. Bugger Doctor Miller, don't you dare serve me up any of that blackcurrant crap, Ziggy."

Nanna told him off and apologised to Mrs Mohammed. With the magic hour fast approaching Mum took her place in front of the telly. She'd already polished the veneer twice but checked it again for dust, glancing at the clock on the mantelpiece and itching to turn the knob. Ink knocked back his sherry and held out his glass for a refill. Dad obliged and he quaffed the second one before leaning across to me.

"One day they'll have regular football on telly, Ricky. Hope it comes soon. Too late for the great push-and-run team, which won the league. There'll never be a team like that again. I'd love to see another Spurs match before I croak."

I replied, "I pray every day that you and Sandy won't croak, Ink."

He quickly changed the subject.

"This reminds me of the Coronation when we all huddled round the telly in the vicarage. He was a good Christian was that vicar. Came from Basingstoke. The Ulsterman should take a leaf out of his book." He looked to make sure Nanna couldn't hear. "That twerp's no more Christian than Sol, the jeweller. And Sol's a bleedin' Yid."

He did his best to lighten my mood but my sulks continued unabated.

I bleated, "Mum made me wash me face and hands and wear this stupid shirt with the tight collar. I can hardly breathe. All that cartoon time wasted, Ink. Don't see the point."

Ink looked upon Mum as the daughter he never had.

"This is a special day for your mother. It's like a grand opening. She don't want to see a cartoon cat and mouse when she turns it on. How happy she looks. You don't want to ruin it for her, do you son?"

I was doing my best to think of Mum.

"Grown-ups always get their own way. But she is me mum... I suppose." His bony hand patted me on the head.

"Good boy."

With that he shoved a sandwich into his mouth. Mum had removed the crust and cut his sandwich into small squares. Ink sucked more than he chewed so that was the end of that tête-à-tête.'

'Mush waited for Ink and me to finish our conversation and said, "Are you sure you're okay, Ricky?" He gently squeezed my knee and then my hand, adding, "If something's troubling you I will always lend a friendly ear."

My discomfort rapidly turned to paranoia and I glanced at the window to make sure Bill and the gang weren't peering in. Ink may have been short-sighted but he didn't miss much.

"Blimey, he's not one of *them*, is he?"

I gave Mush's shirt the once-over. There were no palm trees on it (white with a crisp collar). I wriggled my hand free and had a quick think.

"Don't be stupid, Ink, it's their way."

Realising he'd put me on the spot, Mush said, "Ricky is correct, Mr Ink. It is our custom. Men often hold hands in Pakistan as a token of friendship."

Ink waved his empty glass in the air to get Dad's attention.

"Don't know what the world's coming to. Men'll be marrying men next if we ain't careful… Ziggy!'"

'Mum had another look at the clock and leant forward to switch the telly on. She was waiting for a picture to appear when Fred strolled merrily into the room, a bottle of Double Diamond in each hand. Dad had forgotten to tell her that he'd invited Fred, or tell Fred that the Beakers weren't coming and the Harris's had taken their place. *I Love Lucy* had started but Mum only had eyes for Dad – and they weren't very pleasant eyes either. Fred placed the bottles of beer next to the sherry and, as if governed by some primeval self-preservation instinct, swivelled to catch Reginald Harris hoisting one of Nanna's oak chairs over his head. Ink was too pissed to give a shit but Betty gave an ear-piercing shriek.

And Nanna cried, "Oi! That's an heirloom. Use your own bloody chair Reg."

Fred grabbed Dad's unoccupied chair and hoisted it over his head. But before they could come at each other like runaway forklift trucks, Dad stepped in. He was inches shorter than both men but just as broad and could slug it out with the best of them.

While Mum comforted Betty, he told Reg to back off and barked at Fred, "She's just turned twenty and you're a married man. You should have k'nown better, Fred."

Betty burst into tears and called out Fred's name, but Fred was in too much of a hurry to let contrition hinder his escape. He put the chair down and galloped through the front door and into the street. Betty would have dashed after him if her mum hadn't got hold of her best blouse. Reg apologised to Mum, carefully replaced Nanna's chair, and chased after Fred.'

'I got to the window first. Unlike in the movies, there's very little sound when someone lands a punch. To make up for it, I shadow-boxed and went "pow!" every time either Fred or Mr Harris landed one. The more "pows" I gave the louder Betty's crying got, and after the first half a dozen or so it became a continuous wail. I glanced behind in case Dad was going to drag me away, but he'd gone down on one knee in front of Mum:

"The next time Lucille Ball goes to the Savoy, I swear I'll get you her autograph, Margaret."

Nanna went, "Ha! Forget Lucy. Ziggy better buy her a fridge or the Lea will freeze over before she'll let him lock their bedroom door again."

Ink mumbled, "Fucking doodlebug", and stared into his empty sherry glass.

The Mohammeds, meanwhile, sank into their chairs; heads as immobile as a coconut at a bent coconut shy. I dashed back, grabbed Mush's arm, and pulled him to the window. He didn't want to go but I didn't give him much choice. Ink hobbled over to join us, rummaged through his trouser pocket, and came up with a florin and a ball of fluff.

"My money's on Reg Harris 'cause he's got the longer reach." He nudged Mush in the ribs with a pointed elbow. "Want to take the bet, Malcolm?"

Mush squeaked like a dog's toy as Ink squashed him against the window frame, and then made a sound like Tarzan's chimp as Ink burped into his face.

"Is that a yes in your lingo, Malcom?"

While Mush was recoiling under a gas attack I pressed my nose against the glass.

"Cor! This is better than any cartoon, Mush. Blimey Ink, that was some haymaker… pow! pow!'"

***

'Have a penchant for apes, do you Kuchy?'

'I'm not a racist, if that's what you're getting at.'

'You should send that last scene to the makers of *EastEnders*. Real life drama if ever I heard it.' Raz slapped a hand over my lips. 'Shut it. The Apache are back.'

20

I thought I saw movement, where the orange glow from the streetlight faded into darkness.

'Was that one of them?'

Raz took his hand away from my mouth and whispered, 'Stay put. Don't make a sound and don't try to escape. You wouldn't get twenty yards on the street, chief.' He gave my shoulder a squeeze that might have been mistaken for friendly if I didn't know him better. 'Besides, you'd fall flat on your fat arse if you tried to climb the railings.'

I scanned the street again. When I turned my head back he was gone, as if spirited away. It occurred to me that he could be bluffing and there was nothing sinister out there, that perhaps he'd only answered a call of nature. Drawing inspiration from my heroes, Martin Luther King, Douglas Bader and Mary Seacole, I stretched and rubbed my legs to improve the circulation before setting them in motion. But facts were facts. This chubby Action Man had as much chance of escaping his Colditz as Spurs had of winning the Champions League during the reign of Charles III, never mind during his mum's dotage. I didn't hear Raz leave and I didn't hear him return either. There was no sign of my camera and I was too deflated to ask. He seized me under the armpit.

'Come on Kuchy, we're better off inside.'

'What about the locks, not to mention the alarm?'

'Sorted,' he replied, marching me to the main entrance.

The door was slightly ajar and there was no sign of a forced entry, splintered wood or dislocated hinges. Raz had a quick look behind, bundled me inside, and informed me he was going to reset the alarm. He took a gizmo from his pocket which was somewhere between a TV remote and the latest offering from Q's wacky lab. He secured the door and pointed the thing at a metal box on the wall. After eliciting a series of clicks he led me up the stairs to a corridor poorly lit by two energy-saving bulbs. He cupped an ear and put it to a classroom door.

'Hark, Ricky. Are these Walter Gabriel's rustic tones I can hear? Yes, he's saying in the Ambridge vernacular, "What's up, me old pal, me old beauty?" I do believe your mummy is listening to *The Archers*.' He opened the door a fraction and peered inside the room. 'She is! She's listening to it on a quaint transistor radio. She's wearing a cream dress with a pink sash. How delightful. The flower designs are in blue, pink and red. You'll allow her a splash of red, won't you Ricky? My, how nicely the floral dress contrasts with her brown hair. Oh, and your daddy's sitting next to her reading the racing pages. My, how blond he is. I bet your hair was as blond as his until it turned greasy mouse and started falling out. And Nanna and Ink are sitting behind them. It is them, isn't it? I can see Nanna's bandy legs under the desk. Oh dear, one of her stockings has laddered and I bet the poor old thing can't afford new ones. She's knitting a red jumper and wants you to try it on. Ink's thread-veined nose is almost as red as the jumper. How odd. His white hair is thin and wispy but his eyebrows are dark and bushy, like the furry caterpillars you capture in the backyard to scare the girls with. He's sipping hot water and doing his utmost to burp. If he doesn't retch first, another few sips should do the trick. He's sitting directly behind your daddy. Don't you think you should warn your daddy? Is that a sly grin on your face, Ricky? I hope not. A son should respect his father. Bill and the Tottenham Boys are sitting at the very back of the classroom. There's no sign of Mushtaq. I wonder what's happened to him? Frank is studiously reading the *Encyclopaedia Britannica* while the rest of the gang are launching paper aeroplanes. I'd better move them to the front before they take someone's eye out.'

Call it an act of bravery, call it the last peck of the dodo, either way I took a swing at him. He blocked my punch and I made a grab for his shades. Before I could glimpse the monster behind the mask, he seized my wrist and spun me around, pinning me against the wall and forcing my arm half way up my back. He pushed the classroom door wide open with his foot and frogmarched me inside, flicking the light switch as he went. He closed the door with a back heel and stood me by the blackboard under the full glare of a strip light that had spluttered into life. The papier-mâché dinosaur on a plinth and the crayon drawings that adorned the walls were exposed to scrutiny, yet his features were no clearer to me. It wouldn't have surprised me if he slept in his baseball cap and shades. Tilting his head to the left and the right, stepping back and forth, he compared the kiddie's drawings to Picasso and Modigliani. Banksy, maybe. Picasso at a pinch. But Modigliani?

The last time I was in a classroom I was clearing the personal effects from my desk. The headmaster was standing in front of me scrutinising my every movement, scowl and indignation competing for prime slot on his blubbery face. I was fit then and he took seriously my threat to rip off his head and post it on the railings. Spikes on the old London Bridge were mentioned. He had back up, a hard-tackling Welsh P.E teacher called Dai Evans who'd played hooker for Aberystwyth seconds and could go without blinking longer than Jacque Cousteau could remain under water without air. The muscle man was stationed by the door. His mad eyes locked onto mine as he dared me to have a go. It was a freezing Saturday morning and I wore my Spurs pyjamas under my jeans. Holes in jeans were all the fashion then and I had a cockerel perched on my exposed kneecap. Two days prior to that the judge had given me a three-month suspended sentence for possession of a half ounce of Indian resin. It didn't affect my marriage because Maggie smoked dope, as did most of our friends. She had a well-paid job in publishing and a month later I got a position on the *Evening Standard*, as a rooky journalist. Except for an occasional glass of wine with a restaurant meal I'd been off the booze for years. Indeed, I owned the moral high ground while I was teaching. It wasn't me who came into the staffroom with a hangover and dull, uninterested eyes, downing aspirins and moaning "never again". I wasn't the one who needed two cups of strong coffee before educating the little horrors.

The last lesson I took was on heroism: was the SS soldier who charged a Soviet machine-gun nest a hero? Was he brainwashed? Was his duty to his Fuhrer greater than his survival instinct? Was he mad? Was he subhuman? We went on to discuss, amongst others, Sir Francis Drake, Horatio Nelson, Nelson Mandela, Neil Armstrong, and Florence Nightingale versus Mary Seacole (the black woman won hands down). I doubt if there'd be a man or woman among that little lot who wouldn't get off his, or her, arse and make a dash for freedom. Ink told me that when he disembarked from the ship in France it was the fear of the unknown that gave him the collywobbles. He'd never met a Hun face to face, but had heard stories about rape and pillage in little Belgium. In the same breath he told me about the men who were given white feathers by women, and how the conscientious objectors were shunned because they wouldn't fight.

"Blimey, Ink," I'd replied, "No one wanting to play with you? I'd rather take me chances with the bleedin' Hun.'"

But who were the Hun, or in my case the Apache? Surely they couldn't be any crueller than the thug who had abducted me.

Tiny chairs were stacked on tiny desks, most with scratch marks. Raz removed a chair at the front of the class and put it behind a desk which had the initials R.K carved into it. He ran his finger around the letters.

'This your work, Ricky?'

'No chance. If Mrs Law caught a boy gouging a desk she'd cane him till her arm dropped off. They must have bought new desks since I was here.'

'You're looking peaky, Ricky. Have you got a tummy ache? Or have you seen a ghost? Sit yourself down and we'll commence the lesson.' He selected another miniature chair and put it alongside the first miniature chair. 'One for each cheek. If you refuse I'll send for Mrs Law.'

'You'll need to dig her up first and I don't believe in ghosts.'

'Is that right? Then I'll have to take discipline into my own hands.' He pulled out the long top drawer of the teacher's desk and rummaged through it, removing a hefty ruler. 'Look what I've found, Ricky,' and smashed it down on the adjacent desk.

I almost fitted. Like the time I overdid the vodka and Red Bull.

He screamed, 'Ricky! Do I have your undivided attention? If you're a good boy I might even give you some answers.'

I wasn't sure I wanted to hear his answers. The wrong answer might signal my death knell. K'nell, now that was a word that Dad should have tried to get his tongue around. Walter Gabriel could be found on Google. The caterpillars could have been guesswork, but how did he know about Mum's floral dress? She wore that when we had dinner at the Mohammeds. I was certain I never described it to him. And as for that space-age gismo…

Not wishing the ruler across my knuckles, I eased my buttocks onto the chairs, shifting my weight, trying to get level. But no matter how I positioned myself, my knees remained higher than my hips, something Mike had warned me against. Minutes earlier we were concealed in darkness and lying low. Why had he brought me to this bright classroom? Had he lit a campfire to draw the Apache to us? Was I the bait?

'Excuse me. Won't they see the light?'

'Excuse me *sir*! Don't forget your place, Ricky.'

He strode along the aisle placing chairs on the floor, swishing the ruler and stopping at each desk to correct a spelling or help with a sum. I had an awful feeling that he believed the desks were occupied by children. One of the strip lights started to buzz and flicker causing the dinosaur to shift between light and shadow; the stuff of horror films. He returned to the front and marched up and down in front of the blackboard, ruler held military-style over one shoulder. He came to attention and made me close my eyes as he drew on the blackboard. When he ordered me to open them, I saw six chalk penises in ascending sizes, each with a number above it. They ranged from No. 1, which had no testes or pubic hair, to an erect phallus with an overgrown bush that dwarfed all the others. He smacked the balls on No. 6 with the ruler.

'Men are so vulnerable. These things can be hacked off with a rusty knife, squeezed in a vice. Countless ways a man might be brought to his knees. Now, where were we? Oh yes, the cricket ball. Did Mushtaq replace James Carpenter's ball or did that nasty policeman throw you all in clink? Class! Stop giggling and pay attention.' Smacking his thighs, he continued, 'That's better. Now that you're sitting comfortably, Ricky may begin the history lesson.' He raised the ruler over my head. 'Make it educational, Kuchy, or I'll sprout horns and this ruler will turn into a fucking pitchfork.'

21

'I told Mush that Bill had only borrowed James' ball and it had been accidently lost in the River Lea. I said it was only fair we replaced it.'

Raz gave a couple of loud claps. Another lure for the Apache?

'Stop right there, Ricky. No mention of the police or smashed windows?'

I shot a glance towards the door and strained my ears. Nothing.

'Are you kidding? Not after the incident with the vicar's apple. Mush would have run a mile. I pleaded with him to ask his father if we could have one his balls.'

Raz jabbed an index finger at me. I didn't have time to blink let alone protect myself. Another centimetre and it would have crushed my Adam's apple.

'I'll have no vulgarity in my classroom, Ricky. And pull yourself together. Mrs Law won't pay us a visit. She's busy caning Harry Hooper.'

He slowly withdrew the finger and rubbed it on my arm as if cleaning blood from a dagger.

'Is that how you intend to kill me?' I spluttered.

He rubbed his chin.

'Worth a second thought. I've never killed anyone with a finger before. A dagger would be quicker. Messy, though.' He gently squeezed my shoulder. 'Cheer up, Kuchy. When the talking stops who knows for whom the ball tolls.'

He laughed hysterically and shook my shoulder so forcefully that it was a wonder I didn't get whiplash. 'Well! Did Mushtaq bring a ball along? Did he oblige you delinquents?'

Between gasps, I replied, 'At the next meeting. Unfortunately, it was one of those lightweight practice affairs that didn't have a seam and was as dull as ditchwater. His father said a match ball would hurt our legs and it was only for use with pads on a properly prepared wicket.'

'Very erudite, Ricky. Pray continue.'

I took a couple of deep breaths, which seemed to help. As did the fact that he'd sat in the teacher's chair and was out of shanking range.

'Now let me see. Ah, that's right. We sat in a circle with our legs crossed; disappointment and apprehension etched on our grubby little faces. Mush was all smiles when he arrived but soon picked up on the vibes. Frank's disposition became increasingly sullen.

Eventually he jumped up and screamed, "Tosser! That's no soddin' good!" and threw the ball into Mr Bentley's garden.

Bill made him fetch it. Frank had a devious, scheming mind and in the time it took him to retrieve the ball he'd come up with a plan.'

'I hope you aren't shifting the blame onto this nipper, Ricky. I think you're the one with the devious, scheming mind. I'm keeping a close eye on you, boy.'

Old men are meant to revert to a childlike state, not be induced into it by some bastard when all their faculties are more-or-less intact. I'd have preferred to wait another twenty years before becoming a kid again.

'Frank quoted, "All for one and one for all," and said each of us should undertake a challenge. Anyone who failed would pay for a new ball out of his pocket money. If we all failed or all completed our challenges successfully then we'd pay an equal share. Frank equated it to a trial by ordeal like they had in medieval times. Nobody knew what he was on about but it sounded great.'

'I can see what's coming, Ricky. Or shall I call you Judas? Pauvre Mushtaq. Que Dieu ait pitié de cet enfant. My heart bleeds for him.'

He knew French and his accent was perfect, at least to my ears it was. The only way his coeur would bleed was if I stole his gun and shot him straight through it. It wouldn't have surprised me if he also spoke Latin and Ancient Greek, but I had no intention of massaging his ego and refrained from commenting upon his linguistic skills. As preposterous as it may seem, I considered the possibility that he was a reptilian life form from another planet, then a machine, and finally a genetically engineered human who had escaped from a government facility. The latter seeming the more credible because he had a fine grasp of Terra languages and possessed the strength of a bull elephant. I maintained a semblance of sanity by reasoning that unless it had seriously malfunctioned, a machine or a super-human would hardly be programmed to elicit childhood memories from an irrelevant, ageing press photographer. During my stint as a journalist, I had written an article condemning some of the activities at GCHQ, which was published in *The Guardian*. Surely, I thought, Big Brother or Sister couldn't have been watching me all this time. Could they?

'Mush wondered why we couldn't buy James a ball without completing a challenge.

"Challenges are fun, Mush," said Frank. If the first bit of his response sounded friendly enough, the rest certainly didn't. "If you refuse a challenge you can bugger off and play hopscotch with the sissy girls."

It went to a vote and Mush abstained. It took Frank a good few minutes to explain to Terry what abstained meant.'

Raz leapt up and thrust a stick of chalk into my hand.

'And the nature of these gargantuan challenges? Did Frank fill you in on the labours of Heracles? Pray come to the blackboard Ricky and list them alongside the penises. A gold star if you spell each word correctly. If you fail you will receive the dunce's hat from Terry and take his place in the corner.'

He sprang past me and smashed his ruler down on a desk at the back of the classroom.

'Do you find something amusing, Frank? No? Then stop the sniggering at Terry or I'll tell Ziggy you're of German stock and have him take his belt to you. You've merited six gold stars this week alone. You won't get a seventh if you behave like this.'

As he railed at Frank I seized upon the chance to slip out of the classroom, but my arms couldn't gain much leverage on those junior chairs and my quads felt like they were weighed down with sandbags. Little wonder then that my legs gave way and I slumped back onto my bottom. Before I could make a second attempt he stormed back to the front. As if triggered by some supernatural force the faulty strip light died a death and the dinosaur was once more relegated to extinction. He swung around with what I took to be a weapon in his hand. Sniggering, he tossed a metal pencil sharpener over his head and caught it behind his back.

'Remain in your seat, Ricky. We haven't got all day and I have homework to set. Put the chalk down and tell me of these challenges. Who thought them up? No stumbling over your words now.'

While incarcerated in the toilets, I'd toyed with the idea of killing him. Now I knew for certain: kill or be killed. But if I couldn't kill him then maybe I could blind him. There was a paper knife alongside the ruler in the teacher's drawer. It was blunt but it was also long and thin, capable of taking an eye out. He'd removed his shades to clean them once before and perhaps they'd need cleaning for a second time …

'Each of us had to think of a challenge for the person to their left. Frank made sure he sat to Mush's right.'

Raz's head moved birdlike until it stopped jerking and his gaze centred on a desk.

'Frank! What is 366 divided by 16 in decimals?… 22.875. Very good.' He looked down at me.

'Before we get to Frank I feel we should get the lesser brains out of the way in these challenges. Tell you what; we'll bypass you for the time being, Ricky, and start with the other clever boy in the gang, namely Mushtaq. Who was to his left?'

'Me… but you know that already, don't you? Have you interrogated one of the other Tottenham Boys?'

He slapped me across the face.

'Don't tell me what I know or ask me how I came to know it!'

The blow was gentle by his standards but it caused me to break down and sob: an unbearable accumulation of stress and fear. He hit me again and ordered me to stop blubbering like a girl and pull myself together. When my tears flowed unabated he rested the ruler on my desk, lifted me off the ground by my collar, and shook me. It was lucky I didn't sustain a cervical fracture as we set off down the aisle. I wasn't so lucky when my head struck a polystyrene square in the ceiling and I suffered a gust of dusty, stale air before it dropped back into place. He stopped at a desk and held me up with one arm as easily as if I was made entirely of skin. Hardly any air reached my lungs as his fingers kneaded my lower belly, skirting my pubic hair before unzipping my flies. I thrashed my legs like a man hanging from the gallows, but my collar was touch-tight around my throat and it dug into my flesh. Incapable of speech and on the verge of strangulation, I couldn't look down let alone prevent him from reaching inside my underpants. He pulled out my penis, left it dangling, and lowered me several inches.

The tips of my shoes brushed the ground as he cried, 'Jenny! Stop dreaming of Cliff Richard and pay attention. Now class, which of the penises on the blackboard does this gentleman's sexual organ most resemble? What was that? Number four? Number five? Don't all answer at once. Number one? Was that you, Frank? I might have guessed.' He snapped his fingers and bawled, 'I've got it, Kuchy. Let's pay your parents a visit so they can see what a big boy you've become ... not.'

I tried to direct my head but it wouldn't budge. He shook me again. 'No! Did you say no?'

He lowered me another few inches until the soles of my feet touched the ground, which thankfully eased the pressure on my neck. He glided his tongue along my sweaty cheek, and ran two fingers around my chin.

'When was the last time you shaved, Kuchy? Apart from the pubes there's not much difference between you and Ricky in the cock department. Have you considered a dog groomer for that bush? I wouldn't lie on a lawn when the birds are hunting worms, if I were you. It seems you may need a little encouragement if you're to get a number six. What if I put my fingers in your mouth and we pretend they're my manhood? Would that help? No need to thank me. What are friends for? If you suck me off nicely I might even buy you a Mivvi lollipop. Lime is your favourite, isn't it Ricky?'

It crossed my mind to bite his fucking fingers off. If I were going to be abused or murdered I'd leave him stumps for an epitaph.

Two steps ahead, he hissed, 'I'll tear the tongue out of your mouth before your teeth can even break my velvet skin, white boy.' He tickled my penis. 'Don't worry, Kuchy, I'll send Bill out for some Viagra instead.'

He pushed my penis back inside my pants and zipped up my flies. He crouched, bringing his face level to mine. The smell of coffee mingled with stale breath, probably the product of unbrushed teeth.

'You can see your nearest and dearest, can't you? Take a closer look, Ricky.'

Two of the chairs grew to adult size and out of nowhere my parents appeared. They were showered in golden rays: radiant and fresh-faced, how I imagined them to be when they first met. Before phasing out completely, Mum smiled and Dad did a "V for Victory". I knew it was a signal for me to stay strong.

I exclaimed, 'Yes! Yes! I saw them,' and begged Raz to make them return. He plonked me back on my tiny seat.

'Whether they come back to life depends entirely on you, Kuchy. Now pull yourself together and tell me what horrific challenge Mushtaq set you.'

Hallucination or not, Mum and Dad were real to me. Up until then I'd played for time, slowed the narration down whenever I could and introduced new characters. In the hope of meeting my parents again, I began racing through the story. I was probably hurtling towards my doom but there was sod all I could, or wanted to do about it. I dried my eyes. This was my chance to say goodbye to Mum and Dad.

***

'Mush dithered at first and said he didn't want to upset or hurt anyone. We began giving him the slow handclap, which prompted him to raise an arm in stages and say timidly, "I have one, but if it offends you Ricky, I apologise in advance." My mind boggled. There wasn't much he could that would offend me, except for being asked to wear an Arsenal scarf maybe. And if he asked me to do that I'd either land him one or never speak to him again. When he made me sing *Three Blind Mice* while standing on one leg I thought he'd let me off lightly. I never said it out loud though in case he chose something worse. As soon as I began singing, Bill started squeaking and all the others bar Mush joined in. Mush became frantic and asked me if he'd gone too far. I told him he must be joking and that it was a piece of cake. "Oh dear," he said, glancing at Frank. I think he wanted reassurance that Frank was going to go easy on him. No chance. Frank made hamster cheeks to prevent himself from exploding into laughter.'

'And to your left? Do tell the uninformed of the class who was to your left, Ricky.'

'Roy.'

'And what challenge did you set him?'

'He was to turn Mr Glovers' new gnome upside down. Bill had the old gnome away and put it on a 149 bus while the conductor was upstairs. The 149 went to Liverpool Street Station so hopefully it found a loving home in Cambridgeshire. Looking back, I think the old man must have considered his gnomes a kind of status symbol. Apart from the Nobles, nobody else in the street had the room in their front garden to show off. Roy was fast, but you should have seen him go after he came out of Mr Glover's garden. We'd all moved a good twenty yards further down the pavement by then.'

Raz looked over my head and rubbed his tummy.

'Roy! I'm peckish. Sprint up to Alf's and get me one of his nice pork pies. If you're back within ten minutes, I'll enter you for the hundred yards in the Middlesex trials.'

I felt a draught and heard a click, then glimpsed a shadow in the corridor. My body contorted into a variety of shapes until it adopted the stance of a short leg fielder.

Raz straightened me up by the scruff of my collar and called out, 'Good boy, Roy. No running until you're through the school gates now.' Keeping a firm grip on me, he continued, 'Get on with story, Kuchy. I'll tell you when the Apache are on the warpath.'

***

'Terry was to Roy's left. After Roy had recovered his breath he challenged him to turn the gnome the right way up again. Terry called him all sorts of names. Mush only heard the first "fucker" because he covered his ears after that. Luckily for Terry, Mr Glover was still dozing after his afternoon hot milk and brandy.'

'And to Terry's left?'

'Bill. As I said, Terry loved a scrap, whether watching or joining in. He challenged Bill to fight Jason for a Tom Finney.'

'This may surprise you, chief, but I happen to know who Tom Finney is. But what's a Tom Finney when it's at home?'

'Jason had Finney on a cigarette card and Bill had all the Preston players except for that particular one. Preston North End was our second favourite team because they wore the same colours as Spurs. Terry said he'd give Bill two whole packs of bubble gum to add to the ante, winner takes all.'

171

'Did Bill fight Jason there and then?'

'Later in the day. Jason got a black eye and a cut lip and Bill got his Tom Finney.'

'I take it Frank was to Bill's left? What was his challenge?'

'Bill challenged him to go scrumping in the vicar's garden.'

'And did he?'

'The next day he turned up with a big green cooking apple. As no one saw him scrumping, Bill said he had to do it again, or else. Frank said he wanted a trial by his peers and peers always found the accused innocent as he was one of their own. The only pier the rest of us had heard of was at Southend and the trial was put off for another day (it never happened). Mushtaq probably knew what Frank was on about, but he kept it to himself. I like to think he didn't want to show us up.'

'And now we come to the interesting bit. What challenge did Frank set Mushtaq?'

'Sandy was a little way down the street.'

'Don't tell me. Heracles had to wrestle the Nemean Lion.'

'Sandy was waiting for Mrs Beaker's cat, Tiddles, to come down from a tree. Frank took something wrapped in greaseproof paper from his pocket and whistled. It would normally take half a dozen whistles for Sandy to come when he had a cat trapped up a tree. On this occasion he sniffed the air and obeyed the command first time. Mush saw him hurtling towards us and grasped my arm. Constable Warner had a firm grip but he never left marks when he grabbed hold of you.

Just before Sandy got to us, Frank grinned and said, "Don't run, Mush. Dogs'll have you if you run." He undid the greaseproof paper to reveal a cooked sausage and tossed it in the middle of the circle. "There you go, Sandy. Feast on that, boy." He nudged Mush with his elbow. "And there you go, Mush. Your challenge is to stroke Sandy before he finishes that banger."'

'Mush was shaking so much that he was unable to speak. I tried to break his grip but his fingers bit deeper into my flesh. I don't know if it was kindness or cruelty on my part but I told the gang about what I'd witnessed in Hell Alley.

"Perhaps Mush should show us his knees instead. He wears long trousers during P.E. but I got a glimpse. Bits of bone were pointing in all directions."

Looking horrified, Mush replied, "I was born that way. How could you, Ricky?" He looked pleadingly at Bill. "I can't do it. Neither challenge is acceptable. Please don't make me."

Frank snapped, "Show us your knees instead then, Mush."

Bill had the final say.

"Too late Frank. The banger is the challenge."

If it had been liver, Sandy would have wolfed it straight down. He liked to savour bangers. He flopped onto his tummy and put his paw on the sausage so that one end stood erect. He chomped away a bit at a time, and judging by the look on Mush's face, that sausage could have been a stick of dynamite with a lit fuse. After I wrested Mush's talons from my arm, I tried to put his mind at rest.

"He won't bite, Mush, honest. This is how you do it."

I got up and called Sandy a good boy, stroked his mane, and tickled him behind the ear. He nuzzled my leg and looked at Mush, who was on his feet and hiding behind me.'

'Ink had a brother called Tommy who'd died just before the war started. Mrs Beaker said Tommy had the shakes something rotten. Ink said he died of a disease and that I wasn't to pay any attention to gossip. He said the whisky was for medicinal purposes only. I hoped that Mush hadn't got the same disease. If he had, I thought, he wouldn't be allowed any medicinal whisky else this Prophet geezer would chop his hands off. I did my best to reassure Mush.

"He's never bitten a boy and I've never *actually* seen him kill a cat. He had a swim in the Lea yesterday so he's all soft. He's the brother I never had and I trust him with me life. Go on, have a stroke."

Mush moved his shaking arm towards Sandy's mane. It must have travelled all of two centimetres before it shot back faster than when I accidently put mine on a hot fireguard. Sandy decided that such behaviour required investigation. He sniffed Mush's crutch and his penis poked through the fur as he geared up to hump Mush's leg.

Mush gasped, "Please, Ricky. I'm really scared."

I replied, "His willy looks just like me Mum's lipstick. Dad says you can't colour your lips with it."

Frank chuckled and said, "Mush could have a go though. Can't harm."

Mush replied in the worst possible manner.

"Don't be so vulgar."

Frank went limp-wristed and impersonated Frankie Howerd.

"Ooh, don't be so vulgar."

That did it for Mush.

He bawled, "I hate all of you and I resign from the Tottenham Boys."

As he scuttled away Frank hollered, "Go on, piss off! Come back here and we'll force some bacon down yer throat."

Terry wiggled his arse like Diana Dors and yelled, "Come back this way again and we'll pull yer trousers down and have a gander at those knees."

Mush started to run and so did Sandy, but I grabbed his collar just in time and cried, "Piss off back where you came from! We don't have wimps in our gang. Go and join the flamin' Girl Guides."

I did feel half sorry for Mush but I had to join in the banter. After all, I was a Tottenham Boy.

22

'The next day Mush was waiting for me in the playground. Tears clouded his eyes and his voice was that pitiful it made me want to puke.

He whined, "Why did you betray me, Ricky? You swore you wouldn't tell anyone about my knees."

I didn't owe him an explanation. If he couldn't stroke a dog then he didn't deserve to be in this country, let alone be my friend. I gave him the Tottenham Look and swaggered away.'

Raz grasped the arms of his shades. I feared he was about to rip the sunglasses off his face and give me his version of the Tottenham Look. A few hours earlier, I'd wanted to see his eyes in the hope of unearthing a vestige of humanity and establishing a rapport with him. Since then it had become clear to me that the shades and raised hood – as well as my inability to provide the police with an identikit picture – increased my chances of survival.

He may have kept the shades in place, but my nervous system took another direct hit when he snorted like a bull and bellowed, 'You don't rule the world anymore, white boy!' He ran his hand along his top lip and under his nose, as if wiping away snot, by which time his voice had thankfully calmed. 'And you never spoke to Mushtaq again?'

My mouth was parched and I was drenched in sweat. I couldn't have put a cup to my lips without spilling half the contents.

'I don't know if he or his father requested it, but soon after he was moved to a different class.'

'Did he find a new best friend?'

'No. He kept his head down and got on with his schoolwork. He came top of his class. Teacher's pet and all that.'

Whistling the *Dambuster March*, Raz picked the ruler up and circled the lump on my scalp.

'Did you set your thugs on him, Ricky? If you lie to me you'll never see your mummy and daddy again.'

An imam in Luton once told me that the Devil has as many seductions as tortures. If Raz had conjured up Marilyn Monroe and promised me a passionate night with her, I would have gladly resisted if it meant saving my soul. But I would readily sell my soul to the highest bidder if it meant bringing Mum back to life.

'I won't lie. I swear ... Harry Hooper brought a cosh to school and said he was going to break Mush's arm if he didn't drop his trousers. Dad would've banned me from Spurs if I were involved in anything like that. I persuaded Harry to only scare Mush a bit and he hid the weapon in the bogs until the end of school. Fortunately for Mush he was excused assembly because we sang Christian hymns. Assembly would have given us a good opportunity to stick chewing gum on his seat and put itching powder down his shirt. Even the girls joined in the baiting. Jenny said she'd show him her nipples if he showed her his knees first. Of course, he didn't bite and she had no intention of keeping to her half of the bargain. I was longing for him to play football because shorts were compulsory. I don't know how he wangled it but he was excused soccer. Harry reckoned it must be because "this Prophet geezer only liked cricket". He couldn't escape us forever though and when the teacher on duty got distracted, I helped Harry pull Mush's trousers down in the middle of the playground. The other kids formed a circle around him, giggling and pointing at his long pants and pipe-cleaner legs. He shed tears like you wouldn't believe. Mr Gasson broke it up and asked Mush if he wanted to report any of us for bullying. Mush declined. If he'd learnt one thing about the local customs, it was that no one ratted in Tottenham.'

Raz may have flung me back in time, but I couldn't help wondering if his mind was locked in the 1950s and early 60s. Was he also standing in the playground watching the rabble tormenting Mush? Was he feeling Mushtaq's pain? He put the ruler on the desk and placed his hands on the back of my shoulders.

'Your parents weren't curious as to why you broke off diplomatic relations with Mushtaq?'

'I told them Mr Mohammed didn't want his son mixing with Christians as he thought they were a bad influence. Dad said, "He's lucky Jan Sobieski isn't alive now. He'd tell them where to stuff their Koran." As for Mum, she didn't say it out loud but I think she was glad to be spared a second helping of aaloo keema. Her stomach took days to cease hostilities after she'd had a taste of the Mohammeds' curry. Dad said he'd sleep on the floor if she ate so much as another teaspoonful.'

'Did you re-establish contact with Mushtaq or was that it? Is there anything else of interest ... have you anything else to add? Or is this the end of the line, Kuchy?'

By "end of the line" I knew he didn't mean Epping. The speed of my response could be compared to a sidewinder missile.

'Loads! For starters, Nanna couldn't walk with me to the Co-op anymore because of her bad back. Poor old Ink was faring worse than Nanna. He loved westerns and wanted to buy a second-hand wheelchair so that he could watch *The Magnificent Seven* at the Florida. Nanna said she wasn't pushing him there with her lumbago. I asked Dad what lumbago was and he said he was an Italian general his unit captured in Libya. Nanna did insist on still walking with me to Alf's in Park Lane. I tried to walk slower when I was with her but it wasn't easy, especially if there was a tin can to kick or a pigeon to scare. Nanna held my hand more frequently as time passed. I didn't even let Mum do that. Sometimes Nanna held it to stop me running on ahead, other times she just squeezed it for no good reason.

Often there were tears in her eyes and she would say, "It's not you, Ricky. It's just an old woman being silly."

Even if Ink had bought a wheelchair, I doubt if she would've let Dad push him to the cinema. They'd most likely have argued over the merits of their respective wars and Dad would've let go while demonstrating how to operate a machine-gun on a Cromwell tank. I offered to push Ink there but Dad said I was too small. I told him I'd get the whole of the Tottenham Boys to help me.

He said, "Don't be so ridiculous. Ink has survived two world wars."

Mum agreed with him. She said there was a slope on the way to the Florida and she was worried Ink might join the traffic in High Road. Not to mention the steps. They usually didn't have wheelchair access in those days. Oh, and…'

Raz seized the ruler and crashed it down on the desk with such force that it split the end.

'Stop the filibustering, Kuchy, or that lump on your skull will grow to twice the size. This next bit of the play had better include Mushtaq. Position him centre stage, or else.'

'Okay, but I've got to include Frank.'

'Frank. I think it's time to pick the flesh off that boy's bones. Very well, enter Frank stage left.'

I felt that icy blast shoot up my spine again. Until I'd met Raz, I thought such a reaction to fear was the invention of novelists.

***

'It was around the time of the 11-plus when Frank asked me to meet him at the scout hut after school. That old hut was creepy when it was empty. The building creaked in a strong wind and tree branches scraped along the roof. I imagined a giant with long fingernails, huge furry spiders, worse, an alien invasion. There was no way I would've ventured inside if *Journey into Space* were playing on a transistor radio. Frank had said there was something in it for me and to keep our meeting secret.

When I arrived he produced a key and said, "The sissy scouts won't turn up for another couple of hours yet. None of the other Tottenham Boys know I've got a key to the back door and I want it kept that way."

It turned out that Frank's dad, Barry, occasionally stood in for the Scoutmaster when on leave from the army. He'd been entrusted with a set of keys and Frank had had copies made. Barry was stationed in Malaysia and the whole street wanted to hear about his adventures in exotic climes. Terry was all ears but Frank was totally uninterested. Make of it what you will. Anyhow, we worked our way through the weeds and let ourselves in. Frank looked around the hall, lifted his chin, and put his hands on his hips.

He boasted, "How do you like my gaff? I never nick anything and make sure I leave it tidy so that no one knows I've even been here. Bleedin' Roy would leave a trail of sweet wrappers a mile long, while gormless Terry would stick chewing gum everywhere. As for Bill, he'd try and lift the heaviest thing he could find and make a dent in the floor.'"

'We sat cross-legged on the polished floor and Frank pulled out a pack of candy cigarettes. He tapped the back of the pack until one popped up and offered it to me. It took all my willpower not to bite the pink tip off. I couldn't help having a good suck though and it shrank to half its original size in next to no time. Frank dangled a sugary replica from the corner of his mouth like they did in gangster films, leant forward, and stared at me. His eyes were so dark that I might've been looking at two black holes.

He hissed, "Another lot of Pakis have moved in down Scotland Green. The tide's coming in and we'll be washed away if we ain't careful."

I'd never seen him that riled before. I knew something serious must have gone down.

"Pakis? What are they, Frank?"

He spoke as if they were worse than Arsenal supporters.

"Stupid Paki. Smelly Paki. Stinking Paki. It has more of a bite to it than Pakistani, don't you agree Ricky? Before we know it we'll be overrun with 'em. Bang goes our football. I've checked the list of national teams and they ain't got one. There'll be no more breweries because they don't booze and me mum'll be out of work. That means I won't get that set of encyclopaedias she promised me for Christmas."

He had me going.

"What! No football! Life ain't worth living without Spurs."

He nodded.

"And don't forget man's best friend. Lassie'll be a goner. Football and dogs, British through and through."

I clenched my fist and brandished it in the air.

"They ain't touching Sandy."

"It's a cultural thing, Ricky. The way Mush treats Sandy says it all. As soon as a Paki's born he opens his eyes and do you know the first thing he sees?"

"The ceiling?"

He pulled out a pocketknife and flicked it open.

"A bleedin' man with a long beard about to chop the top of his dick off, that's what.'"

'He got to his feet and jumped onto the platform at the end of the hall, stomped up and down, and ranted like Adolf Hitler at one of his rallies. He gave a Nazi salute and shouted "sieg heil" so loudly that I was afraid we'd be found out. I had the impression he'd have done the very same thing with or without me being there.

He hopped down from the platform and cried, "Not only does Mush have to go but his whole bleedin' family. Time to get rid of the lot. You with me or not?"

I was on my feet now, giving him a stiff-arm salute that nearly wrenched my arm from its socket.

"Say the word!"

He munched his candy cigarette and took a packet of ten Players from his pocket. He dangled one from his mouth.

"The Pakis may need a little encouragement to clear the fuck out."

"What sort of encouragement?"

He took a box of Swan Vestas from his other pocket and struck a match, staring into the flame like Mrs Beaker did her tea leaves.

"Oh, I dunno. There's all sorts of possibilities."

My stomach cramped.

"I ain't setting light to Mush's gaff if that's what you've got in mind, Frank."

"It ain't come to that yet. What we need are more people wanting to serve their country. Then we can go national like the Labour Party. We'll call our party P.A.L.S. and pronounce it Pals. No one can object to that. Friendship, what could be better? Pals can also stand for Pakis Are Lazy Shits. Like it? We'll need funds to help set it up, of course."

He returned the matches to his pocket and tapped the fag back into the packet.

"I'm desperate for a smoke but can't do it in here else it might give the game away. I've got a nice little scam in mind and it don't involve burning things down. Do what I say and you can't go wrong. Just keep it to yourself."

"What about Bill and the others? We can't cut them out."

"Can't involve them yet. We need to keep this hush-hush. Terry's mouth is as big as a gasholder and Roy's ain't far behind when he overdoes the Coca Cola and Mars bars. We'll rope them in as storm troopers later. Besides, this way we need only split the proceeds between the two of us. We'll each give a donation to the party and there'll be enough left over to buy a Scalextric each."

"Did you say a Scalextric, Frank? Wow! But what will the party do with the rest of the money?"

"I'll keep it safe until we've got enough to rent an HQ and buy uniforms. We'll march through the streets holding banners saying Pakis Go Home and the like."

"Cor, uniforms! They'll be blue and white, won't they?"

"Black. And they won't be naff like the Scouts. They'll have long trousers and jackets with medals on. I've been reading up on Hitler.

Don't advertise the fact though because the bloke ain't too popular in these parts."

"If Dad caught me reading anything of his I wouldn't be able to sit down for a year. Did you say medals, Frank?"

"Nice shiny ones, twice the size of the Victoria Cross. I don't agree with everything Hitler said. He reckoned the Germans were the master race. They obviously ain't because they lost."

"If they'd have won, Dad would've been shot and all the Jews here gassed."

"I'll get to the Yids later. As it stands now, anyone white can join the party. Mark my words. We're the future, Ricky."

"Go on, what's this scam, then?"

He shook a key loose from his sleeve. It was a long silver one with a row of sharp teeth.

"This is all we'll need to get going."

"Are we going to rob a gaff?"

"Nah, I found this on the pavement. No idea what it fits." He headed towards the back door. "Follow me."

'We made our way down Park Lane to a bombsite donated by the Luftwaffe in 1940. It was well hidden from the road because the council had erected boards so tall that you needed stilts to see over the top. The land was earmarked for new houses but nothing had happened yet. We squeezed between a gap in the fence and made our way across the rubble. I remember an old pram filled with manky brown bottles and a shocking pink doll's head trapped under one of the wheels. There used to be a wooden cabin in the middle of the site but a group of teenage boys had burnt it down. Harry Hooper's big brother, Ronnie, was doing time in borstal for the arson and a burglary in Totteridge. When Ink read about it in *The Herald* he swore blind that they never had teenagers in his day and the world was a better place for it. By the charred remains of the cabin stood a rusty old car without any wheels. Frank patted the bonnet.

"Do you know how the American gangsters made their dosh, Ricky?"

I knew all about American gangsters from James Cagney and Humphrey Bogart films.

"Booze, weren't it?"

He took the silver key from his sleeve and twiddled it.

"Yeah, bootlegging. But don't forget the protection rackets. Think of all those cars what park in our road on match days. They can't be from around here else they would have walked."

"So?"

He put the key back up his sleeve.

"It's not exactly a protection racket I've got in mind, Rick. Comes close though. We'll offer to look after their motors while they're at the match. Say a tenner a go."

"Why would they agree to that?"

"Because some bastard's been at it and we'll offer to stand guard."

He walked along the side of the old banger, eyes fixed firmly on the Spurs ground.

'I didn't see him take the key from his sleeve, but I heard the squeal of metal on metal. There was a load of scratches on the paintwork but Frank's took pride of place.

"Blimey, Frank!"

"I've been practising getting the key out in front of the mirror."

I pretended to be Matt Dillon drawing on a baddie.

"I do that with me six gun."

He showed me the end of the key.

"There's a bit of paint left behind. That's why we can't use our own keys."

"Smart. But they're still Spurs supporters. It ain't right."

"It's for their own good, Rick. The enemy are already within. Once the Pakis have been exterminated the party will look after all the Spurs. We may even have enough to buy a new centre forward. I'm not convinced about Bobby Smith. He looks as though he's been noshing too many fish and chips to me."

"But where do I fit in?"

"You'll keep a look out."

"But I'll miss the match. Dad's been working Saturdays for a while and he's allowed me to go with Bill and the others."

"Only a tiny bit of it. Tell you what, I'll volunteer to miss out. I'll sit on a wall reading a book while waiting for the punters to come back. We'll have to key a few motors the match before so they're already nervous. Best leave it for a couple of matches after that before we key some more."

Frank often sat on walls with his nose in a book. A bloke came up to him once expecting to find *Playmates* or *Whirligig*, only to find pages full of odd squiggles and numbers arranged in brackets. He thought Frank was reading Arabic. I was good with numbers but Frank was on another planet. Dad said he must come from Mars because he could work out the racing odds in a second flat.'

***

Raz strode down the aisle and stopped at "Frank's desk". He bared his teeth and soured his voice.

'Did this little git key them, Ricky? Or did he con you into doing it?'

I heard a slap followed by a child's yelp. I stared down at my desk, too afraid to look in his direction in case Frank had materialised. Raz marched back up the aisle and lifted my chin with the backs of his fingers.

'Put the frighteners on you, has he Ricky? Is that why you're fidgeting?'

'I'm trying to stop myself wetting my pants and my lower back is killing me.'

He glanced at the clock on the wall and cracked his knuckles.

'Get a move on, Ricky, the bell will go for milk break soon.'

'And you'll bring my parents back to life?'

'Depends. You could always pray to Jesus and see how far that gets you. Carry on at pace, if you would be so kind.'

***

'Frank got off on doing the keying. On match days, cars parked on one side of the road with their bonnets pointing at the opposite kerb. The number of cars was a fraction of what it is now and they could get away quicker afterwards. But it also allowed Frank a fair degree of cover. We waited until we heard the roar, which meant the teams were coming out. He said I wasn't to draw attention to myself by whistling or kicking a tin can. I could never resist a tin can. My heart was going like the clappers while I kept watch, even worse than when we played "knock down ginger". I jumped as a car door slammed behind me, and again when a rattle went off. Frank wore the lumberjack shirt his mum had got him at the jumble. The sleeves were just right, not so big that the key fell out when his arms were at his side, not so tight that it got stuck up there. I gave him the all clear and he stepped between a Morris and a Ford Anglia. He was supposed to gouge the mudguard but he ran the key the whole length of that Morris. He might've run it back again if it weren't for Mr Bentley coming out of his house.'

'Bentley was shaking something rotten, nearly as bad as Dad when his horse lost by a short head.

He squinted at Frank and slurred, "Is that you, Bill?"

Frank slipped the key back up his sleeve and said in a passable Pakistani accent, "It's Mushtaq, Ricky's friend from Pakistan." He repeated the name, but much louder. "Mushtaq. I'm pleased to make your acquaintance."

Mr Bentley replied huffily, "You're sod all use. You lot don't even drink." Bill often ran errands for him, the offy being the first and last stop. Frank observed his handiwork, smiled to himself, and strolled away. I don't mind admitting I was impressed. He was so calm and collected that I honestly believed he was too clever to get caught. He keyed three more motors before asking for money. An artist at work is how he described himself. He'd wait for the other Tottenham Boys to set off for the ground, usually around two thirty, and when a car parked up he'd pull an innocent face:

"Look after your motor, mister? Ain't you heard? Some geezer's keyed motors the last couple of home matches. None been keyed on my watch. Guaranteed."

He finally called a halt when Constable Warner started making door-to-door enquiries. Mr Bentley never mentioned Mushtaq's name to the Old Bill. It was hardly surprising. The old sot couldn't recall what day of the week it was most of the time. I got the collywobbles at the next home match when Ink looked out of his front room window and saw a man in an overcoat walking up and down the street.

He turned to me and said, "Look at those flippin' clodhoppers. I can spot a rozzer a mile off."

I shot off to tell Frank but he'd already sussed the bloke out and said we'd split the spoils in the scout hut. I was well chuffed when he said that we'd made close to a fiver. It was divided up four quid for him and one for me. I protested but he said it was only right because he was the one doing the keying. He went on to say that we needed to cover our arses, but not to worry because he'd devised a scheme that would make us a bundle, and it didn't involve cars. But first I had to get a sample of Mush's handwriting. The following day, I gave him the birthday card that Mush had made for me. He looked at it with admiration.

"Fair play, this is a fine piece of calligraphy. All these wonderful sweeps and curls. Still, a steady hand and a bit of tracing paper should do the trick. Sentimental little Paki, ain't he? Well educated though. A peasant Paki is bad enough but an educated one is like a viper in our midst."

After he'd explained what calligraphy meant, I asked him what it was he had planned. He said I should come back on Thursday and he'd put me in the know.'

'I was having serious doubts by this stage. You might call Frank evil and twisted but he was charismatic and smart. He also possessed a vengeful streak a mile wide. It was obvious that Mush was going to be on the wrong end of whatever dastardly plan he had concocted. Kids in our street could only dream of owning a Scalextric and I turned up that Thursday with fear in my belly and little electric-powered cars whizzing around inside my skull. Frank had made a pamphlet in Mush's hand, and when he placed Mush's birthday card alongside it I honestly couldn't tell the difference between the two sets of handwriting.

I can't remember the exact wording but this is how it started:

Those who attend football matches are an abomination in the eyes of Allah. Let this mark on your car be a warning to all Crusaders. Embrace the Koran and no more harm shall befall you.

Frank said the police would think Mush intended to put pamphlets under the windscreen wipers of the cars he'd keyed. All I had to do was to put it in Mush's desk at school.

"Tell you what, me old son," he said, moving his hands like a barrow boy working a market stall. "Tell you what we'll do. We'll go fifty-fifty on my new scam. Guaranteed."

I planted the bogus evidence at the end of lessons on Friday. It meant Mush would discover it first thing Monday morning.'

***

Raz raised an arm and gave a salute. It started off as Nazi but ended as Black Power.

'Stop right there, Ricky. Frank obviously wasn't as clever as you'd like me believe. What was the point of Mushtaq finding it? For the plan to work surely it'd need a teacher to discover it first, with a little guidance from you perhaps?'

'Frank could've taught Fu Manchu a thing or two. He gambled on Mush handing it in and that Bing wouldn't believe him. He reckoned Mush would think there was a master forger at work who might strike again. Mush would conclude that if there was a next time a teacher might find the forger's handiwork before he did. And who would believe a brown immigrant in that circumstance? The forger might target another innocent soul and handing it in was the right thing to do. Lying to the vicar and the theft of his apple had already stretched Mush's conscience to breaking point.'

The pain in my back had progressed from a dull ache to excruciating. I cursed myself for not doing Mike's stretches and core exercises. The way the story was panning out, young Ricky was coming across as Dennis the Menace and Bart Simpson rolled into one. Not wishing to further tarnish his image, I decided to leave out the bit about Colin and how Frank wanted to fleece the "retard", as Colin was cruelly known by some. Raz had other ideas.

To my amazement, he said, 'Okay, Ricky, stretch your legs and sit on the nice big teacher's chair. Put Mushtaq on the backburner for a while and tell the class all about the retard. I believe his name was Colin.'

23

My eyelids were heavy, mind fuzzy, as if stirring from a deep sleep. I did possess enough of my faculties, however, to know that I daren't risk asking him how he knew about Colin. Curiosity killed the cat and if it didn't kill me it'd probably mean I'd remained cramped on those tiny chairs; the humiliation every inch as bad as those terrible back spasms. If Raz knew that Mushtaq wasn't part of Colin's tale, then why the change of emphasis? From out of the fog quotes from Jean-Paul Sartre popped into my mind: words are loaded pistols. And my new favourite: hell is other people. Groaning, I struggled to my feet and pressed the flat of my hands on the kiddie's desk to stop my legs from buckling. I shuffled around the big desk and gratefully lowered my bulk onto the teacher's chair.

He sneered, 'If it wasn't for Frank and Mushtaq you'd be top of the class. As it stands you're a distant third.' Lifting the edge of the blind, he peered out. 'It'll be light soon. If I were you I'd get a move on, chief.'

The episode with Colin wasn't the proudest chapter in my life. It was one that I'd kept very much to myself. Besides Maggie, no one else knew about it and I was sure she didn't hate me enough to set a maniac like Raz on me. Did she? If I was Sherlock Holmes and my nerves weren't shredded, I might have gleaned a clue from Raz's knowledge of poor Colin. But all it did was muddy the waters even further. We both knew what he meant by "it'll be light soon" and "I'd better get a move on". I had no reason to believe he wouldn't kill me and every reason to believe he would. He was probably involved in arms or drug dealing and that mob make witnesses disappear. They were about to add a fourth lane to the M1 and I didn't fancy being buried close to Luton Airport.

***

'Colin's passions in life were dogs, soppy films, and green Spangles … Spangles were boiled sweets. He was hired by a milky called Dick and, although he'd turned twenty-one, wasn't allowed to drive the float. He had a big head and a jutting jaw like Desperate Dan, features made more pronounced by the fact he wore a baseball cap back to front. We didn't know it at the time but he was a trailblazer in youth fashion. He talked in a slow drawl as if he had a fag dangling from his mouth and possessed legs the size of a baby elephant. Dad reckoned if they were hollow you could fit a howitzer inside and still have room for the shells. Colin was tall. Dad was no dwarf but Colin looked down on him. And he was bloody strong, too. I once saw Colin lift a woman's bubble car when the tyre needed changing. When he first started on our milk round mums kept their kids indoors. His broad smile and chirpy nature soon won Mum over. I might have helped get the coal inside the house when Dad was sick, but it was Colin who humped the sack donated by the street and filled the bunker. Colin would often drop in on Mr Bentley. He'd bring in the coal and light the fire when it was cold. On the rare occasions when Mr Bentley was lucid, Colin would stay for a chat about man's best friend and how he would love to own a pack of them. The same went for anyone else that needed help lifting heavy things. He moved mangles and sideboards when required and put the dustbin out for Mrs Beaker (Mr Beaker had a bad back). Mrs Beaker's dustbin was rusty and smelt like you wouldn't believe. Nanna reckoned it was a miracle that the gunk from her jam hadn't burned a hole in the metal. Ink thought they should put a warning on the side like they did for minefields. Colin wouldn't accept any of her jam as payment. Ink said he ain't that stupid then. Mum always stood up for Colin. She said he had a heart of gold and that anyone who poked fun at him should be ashamed of themselves.'

'Frank said the only thing worse than a Paki was a dumb white re-tard. A retard Paki didn't even class as sub-human in his eyes.

I asked him, "What's a retard when it's at home, Frank?"

He replied, "Colin's a dumb retard… a bleedin' spaz, ain't it obvious? We're going to make a bundle out of that stupid git."

"How do you mean?"

"Dick's been paying a few bob a month into Colin's post office savings account for a good two years now. He lets Colin keep the book. We've all seen it."

"Yeah, Colin's real proud of that book. He says he's going to buy his mum a fridge when he's saved enough."

"There must be over a score in there by now. We're going to have him give it to us."

"How? He ain't that daft, Frank."

"We'll use his love of dogs against him.'"

'Colin always delivered the milk on our side of the road because he wanted to make a fuss of Sandy. There was no need for him to knock because my pooch would sniff under the door and squeal in delight when he heard the milk bottles jangling in their crates. You can imagine how devastating the impact on Colin if anything ever happened to Sandy. Frank's idea was that I should tell Colin that Sandy had cancer and the vet's cure would cost twenty pounds. I was to say that my family couldn't afford the treatment and Dad was going to have him put down. It goes without saying that Colin wasn't to mention a word of it to Mum and Dad. I was to stress that they'd be insulted if he offered them charity and Mum would never speak to him again. A couple of weeks later, I'd tell Colin that Sandy was cured and everyone would be happy. Frank reckoned that the Florida would be the perfect place for the sting. A Lassie film, *The Painted Hills*, was playing there and Colin had seen it five afternoons in a row. He'd asked me if I want to go with him on the Saturday.

When Mum agreed, he said, "Thank you, Mrs K. Don't worry, I'll bring him back safe and sound."

Mum smiled and told him there were fig biscuits waiting when we

191

returned. Just before we set off she gave me a couple of bob to get in and a shilling for a choc-ice.

As Colin lumbered back up the path she whispered in my ear, "You mustn't take advantage. Make sure you buy your own ice cream, dear."'

'In the film, Lassie played the role of Shep and was poisoned by the man who killed his master. It was obvious that Lassie couldn't die but Colin didn't know any better, despite the fact he'd already seen the film five times. If that don't prove he's a dumb retard then nothing does, I thought, trying to forget the fact I kind of liked Colin. The same went for most of the other kids in our street. Bill busted the nose of an Edmonton boy when he started taking the piss out of Colin. Frank told Terry that Colin should audition for Doctor Frankenstein's monster. He only said it the once because Bill found out (Terry snitched on him). The worst part about Colin's crying was when he blew his nose. It started off with his hooter replicating the noise of a train going into a tunnel, and ended up with a bus honking in a peasouper. When Lassie eventually got his man Colin jumped to his feet, extended his arms, and clapped like the clappers. Someone asked me if I'd brought a sea lion with me. As the lights came on and the credits rolled I felt myself weakening. I was out of my seat and wanting to get the scam over with in case I bottled it. But, as usual, Colin insisted on waiting for the music to stop. Before we left, he blew his nose again and by now the hanky had become green and hard. Colin had this nasty habit of holding used hankies up for scrutiny and making them crackle. To spare him any embarrassment I told him to put the hanky away and gave him the clean one, which Mum had neatly folded and ironed for me. And do you know what he did?

He embarrassed me by saying, "You're my best mate, Ricky. And you have the best mum in the whole wide world."

I'd have preferred it if he'd called me a traitorous cunt.'

'My cheeks were still flushed when we left the cinema and sat on the steps watching the cars go by. Having just seen that heart-wrenching

Lassie film I knew Colin was ripe for the taking. I was wavering but the thought of holding a twenty-pound note in my mitt was too great a temptation. The closest I'd come to being rich was when Auntie Sheila gave me a ten bob note for my birthday. My performance wasn't on a par with Laurence Olivier but Colin swallowed it hook line and sinker. I regretted telling him that Sandy had cancer the moment the words left my mouth. Poor Colin, you should have seen his face as he said he'd get the money from his post office account. Glum wasn't the word. And when he started sobbing, I thought he'd never stop. I felt guilty about Colin, but I was more concerned that I'd accidently cursed Sandy and that he'd develop cancer for real. I decided to catch Colin on his milk round on Monday morning to put things right. I was going to tell him that the vet had made a mistake and I didn't need that twenty quid.'

'Just then an Austin A30 pulled up and hooted. It took me a while to realise that Mum and Dad were sitting in the front. I ran straight to the driver's side.

Dad wound down the window and said, "It isn't new and it isn't all paid for yet. It may not be an Austin Princess but it's only the second car in our street. There's a slight knocking in the engine but it drives fine."

Boy, was I excited.

I cried, "Why didn't you tell me, Dad?"

He replied, "We wanted it to be a surprise for when you came home." He paused and his expression became as glum as Colin's as he said, "You'd better have a word with your mother."

I dragged my gaze away from the dashboard. Mum's eyes were red; the rest of her face looked like it was made of alabaster.

She said hoarsely, "Ink has been taken poorly, dear. We're going to visit him in hospital." She dabbed her eyes with an embroidered hanky and observed Colin. "That film must have been a real weepy."

'As I climbed into the back of the car, I remember seeing Colin standing forlornly on the pavement, chin and shoulders slumped. There followed an excruciating silence and then Mum reaching behind her seat to search for my hand. If Mum and Dad spoke a word to each other on the drive, it passed me by. Fear and panic gripped me when we pulled into the hospital car park. Ink had promised he'd live long enough to see me grow up. As we entered the building another emotion came to prominence: anger.'

***

I patted my cheeks which were hot and slippery to the touch.

'Do you want hear about Ink and the hospital? Probably best we move on, eh?'

Raz sniggered.

'That old windbag finally getting his chips? Wouldn't miss it for the world, Kuchy.'

24

'The hospital smelt like Nanna's lav. Mum often joked that Nanna spent as much time disinfecting her lavatory as she did cleaning the rest of the rooms put together. Ink said it wasn't his fault because his old pipes were corroding and his aim wasn't what it was. Nanna suggested he should sit down while he did a piddle. Ink looked horrified and retorted that her suggestion was an affront to his manhood. The first person I saw was a Hattie Jacques lookalike in a lace hat who scared me half to death. The other nurses stiffened and then sped up when she addressed them.

"She's the matron," said Mum reverently.

Dad gauged the breadth of her behind and exclaimed, "I'd rather take my chances with a Tiger tank!"

When we got to the ward Mum squeezed my hand and said, "I'm sure Ink will be fine. Try not to worry, dear."

At least, I thought, Ink ain't copped it. Dad might, but I don't think Mum'd let me see a dead body. Nanna was sitting by Ink's bed. She spotted us, gave a little wave, and smiled. Mum returned the smile, if you can call it a smile. Her mouth flickered like a ventriloquist's when he hadn't got it quite right.'

'Nanna told Mum to stop fussing and kissed me on the top of the head. I was tall enough to see over her shoulder by now. A nurse was checking Ink's notes like they did in *Emergency Ward 10*. So far so good. His face wasn't as white as a sheet and he wasn't gasping for breath under an oxygen mask. Mum put her lips close to Nanna's ear. She tried not to let me hear. Fat chance.

"How is he, Dot?" she whispered.

Nanna appeared fraught and whispered back, "They think it might be his heart, Margaret."

All of a sudden the ward felt icy cold and goose bumps rose up the length of my arms. Auntie Sheila's two husbands had died of heart attacks in bed. Stupid, even for a ten-year-old, but I decided I was going to sleep in armchairs when I got old. The nurse looked along the ward and spoke to Nanna.

"The doctor's here. Perhaps you would like a word."

Mum said, "Ziggy and I will accompany you, Dot. Best they don't tell each other wartime stories. Ink gets quite agitated when they compare horrors. Ricky can stay and keep Ink company."

Everyone was talking as though Ink wasn't there. Nanna continued the tradition.

"That'll be nice. They can chat about Spurs. Ink says they're on the verge of something big with their Yorkshire manager."

Nanna thanked the nurse and Mum handed me the grapes she'd brought from home. She didn't have time to buy fresh ones and some of them were on the turn, although she'd taken the really sad ones out. I was so upset that I nearly lost my grip on the brown paper bag.

She said to me, "You can give Ink these, dear. He'd like that."

As the three of them set off to see the doctor, Dad looked back and said, "Make sure you offer them to Ink first. And no mention of Arsenal and Woolwich. You k'now how it gets him going."

I wouldn't have moved a muscle if Ink hadn't patted the bed and said, "Come and sit beside me, Ricky. Don't worry. I ain't going to kick the bucket just yet.'"

'I offered Ink a grape. He took one look and shook his head, saying he might have one later. There was a twinkle in his eye as he wiggled a finger to draw me closer. He lowered his voice.

"Don't worry, it ain't me heart."

I was old enough to know grownups told lies when they wanted to conceal something from the kids. Santa Claus being a good example.

"What is it then, Ink?"

He raised himself up on his elbows and looked left and right.

"Indigestion."

If Ink had said a runaway Electrolux had careered into his chest, I might have believed him straight out. When I had indigestion, Mum didn't send me to hospital but gave me Milk of Magnesia.

I replied, "Yeah, right."

His arms trembled with fatigue and he sunk back into the mattress.

"It's the truth, son. The man who makes the wills came round the other day. I'd had kippers for breakfast and sardines on toast for lunch."

"What's a will?"

"It tells who you'll leave your things to when you die. They'll be a nice surprise for your mum and dad sometime in the future. Don't worry, son. I'll keep me promise. I'm years away from croaking."

"Did the sardines go down the wrong way?"

"They went down a treat. As you know, I'm going a bit Mutt and Jeff. When the will man put his face closer to mine I burped straight into his face. Nanna's kept the gasmask she used in the war as a memento. She said if it weren't so small she'd make me wear it. The will man spluttered a bit and said if he had a smaller head he'd have a go at putting it on. Anyhow, the bloke didn't throw up but Nanna limited me to two cups of hot water a day after that. When I started getting the chest pains, I thought it must be my heart. Then I realised what it really was. Without regular hot water the acid builds up something rotten."

"Have you told the doctor what's wrong with you?"

"Let them work it out for themselves." He winked. "All these pretty nurses. One of them is going to give me a bed bath later. You won't let on, will you?"

I looked across the ward. Nanna had wrinkles but I'd never seen her face that creased before.

"But Nanna's worried sick."

"Just allow me this one bed bath with the blonde foreign nurse. She's Swedish. Well, I imagine she is. She has such a lovely smile.

That's not too much for an old man to ask, is it? Promise I'll tell them straight after."'

'Perhaps guilt had been brewing in my subconscious and it needed a trauma to release it: the hospital; the fear of death; the thought of Ink never sitting in his armchair again; Nanna lonely and disconsolate.

"Do you reckon Mush should bugger off back to his own country, Ink?"

His brow dropped and his bushy eyebrows covered half his eyeballs.

"Why do you ask?"

"Supposing loads of them come over here and take all the best jobs. I want to be a future Spurs goalie. Mr Mohammed mightn't chop off hands but loads of them do. Poor Bill Brown would let in a stack of goals and I wouldn't even get a trial at Spurs."

"I don't think Spurs would put a man in goal without any hands."

"Don't joke, Ink. I'm being serious. These Pakis…"

"Who?"

"You were in India and you ain't got a good word to say about them."

"Oh, that lot. You shouldn't take any notice of that. Soldiers always moan when they're away from home. Especially if it's hot and there's bugs everywhere. If I'd been posted to Australia I suspect it wouldn't have been any different. There were Indian soldiers fighting alongside us in the trenches. Good blokes most of them. They were just as much our brothers as the Scots. Don't tell the Jock in the next bed but many of us could understand them better."

"What about all these niggers that are coming over here from the West Indies? They're taking all our jobs, ain't they?"

"Don't call them niggers, Ricky. It ain't very nice. Blackies is more polite. As for Paki, that don't sound so bad. These blackies are doing jobs that no one else wants. If the bleedin' Tories paid a decent wage there'd be no need for them. Did you know Spurs had a black player before the Great War?"

"A nigg… a blackie? That can't be right."

"His name was Walter Tull. A good little dribbler he was. Not shoe polish black, looked like one of them half-caste fellers. Dark enough to be singled out, though. We sold him to Northampton."

"Why?"

"He was getting too much abuse and wanted to move to a provincial team. Not from us may I add. Bristol City and Aston Villa spectators were the worse. Those Brummies brought a couple of hundred down and were giving him hell. We soon sorted that lot out. A hobnail boot up the backside does wonders. Walter became a war hero. Don't suppose he'll ever be honoured for it though. What's this all about, Ricky? You ain't seen that Paki friend for a while. Is that it?"

'I blurted everything out. Frank's racist ideas; the keying; the forgery; even what went down with Colin.'

'Ink hummed and thought for a moment.

"Put Colin straight. Tell him the vet got Sandy confused with a cat. Colin don't like cats as much. And keep the Old Bill out of it. That's the way it's done around here, son." Followed by, "That little runt. How could he key the cars of his fellow Spurs supporters? My advice is to tell Frank to sod off and get that forgery back before the Paki finds it."

"It ain't that easy, Ink."

He reached out and pinched my arm. I think he intended it to hurt, but he was a fitter before he retired and his fingers had weakened and gnarled with overuse.

"How could you, Ricky? His dad fighting for us and all. And your dad. He fought the Nazis and now you're mixed up with a member of the Hitler Youth."

"I've heard Dad call them blackies monkeys before now."

"Maybe, but Ziggy's fair. He always gives people a fighting chance. Did he ever tell you the story of the Russian prisoner of war?"

"No."

"Ziggy helped liberate hundreds of prisoners of war from those terrible concentration camps. He hated the Russians almost as much as the Germans but the ones he found there were all skin and bone. He never picked on the helpless because they couldn't give him a good fight. So he gave a Russian slave he'd freed a gun and said he should shoot the Kraut commandant with it. The man was all ribs and couldn't even lift the damned gun. Ziggy had to hold it up for him so that he could pull the trigger."

"I don't understand your meaning, Ink."

"I'm not sure I do."

He clutched his chest. I would have been worried if he hadn't winked at me first. He talked out of the corner of his mouth.

"Look out! They're coming back. Mum's the word. Remember son, do the right thing by your Paki friend."

'Nanna walked back a hell of a lot faster than when she'd walked away. She gave a series of grunts and stood by the bed with her arms crossed. Ink knew the game was up, all right. He tried slithering under the covers but she pulled the sheets back and held up a bottle of Milk of Magnesia.

"The doctor's got your results. You old fraud, up you get."

Mum and Dad had a good laugh but I didn't join in. I was too busy working out ways to get that forgery back without getting collared.'

***

'You know what they say about old soldiers. Never mind, you can't win them all. What happened next, Kuchy?'

25

'I gobbled down my cornflakes and set off half an hour early that Monday morning. Can't remember what excuse I gave Mum, probably something to do with playing football.

I do remember her reply, however: "For one glorious moment I thought it was to do with your schoolwork, Ricky."

Dad looked over the top of the racing pages and chipped in with, "Some hope. You should k'now better, Margaret."

Luckily, the caretaker had already opened the gates by the time I arrived at school. I sneaked around the playground checking for unlocked doors. If I didn't act fast the other kids would arrive and so would the teacher on playground duty. Mr Gasson was on duty every Monday and he had the job of getting us in line at 8.45. Mr Gasson may have been the nicest in the classroom, but he gave the longest blast on the whistle and his voice boomed out if he didn't get a response:

"Form an orderly queue, children! No running once inside the building now!"

As if by magic, yelping jumping beans were grounded; baying hounds reduced to whimpers and thence to silence.'

I could feel Raz's breath on the nape of my neck. A blanket of cold sweat folded around me as he clamped my skull with the flat of his hands.

'Eyes front, Ricky. Thence into a weakness … and into the madness wherein now poor Kuchy raves. I don't recall Shakespeare being on the curriculum.'

I stiffened in anticipation of a horror about to befall me.

'Shall I carry on?'

'If I find you guilty of duplicity the punishment will be severe. To quote Shakespeare again; misery acquaints a man with strange bedfellows.' He squeezed my head that little bit harder. 'But there may come a time when I want to stretch out and have the bed all to myself.' My skull felt as if it was about to pop by the time he removed his hands. 'Yes, you may carry on, Ricky.'

I hadn't heard an "innit" for ages, if he ever said the word at all. His diction was beginning to resemble that of a university lecturer rather than an uncouth gang member. It made him no less scary, but more so, if that's possible. I became so paralysed with fear that I was incapable of begging for my life. What else could I do but seek solace in the past?

***

'As the toilets were in the playground I couldn't give that excuse to the caretaker. I was about to concede defeat when Maureen, the dinner lady, arrived and opened the door that led to the kitchen.

I sprinted towards her, calling out, "Wait up, miss! What's for dinner today?"

She held the door open and smiled at me.

"You're an early bird, Ricky. Sheep's heart and greens with spotted dick and custard for afters."

I replied, "Lovely grub," and meant every word of it.

Bath night was on a Sunday so my hair was soft and shiny. She always stroked my locks when they were freshly washed. I had one foot over the threshold before she'd finished stroking it.

She said, "Be a good boy. Go and play nicely now."

My foot didn't budge as the door closed slowly behind her. The door had one of those attachments which looked like a bicycle pump and prevented it from slamming. She'd disappeared around the corner before it clicked shut behind me and I tiptoed up the backstairs. The classroom doors were made of hardwood and toughened glass, the lower portion of which was frosty. The idea being that a teacher could look in but not a pupil. When I reached Mush's classroom I had to jump up and down to see inside. Having determined it was empty, I grasped the doorknob and said a prayer to our Jesus and their Prophet geezer, figuring two gods were better than one. My prayers were answered, and as the door opened I said ta and promised to call them again.'

'I'd just lifted Mush's desk lid when he walked in. I didn't have time to make up a plausible excuse.

I snatched the paper from his desk and snapped, "You don't want to know."

He stepped closer, cautiously.

"You have taken something from my desk. Please return it, Ricky."

Cornered, I went on the offensive and snarled, "Anyway, what the fuck are you doing here?"

He came closer, a little bolder this time. There was only a desk between us by now.

"It is a special time for Muslims. I'm allowed in to say my prayers before the others arrive. Mr Gasson let me in. He'll be up to check on me at any moment."

A boy in the playground hollered at another kid to give him his ball back. Several screeching voices backed him up. Screwing the paper into a ball, I stuffed it into my pocket.

"It ain't yours and I'm doing you a favour, mate."

He held the lid up and peered inside the desk.

"I recognised my own writing on that paper, Ricky. Tell me what else you have taken."

I felt like landing him one.

"It ain't your writing. Frank forged it. He's the one that's been keying the cars. People got scared and paid him to look after their motors while they were at the football. Don't think about shopping him because that won't go down too well around here."

He replied, "And you were in on it? What about the other Tottenham Boys?"

I hoped that if Mush became aware of the gravity of the crime, he wouldn't risk being put in the dock for it. Even so, he was getting too nosey for my liking and that got me agitated.

I threatened, "The others don't know about it. You'd better keep it that way if you know what's good for you, Paki."

He went through his desk and said. "Nothing seems to be missing, *Kuchy*. Truthfully, were you taking the forgery out or were you fitting me up? I believe that is the correct expression, *Kuchy*."

I snapped, "Don't call me names! I was doing you a favour mate. And I don't give a toss what you think."

He shook his head and held up his hands in apology.

"I'm not one for calling names, Ricky. I should have known better. Forgive me."

I'd have preferred it if he'd taken a swing at me.'

'I wouldn't say that I was inexplicably and suddenly overcome by remorse, but Ink's words had kicked in. His comments about Walter Tull and how a black man had played for Spurs and our supporters had stood up for him. You could hardly call it an epiphany but my acceptance of the superiority of white people had taken a dent. Conflict soon gave way to confusion and confusion to rage. Mush looked at my embittered face and started to cry.

He blubbered, "You were my friend. What have I done to upset you?"

I tried to block my emotions but the tap was turned to full and running green.

"How come you live in a palace? Whites are the ones what taught you things. I saw your big bath with the fancy taps. I ain't never been in one of them." He wiped his eyes.

"My father worked for the government in Pakistan. He tried to change things for the better, to make the country more modern, and we were driven out." I thought for a moment. Then it came to me.

"You mean driven out by the hand-chopper-offers and the stone-you-to-deathers?"

He said, "I wouldn't put it that crudely, but yes."

I took the ball of paper from my pocket and hurled it at his chest. "Here! Take the fucking thing!"

As he started to unravel the paper I charged towards the door. I stopped and looked back over my shoulder.

"'I'd destroy it if I was you, Mush. Remember, if you go to the Old Bill you'll really be for the chop.'"

'I'd never met a kid who could read so fast. He'd finished before I had time to open the door.

He cried, "Wait! I want to re-join the Tottenham Boys. I want you to arrange a vote. I want them to vote me back in and kick Frank out."

That stopped me dead in my tracks, all right.

"You what?"

He clasped his hands together and waved them in front of me.

"I beg you, call a meeting but don't mention Frank's involvement or any of this. Let me present the evidence. Tell them that if I'm voted back in I'll get my father to arrange a proper cricket match with a proper ball. We'll wear pads and gloves and he'll keep score."

The voices in the playground had melded into a wall of noise and it wouldn't be long before Mr Gasson blew the whistle. I flung open the door and hurried along the corridor towards the back stairs, weighing up the possibilities as I went. If I did what Mush wanted I'd be admitting that I'd deprived the others a slice of the action. On the other hand, the thought of playing a proper game of cricket with a proper ball was tempting beyond belief. I got to the top of the stairs and swung around. Mush's head and shoulders were poking out of the classroom.

I pointed at him. "Okay, mate. But I wouldn't hold your breath. Remember, no matter what Frank's done, loyalty runs deep in these parts."

I had a word with Bill after school. He was reluctant at first, but a proper cricket ball swayed him and a meeting of the Tottenham Boys was arranged for the following Saturday.'

***

Raz took the gun from his pocket and sprung towards the door; huge frame scarcely making a sound as it ate up the ground. He checked the ammo clip and put an ear to the glass panel. Had the Apache returned and found a way in? I hadn't heard glass breaking or a door being smashed off its hinges. What if it wasn't them? Perhaps the caretaker had arrived to ascertain if everything was secure. Perhaps the police had been tipped off. Raz looked back at me, a crayon drawing of a train reflecting in his shades.

'Keep talking, chief.'

26

He stood at the side of the door, back pressed against the wall. If the Apache burst in the first thing they'd see would be me, sat shivering and defenceless at the teacher's desk recounting obscure childhood memories. I had a strong suspicion that Mrs Beaker's jam wouldn't go down too well. Why had he kept the lights on? Was I the sacrificial goat tethered to a stake in the jungle clearing? I struggled to my feet with the purpose of creeping towards the back of the classroom before the tiger roared. He fitted the silencer and pointed the gun at me.

'Sit back down like a good little boy and continue talking about the days of yore.'

'I talk therefore I am. But for how long?'

'What's that, chief? Hope you ain't dissing Descartes! Don't worry, they're checking out each classroom in turn. Probably think the light in here is a ruse and don't want to get ambushed from behind. Suspicious cunts.'

He was the boss from the first minute we met, my nemesis, and now, it seemed, my protector.

'You will stop them before they get to me, won't you?'

'I ain't heard the end of the story yet, chief. No story's complete without an ending. Chill, man. Let me worry about them.'

The only way I'd chill was if he'd stuck me in a deep freeze.

I hadn't heard any sirens going off for a while and wondered if things had quietened down. Had the police had retaken the streets and surrounded the school? Maybe one of the residents had summoned the courage to call them. I'd spent a fair portion of my juvenile and adult life locking horns with the law. I was done for drunk and disorderly in my teens, warned for dope in my twenties, done for dope and lost my teaching post in my forties, obstruction in my fifties, and back to drunk and disorderly in my sixties. Whoopee! My life had turned full circle. What I'd have given to be busted and locked away in a police cell right then.

'They may be on my side for all I know. I'll shout out, you'll see if I don't.'

My words might have carried more of a threat if the delivery had been more Noddy Holder and less Enya.

'If you want to die then be my guest, Kuchy.'

'But I'm a sitting duck.'

'What's it to be? The devil you know or the ones who lurk in the shadows? I'll count to three and if you haven't plonked your fat arse down and commenced telling your story by then... one... two...'

***

'The meeting was held in Mr Reeves' coal yard. Bill's dad had gone to visit his brother in Hackney and had taken his wife, little Susan, and the Alsatian with him. The Alsatian always sat on the front seat, its enormous head poking out of the window.

Nanna saw Mrs Reeves huddled on the back seat of their Morris Traveller and commented, "He treats that dog better than he does his poor wife. I hope you don't do that when you become a man, Ricky."

I replied with an innocent's candour, "I'll try, Nanna. But I don't know if I'll be able to help meself. Girls get right up me..."

Before I could finish the sentence she tweaked my earlobe.

"Nice girls need good men to look after them. God made men stronger than women for a reason, but a gentleman should treat a lady with respect. And a pretty bunch of flowers wouldn't come amiss either."'

PC meant police constable back then.'

'Bill had made us promise to stay away from the old stable. The horse had been sold to gypsies and the ramshackle building was now used for storing bags of coal. He said we'd end up blacker than a ... he used the 'n' word … and that his dad would shut him in there overnight. Mr Reeves had replaced the horse with a flat-back lorry. It was a bit smoky and Dad reckoned it would soon conk out. Ink wasn't impressed either:

"You can't get manure from a lorry and you can't beat a horse in times of war and shortages. They don't need petrol and if things get dire you can always eat 'em."

I met Mush at the top of Park Lane and we walked the short distance to the yard. On the way, I reassured him that Sandy was locked in my house and Frank couldn't pull that sausage trick on him again. As we neared the yard Mush put his arm around my shoulders. I felt even more uncomfortable than when Dad took me to his big church up in London. No one smiled there and everyone else seemed to know what they were doing, even when the priests spoke foreign.

Mush said, "This vote means a lot to me, Ricky. I haven't told you before but our lives were threatened in Pakistan. That's why we fled to the home of the free."

I bent to tie up a shoelace, which wasn't undone. When I popped up again I kept a space between us.

"How come? Your dad don't chop off hands but you're still one of them, the same colour and all that."

He didn't respond. I guess he had other things on his mind. Besides, he'd have needed considerably more time to educate someone raised on atlases depicting half the world in imperial pink. It must have taken a lot of courage for him to challenge Frank face-to-face, not forgetting the other Tottenham Boys who'd given him such a hard time the last time they'd met. Before I knocked on the side door (the yard's main doors were massive and padlocked), I checked if he was having second thoughts.

"Do you really want to go through with this, Mush? Fuck Frank. He's a wanker. You don't have to prove anything."

His reply wasn't what I'd anticipated, although it should've been if I'd given it half a thought.

"I don't wish to lecture you, Ricky, but you are swearing more these days." He sounded superior and that got me riled.

"And what makes you think I'm going to vote for you, Mush? I might've been got at."

As irked as I was, he could tell that I wasn't being serious and said jokingly. "If you do that I'm well and truly sugared." He'd heard Mum say sugar instead of a swear word and continued, "The other boys don't know about your involvement in Frank's car-keying operation. They may turn on you when they find out. We can forget the whole thing if you like."

I wasn't going to back down. If truth be known, I drew courage from him. If the gang was under attack Bill would stand his ground no matter what, but Mush displayed another kind of bravery, one that I didn't appreciate till many years later. Right then, it was my contempt for Frank that governed my actions.

"Nah, they're bound to find out sooner or later. And that little cunt has it coming."

I rapped on the door before he could launch the inevitable rebuke.'

'Bill opened the door, peeked up and down the road, and promptly waved us inside. He was probably fantasising that he was Biggles and he and his crew were stranded behind enemy lines, or Dan Dare, or some such boy's comic book adventurer. Roy and Terry were sitting on the old coal wagon previously pulled by the horse. They were giggling, bobbing up and down, and slapping pretend reins. Frank sat on little Susan's swing. It was attached to a branch, which reached into the yard from a tree on the bombsite.

Mush took one look at the smirk on Frank's face and said, "Oh dear. This doesn't bode well."

I hadn't noticed the sunglasses sticking out of the top pocket of Frank's shirt.

He slipped them on and swaggered towards Mush like a Mafioso, curling his upper lip and snarling, "Let's get the rules straight, Paki. If it's a draw I stay and you sling your hook. Challenger's got to get a majority decision in a democracy, chum."

Mush did the last thing I would have expected of him. He squared up to Frank.

"I am Pakistani, actually. And we have fierce hill tribesman who are more than a match for your Grenadier Guards."

I glanced at Bill and we both smiled. A bag of feathers on the noggin would have either one of them taking a ten count.

Mush enquired politely of Bill, "Excuse me, but what happens if I get a majority support? Is Frank expelled immediately?"

Frank sneered, "No sweat. I'll sling me hook. *If* you get a majority."

I cut in, "Who made up these rules?"

Frank shrugged.

"It's the law of the land, mate. Can't get past that ... Paki lover."

The smarmy git clapped his hands in Bill's direction.

"Come on, Mr Chairman, let's get the proceedings underway."

I clenched my fists. Frank had taken me for a ride and it'd just dawned on me how much of a fool I'd been.

I totally lost it when Mush said, "I accept Frank's terms."

I brushed Mush aside and stormed up to Frank.

"I bleedin' well don't. I'll knock the crap out of you."

I might well have done if Bill hadn't intervened. He said he'd sort out the one who threw the first punch and ordered Terry and Roy down from the cart. Terry's clothes were covered in coal dust while Roy's had hardly been touched. Typical Terry. Bill told everyone to sit on the cobbles close to the tree and we all obeyed, except for Frank who hopped back on the swing, replaced his shades, and looked down on us with those coal-black eyes. I expected Bill to order him off. But Bill ignored him and sat cross-legged alongside me.

I hoped Frank would fall off that swing and crack his head open as he threw his arms about and ranted, "A bleedin' Paki wants me to sling me hook. I was born and raised around here. What kind of justice is that?"

Mush countered, "It's Pakistani and you're the one who has done all the bad things." He held up Frank's forgery (he'd done a good job of ironing out the crinkles). "And here is the evidence."

Frank countered by removing a folded newspaper page from his trouser pocket and unravelling it.

"That ain't got nothing to do with me, whatever it is. But this concerns us all." He flattened the paper and held it up. "I found this article in the *Daily Mail*."

Realising Frank was about to put the verbal boot into Mush, I objected on a point of law.

"It ain't the *Daily Mirror* so I don't know if it's admissible in court."

I'd heard that expression when Betty's Uncle Fred planned his defence. He'd been arrested for bashing a scab during a strike at Gestetner's.

Bill responded with a curt, "Overruled. Proceed, Frank."

Frank's probing eyes went from Terry to Roy and back again.

"If ever there's proof of how evil Pakis are then this is it."

He pointed at the article, which had a single word headline. It read: "BARBARIC!!"

After pausing for effect, he continued, "A woman in this Paki village was buried up to her waist and stoned to death. It took her half an hour to die."

Roy asked, "What she do? Bump someone off?"

Frank glowered at Mush.

"Nah. Her crime was that she was found alone talking to a married man. He probably only came round to fix her something or other. Blimey, if Betty lived in Pakiland she wouldn't last more than five minutes."

When Frank kept his gaze on Terry I began to get worried. I'd told Mush we could count on Terry's vote because he hated his clever dick brother.

My worries intensified when Frank said to Terry, "Imagine our own mum being stoned to death. Think on it, Tel.'"

212

'I was desperate to expose Frank for what he was, but didn't want it to appear that a younger boy had duped me into taking part in a scam. Especially one where he got the lion's share and robbed his fellow Spurs supporters.

Frank forced my hand when he turned on me and said, "And you're an innocent little lamb, are you Ricky boy?"

It didn't take a genius to figure out that Frank had already told them about the keying, but had conveniently omitted the bit about framing Mush.

My suspicions were confirmed when he added, "I've given each of the gang their cut from your little scheme. You didn't think I'd do the dirty on me friends, did you Ricky?"

I jumped up and grabbed the page.

"Bloody liar! It was all your idea."

Just in case he'd made it all up, I started reading the article. I only got to the end of the first paragraph before I slung it at him.

"So, what! Mush ain't like that."

'Mush rose to his feet.

"Thank you, Ricky. I'll take over from here." He addressed Bill. "It's true these things happen in my country. My father opposed them and we were driven out. He's written letters to *The Times* and the *Manchester Guardian*."

The point was lost on Terry.

"What? A soldier with a big furry hat in Manchester? How does he know one of them?"

I explained to Terry that the *Manchester Guardian* was a newspaper and went on the offensive.

"Do you know that Frank stole the keys to the scout hut and spends lots of time planning in there?"

That got Bill's attention.

"Planning what, Rick?"

If Bill was slightly agitated, then Terry was peeved off.

He said sulkily, "And he ain't told no one? That ain't fair. We could have had all kinds of fun in there. There's ropes and hoops and those big squashy balls you can bounce up and down on."

Bill told Terry to shut it and repeated, "Planning what, Ricky?"

I couldn't get it out fast enough.

"A new party based on bleedin' Hitler."

But Terry could never button it.

"A new party with Frank as the Further. That ain't fair either."

Frank retorted, "It's Fuhrer numbskull and I think Hitler got one thing badly wrong. We're the master race, not the bleedin' Germans. But whether the master race is German or English it must be whites only. No people the colour of shit and with deformed knees. Hitler would've eradicated Mush and his kind, made us all gods. It's called eugenics." He clapped his hands. "Come on Mr Chairman, get a move on."

'The way Frank spun his words and treated Bill was making me increasingly anxious. On any other occasion Bill would have clocked him one for cheek.

But Bill complied without making a fuss and cried, "All those who want Frank to sling his hook raise your hands!"

Mush and I raised our hands but Terry kept his at his side. I needn't have worried because he was only thinking things through. Frank may have given him a few bob, but that last numbskull had tipped the balance in our favour.

Bill continued, "And those who want Mush to sling his hook?"

Frank's hand went up first and I nipped in before Roy could follow the leader.

"Mush ain't done you no harm, Roy. Has Frank got something on you? There ain't no shame in being taken in by him."

Frank's top lip curled and he exposed his teeth. Picture a rabid Chihuahua.

He bawled, "Keep your fucking mouth shut, Roy, or you know what'll happen."

I doubt if Roy had heard a word I'd said. He'd heard Frank all right because he raised his hand without so much as a glance in my direction.

Frank cried triumphantly, "That's settled then," and jumped down from the swing. He shoved Mush in the chest. "Sling your fucking hook, Paki."

Mush pushed him back and said none too hopefully, "Bill hasn't voted yet."

When Frank saw Bill wavering, the little snide retorted, "Foregone conclusion, mate… Scotland the brave, eh Bill. Now do your duty and serve your country. Hurry it up. Your dad'll be back soon.'"

'If Frank believed his Scotland jibe would keep Bill compliant, he was badly mistaken. Bill shook his head and his brown hair tumbled over his eyes. He swept it back.

"Nah, can't do it. This voting shit ain't for me. Let Frank and Mush slug it out. What did Frank call it? Trial by ordeal, weren't it?"

Frank cosied up to Bill.

"Come on mate, don't you wish to reconsider?"

Bill hadn't got half the temper of his dad but you didn't want to be around if he lost it. When his face went so red that you couldn't see his freckles, that's when you knew you were in trouble. If Frank was a Chihuahua then Bill was a Rottweiler. Bill punched the flat of his own hand.

"Do as I say Frank or I'll spill your fucking teeth. Right, men! Give them some space and let them get on with it."

'Frank and Mush must have beaten the world record for throwing powder-puff punches, most of which were air shots. The fight, if you can call it that, went on for a good few minutes to a chorus of boos and slow handclaps. Things livened up when Frank started fighting dirty. Panting, he stopped dancing and held out his hand.

"Call it a draw, mate?"

Terry shook his head so vigorously that it was a wonder it didn't come off.

"Don't trust him, Mush."

Mush didn't hear him. He went to take Frank's hand and got head-butted across the bridge of his nose for his trouble. I thought he'd crumble but he wiped the blood away with his sleeve and threw a punch that might have knocked Bill off his feet. It caught Frank flush, sending his weedy frame reeling into the gates. Frank slid down a panel and ended up wailing on his backside. I was tempted to give Frank a few slaps of my own but could just hear Mush's response if I had: kicking a man when he's down isn't the gentlemanly thing to do, Ricky. In many ways, Mush was more English than the English, if you get my meaning.'

'Bill went across and glared down at Frank.

"Ricky weren't the only one taken in by this little shit. He promised me a Scalextric if I agreed to be the muscle in a protection racket he'd planned. That Paki…" Bill glanced at Mush and held up a hand. "Sorry, mate. That Pakistani family what moved in down Scotland Green have two sons of our age. Put it this way, their mum gave them two bob a day spending money but they only had a tanner each when they arrived at their school."

He grabbed Frank by the collar and hauled him to his feet. Two of Frank's buttons pinged across the cobbles and Terry kicked them away before Frank had a chance to pick them up.

Terry shrieked, "Just wait till mum sees … numbskull!"

I opened the small door for Bill and he pushed Frank into the street, shouting, "Find a book on Hitler and shove it up your arse, Frank.'"

'Bill told us to stand in the centre of the yard, but Roy held back.

Bill put his arm around him and said, "You weren't the only one to get hoodwinked by that little tosser. Come on, mate. There's something I'd like you to do, something we've both got to do."

Bill went up to Mush and shook his hand.

A broad smile formed on Mush's face, and like a football manager giving a rousing half-time pep talk, Bill cried, "Come on you Tottenham Boys, say it good and loud."

We put our hands one on top of the other with Mush's at the very top.

In unison, we screeched, "All for one and one for all."

After a few hearty back slaps we gave a second rendition that was louder than the first. Except for Terry, that is. He was busy making an aeroplane out of that page from the *Daily Mail*. To be fair it did sail right across the yard and over the gate.

It had just disappeared from view when Frank kicked the gates and bawled, "Paki cunt! I'll fucking kill you no matter how long it takes. Who the fuck do you think you are?"

Mush wiped away a dribble of blood from his lip.

"Me? I'm a Tottenham Boy, mate."

27

For a few minutes Raz hadn't interrupted me. The lull did little to calm my nerves, and with Mush on the verge of departing Tottenham, my fear of death hit critical. The maniac broke the silence by grinning and strolling across the classroom to give me a Chinese burn. It felt as if he'd plunged my arm into a fire, but he knew I couldn't scream for fear the Apache would hear. I choked on the pain as his supersize hands stretched my skin. Just when I thought his intention was to make me shriek he let go.

As I rubbed my wrist he patted me on the back and said, "That's my brave boy. Pray continue, Ricky."

Expert torturers need to have their timing spot on if they're to break the victim without killing him. At least, not until they've extracted all the information they require…

***

'A few days later, Mush told me that his family were returning to Pakistan. The country had a new regime and his father was offered a top post in the government. Mr Mohammed's spy HQ turned out to be a newsagent's that he'd invested in. It was to be run by a cousin of his who'd recently flown over from Pakistan. The day before it was due to open, the Mohammeds held a farewell party there and my family received an invite. Dad had ruined Mum's turning on party by inviting Fred and she was looking forward to dressing up and going out. Dad tried to make it up to her by paying for a new frock, something he regretted after spending hours sitting on stools outside ladies' changing rooms, flicking through the racing pages without being able to place a bet. She eventually plumped for a floral design much like the one she had before. Dad trooped back into the house and told me he could hardly tell one frock from the other. I secretly counted the flowers and informed him that her new frock had three more than the old one with more yellow. He promised to make it worth my while if I told her how lovely she looked and how I preferred the new frock over the old. She only did one twirl but I must have said, "Real fancy," six times before Dad whispered, "K'nock it on the head," and slipped me a florin.'

'They had more cars in Enfield Town than in Tottenham, but there was plenty of room either side of Mr Mohammed's Austin Princess. Dad drove straight past the sweet shop and parked our old A30 a little way down the road.

"It might not be as pricey as his but I'm proud of it," said Mum.

She made Dad turn around and park alongside Mr Mohammed's car. The first time Dad drove the A30 in our street he went slowly up and down three times. Mum told him not to show off but he said he was only checking the suspension. A similar sort of lecture awaited me as I'd got dressed for the party. Mum had me wear the dark grey jacket and trousers she'd recently bought at the church jumble sale (the shirt and tie were purchased at the Co-op).

I'd complained, "What's the point? Mush'll be wearing his flash suit."

She replied, "It's Mushtaq, dear. And be grateful for the clothes on your back and the food that goes in your tummy."

Try telling that to an eleven year old.'

'I got quite a shock when we went inside the shop. I'd never seen so many brown faces and they were all smiling. Their teeth were so white that I thought they must clean them with Colgate three times a day. The men looked pretty much alike, although one of them was very fat and I thought of asking Mum if I could be introduced to him because I'd be able to tell him apart. The same went for the women. I hadn't seen that many head coverings since Dad took me to his Catholic church up London. Mr and Mrs Mohammed came over to greet Mum and Dad while Mush greeted me. After giving Dad a firm handshake, Mr Mohammed directed them to a bunch of people drinking cordial by the counter. One of the Pakistanis was checking how the till worked while another was straining to put things on the top shelf. To break the ice, Dad asked the till operator what he did in the war. When the man said he looked after the family goats, Dad moved on to the stacker, who'd gone from tiptoe to standing on a box. He suggested that the top shelf should be lowered to make it easier to reach *Playboy*. The man thanked him and said he had just ordered twenty copies of *The Beano* but he'd ordered a few *Playboys* to see how the kiddies liked them. Mum gave Dad a proper dirty look and Mr Mohammed dashed over to save the day. Our host offered my parents cordial and introduced Dad to a crinkled old man with a large moustache who used to be a sepoy. If it wasn't for the silver hair and brown skin, the bloke could've been mistaken for Lord Kitchener (a poster of him hung on Ink's landing).'

'While Dad and the old soldier were comparing the various merits of artillery pieces, Mrs Mohammed directed Mum to a gaggle of women who were chattering away in their own language. Mrs Mohammed asked them in English what they were talking about and said it would be polite if they would also speak in English. One of the women replied that they were debating the vagaries of the British weather. I think Mum was glad they weren't discussing curry recipes in case they asked her to join them for a food tasting. She glanced over her shoulder to make sure Dad was behaving himself and took the women through the seasons; how the English might grumble but they should count their blessings (she'd seen a programme on monsoons on telly). She began with bracing March winds and April showers and how it had snowed in June when we got back from Southend.

One of the women shivered and muttered, "Oh dear".

Mum reassured her by saying that was just a one off.'

'Mush said he'd bring me a tray of special sweeties, which were in the storeroom. I told him I'd come with him, but he insisted that it was a holy place and I'd only been a Muslim for an afternoon. Having inspected the chocolate on display in the shop (Dad warned hands off), I'd almost licked my lips away before he returned a minute or so later. The adults were making a hell of a din, but they all heard me groan and say "Oh no", when Mush produced a tray of pink cham chams. He told me to tuck in before the aaloo keema arrived. My face went so pale that Mum made her excuses and asked me if I was coming down with something. I forced down two pink things in quick succession and planned to tell Mush that I was stuffed and there was no room left for the curry of death. I was on my third pink thing when Mrs Mohammed arrived carrying a tray loaded with miniature chocolate bars. There were Mars bars, KitKats, Bounty bars, all my favourites and more. Mum and Dad were in on the dodge and every-one had a good laugh at my expense. I didn't care because I was in seventh heaven. Mum told me to be careful with the wrappers and to finish one bar before I started another. Within minutes, I was rum-maging through a sea of wrappers looking for uneaten goodies. Mush ate more daintily than me and stuck to KitKats. Fortunately for him a KitKat was the last bar left standing. I got my mitts on it first and was about to tear off the wrapper when I caught Mum eyeballing me. Whether I would have offered it to Mush without that look of hers, "do the right thing Ricky", is debatable. I do know that it felt good when I gave it to Mush, and even better when he broke it in half and offered to share.

He said, "Red Indians have blood brothers but we are chocolate brothers, Ricky."

I'd have been a chocolate brother with the Pied Piper but that mo-ment was special. We each put a KitKat finger into our mouths and tried to resist biting it. I likened the showdown to the Old West and who drew first out of Wyatt Earp and Bill Clanton. The argument over which one of us succumbed carried on until the next batch of chocolate arrived. I swear, Mush's jaw twitched and that's the only reason I bit into mine.'

'The last memory I have of Mush is of us hugging each other in a storeroom crammed with boxes of Cadbury's finest. There were tears in our eyes, chocolate smeared around our mouths, and we swore to be friends for life. Naturally, I didn't let on to the other Tottenham Boys about any of that. I did boast that I'd pigged out on more chocolate than Alf stocked in his entire shop. I still think about Mush from time to time. He sent me a postcard when he arrived in Karachi. Mum helped me write a reply but he didn't respond. Ink said my letter probably never got there because their postman nicked it and sold the stamp. I kept checking the mail for weeks, if not months, in the hope he'd write again. He never did. I regret losing touch with him but I was only a boy. You know how it is. I didn't even stay in touch with Bill or Roy when I left school. During my fresher year at university, I moved away from Tottenham to the more salubrious climes of Crouch End. Sometime later, I heard that Bill had fulfilled his dream and become an Olympic weightlifter, while Roy had joined the army and had been posted to Germany. I read an article in *The Guardian* decades later, which related how Mush had taken over from his father as a leading reformer in Pakistan. He was especially keen to promote girls' education in conservative tribal areas. I might have sent him a good luck message if I wasn't in the middle of my second mid-life crisis. If the two sets of parents had stayed in touch it might have been a different story. Dad was more concerned about sending food parcels to his two brothers in Poland, who had been arrested during the Poznan bread riots. Mum was more intent on keeping me on the straight and narrow.'

***

Raz crashed his fist down on my desk. I gripped the sides so hard that my knuckles might have been washed in new-improved Daz. The fact that I couldn't see his eyes didn't mean that I couldn't tell they were ablaze with hatred.

'Frank! What happened to him?'

'Easy, man … after his exile he only ventured out with his mother. I got fleeting glimpses of him at his bedroom window during the ensuing weeks, book in hand usually. Terry was as happy as Larry and did keepie-uppies beneath Frank's bedroom window at every opportunity. Football was the one thing Terry could do better than Frank. The following summer the Lamberts moved down Fulham way and Frank attended that school for gifted children. Terry stayed in touch for a while via his mum and then we lost contact. When I was thirteen Frank turned up at Spurs wearing a Chelsea scarf. This was before the days of the skinheads and widespread football hooliganism so the police were unprepared for what went down. Bill was all for steaming in, but Frank was surrounded by evil-looking men, some of whom must have been nigh on thirty years old. Roy went looking for reinforcements and when Frank saw Harry Hooper's big brother, Ronnie, and his mates charging down Paxton Road, he gave a Nazi salute and hid at the back of the Chelsea crew.'

'Oh, I nearly forgot. Soon after Frank was ejected from the Tottenham Boys, he hired Harry Hooper to sort Bill out - Frank offered Harry a whole one pound note to bash Bill's brains in and to kidnap Mush. Harry and Bill met over Lordship Rec and it was one hell of a scrap. Both ended up with a closed eye and bloody nose and, as referee, I pronounced it a draw. I wouldn't say Harry and Bill became the best of friends after that, but there was mutual respect. So much so that Harry told Frank to stuff his quid "and this kidnapping lark", and said that the next time he saw him he'd bash his brains in. The reason I'm mentioning it is that while the Spurs and the Chelsea mobs slugged it out, Harry tapped Bill on the shoulder and said, "Let's get him, mate." Harry, Bill, Roy and me worked our way around the back of the melee in search of Frank. We were lucky not to be sucked into the fighting and at one point Bill managed to get a good dig into a Chelsea who had his back turned to us. All I can remember of the man is that he had long hair (it covered his ears), and a posh accent. He cried, "You little bleeder" and when he turned on Bill, Harry kidney-punched him. When he went for Harry I kicked him behind the knee, and as he spun in my direction, Roy kicked him in the other knee. Think of a clan of hyenas harassing a lion over a kill. But before we could nab Frank, the biggest Chelsea bloke shouted to be heard. He spoke common, just like us. "Fuck this for a laugh. We'll get 'em at the bleedin' Bridge" and his firm did a runner. The Old Bill had finally arrived on the scene by then and Ronnie thought it better his mob didn't chase after them as he was on probation. I'd grown to despise Harry Hooper at junior school. I especially hated the way he continued to call Mush a Paki while the rest of us had learned to show him respect. Years later, and I still didn't like Harry much - but I could count on him as a Tottenham boy, and as the Chelsea scarpered down High Road, we stood shoulder to shoulder singing North London la-la-la, North London la-la-la.'

A cold draught whipped into the classroom from under the door. My nerves were so raw that it felt as if Jack Frost was massaging my ankles. Had someone opened the door at the end of the corridor? Raz pointed the gun at my head.

'Concentrate. Was that the last time you saw Frank?'

'There… there was one other occasion.'

It occurred to me that my legacy wouldn't be a book, a song or some heroic or altruistic achievement honoured by society. It would be bits of bone and grey matter splattered over kiddies' drawings on a classroom wall. Landscapes and seascapes morphed into abstracts in one blinding flash. Roll over Kandinsky and dig those fragments and sinews. His finger tightened around the trigger.

'When?'

'A few years later… I was in my last year of sixth form when he came back to the street driving a black car. He was spouting racist nonsense about a new far-right party he was setting up. There were a lot more immigrants in Tottenham by then, Afro-Caribbean mainly. I suppose he thought it was a fertile recruiting ground for lumpen whites.'

'Was anyone with him?'

'Surprisingly enough, Terry. He was wearing a gold chain around his neck and a gold watch on his wrist. Talk about a dapper suit. We assumed they'd pulled off a con or a heist.'

'And did any of the Tottenham Boys join Frank's party? Did you? Did you give any more Nazi salutes?'

'Are you kidding? Mush had been our friend and Frank had turned Chelsea. I can't recall the make or model of the car, but it was very sturdy. Bill threw a brick at the windscreen and it bounced off. The paintwork wasn't so lucky, especially after I ran my house key down the side of it.'

'And that's the last time you saw him?'

The way Raz couched the question left me in no doubt that I needed to give him the answer he sought. Not only that, but I needed to deliver it in such a way that he was convinced I was telling the truth.

'Yes, I swear. I never wanted to lay eyes on him again and never did.'

Raz took the gun away from my temple and went back over to the door.

He gripped the handle and said, 'Thank you, Kuchy. That's all I wanted to know. I had to be sure.'

'And what of my parents? You promised.'

'They're dead. Get over it.'

I'd never felt anger like it before, or since. I'd have jumped off London Bridge if it meant taking him with me.

'That's all you fucking wanted to know!'

'Yep. Hush now.'

He ignored the junior chair I'd hoisted over my head and put his ear to the glass panel. I had every intention of crashing it down on his bonce, but after I'd advanced a few strides, my self-preservation instinct cut in (cowardice for short). Next time, I told myself as I put the chair down.

He whispered, 'Stay put,' before easing open the door and slipping into the corridor.

I heard a series of muffled grunts. And then, silence.

28

I lay at the back of the classroom with my feet wedged under a tiny desk. It smelt bad and it wasn't much of a hiding place. For starters, I couldn't be sure that someone entering the room wouldn't see my stomach rising above the desktops or hear my breathing, which was heavier than an Iron Maiden album. The silence was as agonising as the pains which racked my body. The lump on my head throbbed worse than ever and I found it hard to think coherently. How long had it been since he sallied forth to confront the forces of evil? Five minutes? Ten? I clung onto the faint hope that the forces of the law had vanquished him. Better still, that he and his adversaries had stabbed, shot, and throttled each other. Preferably stone dead, but tetraplegia would do nicely.

One of the blinds hung askew, allowing beams of light to stream into the room, and adding a fresh perspective to the cluster of crayon drawings. A halo now hovered over the matchstick man and steam billowed from the funnel of the lopsided train. Flames sheeted from the house and the purple boat was sinking in a tangle of wavy blue lines. I thought the last two artists should reduce their sugar intake and lay off *Call of Duty*. It may not have held a candle to a 60s psychedelic light show, but it did herald the arrival of dawn. I extracted my feet from under the desk and rolled onto my side. Placing the flat of my hand on the desktop, I prayed that whoever constructed that teeny piece of furniture had made a better fist of it than I did with a flat-pack from IKEA. It took my weight and I was up, but hardly away, pushing my stiff back against the wall, taking small sideway steps, aiming to make one drawing at a time. I felt nauseous and that bloody smell was trailing me. From that loftier vantage point I could tell that the boat was still afloat and bobbing nicely in a gentle swell. I crept up to the house, which wasn't burning at all, but had been drawn in bright red using overzealous hand strokes. I stopped and listened again. Nothing. Maybe Raz had gone and taken Oik's body with him. A few longer crab-like steps and I was up to the lopsided train. Whoever drew it should have seen a doctor and had their tiny inner ears examined. As for the matchstick man, it wasn't Lowry-inspired but an electricity pylon, the strands of hair trailing in its wake downed power cables. The sound of my breathing resembled a blacksmith's bellows as I left the wall and opened the drawer on the teacher's desk. I grabbed the paper knife and tucked it into my belt. Grasping the door handle, I put my lobe to the glass panel.

My sweaty palm slipped on the round copper door handle. I wiped it on my trousers and tried the handle again, opening the door just wide enough to poke my head into the corridor. There was no sign of life, or death, and the stairs looked so very far away. Who knew what terrors I'd encounter at the bottom, or if the door to the outside world was unlocked. I settled for the classroom opposite, which I made without coming under enemy fire. Once inside, I closed the door behind me as soundlessly as I could and headed for the window. The daylight, such as it was, passed directly through the vinyl blinds. I reached the second blind from the front without mishap, knelt, and drew the edge away from the glass. The street, like the playground, was deserted.

I inspected them for a second time and mumbled, 'Maybe he's gone. Maybe I'm alone.'

A hope instantly extinguished when I glanced over my shoulder. Light speared into the room through the crack I'd left between the window and the blind. It caught a man full in the face.

Jess sat bolt upright at the teacher's desk; mouth and eyes what you might expect to find on a fishmonger's counter. Forget apparitions and things that go bump in the night; Raz's associate had just been cast into the Underworld by Cerberus and had come face-to-face with Beelzebub. I couldn't see a gun, although his arms were at his side and

228

his hands were out of my line of vision. In the throes of panic, I almost asked him if he was dead. As ridiculous as it may seem, a field trip to Battle Abbey in 1981 sprang to mind. I remembered the year because that's when Ricky Villa scored the greatest ever Wembley goal. One of my pupils, Roger Spate, was more interested in a lifeless badger beneath a ruined wall than the dissolution of the monasteries. He stuck a stick into its ribcage to see if it really had left this mortal coil. Thinking Roger's wasn't such a bad idea, I removed the paper knife from my belt and pondered where I should prod first. Unethical medical practice, maybe. But it sure beat looking for a pulse on that creep.

His ear seemed the logical choice. Ears are sensitive and on the periphery. Basically, I'd have more time to execute an evasive manoeuvre if he came to. It then occurred to me that I really should check if he had a gun before shoving a paper knife into his lughole. I moved cautiously towards the front of the desk, keeping my eyes trained on his sallow face. If his eyes closed and flipped open again I'd have been out of there before he discovered that he was in Tottenham and not the Underworld. Although recent events did suggest they were interchangeable. As I edged closer, I could see that his bony hands were empty; curled fingers and dirty nails digging into low-slung jeans. Sir Francis Drake would have searched the body for a gun, stripped it of all its valuables, and got the drop on Raz if he returned. Mary Seacole would have been more concerned about Jess's wellbeing than her own safety. Me? I jabbed the knife into his ear and hopped back. His body tipped a little to the right but he didn't groan or wince. The ear wasn't a ghastly white and drained of blood, more of a seashell in colour. I thought, that's a good sign, isn't it? But the knife hadn't left a mark and my second thought was that he must be dead. Living or dead, I was none too thrilled about the prospect of rummaging through his effects. I was building up the courage to stick my hand in his pocket when someone tapped me on the shoulder. Have you ever blown into a peak flow meter? That's how quickly the air left my lungs.

Raz made no attempt to lower his voice. If anything, it was even louder than usual, and hideously jovial.

'Easy does it, Kuchy. He surrenders.'

If Jess and Oik were dead, I didn't rate my chances of survival very highly. Two corpses or three? What was the difference to him? And it wasn't as if any emotional attachment had developed between the kidnapper and kidnapped as in the Stockholm syndrome.

'Please tell me he's just drugged. And the same goes for Oik.'

He shrugged.

'Anything to please. They're just drugged.'

Before I could ask him to prove it, he produced a gun from his pocket.

'This what you're looking for?'

I dreaded the answer but had to ask the question.

'What are you going to do with me?'

'Could shoot you but that would leave too much blood. Can't leave any evidence.' He shaped his hands into talons. 'Throttling is a possibility.'

I glanced at Jess to see if there are any marks on his throat. As far as I could tell there were none.

'Is there a third possibility? One where I leave this school breathing?'

'Sure. We get the hell out of here and go our separate ways. But that would depend…'

'On what?'

'If I believe your story and whether you're going to snitch.'

'I won't say a word… and with Jess gone there's one less to share the spoils.'

'And what spoils would they be, Kuchy?' he asked, putting the gun away and moving closer.

I tightened my grip around the knife and slammed it into his chest. When he didn't flinch, I thrust it into his ribcage with all the force I could muster. I followed up with a flurry of blows that got gradually weaker till my arm fell limply at my side. Thinking he must be wearing a bulletproof vest I retreated, reaching blindly out behind, until my buttocks pressed against the desk and my spine attempted the limbo. He held out a hand and I meekly placed the knife in his palm. He scraped the sweat from my forehead and chin, like a barber with a cutthroat razor. Licking the blade clean, he made a movement with his mouth reminiscent of a wine taster.

'I do believe this perspiration is a tad less salty than Oik's or Jess's. Mm, perhaps the slightest hint of whisky, two blends if I'm not mistaken. Your shakes seem to be getting worse, blud. I bet this is the longest you've been without a drink. Kuchy, oh Kuchy, what happened to that liberal teacher, the sober one who wanted to win hearts and minds? We're hoodies. We're deprived and need understanding, heaps and heaps of TLC.'

'And I'd love the opportunity to give it to you. How about we meet in Starbucks a week on Tuesday? We can discuss your socialisation inadequacies over a cappuccino.'

'A joker to the end, eh Kuchy?'

'If you kill me, you'll have three bodies to dispose of. I assume Oik has copped it.'

He looked at Jess and sneered.

'Been to see how the cunt got in. Smashed a window in the caretaker's hut and stole a key to the main building. Lucky I didn't reset the alarm. I've returned the key and put a brick inside the hut. One smashed pane won't cause too much suspicion after last night. As for your story, I'm going to give it a pass mark and write in your report: "Ricky could do better."'

'Does that mean I get to live?'

'If you promise to be a good boy and not tell tales. I've made a call and I'm meeting my business associates in a place far away from here. It was fortunate for you that I got through.'

'What could I tell the police anyway? I don't know what you look like beneath the mask. Tottenham's full of hooded black guys… please don't take that the wrong way.'

He bent the knife till the tip touched the handle, then straightened it again like it was made of rubber.

'You've seen the Devil once, white boy. If he pays you another visit you won't be so lucky.'

He sighed and slid his arms under Jess's armpits, hoisting him over his shoulder fireman fashion.

'Come on, Kuchy, time to split. Hold the doors open for me, there's a good chap.'

'What about my camera? I need it for work. And my mobile's in bits.'

'I did you a favour with that old Casio. If I were you, I'd pay Car-phone Warehouse a visit pronto. You'll get your camera back, although your picture gallery has shrunk somewhat. I've left the snap of the down-and-out sitting in the snow. You really should send that one to *The Big Issue*. Oh, and I also saved the best one of your dick. I thought you might use it to entice wrinkly old girls in retirement homes.'

'The way things are going I might just do that.'

'Come on, let's play follow my leader. You're good at that.'

I flung open the classroom door and dashed ahead to open the one at the top of the stairs. As we went I examined Jess for signs of life and regretted not taking his pulse. His forehead smacked against the base of Raz's back, multiple times, without so much as a groan. If he wasn't dead he must have had his snout in a feedbag full of animal tranquil-liser. Raz pointed at a rucksack hanging on the doorknob at the bottom of the stairs.

'Your gear's in there. If you try to take a picture of me, I'll smash the camera over your head.' He held his nose. 'Your personal hygiene's down to you, chief.'

'Your kindness knows no bounds.'

He approached the alarm panel. I was scared he'd ask me to hold Jess but the deadweight on his shoulder appeared no more hindrance to him than a school satchel. He took the gadget from his pocket and did something that caused the panel to bleep. He nodded towards the main door.

'Shift it, Kuchy. We'll be out of here before you know it.'

Once we were in the playground, he opened a large green commercial wheelie bin and leant inside. He extracted Oik, bound head and foot like a supermarket turkey, and slung him over his other shoulder. I was a good ten yards ahead of him at this stage, but that yardage quickly dwindled to nothing. A second later he was ahead of me, and increasing his lead with every stride. When I finally got to the railings he crouched and made a stirrup with his hands.

'Imagine I'm Bill and you're scaling the vicarage wall, Kuchy.'

Both bodies remained lodged on his shoulders, yet his breathing was so even that he might just as easily have been relaxing in an armchair. I used to squat a hundred and forty kilos in my heyday. I swear that guy could have managed ten reps with an articulated lorry on his back. I slung the rucksack over my shoulder and placed my foot in his interlocked hands, lunging for a handhold like a contestant in that old game show, the one where competitors had to race each other across rubber objects in swimming pools and scale walls with pegs for grips. Clasping the top of the railing, I hooked one leg over at the second attempt, cursing the other leg till it followed suit. Without a thought for my dodgy ankle, I jumped and was in mid-air when Raz and his guests freefell past me. What was that old conundrum? Dropped from the same height, which would hit the ground first, a hundredweight of feathers or a hundredweight of coal? I'd always thought that was a load of bollocks. Somehow, I avoided falling flat on my face and it took four stumbling steps to regain my balance. I steadied and my haggard reflection stared back at me from his black shades.

'Who the hell are you, Raz?'

'Me? I'm just a Tottenham boy, mate.'

29

I looked back to see Raz turning the far corner, the two youths hing-
ing on his broad shoulders showing no more signs of life than the
squished pigeon in the centre of the road. As I reached the crossroads,
an engine fired up from somewhere behind me. If Raz had planned
the whole thing in advance, maybe had he a vehicle parked close by?
Had he hotwired one? Perhaps he was picked up by a person or
persons unknown. The police were stretched that night, some might
say incompetent, but even PC Plod couldn't miss a giant hoodie
humping two bodies halfway across the borough on foot. As the
distance between us grew, but one dilemma occupied my mind:
should I call the cops? I pitted paranoia and self-preservation against
conscience. If I didn't report his crimes I might become an accessory
to murder. But his victims were hardly boy scouts and he wasn't the
type of bloke you'd want to testify against in open court. His true
friends might seek to silence me. But he was a danger to society. A
little child might get caught in the crossfire. It was my moral duty. But
even if I wanted to I couldn't give the police a detailed description of
either the suspect's features or his vehicle. No point involving the cops
just yet, was there? I'd ponder on it again after a good measure of
scotch had slipped down my gullet. All well and good, but first I had
to get clear of Tottenham. For that to happen, I needed my car to be
where I'd left it, and in one piece. Under normal circumstances I'd
have jumped at the chance to put in an insurance claim. That old Fiat
didn't need to be petrol-bombed to produce copious quantities of
black smoke.

It had been my intention to avoid the High Road and weave my way
through the backstreets. But a group of youths heading in my direction
looked far too boisterous for my liking. They were swinging bulging
carrier bags and clutching sealed boxes. One even managed to piss

against a wall with a smart television perched on his shoulder. They obviously hadn't spent their hard-earned dole money at Wood Green Shopping Centre. After a jolly good night's looting perhaps they didn't have the energy to hassle me. I was fragile enough as it was and couldn't take the chance. Keeping a wary eye on the gang, I swung a right and cut into Lansdowne Road. When I reached the junction for the High Road, I found the carpet store reduced to a buckled shell. The structure looked as if it might collapse at any moment and a weary fire crew were dousing smouldering embers from a safe distance. Professionalism and penury dictated that I get the camera out of the rucksack, but I wasn't in the right frame of mind for work. I observed an elderly couple clinging to each other from behind a barrier that had been erected on the opposite side of the road. I got the impression that for them, as for me, it was more than glass, metal and concrete that had gone up in smoke. I imagined them as a courting couple skipping through the Co-op which used to occupy the building; laughing and holding hands as they bounced on beds and inspected the inside of wardrobes. I wondered if the mayhem had triggered memories of an era in which Facebook didn't exist. When front doors were left unlocked and when neighbours were true friends; who would drop in on each other if they were sick or in trouble, to be consoled with a pat, a hug, and a chat over a brew, milk and two sugars, or a glass of warm beer.

Hardly a day goes by when I don't think of Mum. She'd have been heartbroken to see the building torched. When we shopped at the Co-op it would usually be for socks or underpants, the occasional shirt or blouse. The furniture she hankered after was well out of our price range. Sometimes she would run her hand over the top of a table or a dresser and smile to hide her disappointment. I remember a long tube which conveyed the money to the cashier's office. I remember how amazed I was at the speed it travelled. I tried to catch it up once and ran slap bang into a hat stand. Mum knew her dividend number by heart. When our card was marked up at the end of the month, the points we accumulated usually didn't stretch beyond two pairs of cut-price socks.

Raz had sucked a large slice of the happiness out of my past and dredged up memories best left forgotten. Mercifully, he didn't delve into my teenage years or I might have thrown myself out of a window. I could imagine him smirking as he made me narrate the trauma of Sandy's death, when my beloved dog was little more than skin and bone. Gloating, when I told him that Nanna and Ink had become too frail to climb the stairs and were packed off to die in a home (they left my parents their flat and I finally got my own bedroom). Rejoicing, as he made me relive that day in 1967, the lashing rain, the slap of the windscreen wipers, the glare of approaching headlights, the screams as the car veered onto our side of the road and my parents were crushed under the weight of buckled metal. The fear and panic that gripped me as I reached over the back seat and found my mother's limp hand. The bastard had made me bring them back to life and now I'd lost them all over again.

My early days were happy and I'd made them sound awful. Dad wasn't a shallow, uncaring racist. He did hours of overtime to feed and clothe us and to send food parcels to his brothers in Poland. It's a funny thing. I can see old footage of D-day and take the bravery of the men on the beaches for granted. I took Dad's wartime stories for granted, even perceived his ordeals as comical. He was a war hero. Mum a saint. Nanna and Ink the best surrogate grandparents in the whole world, and we, Tottenham, a community which looked after its own. I dabbed my cheeks and smiled through the tears. I hadn't thought about Mrs Beaker in years. And there she'd been, hair in curlers, staring back at me in the gloom of that dismal school toilet; severe eyes and gaunt face, and that angry pimple on her forehead which never seemed to find peace. All of them as clear to me as the picture on my HD TV before it was repossessed. A hand rested lightly on my shoulder.

'Are you all right, sir?' The policewoman handed me a tissue.

'Thank goodness everyone got out alive from the flats above. You didn't live there, did you sir?'

I uttered a "thank you" and traipsed south towards Seven Sisters.

Large numbers of people were milling around, some listless, some angry, and members of both persuasions giving interviews to journalists and TV crews. Locals were helping shopkeepers sweep up the broken glass and board up shattered windows. One shopkeeper howled in front of what was left of his convenience store, shrugging off the attempts of those who wanted to comfort him, praying to a god that I knew didn't exist. I glimpsed a higgledy-piggledy row of burnt out cars and more wrecked shops. The torched bus had crumpled and twisted into a jumble of scorched metal. I reckoned it would make a fine piece of abstract art once it had cooled down a bit. Another photo opportunity missed. In any case, it was far too late for me to cash in. Hundreds of images would already have been circulated of the riot and its aftermath. A little way beyond the bus the police had cordoned off the High Road. They directed me down Bruce Grove, where I passed Mush's old house which had been turned into flats. In my day it was a palace, but now it looked shoddy, and had probably been gobbled up on the cheap by a property investor. I'd already said my goodbyes to Mushtaq and I'd had my fill of the past. One glance, and I hurried on.

I'd left the car a few hundred yards from the party. I imagined the young revellers huddling together when they realised what was going down. The bravest among them taking quick peeks from behind closed curtains, lights dimmed, but not extinguished because the Girls Aloud CD cover had been commandeered by coke-heads and the carpet was thick pile. I'd lost bundles betting on favourites in my time, but it was a dead cert that Mike's son, Danny, no longer considered Tottenham the next up-and-coming place. When I reached Danny's street I hesitated, wondering if I should knock on his door to ask if everyone was all right. I needn't have worried. The curtains were open and I could see a group of them drinking Red Bull and vodka in the living room. Another layer of sweat formed on my face and my hands felt as if they had hold of a pneumatic drill. I was halfway up the garden path when the guy with the vodka held the bottle up to the light and turned it upside down over his tongue. When nothing came out he licked the rim and lobbed the bottle into a wastepaper bin.

I heard a girl scream, 'Not in there, Sean! Danny's puked up in that.' She handed him a black refuse sack, 'His dad will be here soon. We've got to clear up.'

I waited to see if the guy would crack open another bottle, but he took the sack and started loading it with empty beer cans. I set off to find my car. Mike was the last person I wanted to see: too many questions and too few answers.

I found my car where I'd left it. The one next to mine had a cracked windscreen and a small scorch mark on the bonnet. Someone needed to retake their vandalism and arsonist exams. My old banger appeared to be unscathed. It may have looked as if it'd been plucked from a scrap yard but the MOT still had a month left to run. The crazies obviously had more fun trashing motors with blue lights on top and flash ones with gleaming bodywork and pristine bumpers and hubcaps, not ones with large dents and rusted doors. Class war? Unlikely. And there you have it: a psychological profile of your average rioter. I took a cursory inspection of the old girl to validate my hypothesis. The wheels were all there, tyres kind of inflated, and if there were any additional dents I couldn't tell, nobody could. It was unlocked because it didn't lock and the key was behind the sun visor. I kept it there because I'd lost too many keys on social outings, or binges, as they're more commonly known these days. I'm not talking about driving while under the influence, but having a roof over my head to sleep it off. I cleared a pizza box from the vicinity of the gear stick, and a slice of stale Margherita joined the detritus on the passenger's floor. I had to turn the key three times and pump the accelerator before it started. The radio came on automatically and I couldn't believe what I was hearing. There had been riots right across London and they'd spread to Birmingham, Manchester, and a host of other towns. The list, like the violence, was endless.

I took the A10 heading north and maintained a cruising speed of 45 mph, a smidgen below flat out. The A10 heading towards Tottenham was practically deserted. Once I'd cleared the Great Cambridge Roundabout, I focused my mind on what Raz meant by, "I'm a Tottenham boy". Was he a member of a local gang and Jess from a rival one? Had they called a truce to do a drug deal and had one side tried to rip the other side off? Surely there must be more to it than that. Why was Raz so interested in my childhood and Mushtaq in particular? In the unlikely event that he had principles, they were undoubtedly more Malcolm X than Martin Luther King. One thing was for sure, at the first opportunity I intended to Google Mushtaq and re-establish contact with him. Without his moral guidance, I might have become a football hooligan like Harry Hooper. I might never have worn velvet flares and extolled the virtues of peace and love, man. How I wished Mush was around when I hit the booze and made Ladbrokes my second home. A few of his admonishments might have come in handy then.

As cheap Ponders End bedsits go, mine wasn't so bad. I heard the mice more often than I saw them and two rings on the cooker were working. The landlord had promised me a new hob when I was down to one. I could seldom afford to frequent a pub and spent most of my time sitting on the bed drinking cheap wine and cider, watching a television with a back comparable to Dad's prized Bell. I did possess one bottle of Jack Daniels but was saving that in case the new arrival on the top floor, an overweight Romanian, changed her mind about my invitation to wine and dine. I didn't tell her it would be at Ron's fish bar, but I think she guessed.

Forcing the front door open, I stepped over the piles of mail and circulars in the hall. Most were addressed to people nobody had ever heard of, or denied knowledge of if they had; shadows that passed in flight. Usually I'd kick the pizza leaflets and minicab cards around in search of letters addressed to me. If a correspondence came in a brown envelope, I'd scribble: "not known at this address," and stuff it in my pocket ready for posting. It was a little after 8am and the tenants didn't normally stir till past noon. On that morning, tellies blared from almost every room. I opened my bedsit door, added the sounds from my television to the cacophony, and flopped onto the bed. The riots *were* the news; shops and houses ablaze, police charges, police retreats, condemnation, and pleas for calm and justice. It went on and on, town after town, until all the ugliness merged into one. I needed to wash. I needed to think. I badly needed a drink. But my mind was shutting down and I couldn't fight the fatigue any longer...

I stirred many hours later to an image of two faces on the screen. They belonged to men roughly the same age as me. Both seemed familiar, but I couldn't quite place where I'd seen them before. Then it hit me. I sat bolt upright in bed and listened to the commentary...

"Brothers Frank and Terry Lambert were found murdered in Tottenham today along with five white youths. They are all members of the Friends of England, a little-known party with fascist leanings. One of the youths was identified as Jess Ryan, who held the post of party treasurer. Police are linking the killings to a drugs deal. Frank Lambert, founder of the Friends of England, was wanted for questioning over the murder of Mushtaq Mohammed and the desecration of Jewish cemeteries. A leading liberal and reformer in Pakistan, Mr Mohammed had recently arrived in England with the intention of persuading young Muslims to turn away from violence and jihad. In a recent interview Mr Lambert said there could be no peace until all Muslims were expelled from these shores. He called for all those of a Christian background, irrespective of colour, to join together and fight for English values. Opposing gangs of Asian and white youths have gathered near the spot where Mr Mohammed was shot and police appeals for calm have fallen on deaf ears..."

30

Things became fragmented and blurred after I learnt of Mush's murder. I do recall staggering over to the sink and puking up on a pile of dirty crockery. I also have a vague memory of guzzling Jack Daniels straight from the bottle and punching a wall. I think that must have been when my print of Hendrix's guitar sacrifice at Monterey ended up under the armchair. The following morning, I was awakened by what sounded like a pig grunting. Through a thick layer of dust on the tall mirror, I saw the pink bloat roll over, heard its groans, and felt it clutching its brow as it left the sty. Two empty cider bottles and several packets of Nobby's Nuts had been its sleeping companions. Self-awareness is in short supply when the senses are fried and your knuckles are competing with your head for sympathy. I sat on the edge of the bed and imbibed the rest of the whiskey to dull the pain in mind and body. My bum bounced on the squeaky mattress three or four times before I gained sufficient momentum to stand. I even managed to open the curtains without pulling them off the rail or toppling headfirst into the window. Muttering, 'Maybe Jesus did walk on water after all,' I covered my eyes as heaven's light flooded the room. If Raz hadn't trashed my Casio, would I have called the authorities? I'm not sure. But rather than going in search of a phone, I decided to look Mush up on Google.

It took a while to register the images on my laptop. As disbelief turned to outrage, I re-played a clip of Mushtaq giving a speech at a Pakistani university. There were armed guards on the stage and at the entrance. His hair was streaked white like his father's back in the 1950s and though his body was frail his eyes were vital and his voice passionate. The British press hadn't picked up on his struggle against the Taliban or reported the fact that he was shot four times. I suppose fighting for girls to have an education and opposing the excesses of

Sharia Law in the remote climes of Pakistan wasn't as sexy as Hollywood scandals, or as heroic as the war our soldiers were fighting in Afghanistan. Poor Mushtaq had survived all that only to be taken out by English bigots. Before plotting my next move I decided to look up my old pals on Google.

Hard to believe, but Terry was the initial funder of P.A.L.S or Pride in Albion Society, forerunner of Friends of England. I wondered how many members knew the true meaning of P.A.L.S before they joined the party. It goes without saying that Terry came into his fortune through luck rather than by putting his brain to work. He'd won big on Littlewoods pools. Frank probably charmed him with all sorts of promises. A grandiose title would have helped loosen Terry's purse strings. Terry had a little boy complex and it was a fair bet that he had little man complex when he grew up. A picture taken at a recent party rally depicted Frank and Terry standing side by side on a rostrum in a dilapidated hall swathed in Union Jacks. Terry didn't even come up to Frank's shoulder. He had his chin raised and his hands on his hips, Oswald Mosley-style. Terry must have been easy prey for someone as manipulative as Frank.

Raz remained an enigma, as did my sense of morality. Was Frank trying to swell the party coffers by buying drugs or arms from him and his crew? Did the deal go wrong? Or had Raz joined the party with the intention of murdering Frank and his followers? Frank said he wanted all those of a Christian background, irrespective of colour, to join him in fighting the Islamist threat. A tactic designed, no doubt, to expand his party and give the impression that blacks who embraced English values were welcome to join. Did Raz join the party and become disillusioned? No matter his motivation, if Raz had killed Frank he'd done humanity a great service. I thought back to the days of the Tottenham Boys and shed a small tear over Terry's demise.

Of course, my reluctance to call the police may simply have come down to base fear. I could have informed them and even if they had apprehended Raz, there might not have been enough evidence for a murder charge. He wore gloves so the chances were that he wouldn't have left any fingerprints. And what was that gadget he used to disable and reset the alarm? It looked like a television remote, but I was damned sure you couldn't purchase one of them Sci-fi type contraptions in Currys. I chuckled at the thought of Raz as a Trekkie with pointy ears, pushed over the edge when William Shatner took the All Bran challenge. That moment of light relief vanished as rapidly as the inane grin on my face. What if he was working for MI6 or a government organisation not on the radar? That would make him doubly dangerous; a maverick who put two fingers up at the police establishment and said bollocks to public sensibilities. Whoever he was, no matter his motives, he spelt danger. If I had informed on him, I could have been disturbed in my slumbers, witnessed my terrified reflection in his shades just before he snapped my neck. Why upset someone with the strength of Heracles, the intellect of an Oxford don, and the agility of a cat? I knew then what had to be done. I'd brave the day, head down to the offy, and when I came back I'd write a bestselling novel based on my experiences in that school. All the pain that I'd endured had to count for something. Didn't it?

31

Six years later

I never did finish that novel. Mind you, I hit the plonk more times than I hit the word processor. It was a wonder I had any hair left and the bloody keyboard was still in one piece. Wonder upon wonders, after a heroic struggle that surpassed the siege of the Alamo, I managed to complete nine tenths of the damned thing. Try as I might, I just couldn't squeeze out a compelling ending. I called my masterpiece *Tottenham Boys* and sincerely hoped the title didn't offend anyone with violent tendencies (it was also the name of that notorious Turkish street gang).

Set during the Tottenham riot, the protagonists were loosely based on Raz, Mush and me, all aged in our mid-20s. I say loosely because my character, Johnny, had more guile and spunk than Kuchy and overcame Raz in brutal unarmed combat. As you may have gathered, Johnny wasn't a sad, verging-on-alcoholic, scraping-a-living sort of guy. From humble beginnings as a working-class lad, he became a successful fashion photographer screwing gorgeous models left, right and centre. He was in Tottenham because he'd been asked to take pictures of the new Spurs kit, all white with a blue logo. After photographing the sacred shirts on his harem, he fraternised with the players and was given a complimentary seat in the director's box. Raz was called Jason after the nutter from my childhood, and I depicted him as a schizophrenic who'd run out of medication and had acquired the habit of head-butting walls and human skulls. Try as I might, I couldn't think of ways to make him any scarier without delving into Gestapo methodology. Mush was called Mohamed, a demure figure who bravely halted the spread of Jihadist theology in this country almost single-handedly and received the Nobel Peace Prize. One of his many accomplishments was to act as mediator between Johnny and Jason during a standoff in a church - Jason had head-butted the vicar and was licking blood off a pew when gallant Johnny arrived on the scene. To give Johnny the ending he deserved, I decided to pay Waterstones a visit for a touch of plagiarism. My purpose was to find novels of the right genre, read the blurb on the back, and digest the last few pages before I'd overstayed my welcome. To bolster my flagging ego and purge my conscience, I'd convinced myself that J. K. Rowling and Stephen King must have done it, and William Shakespeare certainly did.

***

I'd come to fully clothed, no need to dress, just a quick splash at the sink and a sprinkle of the eau de Cologne Mike got me for Christmas. I did lift my shirt above my tits so most of the scent went close to my armpits. My stomach caught any surplus before it hit the carpet, and I had the sweetest smelling bellybutton in the whole of Ponders End. In my defence, I usually kept a set of clean clothes in the rare event that there was a text containing a job offer. Okay, sometimes I forgot and life became a scramble to find laundry money. Most of the time there wasn't enough in the kitty to buy booze and do a service wash. Heads I got pissed; tails I got rat-arsed. To hell with it. I was going to be evicted soon anyway. I'd spent the last of my savings on a Spurs season ticket even though I was two months behind with the rent. The new stadium couldn't possibly hold the same memories and emotions for me as The Lane, but it looks might impressive. Mike said I should have spent it on razorblades. I retaliated by calling my growth retro designer stubble and asked him if he had any idea how much razorblades cost these days. He has a beard.

I stepped over an empty Toro Loco bottle and donned the Paul Smith cashmere overcoat which took pride of place in my wardrobe, reserved for funerals and jobs in posh locations. Freud might have surmised I wore it indoors because of a string of rejections and to hide my shame; notably the booze and kebab stains on my shirt and trousers. I prefer to think it was because I was cold and often there wasn't enough money to feed the metre, and certainly not because I fantasised that I looked like a man at the top of his profession. Admittedly, there were moments when I gazed into the tall mirror and saw my alter ego, Johnny, with a coterie of scantily clad models clinging to his arms and shoulders. Most of the time all I would see was a sad old man staring back at me. The mirror had a wooden surround with robin redbreasts carved into it. Maggie had chosen it when she still professed to love me. How I wanted to smash the whole bloody piece, birdies and all.

I thought I'd better check on the weather before leaving the bedsit. I looked out of the window, saw the rain, and discarded my Paul Smith for the mac I'd bought at the charity shop (Orson Welles might well have worn it in *The Third Man*). It was recycling day but I thought screw the empties, they'll be waiting for me when I get back from Waterstones, as will that pile of manky washing up. To be on the safe side, I listened at the door before opening it. A big Afrikaner had moved into the bedsit next to mine. Put it this way, he didn't have a picture of Nelson Mandela gracing his wall. Nothing much changed in my life, except my neighbours and they changed every few months, weeks sometimes, mostly keeping themselves to themselves. If I happened to learn a name it was soon forgotten. I prayed the Boer didn't buck the trend and I was dreading him catching me in the hall with a six pack of lager, a wide grin spread across his ruddy face. Knowing me, after downing a few, I'd sing that classic from *Spitting Image*...

The stench inside the building wasn't entirely of my making. The loo on the landing was blocked and the plunger had gone missing. At such times, there's something to be said for going outside and breathing in hydrocarbons. Negotiating the stairs without mishap, I trampled on the junk mail and unclaimed post, forced opened the front door, and slammed it behind me (it wouldn't close if you didn't slam it). I bumbled along the noisy High Street, fighting the gale force wind and the torrential rain, trudging gamely on until my umbrella turned inside out. It felt as if I'd been slapped across the face with a cold wet flannel. Sobered by the forces of nature, a chain of unwelcome images burst into my mind: those gloomy school toilets, Oik's pathetic groans, Jess's glazed eyes and gaping mouth, the physical pain Raz had delighted in inflicting on me, the humiliation and psychological torture. Sometimes when I had these flashbacks, one of the Tottenham Boys would materialize in the middle of everything. Especially Terry, with his grubby face and scraped knees, whooping and hollering as he played football or cowboys and Indians. The horrors could arrive when I was making a cup of tea, sitting on the loo, or when I was on a photo shoot. It cost me a day's pay when I heard a death rattle and saw Mush as a skinny kid through the lens: spread-eagled, body riddled with bullets on a road just off Park Lane. It was a hot summer's day and I could smell the melting tar, which sucked him in like quicksand. I pulled such a harrowing face that the bride thought I found her unfit for purpose. I was told to "fuck off" and the groom's brother said he would take the photos, once the bride had stopped wailing, that is.

At other times, I awoke to a sickening terror that rose from the pit of my stomach and crushed my chest till I gasped for breath. I had hoped the novel would be cathartic, a healing process designed to banish, or at least reduce, my panic attacks and nightmares. When I felt bold enough, I tried to figure Raz's motives and make sense of things that didn't add up. For example, how did he know about Colin? I could swear I never told him beforehand. Was I drugged or possibly too freaked to know what I was saying? As for his interest in Mush I feared that would remain a mystery – if, indeed, it wasn't just the product of a delusional mind. I'd done my research and discovered that Mush hadn't stepped onto these shores from the time he left junior school till the days just before the riots of 2011. I doubted very much that Raz worked for Christian Aid or Save the Children and had met him in some impoverished village in the Hindu Kush.

Waterstones was two miles away, but in my lamentable state it might as well have been ten. My mac was sodden and weighing me down and a Zulu could have used my umbrella on the defenders of Rorke's Drift. I dumped it in the rubbish bin by the bus stop. I would have queued for a bus if my oyster card had any credit left on it. By the time I'd braved the dual carriageway and tramped to the bookshop the cracks in the pavement were like bear traps, kerbs precipices. Water dripped into my eyes and it was difficult to discern the images on the cover of the book that formed the centrepiece of Waterstones' window display. Running a sleeve over my face, I was certain I could see the words *Tottenham Boys* and squashed my nose against the glass to be certain. Sure enough, some bastard had ripped off the title of my novel. I cursed *The Mirror* for not having better literary reviews. I could have gone down the pub and prepared myself for this. I executed a rugby-style hand-off on the glass and stumbled on squelching shoes into the store. Blowing into my hands, I snatched the plagiarist's book from the top of a pyramid.

The writer was someone called Raymond Deane and the strange cover depicted a violent hoodie casting a shadow which resembled a cricketer. I turned it over and on the back cover there was a picture of two men with their arms around each other's shoulders. I raised the book closer to my eyes. One of the men wore some sort of tribal headdress and his face appeared weather-beaten. Mush! An image on the Internet depicted him wearing that clobber when he reopened a school laid waste by the Taliban. The other man was black, huge in comparison, and wore army combat gear. In the background I could make out a range of barren mountains set beneath a bright blue, cloudless sky. A slight, young woman with a ponytail appeared from God knows where. In my agitated state, I wouldn't have seen an army of Klingons beaming down brandishing bat'leths. She was transporting a life-size cardboard cut-out of a man which she plonked by the pyramid, sliding it a few inches to the left and a few more to the right, until, arms folded, she gave it a nod of approval. The cardboard bloke was wearing slacks and a short-sleeved shirt. There were two criss-crossing scars low on his forehead and a patchwork of pink scars high on his right cheek. I'd taken pictures of fire victims as evidence for insurance claims and was familiar with burn marks. Both of his muscular arms were similarly disfigured and the damage to his skin had obviously been enhanced rather than airbrushed out. I looked at the soldier on the cover and compared him to the figure on the cut out. My gaze went rapidly from one to the other until they became a blur. Through the muddle, an image of Raz in the school toilets embedded itself in my mind. It was the one of him cleaning his shades when I saw what I perceived to be pink scales on his cheek. I blinked and tried to home in on the pink scars on Raymond Deane's cheek. My head felt as if it was clamped in a vice and all the air was being sucked from my surroundings.

The onset of my panic attack in Waterstones closely resembled Mum's symptoms when she first partook of curry. Rasping, I clutched my throat with both hands and panted like an old dog in a sauna.

I was close to passing out when a hand squeezed the back of my arm and a familiar voice said, 'Hello, Kuchy. Remember me?'

Another hand landed on my other arm and together they guided me through 180 degrees. And there I was, face-to-face with the man whose performance had me scuttling to the doctor's in search of diazepam and statins. When the beast held me hostage I imagined that he had cornrows, a Mohican, or a shaved head maybe. But like his two-dimensional doppelganger, his curly hair was short, neat and conventional. Pursued by a cackling, mostly female entourage, he thrust a hardback copy of his book into my hand.

A bolt of fear pinned me to the ground as he said, 'Meet me in the

Black Horse in an hour. Before I get there you should have enough time to read chapter one and chapter six from the top of page 254.'

Lost in a whirl of hatred, I watched him saunter towards the back of the store, along a line of people snaking towards a desk, each of them clutching a copy of *Tottenham Boys*. I stood shuddering, assailed by a wall of exuberant chatter, and through a sea of shoulders and heads I glimpsed him lift a hand to acknowledge the accolades. The beast took his seat, had a sip of water, and each time he signed a book he flashed his fangs at a member of his adoring public.

I deepened my breathing and tried to rein in my mind and slow my heart. A psychoanalyst friend of Mike's told me that a person's anger and thirst for revenge can become a palliative if challenged by a reasoning mind. I'd lost my fucking mind and toyed with the idea of running him over. But that would have been difficult because my latest old Fiat was in Winter's garage. Mr Winter said that if I didn't pay up soon he'd find it a new home in a Brimsdown scrapyard. I flipped open the book and glanced at the credits at the front. My name was there and he'd spelt it correctly. Below it he'd written: *"I owe him a great debt which I hope to repay in the very near future."*

Tell you what, arsehole, I thought. Give me half the royalties, have a good feel of the live rail on the Victoria Line, and then we'll call it quits. I turned the page and read the prologue:

At Oxford, my fellow philosophy students unsurprisingly called me Ray. Things weren't as straightforward in the army and I was either called Sunshine (ray of) or Raz by my comrades. I commenced writing this book in 2014, three years after Mushtaq's murder and five years after the mission to rescue him. The records will state that I freed Mushtaq from the clutches of the Taliban in 2009. In truth, it was he who liberated me. The time we spent together escaping the insurgents had me in awe of a special human being with an indomitable spirit. I was trained in survival techniques and could jog two marathons in quick succession while sporting a full pack. He was skinny and a fraction of my size, not to mention twice my age. By sheer determination he matched me stride for stride.

Soon after the rescue mission, I left the army for reasons stated in the book and became a reporter specialising in war zones which included Afghanistan, Pakistan, and the Middle East. While on assignment to interview Mushtaq, I was captured by Jihadists in a region of Pakistan close to the Afghan border. My helicopter had been shot down en route and I had to endure months of incessant interrogation and torture. The physical tortures ended when the Jihadists broached the idea of a ransom and a prisoner exchange. The psychological tortures carried on unabated until the day of my release and beyond. I keep telling myself that I'm the lucky one because I was thrown clear, while my colleagues were burned beyond recognition after the copter spiralled onto that barren hillside. I survived the ordeal by utilising my army training and drawing upon the inspiration Mushtaq provided me. As my ex-wife Samantha can testify, his murder hit me very hard and I wasn't quite myself for a long time after that.

I don't believe in fate, but how strange that Mushtaq and I attended the same school in Tottenham, albeit thirty-odd years apart. He was a humble man and didn't go in for self-flattery or personal gratification. He would talk openly about politics and the need for social change in his country, rarely about his good deeds. In consequence, the facts laid out in this book were largely gathered elsewhere. I must thank his colleagues and acquaintances for putting the flesh on the bones of this great man. Mushtaq did tell me a little about his boyhood years in Tottenham but there were gaps. Luckily, I stumbled upon an old schoolmate of his with a keen retentive memory. If it wasn't for Ricky narrating his childhood memories so cogently, Mushtaq's formative years might have been lost to posterity. I have reported the events laid out in the book down to the minutiae, and certain passages are in the form of a documentary-novel. I am blessed, although some may call it a curse, with an exceptionally rare condition called hyperthymesia. I never forget …

The fucker had had the last laugh. He was venerated and I was alive because he allowed me to live; given me permission to carry on breathing.

I hissed, 'Playing the hero, are we? That right, black boy?'

Spittle sprayed from my mouth as I laid into cardboard Raz with a flurry of wild right hooks. He rocked violently on his base and each time he sprang back, I clubbed him with even greater ferocity. The last punch had him on the canvas and I stood over him, snarling and gasping, imagining the book in my left hand to be a pulsing heart ripped from his body. But instead of taking a ten count the bloody thing shot upright again like a giant Subbuteo player and bashed me on the nose. So great was the anger and confusion pin-balling in my brain, that I couldn't feel the pain in my chafed knuckles or tell you if I articulated my rant or not: fucking philosophy student! Kindly volunteered, did I? You had that hi-tech gadget. Did you also have a mic secreted in the peak of your fucking baseball cap? Not that you needed it, seeing as you've got the memory of an elephant. Was "I never forget," meant as a warning to me? Wasn't quite yourself... You can say that again, squire! I do know that I tossed his book onto the pile and it caught the edge of the pyramid. Several copies tumbled to the floor and I kicked the nearest one into the children's section, just missing a girl who was giggling into a copy of *The Queen's Orang-utan*. I would have kicked a second if I were any good with my left.

The young woman with the ponytail re-appeared. She shot a glance at a security guard who'd taken up a position by the entrance. I suspect he'd been having a pee while I did my Mike Tyson.

Unable to catch his eye, she said nervously, 'I'm sure it was an accident but please try to be more careful, sir.'

I grunted and tapped my pockets until I heard the jingle of coins. For one awful moment I thought I'd put them in the fruit machine at the Dog and Duck. My wallet may have been devoid of paper currency, but I had enough shrapnel to purchase a couple of pints. I'd just put a shaky hand inside a sodden pocket when the security guard grabbed my arm.

The guard, a rotund man with a bigger bald patch than mine, rolled out a rehearsed, "I'll escort you to the exit, sir." Adding, "Now run along home like a good boy."

Old men might revert to childhood, but there's no need to throw it in our faces. I gave the condescending bastard an "up yours", and slogged towards the Dog and Duck.

The sky remained black and threatening but it was only spitting when I made my ignominious exit from the bookshop. I didn't get far, stopping in front of a betting shop handily placed two doors along. Maggie once said I was like a giant homing pigeon and Paddy Power and Corals were my lofts. A punter inside the shop waved at me and gestured that I should join him. I'd spent many a fruitless afternoon with Spanish Bob looking at the plethora of screens, jumping up in expectation as the horses neared the winning post, slumping back onto our stools if we'd lost. I hate to think how many betting slips we'd screwed up or ripped to shreds between us. Bob was of a similar age to me. He had an Alex Ferguson nose, a large pate with tufts of fine hair, and sagging jowls. Imagine a bloodhound with alopecia. For some reason, after my split with Maggie I'd started comparing people to man's best friend. North London through and through, Bob couldn't speak a word of Spanish and had only visited the Iberian Peninsula once, a package holiday to Benidorm if I remember correctly. He'd acquired the handle because his old mum had passed on the necessary survival skills by teaching him how to make Spanish omelettes which, she said, were cheap and nutritious and could be eaten every day without the need for a woman.

Never mind that your mac is steaming, or that you look and smell like a hobo who's slept in a McDonald's wheelie bin. If you flash a bundle most betting shops will welcome you, providing you're not slurring *Eleanor Rigby* or *Danny Boy* at the top of your voice. I may not have smelt like a Big Mac, but my attire left much to be desired and my nine quid could hardly be termed a bundle. I gave Bob a thumbs up and if he'd returned the gesture I'd have tapped him up for a few quid. He frowned and gave me the thumbs down. I shrugged, mouthed 'hard luck mate', and debated whether to have those two pints or have him put the last of my dosh on a nag in the second race at Kempton Park. I chose neither and did something quite out of character. I plodded on for a few yards and stopped to have a good think.

The first thought I had was, what the hell am I going to do after the Dog and Duck? There followed a series of musings nourished by desperation and paranoia. Raz had to know I never squealed on him and he might give me a percentage of the royalties. A couple of grand would come in very handy. After all, I was a contributor. Blackmail was out of the question. I didn't have the guts for that. But needs must and if he looked at me through a killer's eyes I could always drop just the tiniest hint involving the Old Bill. I could sure have done with the readies. As I said, work was thin and my bloody ankle had started playing up on my last assignment. It was all I could do to keep up with Wayne Rooney and he had his injured foot in a protective boot. *The Sun* photographer got a scowl and a mouthful while all I got was a shot of a fat Scouse backside. What did I stand to lose?

I turned and crept back into Waterstones. It was hardly a grand entrance; I stumbled twice before grabbing a copy of *Tottenham Boys* from the top of the pyramid, which had now been rebuilt and made fit for Tutankhamen. But the security guard had me in his sights and there was no way that I would have made the street if the shop assistant hadn't intervened.

She looked starry-eyed at Raz signing copies of *Tottenham Boys* and cooed, 'It's okay, Sid. Mr Deane has given this man a copy. Did you know Mr Deane has started a charity for orphaned children? He's calling it "Rays of Sunshine". How sweet is that?'

Cunt.

32

On the surface Raz appeared to be without a care in the world, a successful author revelling in the adulation. Strangely, for an action book, most of his fans in Waterstones were women; the only surprise was that they didn't hurl their knickers at him. Little did they know that he was a murderer who tortured his victims. Just because he'd written a book, it didn't make him less dangerous (take Adolf Hitler and Alice Cooper, for example). I tried to weigh up the odds on my survival as I headed at a snail's pace towards the Black Horse. How many people had he killed? Whatever the number, I expected his conscience could accommodate one more. But surely he had more to lose than before. Did that mean he was more likely to cut a deal with me or more likely to bump me off? I repeatedly looked over my shoulder. He'd been in the army, SAS at a guess, and I probably wouldn't hear him coming.

I reached the junction where I needed to turn left for the Black Horse, and froze. Ahead, I could see an Indian restaurant and a snooker hall. The last time I was in an Indian restaurant I had a korma. I was with Maggie. If aaloo keema had been on the menu, I'd have taken her to the Chinese next door. It was soon after my encounter with Raz, and I had pleaded with her to give me one last chance. I was tempted, desperate, to tell her of my experiences during the riot, to play on her sympathy. But as was the case with Mike, I couldn't risk putting her life in danger. Or mine, because one of them was bound to go to the police, and Raz could be anything from James Bond bingeing on martinis to a serial killer on crack. Some may argue they are the same thing. Instead, I told her I'd always love her. A smile flickered on her lips, that died as she casually mentioned the division of joint assets. I'd forgotten about our hundred shares in British Telecom. I rallied slightly when she said she'd like to be friends and perhaps we could go out for another meal in a month or two. Providing, she insisted, that I was sober and we didn't dredge up the past. She meant what she said, about being friends, but I clung on to the dream that we might get back together again. I gave up the booze, and days later, emailed her with the news that I'd joined AA. A few weeks after that, I emailed her again and told her that I'd turned my hand to wildlife photography. Stalking rutting stags is how I screwed up my ankle for the third time. It was on the day when Mike strapped up my sprained appendage that I received news of her forthcoming marriage.

Mike told that he'd drop in on me after work. By the time he showed up I'd ripped into my second bottle of scotch. He suggested that I should stop wallowing in self-pity and that I should pull myself together. The "sod" was slurred at an angle of forty-five degrees, the "off" supine. He put me in the recovery position and slept on my floor that night. In the morning, he produced a packet of aspirin and a list of dating agencies. I screwed up the list, missed the bin, and reached for the scotch on the bedside table. He emptied the scotch down the sink, left two aspirin, and took the packet away. On leaving, he said, "Friggin' kill yourself if you want, but I'm not going to help you do it." He came back minutes later and sat by my bed. The last time I went to a snooker hall I was with five mates and the beer was half price. Mike broke and the cue ball left the table and hit Neville in the balls. Neville wasn't laughing, but the rest of us nearly choked on our drinks. Of that merry bunch only Mike has stuck by me, and he keeps harping on about retiring to his birthplace, Barbados.

I was at the proverbial crossroads, and from where I stood all directions led to purgatory. If one of the roads had led to California, I'd have headed for the sun and slept out under the stars on Malibu Beach. But I was broke and in good old London Town, where the weather was miserable. Retracing my steps was out of the question, and treading the same life path would have seen me kipping in dank shop doorways, glugging cheap cider. I unbuttoned my mac and extracted the wallet from my trouser pocket. Flipping it open, I examined the various credit and debit cards lodged in their tiny sleeves. None of them were of any use; several had expiry dates going back to the time when Tony Blair pulled that fast one on Gordon Brown. Only one card was valid: my Spurs season ticket. Raz could threaten to cut both my little fingers off, but I was buggered if I was going to flog that.

A single-decker bus sped from the road to my right. I'm sure the bus driver had a mischievous grin on his face as he steered tight to the kerb and ploughed his vehicle through a large puddle, better described as a small lake. A sheet of dirty water soaked my shoes and the bottom of my trousers, and I seriously considered jumping under the next bus. I sighed, slumped my shoulders, and muttered a defeatist 'what the fuck', before turning left towards the Black Horse. I trudged on, head down, my squelching footwear sparking a memory of the time when my flapping shoe made a sound like a wet fart in Mr Mohammed's car. He had come to my rescue in my moment of need. Sixty years later: three relationships, which had fizzled out, one failed marriage, countless lost friends, and I was all on my own. I may not have had the guts to jump in front of a bus, but maybe I didn't need to. Maybe I'd ask Raz to do me a favour.

The pub was quarter full at best. I bought a cheap Australian lager and finished it at the bar. I can't say I drank it in world record time, but it came close to my personal best. After wiping the thin froth from my lips, I ordered a proper pint (London Pride), paid the barman in coins, and selected a table in the far reaches. Clutching the glass in both hands, I steered a course which took me well away from the fruit machine; I was saving my last quid for a tin of spicy baked beans to go with my jacket potato and tuna in brine. My table was next to a Kentia Palm. Maggie was fond of indoor plants and we'd had two of those things. I'd urinated on the larger one of the pair when she gave me my marching orders. I couldn't remember a thing about it when I came back a few days later with a bunch of flowers. My meagre belongings were scattered along the garden path and she stood in the doorway, arms folded. She wore the blue and gold-trim tracksuit I'd bought her when she said she needed to get fit for middle age. Her auburn hair looked windswept and her face was sweaty because she'd just finished one of her gruelling interval runs. I told her what a moron I'd been to put the last of our savings on a dead cert (if only Tartan Bearer had won the bleedin' Derby). I said that if I'd won a bundle, I would have replaced the money we'd set aside for the mortgage and paid for a new kitchen and bathroom. I blamed Dad for passing on his gambling gene, and swore that I'd seek treatment and never go near a bookies or a racecourse ever again. I told her I understood how much I'd let her down, and said she was right: who can trust a partner who swears he'll never bet again more times than he says "I love you"? I told her how much I missed her, how much I'd suffered in how ever many days I'd been away. Moody, sulky, and self-pitying were some of the things she'd thrown at me before losing patience and beginning the affair with Jim Squires, that journo bastard. She kept the self-pitying bit, added loser, tosser and lying bastard, and slammed the door in my face.

The publican had joined his barman, who nodded towards me as he polished a wine glass. He clearly reckoned I couldn't afford a third pint and was bad for business. Never fear, I had my defence planned. If challenged, I would tell them that I was a *Big Issue* seller. There was something about the publican that was familiar. He obviously thought the same about me, because his forehead crinkled and his jaw jutted as he leant across the bar to get a better view of what the cat had dragged in. Then it came to me. He had the same short, powerful frame and cropped hair, but it was the mad, unblinking eyes that gave him away. The bloody publican turned out to be Dai Evans, the PE teacher who'd acted as the muscle for the headmaster after I was dismissed from my teaching post. All I could do was to put my faith in nature and hope he couldn't see through her disguise: hair loss on top, hair gain in nostrils, large ears, and an abundance of adipose tissue. I took two sips of ale and pretended to be fascinated by the Kentia Palm. At least I could tell him the name of the triffid if he asked me.

Before I knew it the level of ale in my glass was down to less than half. At that rate of consumption I'd finish my drink before I'd even started reading Raz's creation. Try as I might, the glass would insist on coming up considerably quicker than it went down. I gripped the book and held it in front of my face, fumbling through the pages with my thumb till I found chapter one. Before I began reading I wondered if there was something sinister underlying Raz's desire to have me read his book. Was it some kind of test? What if he asked me questions and I gave him answers that weren't to his liking? I'd had a taste of how he dealt with failure…

TOTTENHAM
BOYS

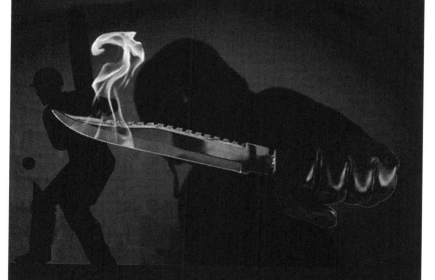

Raymond Deane

Chapter 1

During my research into Mushtaq's formative years, Ricky furnished me with anecdotes of Tottenham in the post-war era. His accounts were entertaining and shed light on how the first non-white immigrant boy was greeted and treated in a school in which British imperialism was taught with pride. The interaction between Ricky and Mushtaq, and the events that set them asunder and drew them together, will be narrated in future chapters. For now, I would like to utilise a few of Ricky's descriptions of school and street life in the 1950s, and make a comparison between then and the 1990s when I attended the same school. In doing so, I hope I will give the reader an insight into my formative years and a better appreciation of what influenced our respective behaviours, when I encountered Mushtaq Mohammed many years later in a remote part of the world.

Ricky and I are both only children, but that's where the similarity ends. At the age of ten, Ricky wielded a spud gun, stole big green apples from the vicar's garden, and pretended his candy cigarettes were Benson and Hedges. At the age of nine, I was lifting purses from women's handbags and stealing booze from off-licences. Aged ten, the local gang let me have a drag on a joint and fondle a home-made gun that could drill a hole in your skull. They were my rewards for riding off with, and hiding, their stash of crack and brown moments before the feds raided their lockup on my estate. As time went on they didn't push so much weed, as it was bulkier and less profitable, but kept a good supply for personal. At fourteen, I was taught how to "whip" coke and turn it into crack, and the art of flipping, or selling drugs.

I was aged seven when I began conveying drugs for the gang. Sometimes I collected the money when they were passing their "bitches" around or were too smashed to function. I had no need to write anything down because I never forgot the amounts and locations. That's why they called me "baby elephant". Our best clients were junkies because addiction needs regular feeding and they required funds to pay for the brown. Most of the money they handed over had been stolen during muggings and break-ins. The gang hiked up the price and increased the stocks when they knew they were flush. To quote Keynes: successful investing is anticipating the anticipation of others.

According to Ricky, the people in his street were big on community spirit and many of them had lived in the same house all their lives, social mobility being rare if non-existent. He insists this inertia didn't breed a race of Andy Capps, far from it, and that hard graft and altruism flourished. Front doors were kept unlocked and neighbours looked out for one another. The estate I grew up on didn't exist when Ricky was in junior school. Promoted as a model for the future, within ten years its walls were covered in graffiti, the walkways the domain of drug dealers, the residents for the most part dumped there by the council. Result: they couldn't wait to get out.

The gulf between Ricky's period and mine similarly applies to family life. His mother and father stuck together while my father, as is the wont of many Jamaican fathers, preferred to sow his seed far and wide. It was no secret that I had many half-brothers and sisters that I would never meet or even know the names of. My father did make one appearance after he'd abandoned us. He stank of rum and slurred his speech, and delighted in beating me till I couldn't stand. He was angry that my mother had bought me a new bike and couldn't help him pay off his gambling debts to a vicious bookmaker from Brixton. Little did he know that I had £3000 stashed under the bed which I was minding for the gang. My mother was bruised and in tears when he left, and I swore that if he came to my hood again I'd kill him. From what I gathered, Ricky's father, although a gambler, was a devoted family man who never drew blood or had an affair, never mind numerous affairs. Establishment prigs continually harp on about the importance and benefits of the stable nuclear family. Perhaps they have a point.

If Mushtaq had arrived in England during my stay at the school he wouldn't have been subjected to such racist abuse. Conversely, he would have stood a far better chance of being mugged or shanked with a knife. I hate to admit it, but I'd probably have been the one doing the mugging, or at least organising it. I have no wish to brag, certainly not about those days, but I was the strongest and easily the most intelligent of the gang. At fifteen, I became their leader and demanded and got respect, relishing the fear I engendered, the power I had over others. On the flip side, it meant that I was the main target for the feds. I had two spells in borstal and would have ended up in prison if it hadn't been for the efforts of one man.

When I interviewed Ricky I neglected to tell him that I had attended the same school, or that there was one notable constant between his time there and mine. Mr Gasson had been his teacher and for one solitary day he was also mine. We'd had supply teachers for most of the year and when I heard the regular teacher, namely Mr Gasson, was coming off sick leave I thought I'd show him who rules the roost. Ricky described him as caring, beatnik in appearance, with a shock of black hair. In my time, he was bald (due to chemotherapy), beardless, short of breath, and frail.

I strolled into his classroom smoking a cigarette. When he ordered me to put it out I adopted "the attitude", told him to keep his hair on, and swaggered between desks, offering some of the other kids a draw on my smoke. The class was evenly split between white and non-white and there wasn't one black boy who didn't accept my offer. The local gang who I ran errands for were all black, and it was common knowledge among the "niggers" that they wouldn't let anyone diss me. Mr Gasson hobbled in my footsteps and each time a boy took a drag from my cigarette he showed them his fingers, which were stained brown, and a picture of lungs that had been ravaged by cancer.

He returned to the front of the class and said, 'You will never forget the image I've just shown you. They will be your lungs in years to come if you keep on smoking. Please don't make the same mistake I did. My cancer is of the blood, but all cancers have the ability to grant you a slow, agonising death.'

Irrational maybe, but I got feeling that he had dissed me. I stormed up to him and pulled a blade. I think I would have shanked him if he hadn't stared unwaveringly at me. Have you ever played that game when you try to outstare someone and the first one to look away or blink loses? Well, it was like that. I widened my eyes, put on what Ricky described as the Tottenham Look, and still the old man wouldn't budge. The standoff went on for what seemed like minutes before my grip on the knife weakened and I turned my head away. Some white kid at the back shouted, 'You lose!' and a few of the girls jeered at me. I called them slags and ran out of the classroom. It was my intention to head to the estate and ask the gang to sort Mr Gasson out, but before I got there I was waylaid by the police and taken into care. The next time I saw Mr Gasson was ten years later, two years after my mother had died from an overdose, and weeks after my second stay at borstal.

It was a spur-of-the-moment robbery, Enfield Chase in mid-afternoon. I'd been shopping at Edmonton Green and couldn't find the trainers I wanted. Frustrated and bored, it was as simple as that. I didn't need the money because I was loaded from the sale of brown. It was one of those mock-Tudor semis, built in the 1930s for middle-class families who had the means and wanted to escape

265

the inner-city grime and smog. Milk and eggs were on the doorstep, and the curtains were drawn. Someone had forgotten to cancel the milkman. Normally I would walk past a mark a few days before to check for alarms, dogs, and open windows. No need because this was a cinch. The house was at the very end of a quiet street so it only had neighbours on one side and a paved path that ran to the back. I was expecting to scale the fence, but not only had they forgotten to cancel the milk but also to lock the side gate and back door.

I began in the upstairs bedroom because more often than not that's where the spare cash and jewellery's kept. There were no women's things in any of the drawers and all I could find of interest was a bronze medal. It had a blue and white ribbon and the word Korea inscribed on it. I didn't think it was worth much, but thought I might give it as a reward to a sharp-eyed nipper who acted as lookout on the estate. My next port of call was the front room and with the curtains drawn I felt secure enough to turn on the light. I opened the door and was just about to flick the switch, when a brilliant light blinded me.

As I shielded my eyes a voice said, 'I left the back door open for my carer but somehow I don't think you're here to care for me, Raymond Deane.'

I switched on the overhead light and saw a skeletal old man in pyjamas propped up on pillows in a single bed. There was a large canister by the bed and an oxygen mask resting on his chest. The torch in his hand cast a light that tinged his skin a ghastly blue-grey. He turned off the torch and spoke in broken sighs.

'Be a kind boy and pass me the water on the little table by my bed, would you Raymond?'

I hadn't the slightest notion who he was, until he said, 'Still puffing away, Raymond? When you ran out of my class I feared you would end up this way.'

Freaked out by the fact that he'd remembered my name, I closed in on him. That pile of bones could put me away if he called the feds.

I snarled, 'How come you're not dead?'

He told me he had been in remission, but the cancer had returned and the doctors had given him six months to live, at most. Knowing this made my decision a whole lot easier. I'd practically be doing him a favour. I picked up a cushion from the settee.

He saw what I was planning and said, 'There is another way, Raymond. Why risk being convicted for murder?'

There wasn't enough air in his lungs for him to scream for help, so I decided to hear him out. And what he said next changed the course of my life.

He fitted the mask over his face and pointed at the bookcase.

After inhaling oxygen, he put the mask back onto his chest and said, 'Please take the second book from the right. It's called Oliver Twist. If you read it and can prove to me that you've read it then I will not call the police. You have my word.'

I was within a few feet of him by now, cushion still in hand. I stopped and thought for a minute. I was wearing gloves and nobody knew me in that swanky hood. I'd inflicted some serious damage on rival gang members, premeditated a lot of it, but I'd never killed a helpless geriatric before. The advantages were obvious. The poor bastard couldn't shoot or shank me, and if I smothered him they might think the cancer had killed him. What was I waiting for? I took a few more steps and loomed over his bed.

He looked up at me and said, 'Are you sure you want to do this, Raymond? Why not read the book? A man called Charles Dickens wrote it. Have you heard of him?'

He held the mask to his face, inhaled, and then added, 'Come back in a week's time and prove to me that you have read it by

267

answering a few simple questions. The back door will be unlocked.'

If he'd made me promise to abandon the gang and stay out of
trouble, I'd have smothered him there and then. But all he wanted
me to do was to read a fucking book. With my memory it would
only take one quick read and he could ask me any question he
liked. It all boiled down to whether I trusted him or not. I peered
into his eyes. In his classroom they were bright and alert, but
these things were dull and bloodshot. Lifeless maybe, but they still
unnerved me and for a second time it was me who turned his head
away first. I had a mind to threaten him, to tell him that if he
stitched me up the rest of the gang would slice him up. It would
have done no good. What could they have done to him that the
cancer already hadn't? I got his medal out of my hoodie and
placed it alongside his plastic beaker of water.

'Here. What is it? Some kind of war medal?'

'The Korean War,' he replied.

'Kill many?'

'I was a young medic. I don't believe in killing.

I swear it could have gone either way. I put the cushion down
and grabbed the book from the bookcase, then stood there like a
dummy, shuffling and agitated. Supposing I came across a word I
didn't know? Supposing I couldn't pronounce it properly? Clutching the book, I fled out of the front room and through the back
door before I changed my mind.

There was no way I was going to tell the gang what had gone
down. Later that day, I found a quiet spot by the Lea and read a
fair bit of the book. I came back to the same location the following
day and read the rest. They were mere words to me then and any
deeper significance passed me by. I figured the sooner I got him
off my back the better, so I didn't wait a week to revisit Mr Gasson.
I had them all off pat: Oliver Twist the orphan, Mr Bumble the

workhouse bloke, Jack Dawkins, Sikes, Monks and Fagin, the head of the gang, who used his nippers pretty much like I did on the estate. I knew the names of all the locations and characters down to the ones who made fleeting appearances.

I found Mr Gasson in bed, but this time he was motionless and lying flat on his back. Half of me hoped he'd snuffed it but when I shook his pyjama sleeve he stirred. He gave a grunt and his eyes flickered open. He smiled when he saw me. I suppose he was glad I had his book and not his cushion in my hand.

I said cockily, 'Ask me anything. Test me all you like.'

'I have only one question, Raymond Deane. Assuming Charles Dickens didn't write *Oliver Twist* for money, what other motive could he have had?'

Chapter 6

Page 254

The storm shrouded the desert in shadow; a hot wind stung our cheeks and parched throats. We each took a drink of water from our canteens and then adjusted our goggles and covered our faces with cloth, securing it behind our heads with ties. Sergeant Jacks gave me the signal and the two of us scrambled out of our foxhole to plough through the choking sand. It's an odd thing. You can survive a hail of bullets unscathed and yet a stray bullet may ricochet off a rock and find the tiniest opening in your body armour. With only our packs to carry and with no body armour to weigh us down, we could move a hell of a lot faster, but how we made the wadi without being hit, I'll never know. Jacks had made a judgement call and it had paid off. In the field you learn to trust your instincts and your superiors, if they warrant your trust. I hated Jacks's guts even before he put Ronnie "out of his misery" like some old nag, but I respected him as a soldier and that's what counted.

The storm had given us some respite from the Taliban onslaught but air support was now out of the question. The sand would have clogged up a Chinook's engines if they'd attempted a rescue. As we ran along the wadi, I kept glancing up, expecting to see the outline of a bearded man pointing a Kalashnikov. The cloth covering Jacks's large, square face was flapping like a sail by the time he flung out an arm and ordered me to stop. He removed his goggles and wiped his face with the cloth, but his flushed skin still glistened as he shaded his eyes to observe the sun. Every growling sentence that came out of his mouth sounded like a curse even if it didn't include an expletive.

'It just would, wouldn't it? Directly overhead and visibility's improving fast. We need to find our man before they get us in their sights again. Follow me, private. Go!'

I removed my cloth and goggles and clambered after him up the slope, losing and finding my footing as I fought my way to the top.

Despite running for over thirty minutes he'd judged the distance perfectly and the house was less than a hundred metres from our position. We lay side by side, sweeping the house and the surrounding desert with our binoculars, straining to pick out movement within the heat haze.

'Clear, sergeant.'

'Clear,' returned Jacks, scrambling to his feet and waving me forward. 'Make yourself a hard target! Did you hear me, Deane? If Corporal Rainer had done what he was told he'd be alive now.'

As we zigzagged between the rocks and boulders he continued barking out commands. But my mind was elsewhere, replaying the worse five minutes of my life... the black dart with a crimson tail... the blinding light as it struck the Scimitar... the mortar rounds... the screams... clawing at the sand... an arm... a mouth... curly hair streaked red... my best mate straining to look at feet that I knew weren't there... the panic that gripped me... throwing up... fumbling for the morphine... the phantom hordes that materialised as if from Hades... Jacks firing a round into the side of Ronnie's head ...

'Was Ronnie a fucking hard target, Jacks?' I screamed through my tears. I seized his shoulder and spun him around. 'You don't know he would have died.'

He threw my hand off.

'It's my job to know, private. Lost too much blood. Wouldn't have lasted twenty minutes. Didn't want those savages getting to him before he croaked.'

271

I hurled my pack to the ground.

'You're the fucking savage, Jacks!'

He discarded his pack before I launched myself at him and we ended up on our knees like two grunting wrestlers, neither gaining the upper hand.

The last time I'd lost it like that was when I was leading the gang in Tottenham. There was a longstanding beef over turf and before taking on the rival gang, I psyched myself up, did a little crack, a shot of vodka, never weed, no place for mellow, and when the time came, I thrived on the rush and took delight in the screams and pleas of the enemy. How I wanted to hear Jacks scream and plead for his life. I'd only just moved in with Mr Gasson when I was stopped and frisked by a cop who recognised me from my Tottenham days.

He mocked, "You can take the boy out of the gang but you can't take the gang out of the boy."

Those words reverberated in my brain as I fought to get the better of Jacks. If he hadn't been Midland Counties' heavyweight boxing champion, I swear I would have rammed my fists into his face until it turned to mush, or worse, shanked him with my army knife. But the stalemate allowed my army training time to kick in and Jacks was as professional as I was animal. He pushed my arms aside and got to his feet, scouring the land between the house and us.

'We're sitting ducks out here. We'll sort our differences out in a boxing ring, if you've the guts.'

I didn't resist as he took my arm and hauled me to my feet.

He continued, 'The house is single-storey and too small to hold many of the bastards. Can you see movement in there, private?'

I scanned the adobe building again. Part earth-coloured, part whitewashed, it had two dirty windows and a door.

'Negative.'

'Neither can I. Move!'

We made the house without coming under fire and pressed ourselves against the wall on either side of the door. You can take as many satellite images as you like, but none of them can guarantee that a door isn't booby-trapped. Jacks checked his rifle and indicated that he was going to enter on the count of three. I nodded. We'd done this manoeuvre a dozen times but there was no adrenaline surge on that occasion, no pumping heart or taut muscles other than from my physical exertions. I tried to clear my mind and focus, but images of large birds feasting on Ronnie's body and my hatred for Jacks made that impossible. The moment his third finger went up he turned the handle, and we burst inside.

In a recent operation we'd raided a jihadist stronghold and found a torture chamber in the basement. The walls were splattered with blood and severed body parts were piled in one corner. With this cramped dwelling the jihadists had had to make do and three people were hanging by their wrists from beams in the living area. We stepped around them and went speedily from room to room, covering each other as we went. Jacks was checking a recess containing a potter's wheel when he glanced over his shoulder. A second earlier he would have caught me, knife poised. If I hadn't seen his body tense would I have shanked him in the back? Doubtful. I wanted to savour the look in his eyes as the blade penetrated his thick hide.

We returned to inspect the victims and Jacks ordered me to proceed with caution in case they had been rigged with explosives. He circled the trio and went down on his haunches, examining them from various angles. They consisted of a middle-aged couple and a bareheaded younger woman, all in blood-stained tunics. The three had their eyes gouged out and their ears cut off. The front of their tunics had been ripped open and a cross had been carved into their chests. The torturer had made sure that the knife sliced through the young woman's nipples. Jacks ignored the women and lifted the man's chin.

'Ain't him. Too young, and our man has a scar on one cheek. Lucky bastard by all accounts that Mushtaq Mohammed. Reckon they've taken him with them. Bet he won't be so lucky this time.'

The words had hardly left Jacks's lips when the frayed carpet rippled. The waves grew larger until one rose above all the others, and when the carpet would stretch no further the bulge became squarer and pegged in suspended animation. Jacks aimed at the bulge but didn't dare pull the trigger for fear of bringing the enemy down on us. He drew his knife and signalled for me to pull the carpet back. Imagine a magician whipping a tablecloth away and leaving the tea set in place. That's how much time it took me to reveal a trapdoor and the brown, wizened face poking out of the cellar. The man climbed a couple of rungs and bowed his head.

'Blimey,' cried Jacks. 'It's bleedin' Gandhi risen from the grave.'

The man splayed his elbows and pressed his palms together.

'Please don't shoot. I am Mushtaq Mohammed, not Taliban. It appears that I haven't quite used up all of my nine lives.'

'You will have if you don't grab hold of that bleedin' ladder,' barked Jacks. He strode up to the man and twisted his chin to reveal a white scar on his cheek. 'It's him all right,' he continued, not bothering to disguise his annoyance.

As far as he was concerned, Captain Manley and two of his men had died for nothing ... for this.

I agreed with Jacks. Mushtaq Mohammed wasn't top priority. He had no intel of any real value to us in Afghanistan and he wasn't a Brit. The rescue attempt was made at the request of the Pakistani government, which had promoted his educational reforms in regions previously controlled by the Taliban. The fact that he'd been abducted and taken across the border into Afghanistan was a slap in the face for them, and something they wanted resolved as soon as possible. Our relationship with Islamabad had been somewhat strained of late and it was a way of smoothing things over.

Mushtaq became aware of the three bodies hanging from the hooks. What he did next I haven't seen since and don't expect to witness again. He crossed himself.

'These people are Christians, apostates worthy of death in the eyes of this backward society,' he lamented. 'I escaped from the Taliban during an air raid and they hid me, a devout Muslim.'

'Must have liked your ugly face,' snarled Jacks.

'It is to my eternal shame that I remained hidden while they screamed in agony. Their torturers shouted Allahu Akbar, Allah is Greater, as they went about the Devil's work. These kindly souls fled to the desert to live like their people did thousands of years ago. May I find forgiveness in their Christ as Saul the persecutor did.'

'I heard you do a lot of good work in Pakistan, Mr Mohammed,' responded Jacks. 'Giving yourself up would have done no good. These poor blighters still would've copped it and you'd have joined them.'

Jacks was the last person to lend a friendly ear, but he'd registered Mushtaq's distress and was doing his best to sound sympathetic. A cynic might surmise he figured the mission would go more smoothly if the rescued felt valued. But Jacks could only turn on the charm for so long and quickly reverted to form.

'What did you say before we set off on this mission, Deane? The downtrodden and exploited need men like old Gandhi here.'

I'd read up on Mushtaq's exploits and found them inspiring. Now they were as irrelevant as my life.

I replied with a miserable, 'Something like that, sergeant.'

'Only an educated black man would use downtrodden and

exploited in the same bleedin' sentence,' sneered Jacks. 'You two should get along like a house on fire.'

I could have shanked Jacks there and then, but I would have been lumbered with Mushtaq, and didn't trust myself not to abandon him in the desert. That was as good a reason as any for keeping the sergeant alive. For the moment, at least.

I detected it first, a slight tremor soon to be followed by vibrations that shook the earthenware pots and jugs stacked against one wall. Seconds later, and it was as if Formula 1 cars had left the grid and were hurtling towards the first bend. I crouched and peered out of the grimy back window. A convoy of cars and small trucks, some with mounted machine-guns, were speeding towards us kicking up clouds of dust. I rushed to the front window and observed scores of insurgents in robes emerging from the wadi. The cars and trucks slowed and manoeuvred to form a perimeter while the men on foot crept towards the house.

'Too fucking many! They'll be on us in minutes. We'll never hold them off.'

'Only one thing for it,' growled Jacks. 'One of us'll stay up here and the other two will hide in the cellar. The unlucky sucker can replace the carpet and put that table on top of it.'

'Let it be me,' pleaded Mushtaq, his modest linen shirt and the top of his baggy linen trousers visible as he strained to leave the cellar. 'I can fire above their heads.'

Jacks sniggered, 'With those spindly arms I doubt if you can lift a gun, let alone fire one, chum. No time to draw lots. Looks like I shall have to pull rank, Private Deane.'

He bent and gazed into the cellar.

'Get your black arse down that rope ladder and take Mr Mohammed with you.'

I could see that Mushtaq was about to protest. As could Jacks. He put a hand on Mushtaq's head.

'Go down on your own accord, Mr Mohammed, or I'll push you into the bloody cellar.'

I believed him, but Mushtaq remained undecided. At the time I thought it would be an act of mercy if Mushtaq broke his neck in the fall. You can tell that I didn't rate our chances of survival very highly.

'Now, if you please, Mr Mohammed,' commanded Jacks.

Mushtaq looked down at the drop and then into Jacks's eyes.

'Very well,' he muttered, starting the descent. As his head disappeared he added, 'I will pray to God for you, Sergeant.'

Jacks glared down at him.

'Ta, but I've made other arrangements.'

'Your English sense of humour,' echoed Mushtaq's voice. 'It has been an honour to make your acquaintance, sergeant.'

Jacks waited until Mushtaq was standing on the cellar floor before confronting me. I guess he figured he wouldn't survive the attack and wanted answers to questions that had been bugging him. He crouched and looked through both windows in turn before directing me into a corner of the room.

'You're an odd one, Deane. The other lads ain't thick, some even read *The Telegraph*, but I ain't seen any of them reading that frog's *Social*... what was it?'

'Rousseau's *Social Contract*. He was a philosopher.'

'So why didn't you stay philosophising at Oxford? You weren't recruited by the men in grey suits, were you? Are we on two separate missions here?'

'It's personal. Keep your Brummie nose out.'

'There's something not quite right about you, Deane. Just can't put my finger on it.'

'There's nothing to tell, and if there was you'd never get it in a million years. You sure you want to do this, Jacks? In a year or two you could be dining in the officer's mess.'

'Not me, Deane. They don't like you putting brown sauce on their caviar.'

'It's suicide and they might discover the cellar anyway. We could go out blazing like Butch Cassidy and the Sundance Kid, leave Mr Mohammed in the cellar.'

The sergeant scowled and checked his ammo.

'He can't stay in the cellar forever and wouldn't last ten minutes alone in the desert. Besides, for all we know they might think I'm the only one to have survived their ambush.' He ended with a curt, 'I hope the Villa stuff you bleedin' Yids.'

His eyes told me his course was set. He'd gone into the zone, as I called it, and would kill without compunction. I saluted, but instead of returning my salute he reached out and shook my hand.

'You should know better than to salute a sergeant, Raymond. Suppose we'll never know who'd have won if you'd stepped inside a ring with me. Now piss off and let me get on with killing these tossers.'

I took the rungs three at a time and jumped onto the earth floor. Bereft of furnishings, the cellar couldn't have been more than eight by six, the square of white light overhead sufficient to expose the paintings of Jesus, Mary and the disciples, which adorned the walls. I jettisoned my pack and checked the base of the walls to see if I could dig my way out with my knife. I looked up at Jacks and shook my head.

'We'd need a fucking pneumatic drill.'

Resigned to my fate, I gave Jacks the signal and he closed the trapdoor to leave us in total darkness. I heard the table being dragged across the room, followed by the sound of army boots on the ceiling as Jacks went hastily between the front and the back. Jacks settled for the front window and bellowed a curse at "God or whoever the fuck!" before opening up.

He ran six times between the front and the back. The enemy

must have thought there was a whole detachment inside the house. When his gun fell silent I saluted and held the salute as the cellar shook and the enemy convoy roared up to the house. The front door crashed open and harsh voices yelled in what I knew to be Pashto (we'd been taught some basic words so as not to inadvertently offend the locals). A gruff, brutal voice could be heard above all the others and then something was hauled overhead. At first I thought it was the table and aimed my rifle in the general direction of the trapdoor. It was only when I heard the thump, thump, thump that I realised it was the sound Jacks' boot heels striking the floor.

Mushtaq whispered in my ear, 'I speak many languages. Their leader is angry. They cannot torture the sergeant for information because he is dead. The sergeant killed twelve of his fighters and was hit many times before he fell. May he find peace in heaven.'

If the first thing moved across the floor was a body, the next object was the table. Mushtaq put a hand on my shoulder to get his bearings and stepped in front of me.

'If I am your shield, Private Deane, then you can get many more of them before they get you. For the coward that I am, it would be a blessing for me to be killed quickly.'

I grabbed his arm, reaching out like a blind man until I touched a wall. Guiding him to the wall, I pushed his shoulders down till he was resting on his bony backside.

'Stay there and don't get in my bloody way. Don't worry, I'll find myself another human shield. If you can call it human. Then I want you behind me and not in front. Do you understand?'

He replied with a grudging, 'Yes', and fell silent, most likely in prayer.

The first part of my plan went smoothly enough. I located the rope ladder and climbed it till the top of my head pressed against the trapdoor. The moment it opened, I intended to grab whoever appeared and pull him into the cellar, the idea being that I would then jump down after him and disable the man before using him as a shield. If my luck was in it would be their leader and I could negotiate our way out. Of course, going on my past experiences the chances were that he would tell his minions to shoot, because Paradise awaited him.

The jihadist who operated the trapdoor obviously wasn't so keen to meet his maker because it opened a few inches at a time. I got a whiff of spicy breath and had just made eye contact with the man when there was a loud explosion.

Someone shouted, 'Airstrike!' in Pashto.

Another explosion and I was flung from the ladder. The ground quaked and chunks of hardened mud and straw broke loose from the ceiling. The weather-beaten face peering down at me vanished, his frantic wails lost amid a frenzy of agitated voices and stampeding feet. Another explosion rocked the cellar, hurling me against a wall. I stumbled, grabbed Mushtaq, and together we scrambled towards the rope ladder.

Climbing the rungs, I screamed, 'They're taking out their vehicles first! A direct hit on the house and we're finished!'

My head had cleared the trapdoor when there was yet another explosion. Mushtaq swung wildly on the rope ladder and a painting of Jesus crashed to the floor. I reached down and shouted for him to take my hand. He was so light that if I hadn't felt his hand in mine, I wouldn't have known he was attached to me. I'd just hoisted him into the living area when there was a fourth and truly deafening explosion. A side of the house collapsed and part of the roof caved in. I was engulfed in a dust and all the noise and chaos melted away...

A voice resonated, faded, and resonated again. I couldn't make sense of the meaning, no matter how many times it repeated itself. I opened my eyes, blinked, and saw Mushtaq lifting small chunks of masonry from my chest. He sounded quite calm, if a little out of breath from his exertions.

'I was thrown well clear, Private Deane. I think I must have more than nine lives. Are you injured?'

I patted my uniform and rose unsteadily to my feet. After transferring my weight from foot to foot, I took a few sharp intakes through my nose and exhaled fully through my mouth.

'Some bugger's stuffed cotton wool in my ears; other than that, just a headache and few bruised ribs by the looks of it.' I stuck two fingers up at the sky. 'God! I hate Yanks.'

Mushtaq dropped the last piece of masonry onto a pile of rubble and stooped to pick up a tiny bird with matted, dark red feathers and curled feet. He stroked its limp neck.

'Oh, dear. I think this little chap isn't so lucky.'

He might have been playing Saint Francis, but survival and completing the mission were foremost on my mind. I observed the burning cars and trucks in case any were salvageable; and then the corpses, some smoking, others dismembered. The Americans had done a thorough job. I was watching the surviving vehicles retreating across the desert, plotting my next move when someone groaned from within the shattered shell of the house. Unable to locate my rifle, I drew my knife and worked my way between the fires and smouldering debris. I found an insurgent trapped under a beam, one arm pinned, struggling to reach an AK-47 with his free hand. It wasn't the beam that thwarted his efforts but the body of the young woman they'd tortured, still secured to the wood by her chains; hollow eye sockets and bloodied features no more than a foot away from his petrified gaze. Every time he tried to push her body aside she rolled closer towards him, until her cold flesh touched his warm sweat and he pleaded in the name of his god. I gripped him by the beard and raised his chin, twisting my knife into his throat, not quite deep enough to pierce an artery but deep enough to create a trickle of blood. He may have craved martyrdom but I don't think he wanted to carry her image with him to Paradise. I would have delighted in smearing pork fat over his nostrils and nailing him to a cross, but there wasn't time for retribution. I cut his throat in one movement and wiped my knife on his robe. Seizing his AK, I removed the ammunition from the pouches in his chest webbing and when I turned around Mushtaq was standing behind me. He knelt and uttered a prayer for both corpses in turn. I didn't have the patience for any of that crap.

'Move! We can't afford to let them know we're here. I'll have a quick look to see if I can find our army packs, then let's get the hell out before the bastards come back.'

I found Jacks's night vision goggles and binoculars, both with hardly a scratch on them. I never did find his body or pack. To make matters worse, when the house was obliterated, the drinking well had caved in and my pack had been buried. Fortunately, besides his AK, I'd also relieved the insurgent of a canteen, which was over half full. I estimated that if rationed, our water supply would last two days. I didn't inform Mushtaq that two days' worth wasn't sufficient and the chances were that we would die of thirst.

We had no choice but to head off when the sun was at its hottest, and every few minutes I shook the front of my shirt which stuck to me like Elastoplast. Expecting Mushtaq to lag behind, I factored in the possibility of having to carry him at some point soon. But he doggedly kept pace, and if he did stumble or fall he waved me away and got to his feet unassisted. When we rested, I even had to force him to take a second drink of water. If I'd asked him from where his strength derived he'd have probably said God. I wouldn't have given a shit if he'd made a pact with the Devil and all his demons as long as his legs functioned.

Where possible, we kept tight to the wadi walls. Comprised of red rock or scree, sometimes tiny stones would break loose and roll down the slope to land at our feet. Then I would urge Mushtaq to push on, and when he reached the limit of his endurance, I'd climb to the top for a recce while he recovered his breath. I saw nothing sinister until I caught sight of a stationary jeep with its engine running. There was one hostile in the vehicle, slumped over the steering wheel. Carefully scanning the jeep and its surroundings, I found no obvious signs of damage or evidence of a trap. I told Mushtaq to wait in the wadi but he insisted on coming with me. He said four eyes were better than two. I replied that he'd better not pray over me if I copped it, suggesting he'd be more usefully employed putting a bullet in his brain before they got hold of him.

The flies crawling across his tortured face indicated that the man was dead. Even so, I instructed Mushtaq to stand behind me and kept my gun trained on the man until I could grab him by the collar and haul him back into his seat. There was a large gash in his head, probably the result of the bombing. I went through his pockets, took a lighter, some Turkish fags, and a picture of a burka-clad woman with two small boys. I fended the flies off with my hands, but they swarmed again almost instantaneously. I burnt the picture and used the smoke to dispel them – a gesture that had little effect on the flies but gave me satisfaction. Of no further use to me I flung him from the jeep, and as he lay sprawled on the desert floor I noticed that one of his legs was busted. A bandage around his foot was stained with congealing blood and a splintered shinbone protruded through his tanned skin. It must have been agony for him to drive the jeep and I was glad that he'd suffered. A canteen lay on the passenger's seat. It was empty, and I conjectured that he'd drunk some of the water and used the rest to clean his wounds. I suppose he expected his mates to come back for him. I checked the fuel, which was three quarters full, and if our luck held it would take us close to the allied zone. Head bowed, Mushtaq approached the corpse. I'm sure he would have fallen to his knees and said a prayer over it if he hadn't seen me pointing south to a glint in the desert. Like twinkling stars, more glints appeared.

'Sun's reflecting off windshields. They're coming back!' I looked to the east. 'Damn it! We'll take the jeep over rockier terrain so they can't follow our tracks. We'll have to travel at night without using lights. It won't be easy even with night vision.'

Mushtaq took a makeshift crutch from the back of the jeep. It consisted of two rough pieces of wood tied together with string, the work of the dead jihadist no doubt. He pointed it at the sky.

'God will be our guide.'

I gunned the engine to maximum revs. It was better than cursing and I'm pretty sure it drowned out my response.

'Yeah, right. Perhaps God will let Lawrence of Arabia return from the dead to lead the way on his camel.'

We'd only travelled a few miles when the jeep spluttered to a halt. I opened the bonnet to be met by a plume of scalding steam. I kicked a tyre in frustration.

'Can God fill fucking radiators?'

Mushtaq tutted and shook his head.

'What is it with you English? You can't go more than two sentences without uttering a profanity or an expletive. When I was a boy in Tottenham the mother of my best friend used the word sugar as an alternative. Have you tried utilising that?'

The last time I smiled was at Ronnie after we'd dug in and were surrounded by the Taliban. It was one of those smiles that brushes lips and is accompanied by a thumbs up: we'll be okay mate. I looked at Mushtaq's silly, beaming face with its crinkles, scars and missing front tooth, and couldn't help but smile. But rather than lifting my mood it made me even more irritated. What I needed was a fight, and I wasn't going to get one from this guy.

284

'Sugar off! Is that any better?'

'Much better, Private Deane, but you might have said it with a jot less aggression.'

'Did I hear you right? You lived in Tottenham?'

'Bruce Grove, do you know it?'

'I was raised just down the road off Lordship Lane.'

I sat with my back against a wheel to get the benefit from what little shade there was. He sat beside me and became reflective.

'I must remember to look up my old friend Ricky. And there was a young man called Colin who I met through Ricky. He had a mental disability but was one of the sweetest people I've ever encountered. My father trusted him enough to let him take me to the cinema, providing the film didn't contain immoralities. It's been such a long time but if Ricky's still alive I bet he doesn't live too far away from Tottenham Hotspurs. He was nicknamed Kuchy. My nickname was Mush, at other times Tonto. If we survive maybe I'll tell you all about my childhood there and our gang. It was called Tottenham Boys.'

'Ruled the hood, did you?'

'The hood?'

'Your patch... your neighbourhood.'

'Oh, I see. Well, I was only eight when I joined and eleven when I left.' He saw the amusement on my face and added hastily, 'But we were right little scallywags. Once I stole an apple from the vicar's garden. It may not seem much but you should have seen that vicar. Have you ever played Subbuteo? Ricky always got the better of me, but I suspect he didn't play the game like an English gentleman. I'll buy a set and give you a game after we reach safety.'

'I'll look forward to it. When we reach safety, you said? I only wish I shared your optimism.'

Unwilling to use all our water on the engine, I decided to let it cool down of its own accord. I clambered from the jeep and climbed a ridge to get a better view of the enemy. In a distortion of yellows and reds, the twinkling stars had multiplied and the way they were dispersed, the disorganised manner of their approach, convinced me they were hostile. When I descended the ridge Mushtaq was waiting for me at the bottom.

I cried, 'They're definitely heading our way. We've got to get out of here fast. Have one last swig of water and the rest's going in the rad.' He raised a hand.

'I think a more sedate retreat is in order.' He prodded the sand with the crutch and a triangular head with cat-like pupils popped up. The hissing snake had two spiny horns above each eye. 'Step carefully, Private Deane, for I fear we have disturbed another nest of vipers.'

We slowly retraced my footsteps back to the jeep. As we went, Mushtaq sang an upbeat song that I didn't recognise. He told me that when he was in England, parents didn't like their children listening to this type of music because the dances were suggestive and the artists wiggled their hips. It was called "rock and roll" although he had no idea why. He couldn't remember the name of the song but it was by someone called Cliff Richard. It wasn't his singing that bothered me, which, by the way, was bloody awful. It was his mood, which bordered on the euphoric. Stranger still, as soon as we got into the jeep he started chanting in Arabic. Thinking I might be posted to Iraq, I'd done a crash course in the language. Yet again my ability to remember everything I'd learnt came in handy and I was soon teaching my mates the rudiments. Although I recognised many of his words, none of them seemed to form coherent sentences. At first I put it down to my ignorance or his pronunciation, but a short while into the drive I realised he was slurring his speech and that he was making fists with his left hand. I stopped the jeep and grasped his wrist. I rolled up his sleeve and on the forearm there was a red blotch like a love bite. In the centre of the discolouration trickles of blood seeped from two puncture wounds.

'Why the hell didn't you tell me?'

'Because I can still function and I didn't want to hold us up.'

'Is there an antidote to the venom?'

'We have similar snakes near my home. There is no antidote out here.'

'How long before it becomes fatal?'

'Ten hours, if I'm lucky. Pain comes before paralysis and I can stay alert through pain. Another pair of eyes and all that.'

The sun was low in the sky; a pale orange rim hovering over a desolate moonscape. As the wheels spun I slammed the gears into third and decelerated, coaxing the jeep into motion. Finding traction on bedrock, I switched on the headlights and hit the accelerator, weaving between an assortment of small rocks and mounds of pebbles the size of anthills. Mushtaq raised his voice for the first time since I'd met him.

'No! Please don't risk your life for me, Private Deane. It will be dark in less than an hour and you can use your goggles to see. Even with medical assistance my chances of survival are slim.'

'Call me Raz, and I'll be buggered if my comrades have died for nothing. I'll get you help...' I clutched my chest, which felt as if a hammer had struck it above the first rib. Holding a hand up to my face, I licked the blood from my fingers. 'Fuck! Must stem the flow.'

Searchlights crisscrossed the ground and more bullets fizzed overhead. I pushed the pedal to the floor and the engine screeched in protest, black smoke billowed from the exhaust. A mortar round landed with a muffled thump; another with a loud crack, the third exploded with a boom and clouds of dust obscured my view. Two shapes materialised and like wraiths they vanished in a flash.

'Maybe the angels have come to guide us,' muttered Mushtaq, fighting to keep his eyes open.

'Some fucking angels!' I exclaimed, as a snarling insurgent landed on the bonnet.

I slammed on the brakes and his body hurtled forward. His face smacked against the windscreen before he was thrown from the jeep and mangled under the wheels. The impact caused the jeep to balance on two wheels and we were within an ace of rolling over.

I had my first joy ride at the age of fourteen when I nicked my father's car – the Victoria Line to Brixton and his old Ford Corsair for the return journey. The car was a burnt-out shell by the time it was found over the Marshes. By the age of sixteen, I'd been involved in half a dozen high-speed chases and the police had only caught me once. Self-taught has its advantages when it comes to doing wheelies along the North Circular or regaining control of a jeep in the desert. We landed on four wheels with a thump and, although Mushtaq bounced and jolted in his seat, he remained drifting in and out of consciousness. I slapped his cheek.

'Stay awake! Don't give in!'

He stirred and tried to move his fingers.

'Oh dear, I appear to have lost sensation in another digit. Do not worry, Raz. I still have one left to stick up at the enemy.'

'I'd like to stick a stick of dynamite up the arse of the fucking bastard who shot me.'

He sighed, mumbled, "Language", and slumped back in his seat. If he thought our soldiers swore a lot he should've spent some time with the bloody Yanks.

I drove flat out until steam rose again from the bonnet and the engine spluttered and died. I managed to steer the vehicle down a gradient and park it beneath an outcrop ominously shaped like a coffin. I got out, examined my wound, and cut three strips and a patch from my sleeve to serve as bandages. I tied the strips together, placed the patch over the wound, and wrapped the extended bandage around my body to secure it in place. Woozy and fatigued, I circumnavigated the outcrop and crawled to the top of a rise.

A tourist would have found the view stunning, for bleak desert had transformed into an ocean of mauve and white flowers. At the edge of the poppy field a plane stood on an improvised runway. It was next to a drab building with a flat roof and open iron shutters. A track cut through the poppy field to the building. It originated from a complex on the far side of the valley, which I figured was the processing factory that turned the goo from the seedpods into morphine. In the cool of the late evening, the pickers were busy snapping off the pods. Among them were men and women, some elderly, and children whose heads bobbed above the flowers. Six armed men wearing robes and tribal headgear were loading the bricks onto the plane, ready to be synthesised into heroin in a lab possibly located in Pakistan. An idyllic scene – if you can call it that – but the way ahead was impassable. Knowing it wouldn't be long before the jihadists discovered us, I slid back down the slope on my backside and jogged to the jeep; each stride felt as if a red-hot knife was being jabbed into my flesh. My body trembled and almost buckled with the exertion of reaching inside the jeep and lifting Mushtaq over my shoulder. Feverish and gasping for air, I ploughed through the sand, and when my strength failed I placed him in a dip and collapsed alongside him. He appeared comatose and I knew I was losing too much blood to last much longer.

I'd taken part in numerous actions, had many a close call, but I had never thought death inescapable before. Helpless, the prospect of my own demise forced me to re-evaluate my life; my inner turmoil manifesting itself in a string of bitter utterances:

'Bollocks! I am who I am. What's the soddin' point in putting myself on trial now?' The first stars appeared as representatives of the cosmos. I raged at them. 'I'm a coward and plead guilty on all counts. If you'd just hurry my passing, I'd like to meet up with Jacks in Hell.'

Death was creeping up on me and I would've much preferred to die in battle, charging a machine-gun nest head on or throwing myself onto a grenade to save my comrades. Quick and glorious: death with purpose. Not on a failed mission where my best friend was murdered by one of his own. I was gathering the energy to check on Mushtaq when he rolled over and took my hand.

He said softly, 'The sun is sinking fast, Raz. Unless you free yourself of guilt, I fear the night sky will remain mere spots of light on an empty canvas.'

How he found the strength I had no idea. I directed my anger at him.

'Save it for bleedin' Allah.'

He had a message for me and was determined to get it across.

'I believe the Catholics need to confess their sins to a priest. I'm no priest but I try to be holy.'

What really got up my goat was that he wasn't going to let me die in peace.

'I'm not a bloody Catholic and I don't believe in God. I hate to tell you this but you're delirious and we're about to snuff it. What about you dying your way and me dying mine?'

The light was fading fast and I could just make out the deep lines on his face.

I had no idea whether he intended a joke as he enquired, 'Wasn't that a Scottish song?' But what he said next was no joke. 'I'll unburden myself first, if you like Raz.' He paused as the words jammed in his throat. He took a deep breath and threw them at me. 'I like men. It's true. For my sins I like men.'

Nothing had been lost in translation: he fancied men. When you think you're dying, revelations such as that don't have quite the same impact. I'm sure "so what" would be the response on the deathbed of all but the most incorrigible of homophobes. I was tempted to say "each to their own, mate," except for one thing: I too preferred men. I'd trained myself to avert my gaze in the barrack showers for fear of being found out. Now and then I would sneak a glimpse into a man's eyes to see if I could perceive the same urges. If there were others like me they'd also kept it well hidden. That was in the days when gays were frowned upon in the army and it was much safer to join in with the smutty boasting – like having sex with that "bit of all right". If we were anywhere else, I might have kept my sexual preferences to myself. Or tried to. He moved his face so close to mine that his breath tingled my cheeks. In the last of the daylight, I peered into his mournful eyes. He already knew.

He said, 'For the sake of my work, I haven't acted upon my carnal desires for many years or told another soul. Pakistan is a very conservative country and I would be totally discredited, maybe killed. I think we are in the same boat, or should I say closet, Raz? At least we can step out without suffering the heat.' Shivering, he tried to defuse the tension. 'It's getting chilly. Ricky would object, but what I wouldn't give for Nanna's red sweater.'

I had no idea who Nanna was and my secret would die with us. I thought, what the heck and blurted it all out.

'On my last leave my wife, Samantha, caught the dead expression in my eyes and rolled away while we were having sex. Not for the first time, I'd hoped she'd mistake mechanical vigour for passion. It wasn't as if I didn't want her to have orgasms or to be fulfilled by love. It was just that my fondness for her was incompatible with the physical side of our relationship. The best bit for me was when it was over. She burst into tears and accused me of having another woman. I was the great macho war hero. The fact that I needed to fantasise about men to have an erection would be inconceivable in her eyes. One night, after a gutful of wine, I nearly let my guard slip and came close to whispering Ronnie's name as I made love to her. He was in my unit and was killed just before we rescued you. Soon after, I married her because I wanted to appear "normal", and I blamed my lack of interest on the terrible events I'd witnessed in Iraq and Afghanistan. I told her things I had sworn to keep to myself, about the sniper's bullet, which had grazed my cheek and killed a small child. About how she'd died in my arms.'

Mushtaq needed to catch his breath before commencing each sentence.

'I too am a coward, Raz. Shame on me.'

Self-loathing was an emotion I was all too familiar with.

'At least you acted honourably by not deceiving the people you love. I wanted to tell Ronnie about my feelings for him, but he was as straight as they come and I didn't want to risk our friendship.'

He squeezed my hand that little bit harder.

'I killed a man who loved me. We were young, in our twenties, when I ended the relationship. At the time, I thought it went against the teachings of the Prophet and would have brought the wrath of Allah upon me. Arif begged me not to leave him, and when I refused to change my mind he threw himself under a train. I've lived with the guilt ever since.'

'How long have you known you were "different"?'

'A long time I suppose, but without understanding what drove my behaviour. When I was a Tottenham Boy I was forever touching Ricky, even though I knew it made him uncomfortable. At least he won't have a chance to carry out his threat if I visit England again.'

'Ricky?'

'No. A boy called Frank who was expelled from the Tottenham Boys. He had eyes which turned the colour of coal when his hatred boiled over. A peasant from my village might think him possessed by the Devil. Frank called me a Paki and tried to frame me for a crime I didn't commit. I'm not saying he invented the insult, but it certainly has become popular among certain elements of British society. I beat him in single combat and he swore he'd kill me no matter how long it took.'

I thought pillow fight but kept it to myself.

'This Frank was only a kid and kids say all kinds of nasty things without meaning it.'

'Frank Lambert may have been only ten at the time, but I believe he would carry out his threat if I went to England again. I'm glad I haven't given the little Hitler the opportunity. Somehow I don't think he'll appear over that crest riding a camel.'

'Don't suppose he will.'

He had stood up to the Taliban, been shot, yet the threats of a ten-year-old English boy dating from the 1950s were freaking him out. I put it down to paranoia induced by snake venom. He was having a bad trip and I was tempted to blame Cliff Richard. I wanted to laugh but it was too painful.

So it appeared were our confessions, because he said, 'I hope we live long enough to take in the wonders of the night sky, my friend.' And with that we both fell silent.

It's difficult to put into words the raft of emotions I experienced as night descended. The desert sky was a blaze of stars, mesmerising, lending a sense of vastness, of wonder, of how small we humans are. I could use hippy-speak and say I was at one with the universe, or take the hard-headed approach and say that what I felt was the result of delirium. For whatever reason, the love I experienced was all encompassing, untouched by the brutality of Man or by guilt. The spell was broken when a savage coldness came over me and I started shivering uncontrollably. Mushtaq wrapped his arms around me, gently rocking me until the pain in my chest melted away, evoking the same feelings as when my mother held me; comforting, dispelling fear, a feeling of being safe and cared for. He quoted extracts from the Koran, the Bible, the Torah, and recited the words of John Lennon's *Imagine*. Hallucinating or not, his sentences flowed effortlessly one into the other, as if penned by the same author. As my strength failed he told me to close my eyes and that my journey wasn't over. That it had only just begun. I didn't believe a word of it but couldn't care less. What a beautiful way to die.

***

I never did make Hell because when my eyes flickered open I was attached to a hospital drip. There was a medical bandage wrapped around my chest and over my shoulder. The first person I saw was Mushtaq who was sitting on a chair by my bed.

I croaked, 'How long have I been here?'

'Two days, and I've been at your side praying and dozing for most of that time. The female nurse is pleasant enough but the male nurse is very testy.' He glanced over his shoulder in case he'd been overheard. 'There's no need to thank me. I needed the rest after what you put me through.'

I propped myself up on my elbows and squinted.

'How come you aren't dead?'

He stretched out his arms and wiggled his fingers, making a woo sound that was meant to be ghostlike, but was more like a rider pulling up a runaway horse.

'When you drifted off under the stars I set fire to the jeep. The lighter you confiscated from the dead jihadist didn't do the trick, so I used your rifle. Allah was with me, because I hit the petrol tank with the last bullet and the flames alerted American soldiers who had arrived to raid the poppy factory. If it wasn't for their medic you'd be dead now.'

'It would have to be a bloody Yank, wouldn't it? Ingenious, but I meant why aren't you dead from the snake bite.'

'Oh. I saw a cowboy film once where the hero was bitten by a rattlesnake. He used his knife to dig out a little of the flesh, sucked out the poison, and spat. I thought I'd give it a go. While you were watching the Taliban's approach, I took a long splinter from the crutch to use as the knife, said sugar several times, and gave my arm a jolly good suck. I then had a jolly good spit and offered a little prayer. I knew it was working when my fingers relaxed and I was able to hold your hand under that heavenly night sky.'

'It's okay for you. I nearly turned into a bleedin' hippy out there.'

He shrugged and his voice saddened.

'I've got important business in Pakistan and I have to return immediately. The Taliban are up to their old tricks again, forcibly denying girls school places. If I weren't such a pacifist, I'd arm the women and get them to shoot the misogynists where the sun doesn't shine. I learnt that expression in Tottenham. Maybe you would like to visit me at my house in the foothills? We can swap stories of Tottenham.' He chuckled. 'From what I'm hearing there are more of us than those white boys nowadays.'

I accepted the invitation feeling excited yet apprehensive. Was it a friend asking a friend or did he intend something more? His demeanour had remained the same when he said it, but maybe I'd missed some subtle hint? Maybe his motives were akin to those of an old man pursuing a young woman, encouraged by the fact he hadn't got the brush off. I almost laughed out loud at the absurdity of the notion. Perhaps it would've made life easier if I'd asked him outright whether it was sex he was after. Scared of what my reaction would be if he'd said yes, all I could do was nod.

'Good,' he said, flashing what were left of his teeth. 'You are most welcome. Not so long ago, I was informed by an old friend that my eyes had lost all their humour. Now I think they are sparkling once more.'

I was pleased that I'd made him happy. The bond between us, his bravery in confronting prejudice, had me thinking about the direction of my life.

'Your story needs to be told. Instead of shooting the Taliban perhaps I could inflict more damage by exposing them as the medieval barbarians that they are. Maybe I'll quit the service and try my hand at reporting. Besides, it'll be a hell of a lot easier to step out of that closet.'

'A noble profession if the pen is wielded on the side of justice.'

He rubbed his hands together and said gleefully, 'It could be such fun swapping anecdotes about my life in Tottenham. And I simply must tell you about the time I tried to teach Colin to play cricket and he showed me how to make friends with a dog. Ricky was so very pleased when I stroked his dog, Sandy. By the way, how are Tottenham Hotspurs doing? If I can locate Ricky, perhaps I'll ask him to take me to a game when I visit London. I could return the favour by taking him to Lords to see a Test Match. Far more civilised. The MCC made my father an honorary member, you know. That's if Ricky still wants to be my friend and hasn't come under the influence of evil Frank again. It was such a long time ago but it seems like yesterday.'

33

Before I'd finished wiping the tears from my eyes, a third pint materialised in front of me. I looked up and saw Raz drinking fruit juice in the chair opposite. At least he wasn't clutching a knife between his teeth. I caught sight of Dai Evans heading in my direction. Raz glanced over his shoulder, rose to his full height, and stretched. When Evans saw the wingspan of my "friend" he didn't fancy coming any closer. Luckily for me (and Dai), the days when the little scrum half could tackle the big lock forward had long gone. Raz sat down and leant across to offer me his hand.

'Hello, Ricky. Sorry I took so long. I had a little errand to run. Don't worry, you're perfectly safe.'

And so were the passengers on the Titanic. With both mitts wrapped around my empty glass, I stiffened and slid back in my chair. Though I had to admit he did look a lot less threatening in smart casual gear and without those god-awful shades. The very thought of him in that hoodie outfit had brought on many a panic attack. He withdrew his hand and shrugged.

'As you wish.'

I flicked away the tears from my cheeks and tried to focus. There wasn't a shred of hubris in the eyes of the battle-hardened warrior and beads of sweat had clustered on his scarred brow.

'Tell me, when did the human being become a monster? Judging by your childhood exploits he was never human to start with.'

'How much have you read, Ricky?'

'Enough.'

'If you'll allow me, I'll move it on a few chapters. When I was captured my interrogator, Ahmed, tried to get me to confess to being a homosexual and a sodomite.'

'When you were a reporter, right? You'd have been better off staying in the army. As a matter of interest why did you enlist in the first place? It's a far cry from the hallowed quadrangles of Oxford to Afghanistan. Wouldn't rent boy on Hampstead Heath have been more to your liking?'

Expecting retribution, I flinched.

'One of my mates on the street was shanked to death. He'd saved my life when I was fifteen. I was asked by the gang to come back to my old hood and help get even.'

As distressed as I was, I couldn't let the opportunity to "get something on him" pass me by.

'And did you get even?'

'I was honour bound. But we'll save that for another day. One thing was for certain, there wasn't going to be a second time. I needed to escape my past, or else I'd have ended up dead or behind bars. At Oxford, I was easily accessible, just a short ride along the M40. I had to be much further away than that so the gang couldn't play the loyalty card again.'

'That question Mr Gasson posed. What was it? Ah yes, assuming Charles Dickens didn't write Oliver Twist for money what other motive could he have had? Tell me, how did you reply?'

'When I couldn't give Mr Gasson an answer, he asked me to read the book again.'

'Did he say "or else"?'

'He praised my efforts. I wasn't used to praise from someone like him. I didn't return for three weeks and during that time the riddle he'd set churned in my mind. Just as he'd hoped, the more I thought about it the more the book became relevant to the way I conducted my life.'

'Ah, I get it now. When you went back you had a protracted philosophical debate involving capitalism and Victorian morality. After that you took your O and A-levels and sailed through them. That right?'

'If you really want to know, I got all A grades and he rewarded me with his Spurs season ticket. He obviously couldn't go any more. None of the gang were much into watching football. Only white people and Uncle Toms did that. They preferred rap videos and hood wars, but I gave it a go.'

'Ah, the slippery slope.'

'I told him to stuff his learning a few times, but kept returning. The exams were a doddle, although Mr Gasson insisted I incorporate the subjective and didn't just regurgitate facts. He said I had a gift that I should build upon.'

'I bet you were popular with the rest of the gang when you turned into a teacher's pet. Did they know you were gay? Had enlightenment reached Broadwater Farm or wherever you lot hung out?'

'When I was in my mid-teens one boy called me a queer. He kept on baiting me with "Where's your bitch, Raz?" I got drunk, fucked his girlfriend, and closed my ears to her pleas as I thrust deep into her. I'd seen the joy on women's faces in films when they were having sex, but her expression was like that of a rival gang member after I'd pinned him down and threatened to carve my initials into his chest. The anger I felt was immeasurable, with myself for not being normal, with her for not making me normal. After I'd puked up, I found her boyfriend and rearranged his face.'

A sentence from Raz's book sprang ominously to mind: You can take the boy out of the gang but you can't take the gang out of the boy. He was on the edge and luckily for me his fury was directed at himself… but for how long?

I uttered a subdued, 'Go on. What happened next?'

He swiped the sweat from his brow with the back of his hand.

'I left the hood to avoid the same thing happening again, took a rent-free room in Mr Gasson's house and helped with his care. He was a wonderful man.'

'Don't tell me, he was the father you never had.'

'He was a friend, Ricky. Did you know that there were hundreds of his old pupils at his funeral?'

'He was my favourite teacher, but where's this getting us? Bottom line. Why did you abuse me in those fucking toilets?'

I wondered if he wanted me to feel sorry for him. If he did he was crazier than I thought.

He replied, 'If you'll hear me out I'll try to explain. It's complicated.'

'Do tell me all about those interrogation sessions. I might get to like this Ahmed character.'

'I don't know what made my captors suspicious. Maybe they were tipped off by one of Mushtaq's servants. Mushtaq employed three gardeners when one would do, the same with his cleaners, and paid them double the standard wage. He called it a kinder form of charity. Whatever the reason, Ahmed tried to make me say that Mushtaq was my lover. He wanted a video of me giving a full confession to that effect. If people in Pakistan thought Mushtaq was gay and had an English boyfriend it would have finished his political career. He may even have been put on trial for his life or assassinated by some madman. Ahmed tried waterboarding, whipping, electric shocks, but I wouldn't give in. Incensed, he then gave me Viagra and took pictures of me naked, coerced me into adopting lewd positions, which included putting objects in my anus. Under the threat of crucifixion, he got Christian boys to give me blowjobs while his photographer snapped away.'

'You didn't happen to notice if the chap used a Hasselblad H4D, did you?'

Raz pressed the flats of his hands together. At first I thought it was to stop them from making fists, but I soon realised it was to prevent them from shaking.

'Ahmed informed me that the photos would be sent to Mushtaq, one snap at a time. When Ahmed had completed his gallery of obscene photos, he told me he had posted the last of them first class to Mushtaq.'

I could've hugged the Kentia Palm. The abuse he'd endured was

300

truly horrific, but nothing could excuse his sadistic behaviour towards me at my old school. My tormentor was vulnerable and on the verge of breaking down before my very eyes. That was as maybe, but I still feared him and wanted proof that he'd become a humble writer, if there is such a thing. Wary of pushing him too far, I continued to probe his defences. A General must know the strengths and weaknesses of his enemy before commencing an attack. In age-old military tradition, I sent out the skirmishers.

'Did you go to Mushtaq's house in the foothills after you were released? Had he enjoyed Ahmed's photos?'

This time it was him who stiffened and pushed back in his chair.

'He was enraged and horrified. Mushtaq was the most centred man I'd ever met, but he smashed every piece of crockery on view in his kitchen. He called the Taliban a scourge and an infestation that needed to be eradicated. When he eventually calmed down he apologised and spent days comforting me. I stayed at his house for over a month on the pretext of writing articles about his work.'

'But that was plenty of time to find out about his childhood, about me.'

'He told me bits here and there. I was too fucked up to concentrate properly. We explored ourselves mainly; walking, meditating, healing. I thought there'd be many other opportunities to research his past.'

'Wore a string of beads around your neck and a garland in your hair, did you? Did you tell Samantha that your arsehole was ten times bigger than when she last saw you?'

'I tried to tell her that I was gay but she just couldn't get it. She said I should seek medical help and that it would pass. I told her being gay wasn't like having flu but she wouldn't listen. She tried to convince me she enjoyed making love with me but I couldn't see how.'

'Why the hell did you marry her in the first place?'

'I was worried that some of the men were getting suspicious about my sexual preferences. I convinced myself that, in time, I could learn to enjoy making love to her. I married Samantha six months after joining the army. I liked her a lot. We had a laugh and could talk about all sorts of things, including football and politics. She was an Orient supporter and couldn't stand West Ham. Always a good start. She's bright and well-read and, man, you should see her moves on the dance floor. If she doesn't tie her long blonde back it acts like a whip. She deserved better.'

'Gay's cool. Are we talking love triangle? Or did you abandon her the moment you got back from Mushtaq's?'

'Sam wouldn't let me go and my relationship with Mushtaq was platonic. When alone we held hands and kissed each other on the lips but that's as far as it went.'

'So that's why you've got so many female readers. Women aren't usually as interested in action books as men. The later chapters more Mills and Boon than *Rambo III*, are they? Did your old comrades know that you touched up a geriatric before you wrote the book? Come to think of it, did you have a good feel of Mr Gasson? The lack of women's things in his bedroom might suggest he had similar leanings.'

'You can't provoke me, Ricky. But carry on trying if it makes you feel better. If you're asking if I told my mates in the army that I was gay, then the answer is yes. If Jacks were alive… well, you can imagine his response. By and large they were supportive. It wasn't easy leaving Sam, but I'd fallen in love with a very special person. Age didn't come into it. We'd arranged to meet after he'd completed his work for the Muslim Council in London. I thought I might rent a cottage in the Lake District. I have no idea how things would have panned out. He still had his political career and we were both on guilt trips.'

What I wasn't prepared to do was disrespect Mushtaq any further. I'd already overstepped the mark. That said, I found Raz's inner turmoil simply exquisite.

'Go on. I think I could learn a lot from this Ahmed.'

'When the negotiations for my release began, Ahmed changed his approach and played the good cop. He allowed me to take baths and offered me chocolate and hot soup. It wasn't until the prisoner exchange took place and the ransom money was paid that I found out for sure that Mushtaq was alive.'

'Mushtaq paid your ransom, didn't he?'

He paused and moved on.

'During "re-educational" sessions Ahmed called me Mandingo and told me I was a victim of a corrupt western system, that it was the crusaders to blame. He showed me pictures of devastated villages, charred corpses of men, women and children who'd been celebrating a wedding. He preached that it was the result of British and American bombing that black and brown people were still slaves to the white boys. "Come and join your brothers, Mandingo, and embrace Islam," was his mantra. He said it often enough.'

'And have you? Did Ahmed groom you into becoming a jihadist?'

Now he did clench his fists. If his glass hadn't been on the table it would have shattered in his hand.

'The bastards killed Ronnie. What do you think? I'm sorry, Ricky. The monster at the school wasn't me. I was still disorientated at my debriefing and only returned to something approaching normality during counselling sessions with a shrink. I took strong medication after I'd heard about Mushtaq's murder. The kind you can only buy on the street.'

'Did you inject yourself at the school? And what's with the coffee? I expected to smell skunk on your clothes and booze on your breath.'

'I like coffee and wasn't in the mood for weed. Other than that, I did the lot that day. Shot up, popped, snorted, and needed a top-up.'

I glanced at the pink scars on his cheek.

'You think you went crazy. When you removed your shades I was over halfway to believing you originated from a water world.'

'You have no idea how much his death affected me. I was suicidal when I decided to write the book. It saved me from an early grave and Mushtaq's story deserved to be told.'

I thumped the table so hard it was a wonder the glasses didn't take off.

'You weren't the only one who loved Mushtaq! We could have grieved together, you bastard. If I'd got in Frank's car when he came back to Tottenham recruiting, would you have…?'

'Killed you, Ricky? With pleasure.'

'Like you killed Frank and the others?'

'What makes you think that? I was camping with two old army mates at the Brecon Beacons when that happened. I'd saved both their skins in Afghanistan and to repay the debt they'd asked me there to recuperate. After Frank's murder the police interviewed his inner circle and my old comrades confirmed my alibi.'

'And the cops believed that? Who did they put on the case? Inspector Clouseau?'

'Before you ask, I was Frank's prized black, a war hero with a Baptist mother. Onward Christian soldiers and all that shit.'

'How many people did Frank have in his party? How many were black?'

'Around two hundred and five niggers including me. The other four brothers had one brain cell between them.'

'Did you have access to arms through your old comrades? Maybe you only needed a couple of assault rifles as samples? Did you tell Frank more were to follow?'

'I told you, I was camping at the Brecon Beacons when Frank was killed.'

'We both know that's impossible. I've done some research and there was about thirty minutes between the minute you left me and the time of Frank's death. Why the hell did you kill Terry, Jess and the others?'

'Wouldn't you have snuffed out Himmler and Goebbels given the opportunity? Best cut off all the Hydra's heads.'

'Poor Terry would've thought Goebbels a rodent. Why didn't you kill me?'

'You were Mushtaq's best friend, Ricky.'

'How did you know I wouldn't squeal?'

'Didn't.'

'If Frank's followers didn't come from Tottenham, then where did they come from?'

'Frank recruited them from all over London. Some were in gangs, some weren't. He was very persuasive and they were very greedy, and very thick.'

'Why shouldn't I call the cops?'

'Do you think the police would take the word of a drunk?'

I'd always denied being an alcoholic, even during the love-in at my one and only AA meeting. I certainly wasn't going to change tack now. Playing blasé had become second nature to me.

'I'm not drunk all the time. In fact, these days I can take it or leave it.'

'Just can't help yourself, can you Kuchy?'

'What happens now? Am I in danger?'

'Of cirrhosis of the liver? Most certainly.'

'You know what I mean.'

'Could've bumped you off in your bedsit if I'd wanted to. By the way, that Afrikaner won't bother you again. He's packed his bags and limped off.'

'You've been watching me! For how long?'

'Long enough.'

'Have you been in my room? How did you find me?'

'The beer at The Lane ain't a patch on the draught in your local. I won't ask how you can still afford a Spurs season ticket.'

'You followed me from the football!'

'Relax, I was merely checking on your progress. Ricky, I'm giving you a D minus, you could do so much better.'

'I never saw the bastard who bashed me over the head. You obviously didn't have a girlfriend. Was it you?'

'Some bloke who'd just torched a car. You pointed the camera in his direction at the wrong time.'

'That gadget which deactivated the school alarm. How did you get hold of it?'

'Bought it on eBay.'

'Yeah, right. And the keys?'

'Borrowed them.'

'You seemed surprised when you saw the name Kuchy on my camera strap. Or are you just a bloody good actor? Don't tell me, you were into amateur dramatics while you were at Oxford. Othello, was it?'

'Roderigo, actually. Othello was already taken and Shakespeare didn't pen a golliwog for the play. Let's put it all down to random futility, shall we Ricky? It's amazing what one can unwittingly let slip under interrogation. I think you must have read *The Dice Man* on acid when you were at university.'

Once or twice in the recent past, I'd had the feeling that someone was watching me. I was worried it was a snoop from the dole office. Without thinking, I took a large swig of the pint he'd bought me. Recoiling, I thought supposing it's poisoned and my life is slowly ebbing away right before his cunning eyes? I jumped as he reached inside his jacket and produced two padded envelopes, one coloured blue, one red. He found a dry patch on the table (I'd been messy with my second pint) and slapped them down side by side.

'The little errand I had to run. The envelopes are in Spurs blue and Arsenal red. Symbolic of the yin and the yang, wouldn't you agree, Ricky?'

'That shrink who gave you the all clear should be struck off.'

'I'll give you a choice. Inside the red one there's twenty grand in cash. Call it payment for your contribution to my success. Take it and you'll never see me again. If you don't blow it all at the bookies you can drink yourself into oblivion.'

'Feeling a little guilty, are we? And the blue?'

'That's the hard option. Like supporting Spurs over the years, though I must admit, things have certainly picked up recently. How I envy you, Ricky.'

'You envy me?'

'What I would give to be transported back in time. The thrill of watching the great Double Team, no gloating Gooners or Chelsea millions: Dave Mackay, Danny Blanchflower, John White, and Jimmy Greaves. I know Jimmy joined the following year – but what a finisher! I've seen so many clips. I especially like the one where he beats the entire Manchester United defence and rounds the goalkeeper before slotting it home. I might even drop in on your old house and say hello to your mum and dad. Margaret sounds like an angel and I could discuss battlefield tactics with Ziggy. I wouldn't know what to say if they asked me how you've turned out. But all is not lost just yet, Ricky. The blue envelope contains keys to a rented flat in Muswell Hill and five hundred pounds in advance of your first pay cheque. A year's rent has been paid in full and it has a fully stocked wardrobe in your size.'

He was making me exceedingly nervous. Enter the joker.

'I'd prefer a fully-stocked wine cellar. New Zealand not Chilean Sauvignon Blanc, preferably.'

'I'll also pay for gym membership and a course of physio for your ankle. I'm sure Mike would appreciate getting paid for a change.'

'What's the catch?'

'No boozing or gambling. One slip and you'll be back in your squalid bedsit. Though not for long, I suspect. Dossing on the street surely beckons.'

'Am I also to turn vegan? It'd better be one hell of a job. Will I be taking snaps of copulating adulterers in hotel rooms? I think I can manage that.'

'We'll be working freelance, travelling the globe following leads. Those two old army mates will be joining us.'

'And just who will be hiring the A Team?'

'That's my concern. I will say that we try to be on the side of the good guys.'

'If you mean governments, I don't know one that communes with the angels. Military intelligence, is that how you came to possess that gadget? I'm sure someone with your army background and memory might prove very useful to that organisation. Perhaps Jacks was right and you do work for the men in grey suits. Either that or you're a mercenary.'

'Keep fishing, Kuchy. All you're liable to catch is a tiny gudgeon rather than a dog of war.'

'Why me? Why not someone younger and braver?'

'I've trawled through your archive. You're a bloody good photographer and I can trust you to be discreet.'

He leant forward again.

'I can, can't I Kuchy?'

Perhaps it was the flattery that offset my fear of those giant hands tightening around my turkey neck. The last person of note to pay me a compliment was Ian Hislop, after I'd snapped the Duke of Edinburgh standing in a cowpat with a finger up his nostril.

'You forgot to narrow your eyes.'

'I didn't intend to be threatening, Ricky. Please be aware that our work requires absolute secrecy.'

'Don't you want to write a sequel?'

'*One Flew Over the Cuckoo's Nest, To Kill a Mockingbird…* It may not be up there with the greats but *Tottenham Boys* is definitely a one-off. I can't sit at a bloody word processor all day long waiting for the muse. Well, Ricky, what's it to be? The blue or the red envelope?'

'Twenty grand in cash, you said? And I'll be safe, you guarantee it?' He nodded.

'All you have to do is choose the red envelope and wait for the fairies to come and carry you away.'

'You could've chosen blue and white envelopes. You know I hate red.'

'Didn't I read somewhere that alcoholics can go colour blind?'

What to do? If I chose the red envelope, I could rent a nice flat and set aside a couple of grand to have a flutter now and then. Who knows, I might get on a roll and win enough to buy a small place of my own. The blue wasn't nearly so appetising, more Marmite than Robertson's strawberry jam. Travelling the globe? Somehow I didn't think I'd be sunning myself on a sandy beach in the Maldives or Florida, taking pictures of bikini-clad beauties. It was odds on that I'd be tramping through steamy jungles in pursuit of Spanish-speaking coke bosses. Worse, I'd be taking a camel ride across a parched desert to take snaps of a Jihadist with a South London accent. Even with fitness training my getaway speed couldn't exceed waddling penguin. It followed that I'd probably be using a zoom to capture the layout of a building and the people who frequented it. That was on the assumption that the inhabitants were still breathing. My greatest fear was that I'd be taking pictures of corpses, maybe as proof that Raz had fulfilled a contract. I'm not good around guns. I'm not good with heights unless I'm behind glass. If he wanted me to take a picture of a deal going down on the windswept roof of the Shanghai Tower, he'd got another think coming. Choosing the blue envelope would be the most absurd thing since the Polish cavalry charged the German tanks in World War Two. My Great Uncle Leon broke his lance on a Panzer. Dad said Leon would knock back the vodka and re-enact the event using two broomsticks. The red envelope may have been in Arsenal colours but it was a no-brainer. With that twenty grand I could rent a swell flat, join a gym, and pay for Mike's physio treatments in advance, thank you very much.

What was stopping me? I reached forward, my hand hovering over each envelope in turn. I hadn't let anything red near me since Nanna had one of her funny turns and tried to foist that horrible jumper on me. Sandy was born in 1951, the year the great push-and-run team won the league. Mum told me Nanna knitted him a blue and white puppy coat to celebrate our success. Times were hard and Nanna couldn't afford to wait until he was fully grown (when Sandy outgrew his coat she made a pair of socks for Ink out of the wool). When I was three, Dad would take a cushion to the match and sit me on a bar. When I was five, he would take a wooden box and stand me on that. It cost a florin for Dad to get in and zilch for me because the man would let Dad lift me over the turnstile. Mum complained that Dad and I didn't spend enough time together. She was pleased when we went to watch the Spurs and would shoo us out of the house on Saturday lunchtime. Then she could have "a bit of peace at last" and settle down to listen to the radio with a fag and a bottle of stout.

Dad and I would go to Beryl's Cafe in Park Lane before the match started. He rarely talked about the war while we were drinking our tea and eating our bacon sandwiches. Mostly he'd talk about his family in Poland and how lucky I was to be born in England. He thought that, along with Poland, England was the greatest country in the world. I'll never forget the time when he removed the bacon from his sandwich and held up a slice of bread:

"My brothers are in a Russian prison because they wanted more of this."

The man on the next table scoffed, "They can have mine, chum. It's stale."

If Beryl didn't land him one I thought Dad might.

But he said wistfully, "And they'd bite your hand off for it."

We were late for the match that day and the crowd was packed solid behind the goal.

Dad thought about relocating to the long Worcester Avenue stand, but a man at the back saw our dilemma and shouted, "Nipper for the front!"

Dad lifted me up and I was passed over the top of the heads.

I heard Dad yell, "Wait for me in our usual place in front of that long bar with the other kiddies. You k'now where."

I had my arms outstretched like aircraft wings and pretended to be a Spitfire shooting down Messerschmitts. We took a flask of tea with us at mid-week matches during the cold winter. Before we went inside the ground, we'd buy hot roasted chestnuts and peanuts in their shells. Sometimes you'd break the shells only to find a burnt peanut, which was half the size of the rest. Dad didn't like those, but I did.

Mum did come with us to the FA Cup semi-final against Manchester United. It was played in Sheffield and they put on a special train from White Hart Lane Station. Half the street went and even Mr Bentley said he'd join us (he never made the train). We won 3–1, but I can't remember much about the match because at four feet nothing, I could see sod all. I do remember a family wearing red scarves and rosettes crossing the road from the opposite direction. Mum gave the Manchester mum a little wave and she gave a little wave back. I gave their son the Tottenham Look and Dad gave me a clip around the ear. The 60s began with "Glory, glory hallelujah and the Spurs go marching on". We started singing it at school during music class. The teacher never made us sing *The Battle Hymn of the Republic* again. When we won The Double there were street parties with bonfires and huge kegs of beer. People used doors and window frames from condemned houses for firewood.

It's very sad. My old community has been scattered the length and breadth of Essex and Hertfordshire. Some of their descendants might even drive white vans and vote Tory. When I was growing up the club was the adhesive that bound us together. It's ingrained in my psyche and has an entry in every chapter of my life. I know my dislike of Arsenal and anything red is illogical, irrational, idiotic, pathetic, bigoted, random futility gone haywire. I'm sure many Arsenal supporters give generously to charity and support noble causes. When I called the Samaritans the guy on the other end of the phone might've been a Gooner but ...

The whole pub turned their heads when I screamed, 'Get rid of that red shit!'

Raz passed me the blue envelope and clapped.

'I can hear Ink applauding in heaven, Kuchy.' He held up a hand. 'Give me a high five. Tottenham Boys forever, mate.'

I informed the Kentia Palm that it could have been a whole lot worse and tipped my pint into its pot. I swear I could hear the crowd singing "Glory, glory, hallelujah" as the pool of real ale slowly sank into the soil. I gave Raz that high-five.

'Damned right we are, bro.'

ACKNOWLEDGEMENTS

My thanks to Debbie Scott for her brilliant artwork, to Dominic Walker who did the inside cover, and Katya Rosenberg who did the front cover.

Printed in Great Britain
by Amazon